Pokémon™

Pokémon the Movie
The Power of Us
Zeraora's Story

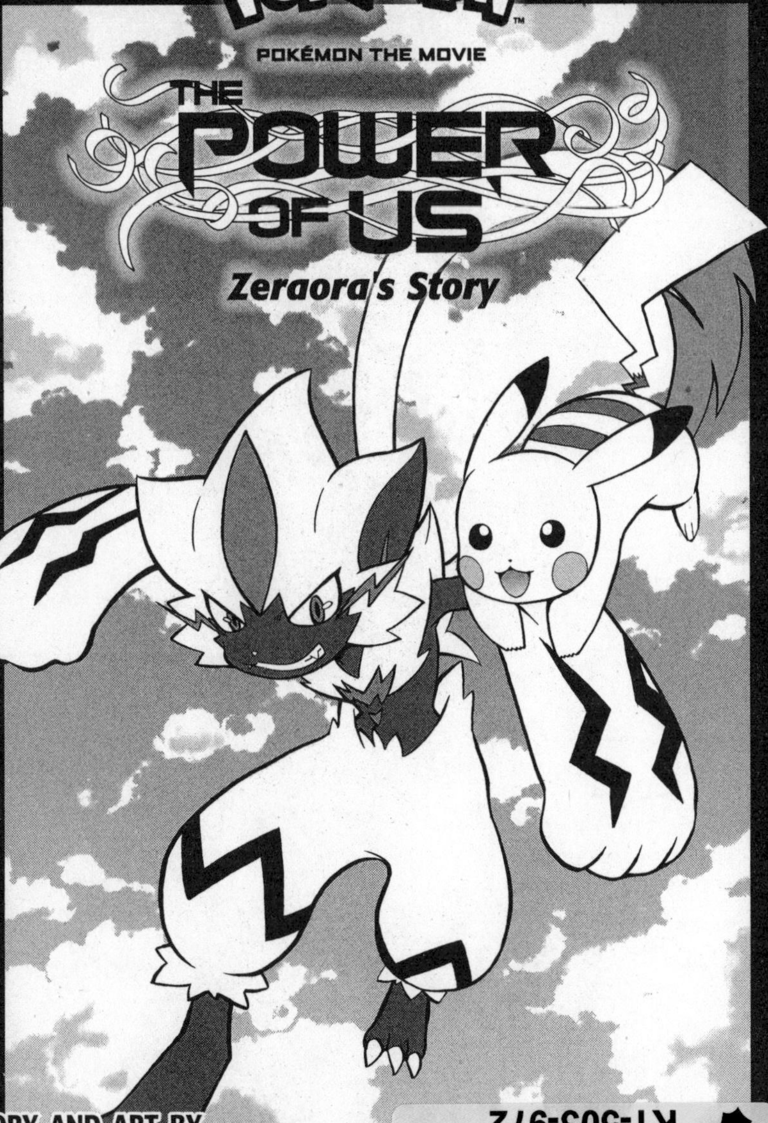

STORY AND ART BY
Kemon Kawamoto

Original Concept by
Satoshi Tajiri

Supervised by
Tsunekazu Ishihara

Script by
Eiji Umehara, Aya Takaha

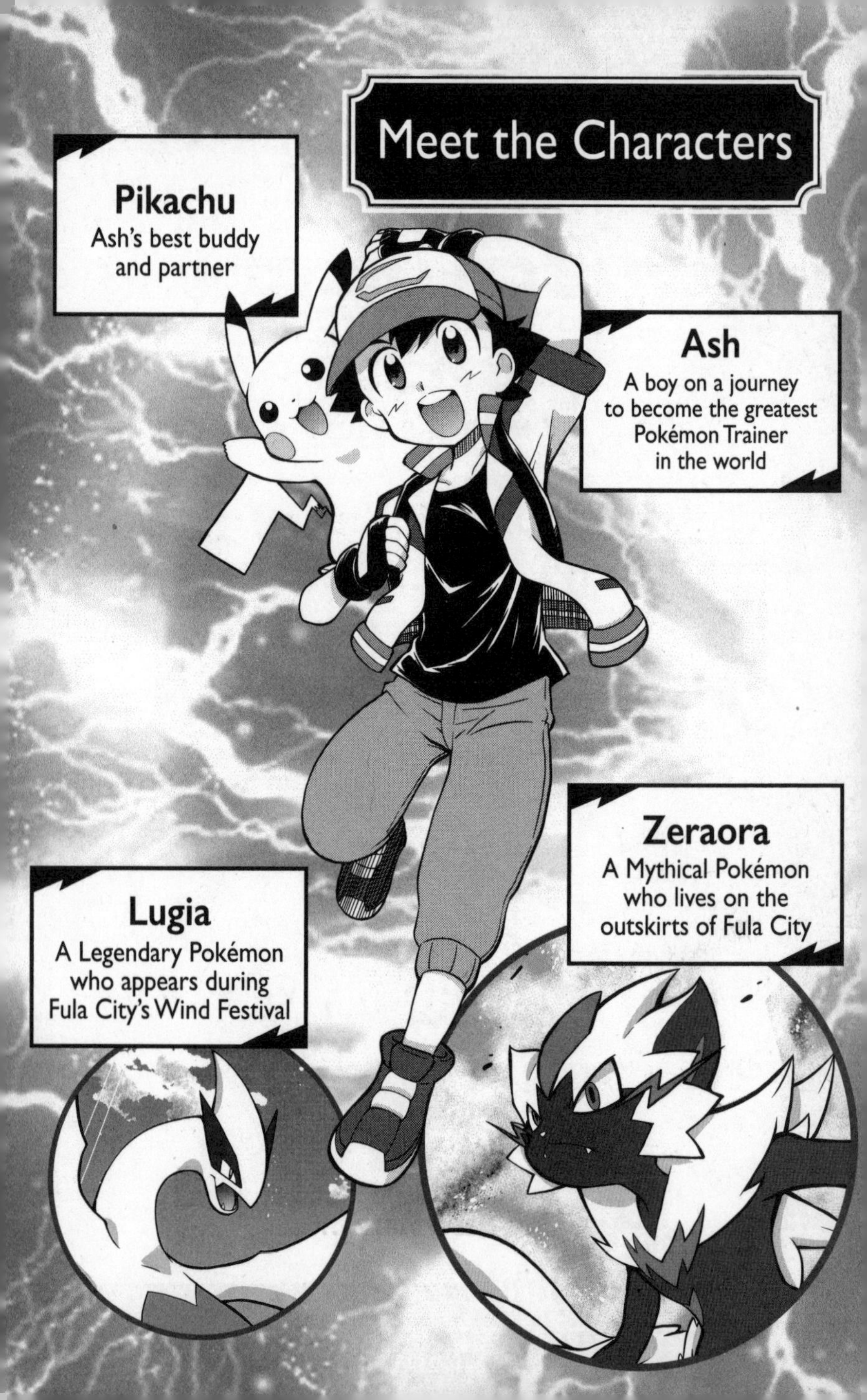
Meet the Characters
Pikachu
Ash's best buddy and partner
Ash
A boy on a journey to become the greatest Pokémon Trainer in the world
Zeraora
A Mythical Pokémon who lives on the outskirts of Fula City
Lugia
A Legendary Pokémon who appears during Fula City's Wind Festival

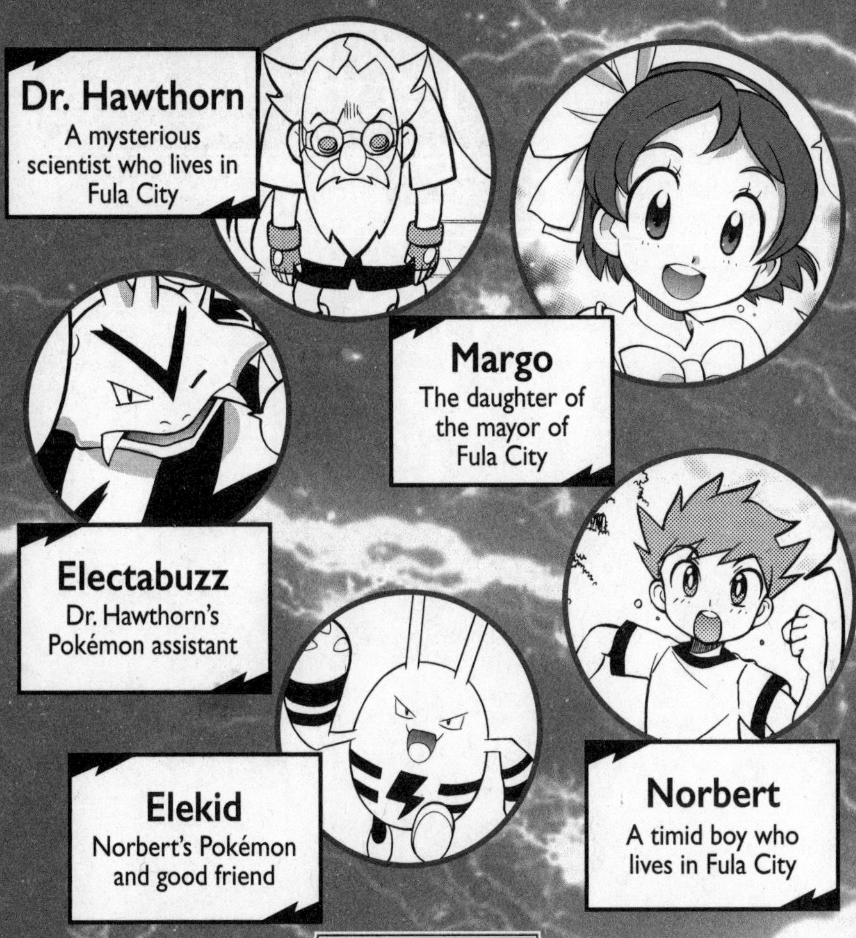
Dr. Hawthorn
A mysterious scientist who lives in Fula City
Margo
The daughter of the mayor of Fula City
Electabuzz
Dr. Hawthorn's Pokémon assistant
Norbert
A timid boy who lives in Fula City
Elekid
Norbert's Pokémon and good friend

CONTENTS

Chapter 1
Zeraora Is Born!

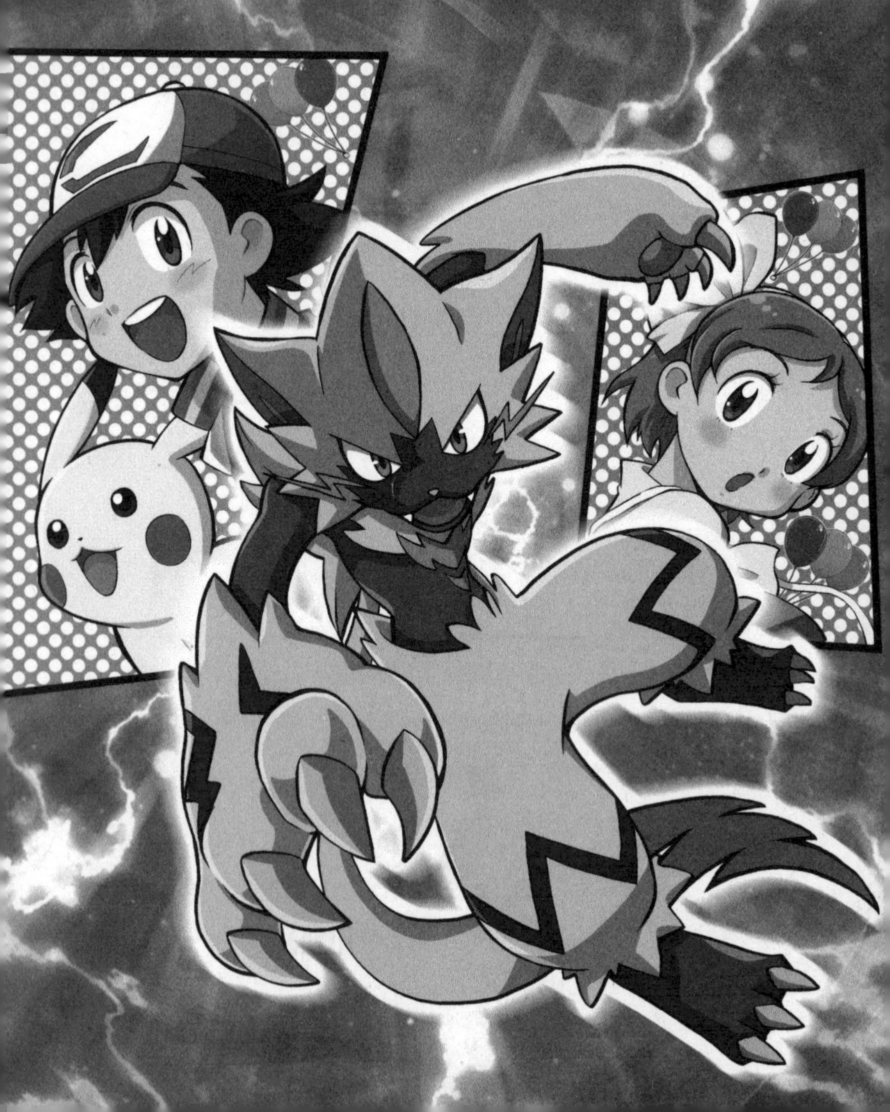

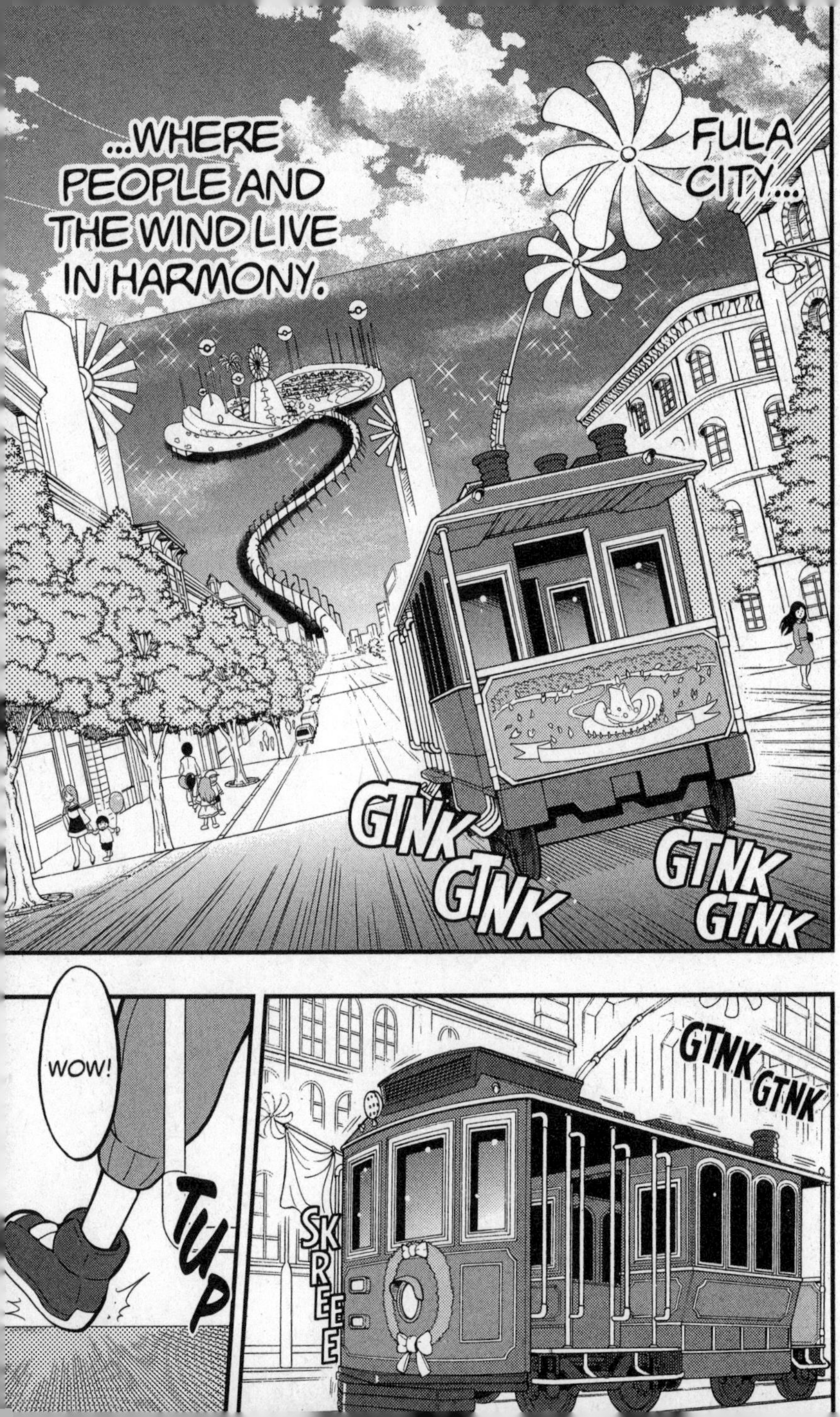
FULA CITY...
...WHERE PEOPLE AND THE WIND LIVE IN HARMONY.
GTNK GTNK
GTNK GTNK
GTNK GTNK
SKREEE
WOW!
TUP

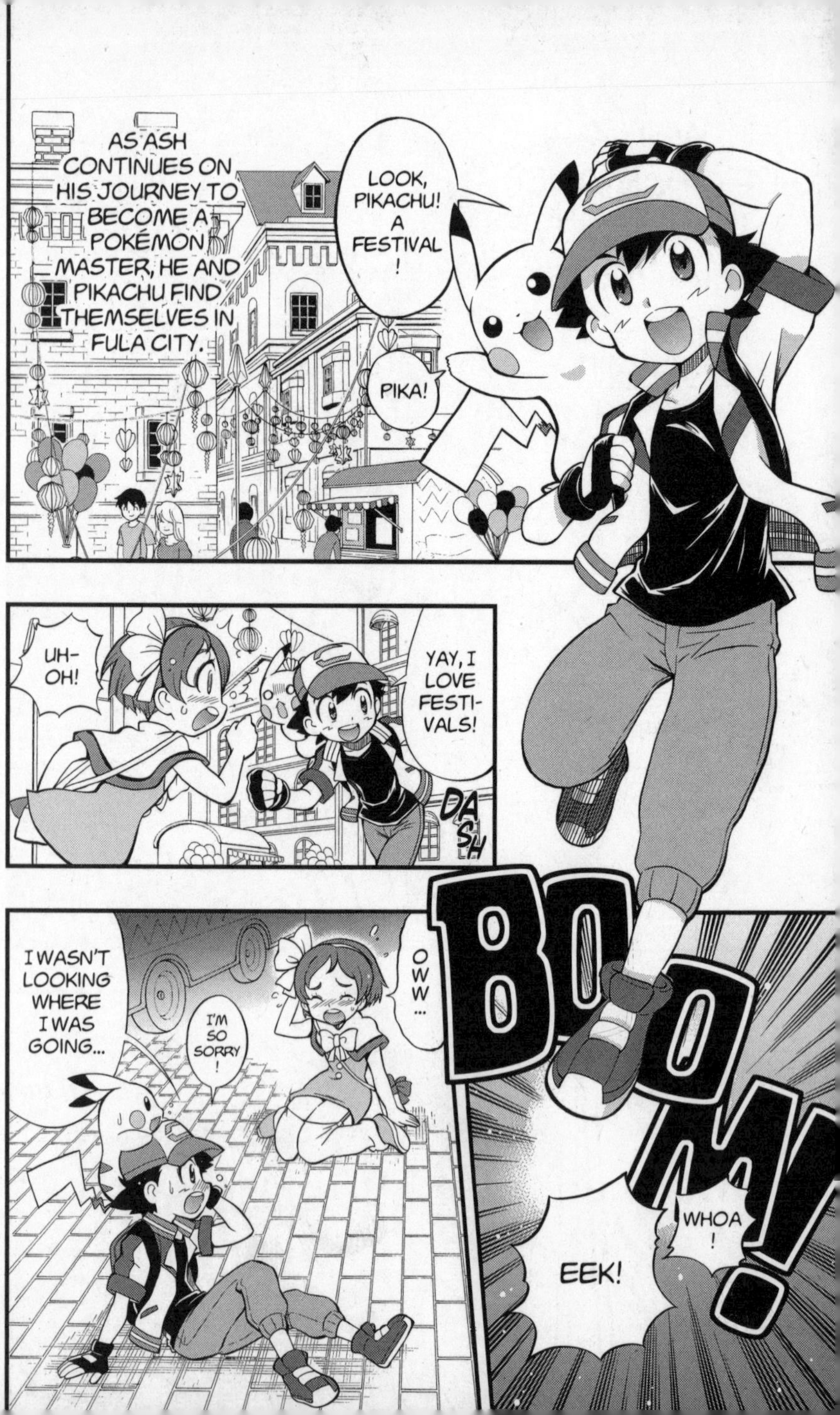
AS ASH CONTINUES ON HIS JOURNEY TO BECOME A POKÉMON MASTER, HE AND PIKACHU FIND THEMSELVES IN FULA CITY.
LOOK, PIKACHU! A FESTIVAL!
PIKA!
YAY, I LOVE FESTI-VALS!
UH-OH!
DASH
BOOM!
WHOA!
EEK!
OWW...
I'M SO SORRY!
I WASN'T LOOKING WHERE I WAS GOING...

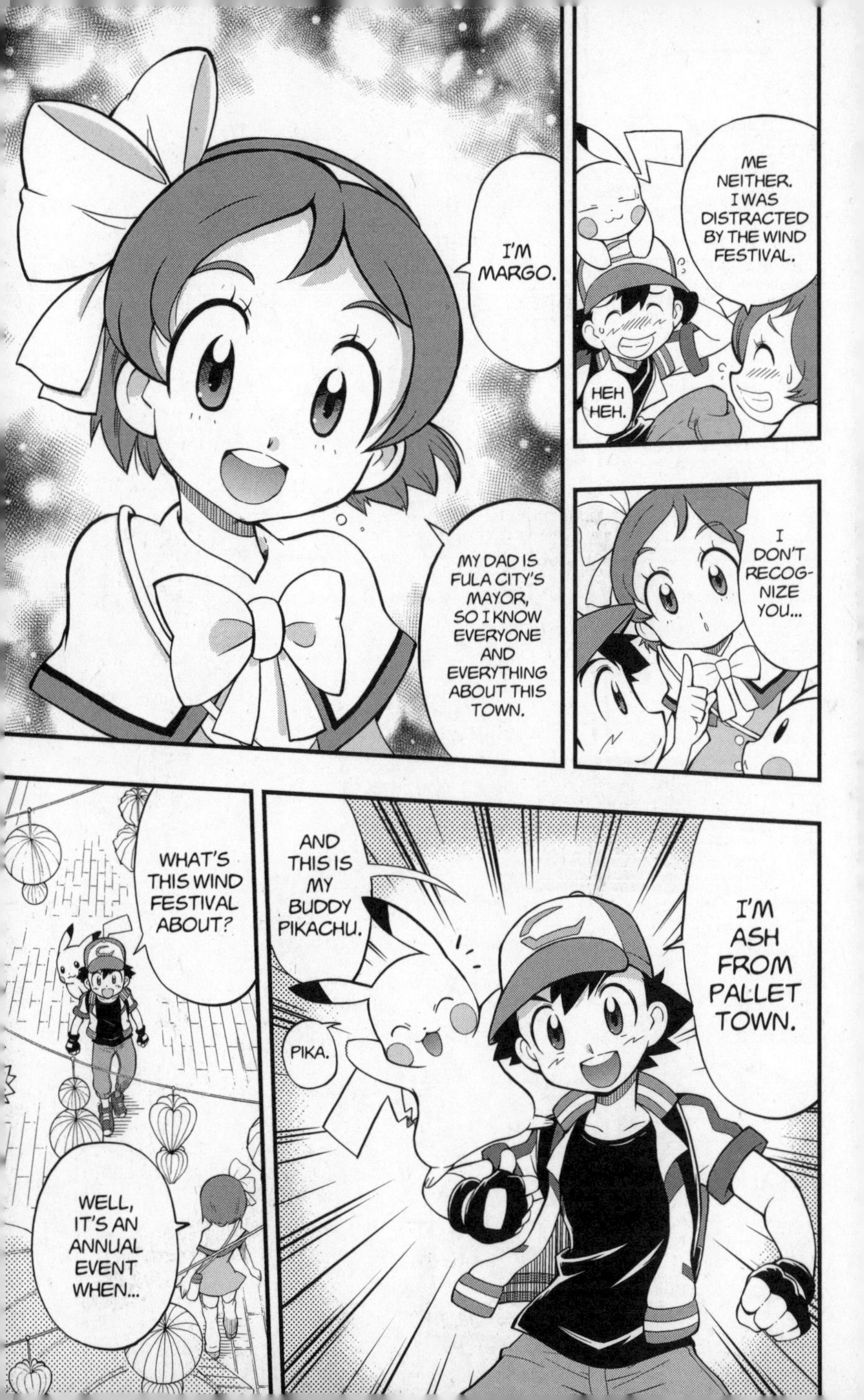
ME NEITHER. I WAS DISTRACTED BY THE WIND FESTIVAL.
HEH HEH.
I DON'T RECOG-NIZE YOU...
I'M MARGO.
MY DAD IS FULA CITY'S MAYOR, SO I KNOW EVERYONE AND EVERYTHING ABOUT THIS TOWN.
I'M ASH FROM PALLET TOWN.
AND THIS IS MY BUDDY PIKACHU.
PIKA.
WHAT'S THIS WIND FESTIVAL ABOUT?
WELL, IT'S AN ANNUAL EVENT WHEN...

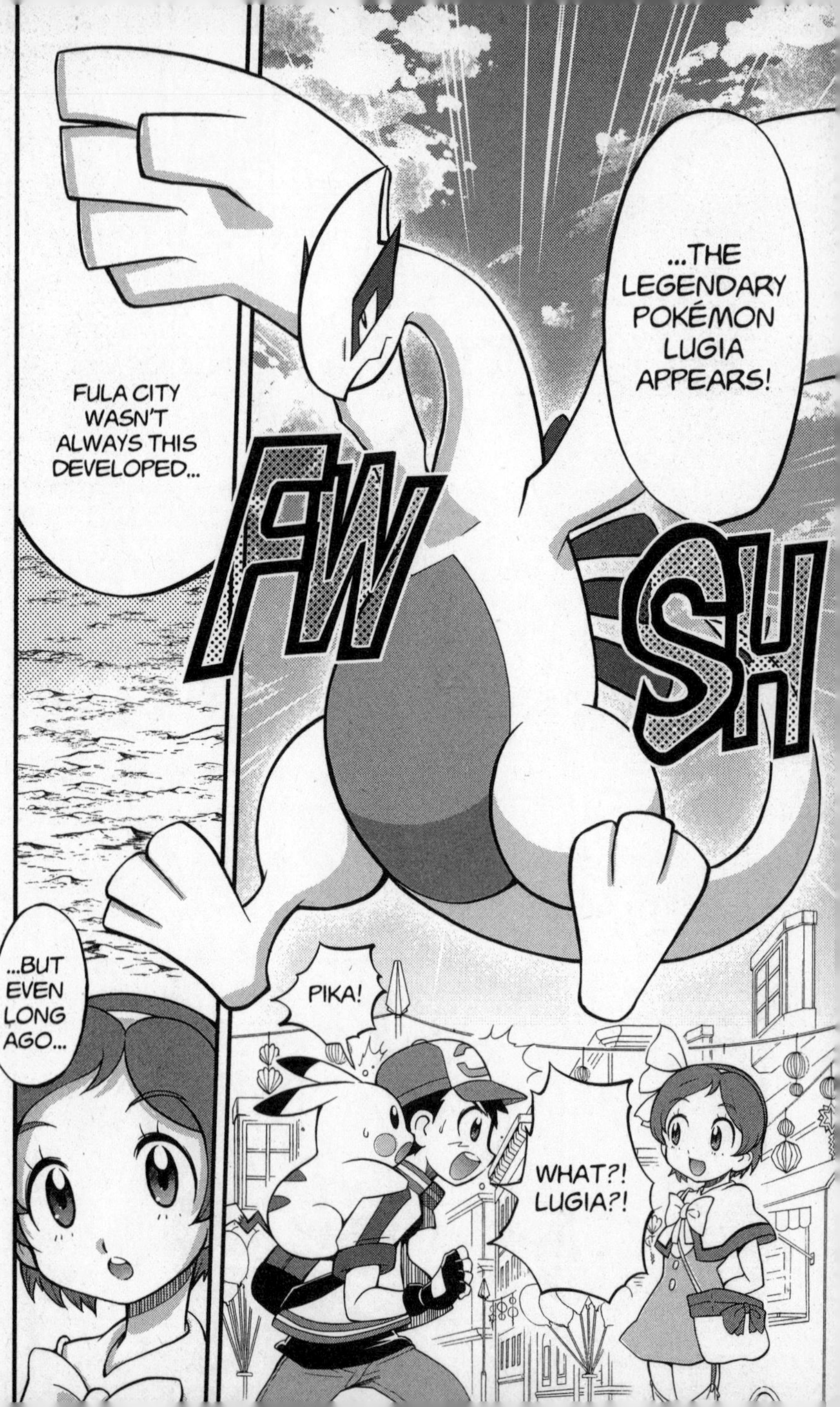
...THE LEGENDARY POKÉMON LUGIA APPEARS!
FWSH
WHAT?! LUGIA?!
PIKA!
FULA CITY WASN'T ALWAYS THIS DEVELOPED...
...BUT EVEN LONG AGO...

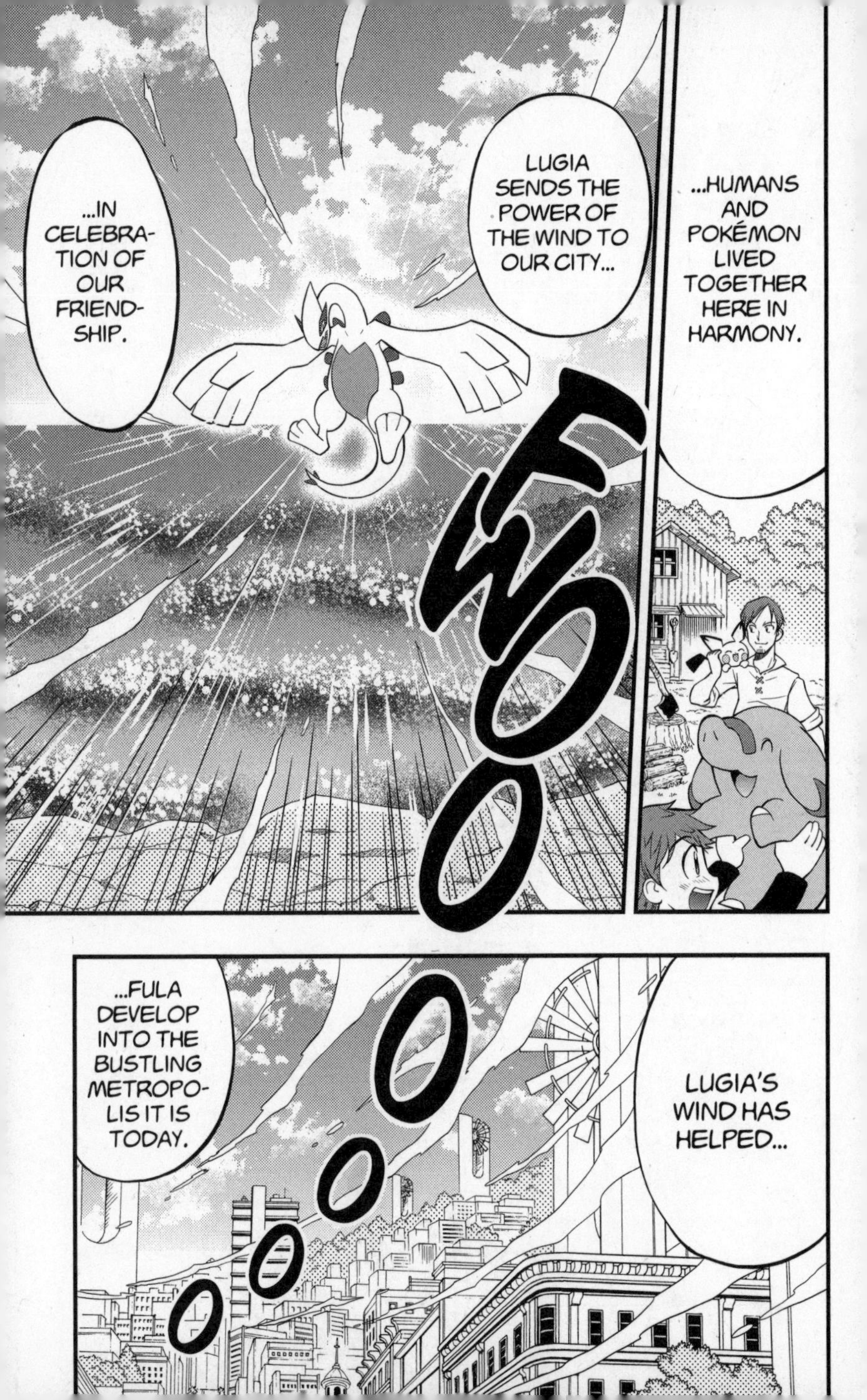
...HUMANS AND POKÉMON LIVED TOGETHER HERE IN HARMONY.
LUGIA SENDS THE POWER OF THE WIND TO OUR CITY...
...IN CELEBRATION OF OUR FRIENDSHIP.
LUGIA'S WIND HAS HELPED...
...FULA DEVELOP INTO THE BUSTLING METROPOLIS IT IS TODAY.

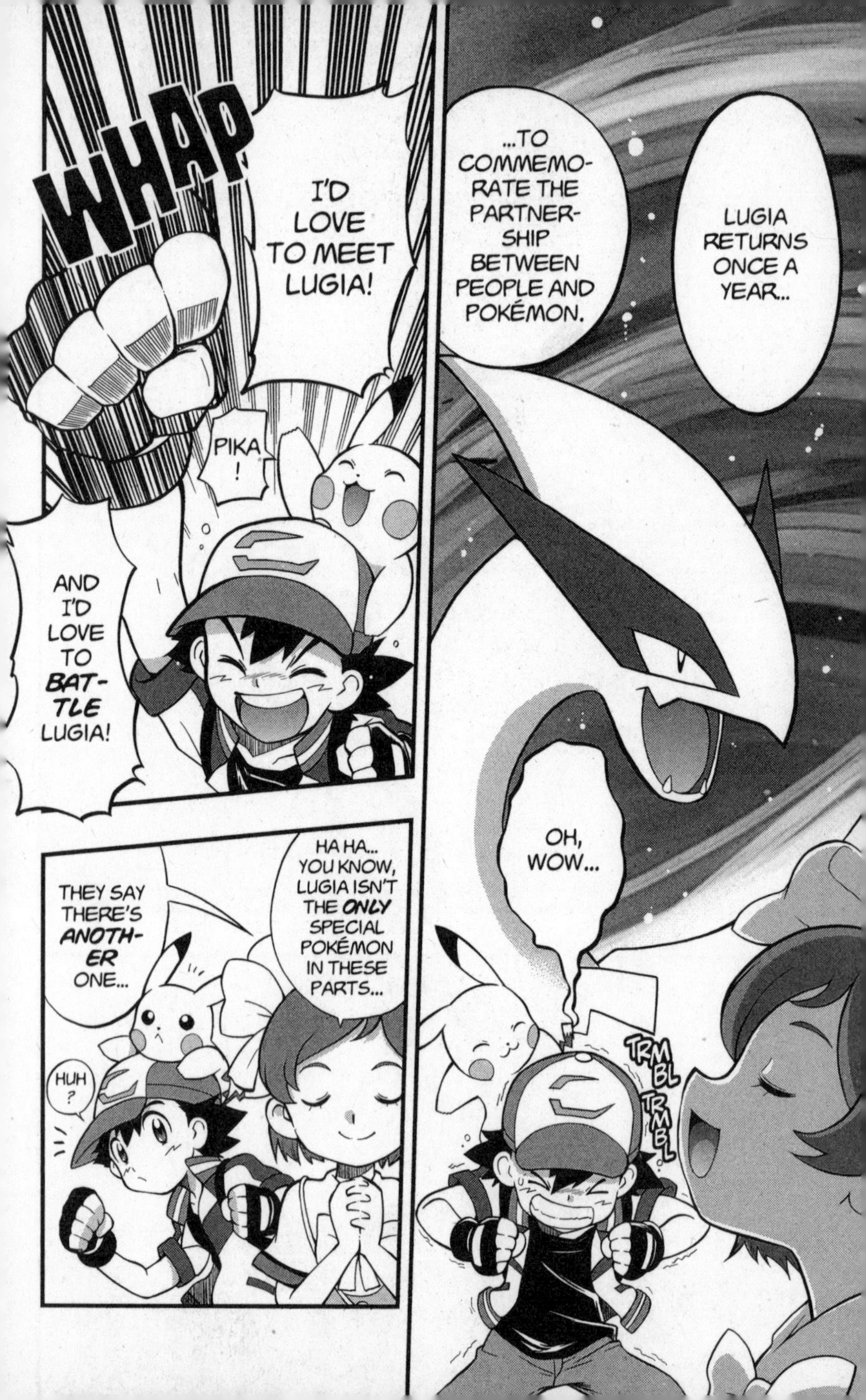

LUGIA RETURNS ONCE A YEAR...
...TO COMMEMORATE THE PARTNERSHIP BETWEEN PEOPLE AND POKéMON.
OH, WOW...
TRMBL TRMBL
WHAP
I'D LOVE TO MEET LUGIA!
PIKA!
AND I'D LOVE TO **BATTLE** LUGIA!
HA HA... YOU KNOW, LUGIA ISN'T THE **ONLY** SPECIAL POKéMON IN THESE PARTS...
THEY SAY THERE'S **ANOTHER** ONE...
HUH?

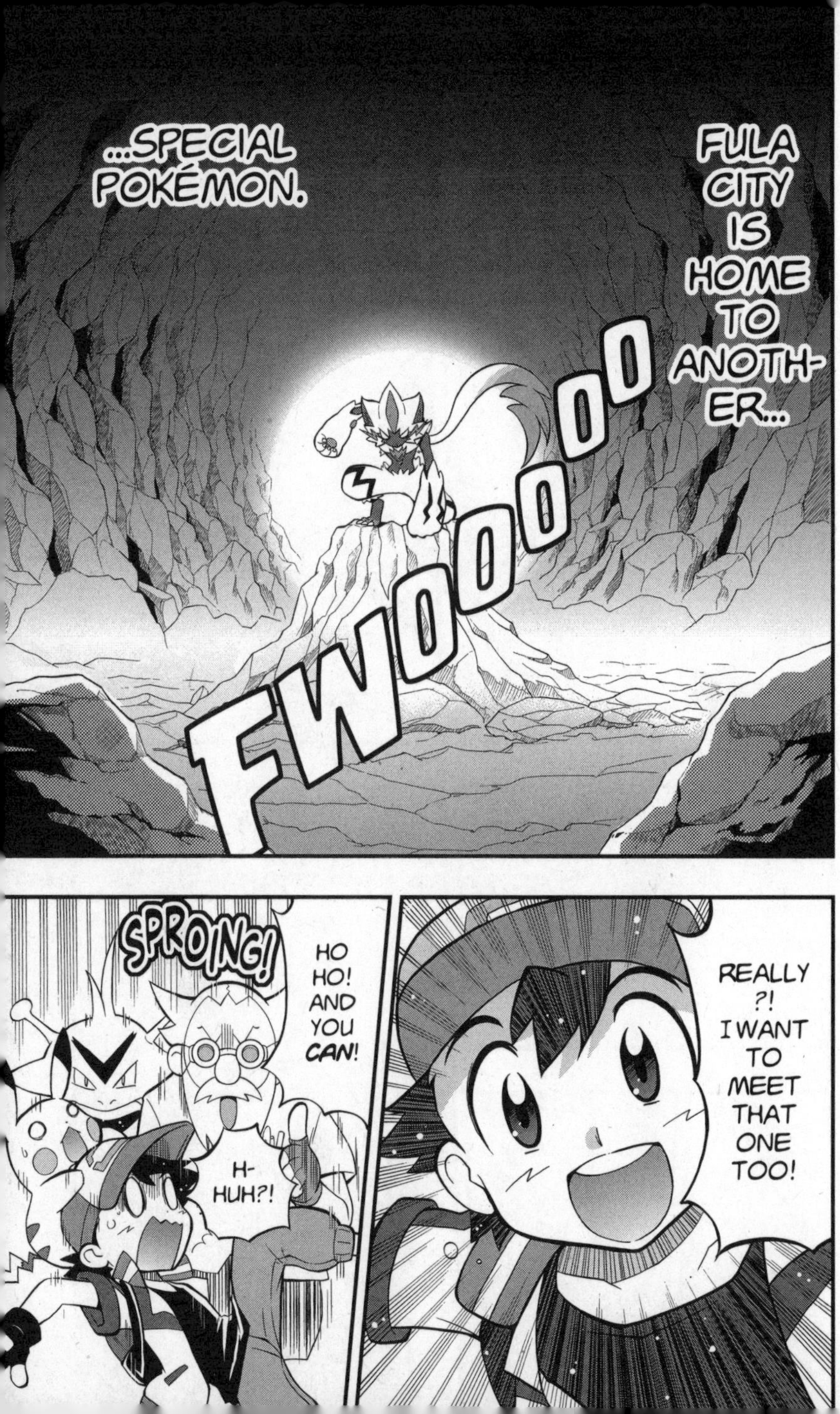
FULA CITY IS HOME TO ANOTHER-ER...
...SPECIAL POKÉMON.
FWOOOOOO
REALLY?! I WANT TO MEET THAT ONE TOO!
HO HO! AND YOU CAN!
SPROING!
H-HUH?!

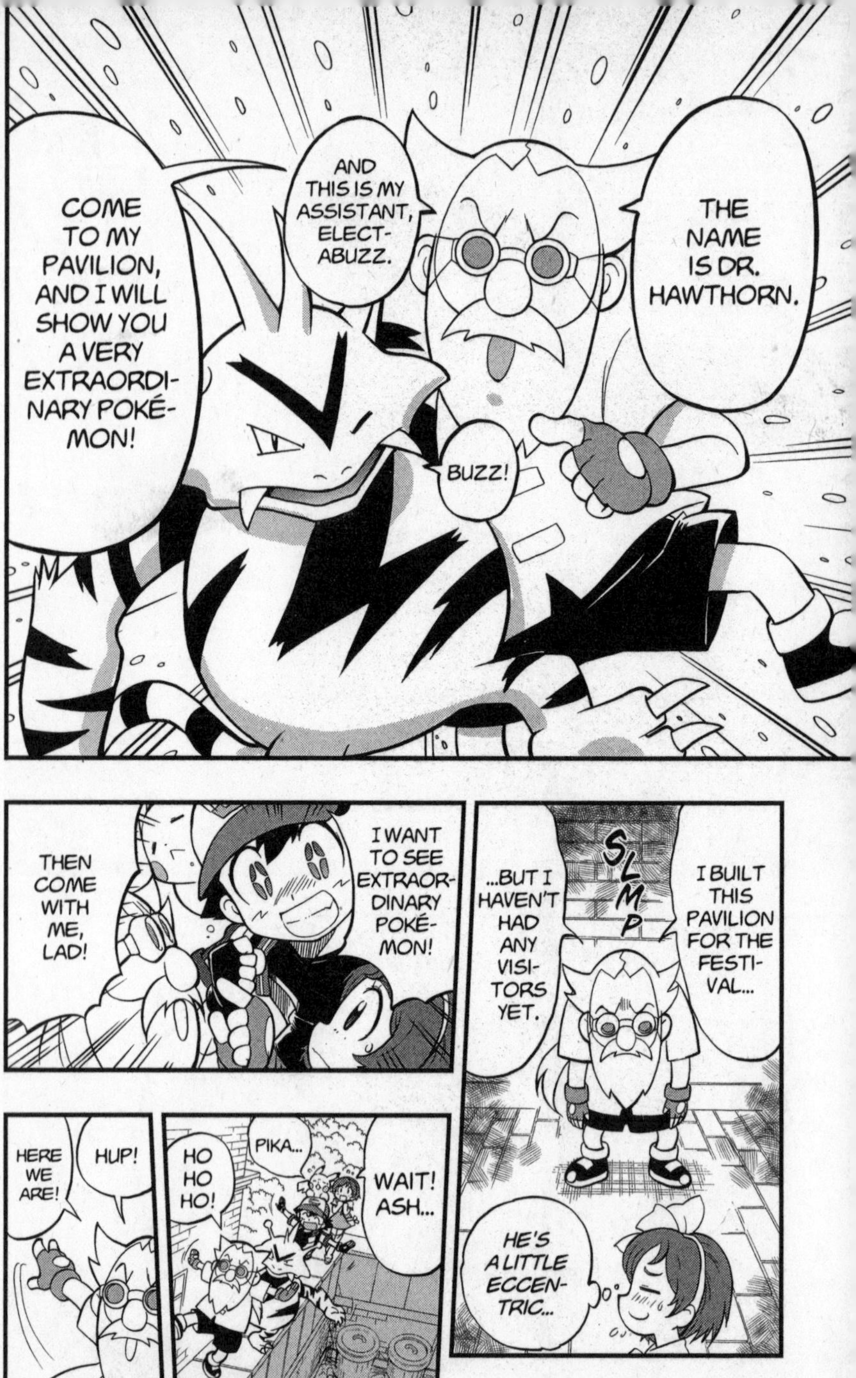
THE NAME IS DR. HAWTHORN.
AND THIS IS MY ASSISTANT, ELECTABUZZ.
BUZZ!
COME TO MY PAVILION, AND I WILL SHOW YOU A VERY EXTRAORDINARY POKÉMON!
I BUILT THIS PAVILION FOR THE FESTIVAL...
SLMP
...BUT I HAVEN'T HAD ANY VISITORS YET.
HE'S A LITTLE ECCENTRIC...
I WANT TO SEE EXTRAORDINARY POKÉMON!
THEN COME WITH ME, LAD!
WAIT! ASH...
PIKA...
HO HO HO!
HUP!
HERE WE ARE!

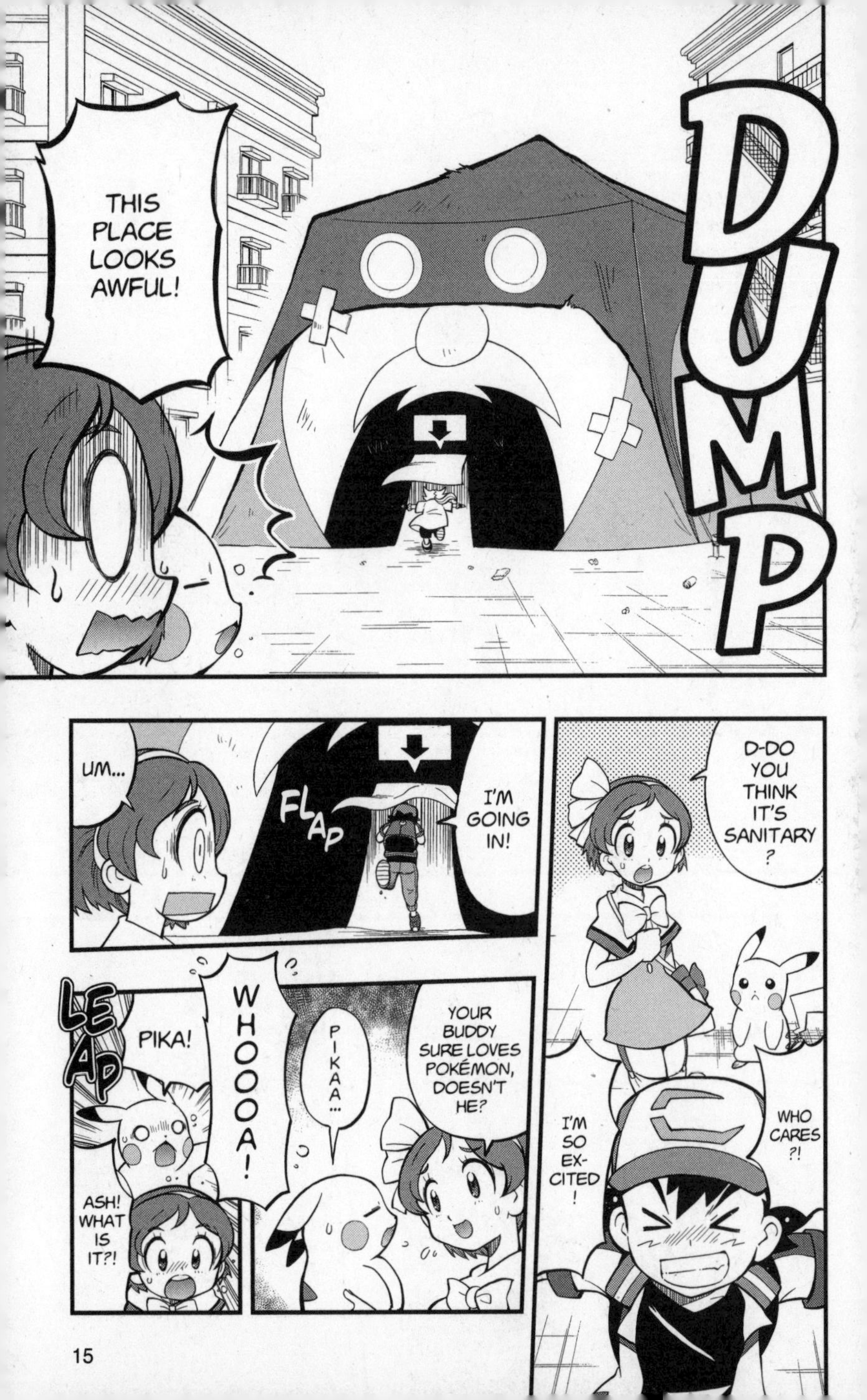
DUMP
THIS PLACE LOOKS AWFUL!
D-DO YOU THINK IT'S SANITARY?
WHO CARES?!
I'M SO EX-CITED!
I'M GOING IN!
FLAP
UM...
YOUR BUDDY SURE LOVES POKÉMON, DOESN'T HE?
PIKAA...
WHOOOOA!
PIKA!
LEAP
ASH! WHAT IS IT?!

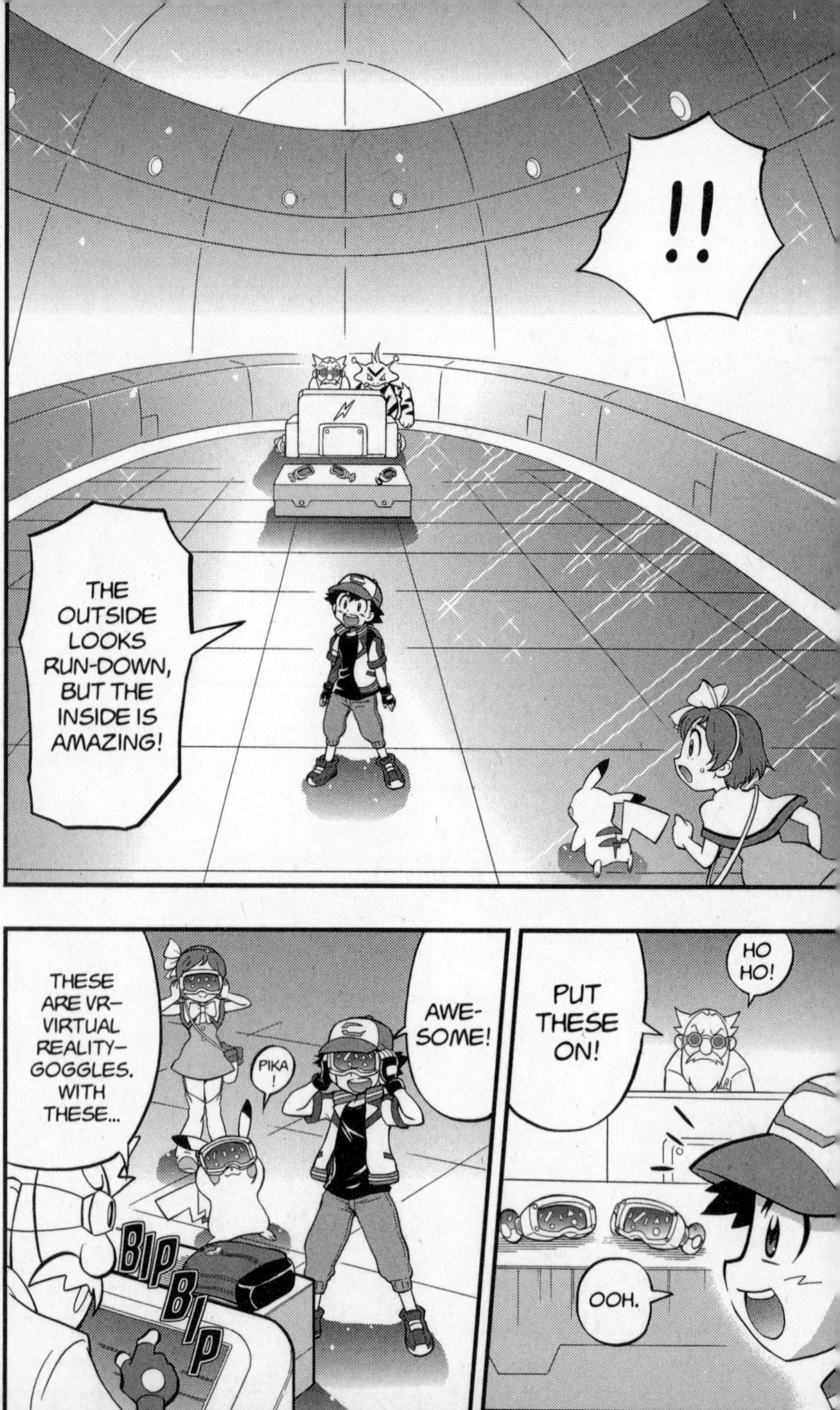
!!
THE OUTSIDE LOOKS RUN-DOWN, BUT THE INSIDE IS AMAZING!
HO HO!
PUT THESE ON!
OOH.
AWE-SOME!
PIKA!
THESE ARE VR—VIRTUAL REALITY—GOGGLES. WITH THESE...
BIP BIP

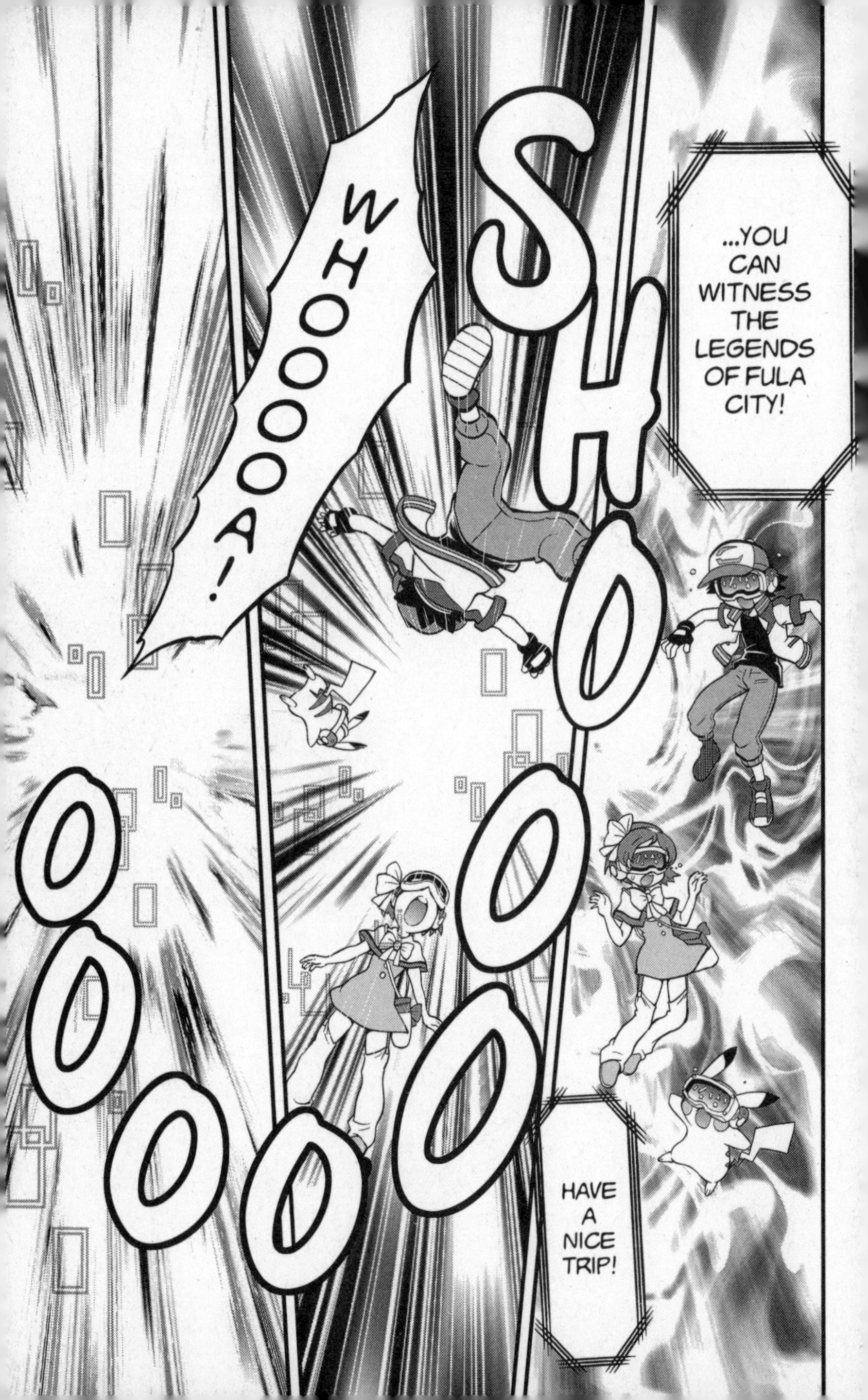
...YOU CAN WITNESS THE LEGENDS OF FULA CITY!
SHOOOOOOOOO
WHOOOOOA!
HAVE A NICE TRIP!

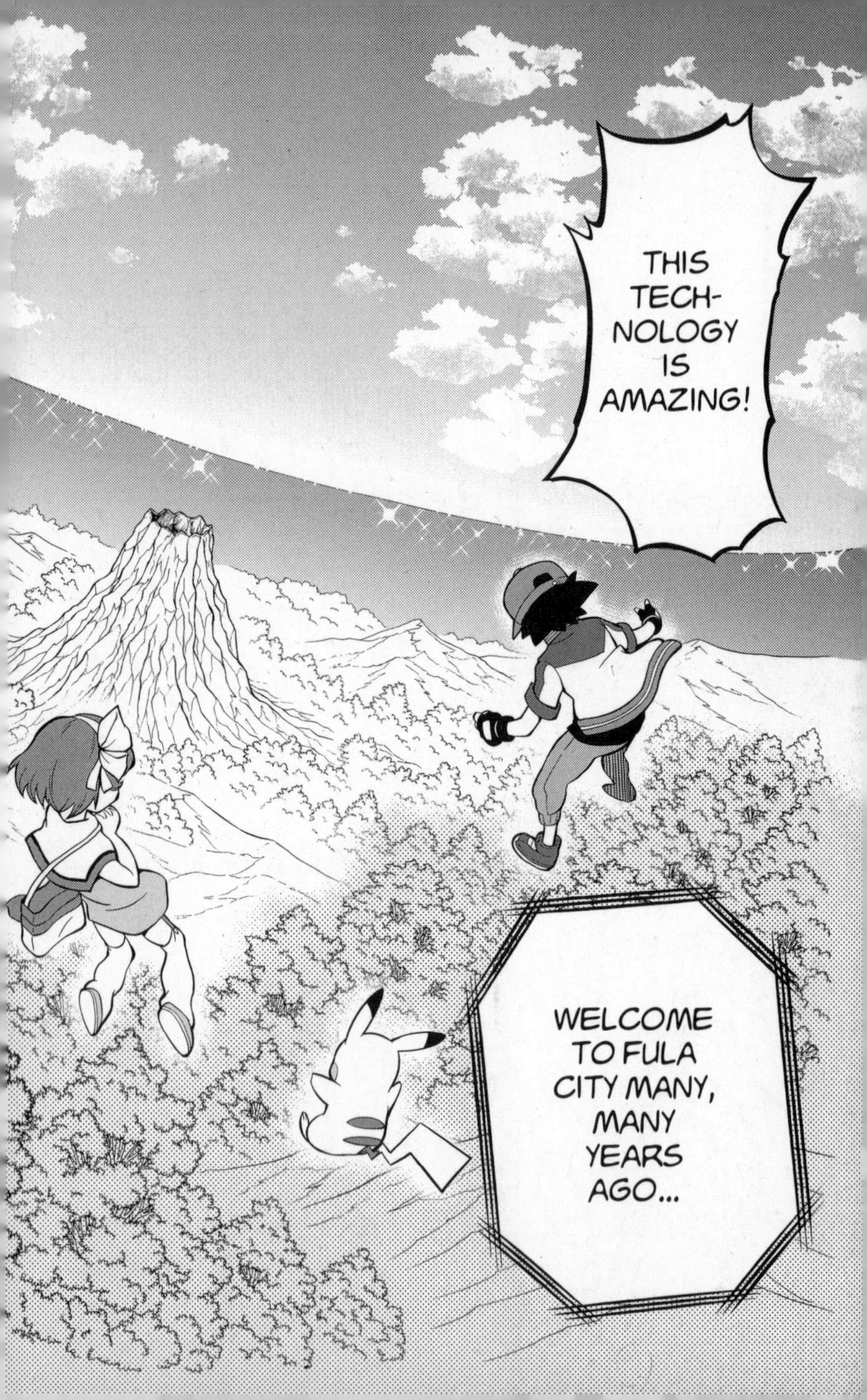
THIS TECH-NOLOGY IS AMAZING!
WELCOME TO FULA CITY MANY, MANY YEARS AGO...

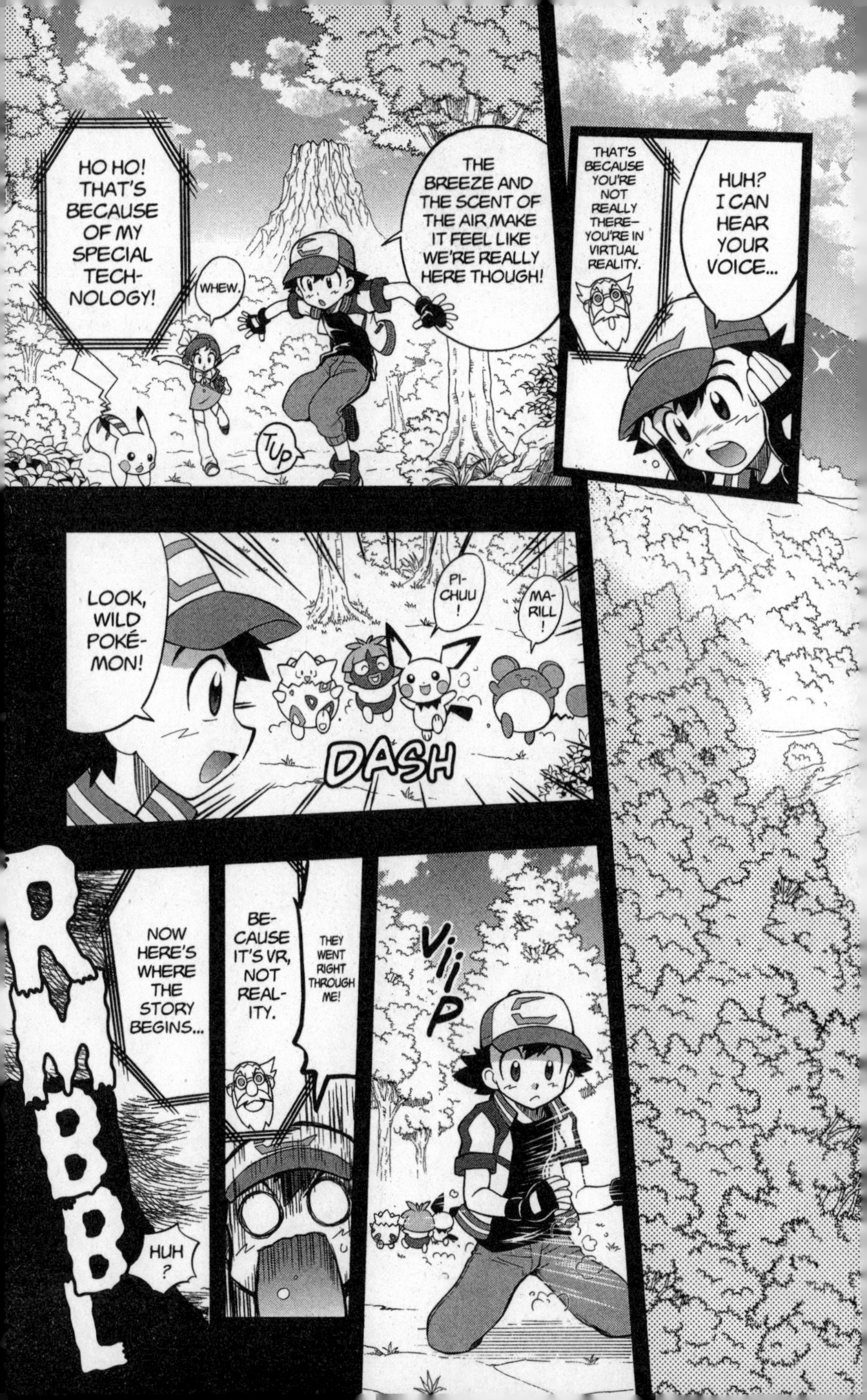
HUH? I CAN HEAR YOUR VOICE...
THAT'S BECAUSE YOU'RE NOT REALLY THERE—YOU'RE IN VIRTUAL REALITY.
THE BREEZE AND THE SCENT OF THE AIR MAKE IT FEEL LIKE WE'RE REALLY HERE THOUGH!
WHEW.
HO HO! THAT'S BECAUSE OF MY SPECIAL TECH-NOLOGY!
TUP
MA-RILL!
PI-CHUU!
LOOK, WILD POKÉ-MON!
DASH
VIIP
THEY WENT RIGHT THROUGH ME!
BE-CAUSE IT'S VR, NOT REAL-ITY.
HUH?
NOW HERE'S WHERE THE STORY BEGINS...
RMBBL

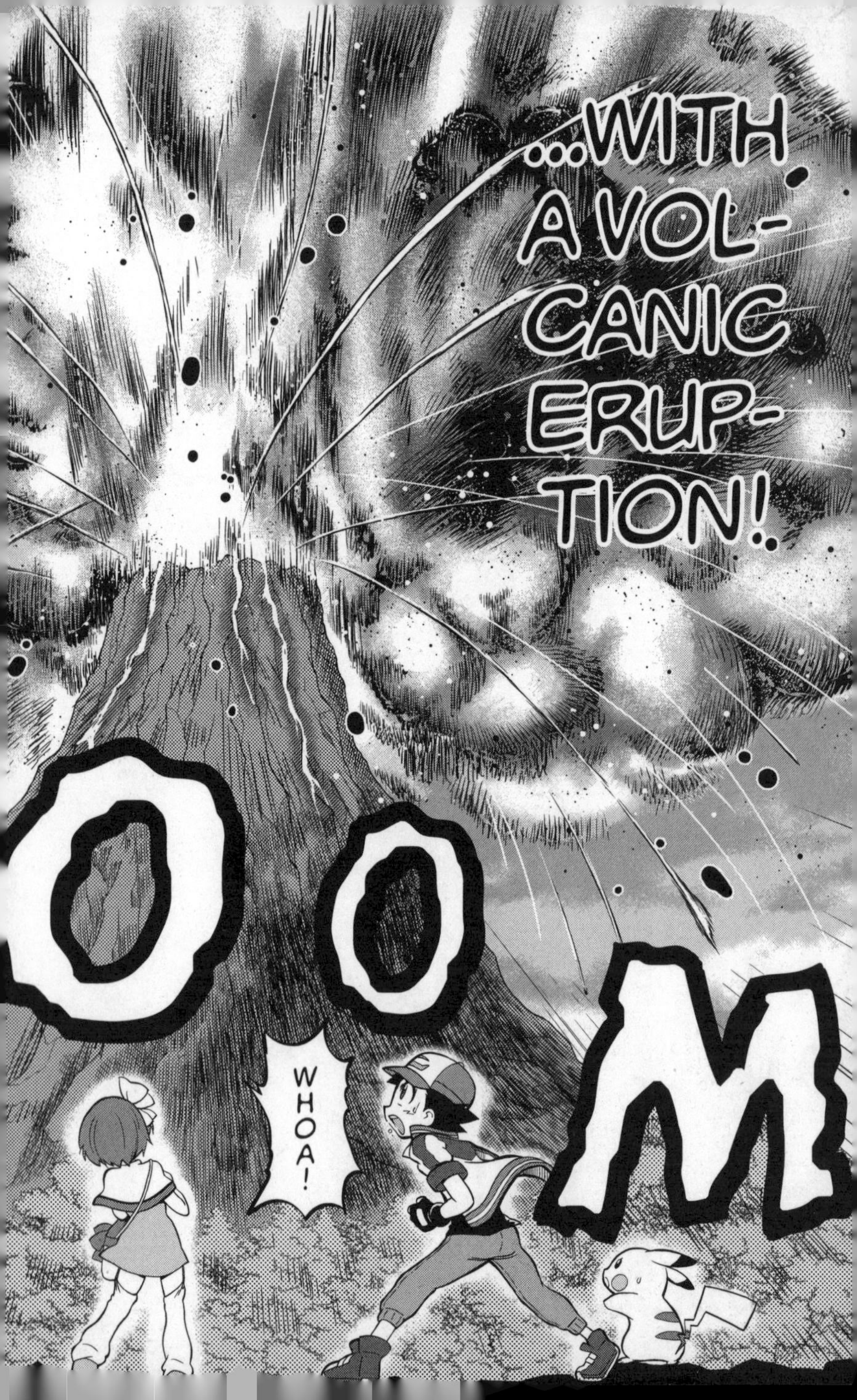
...WITH A VOL- CANIC ERUP- TION!
OOM
WHOA!

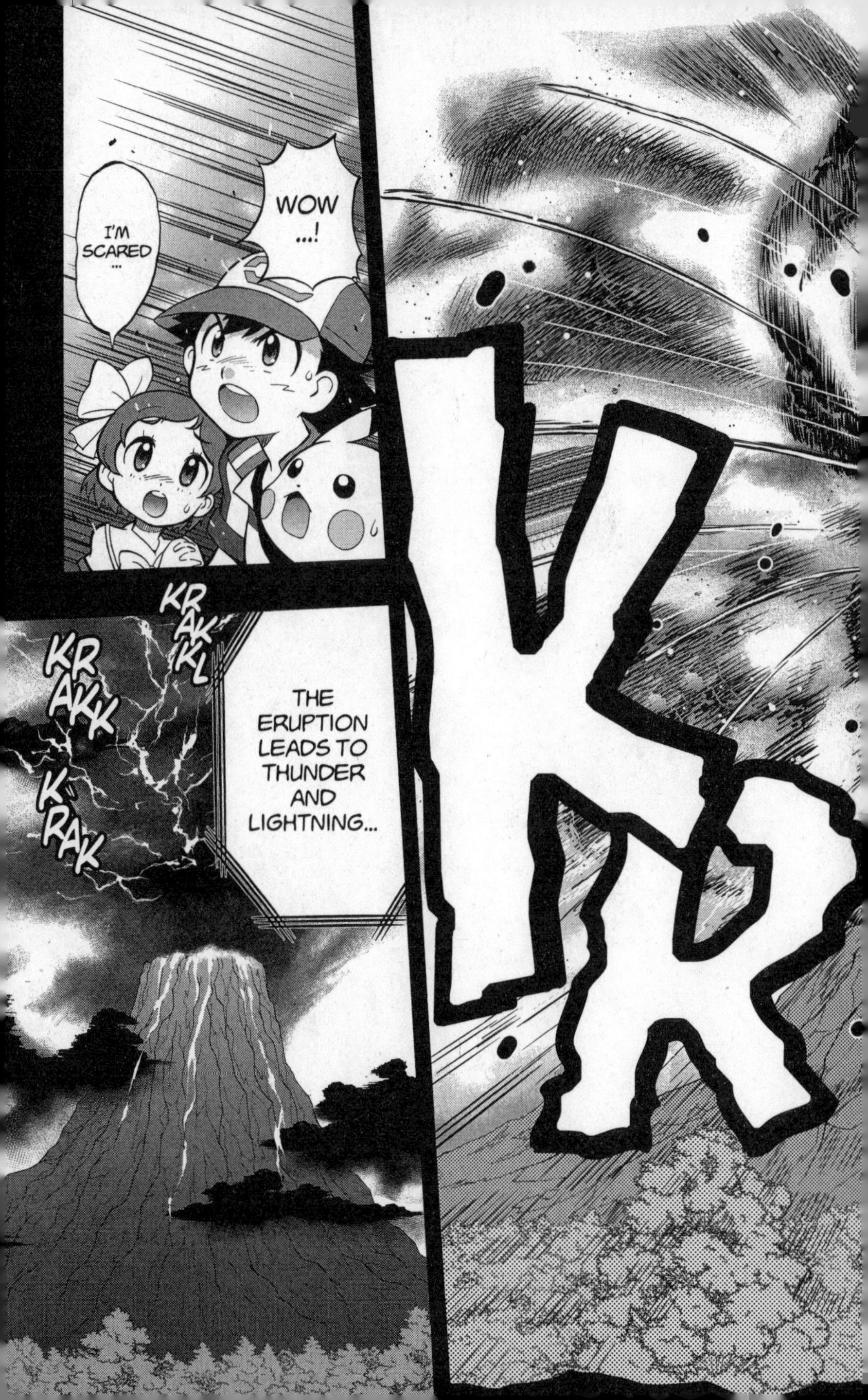
KR
WOW ...!
I'M SCARED ...
KRAKKL
THE ERUPTION LEADS TO THUNDER AND LIGHTNING...
KRAKK
KRAK

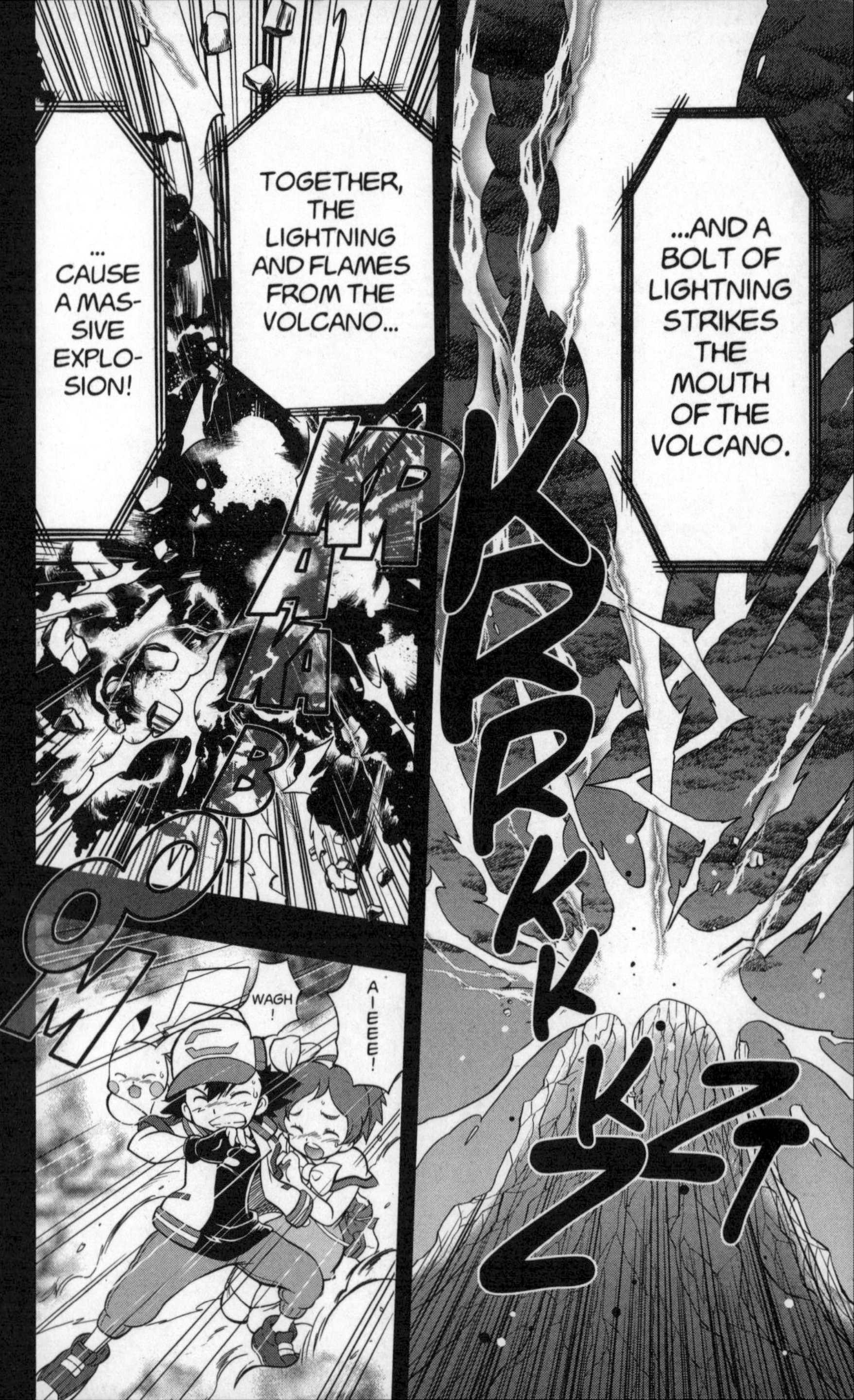
...AND A BOLT OF LIGHTNING STRIKES THE MOUTH OF THE VOLCANO.
KRRKKKZZT
TOGETHER, THE LIGHTNING AND FLAMES FROM THE VOLCANO...
... CAUSE A MAS-SIVE EXPLO-SION!
A-IEEE!
WAGH!

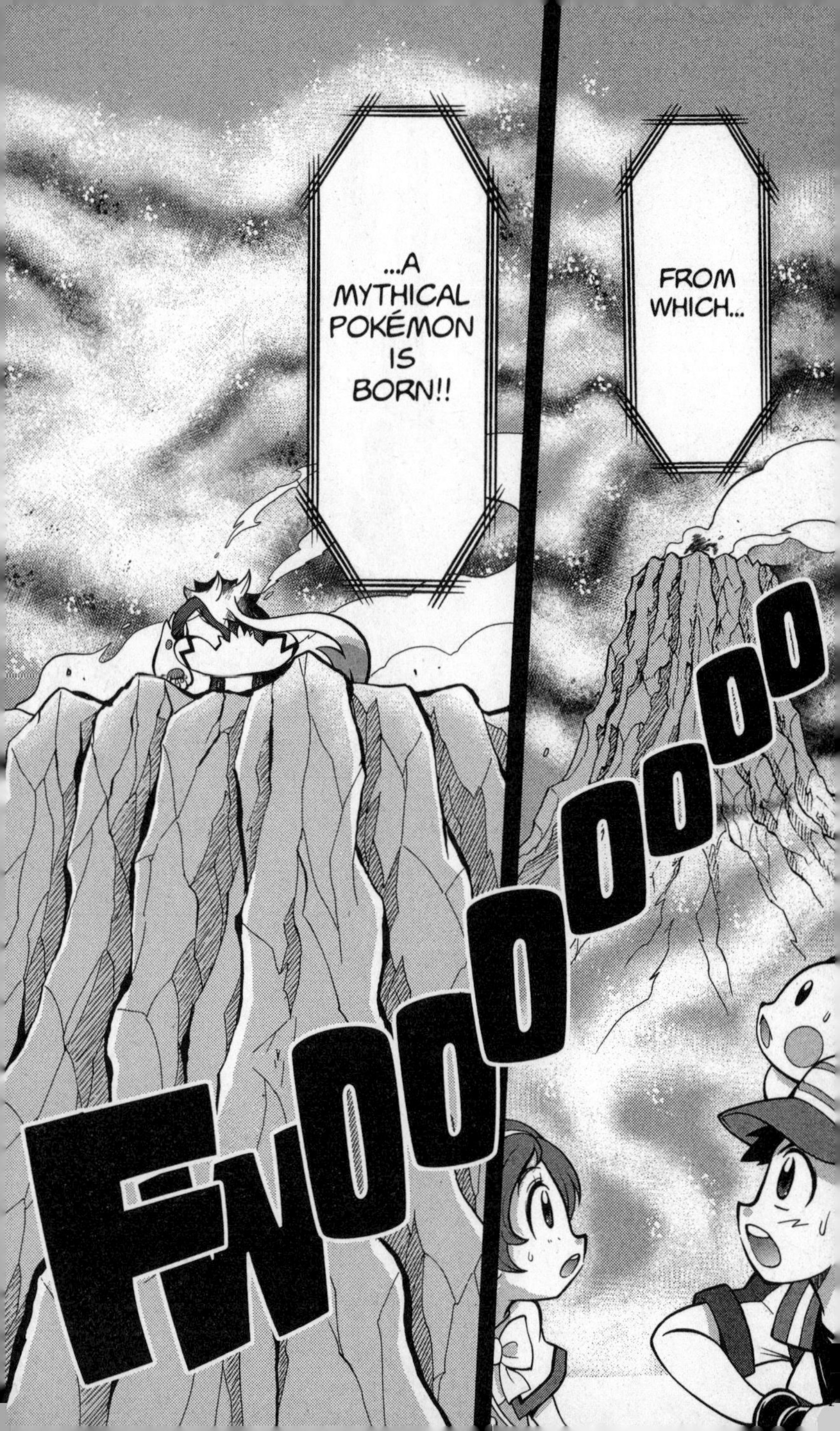
FROM WHICH...
...A MYTHICAL POKÉMON IS BORN!!
FWOOOOOOOO

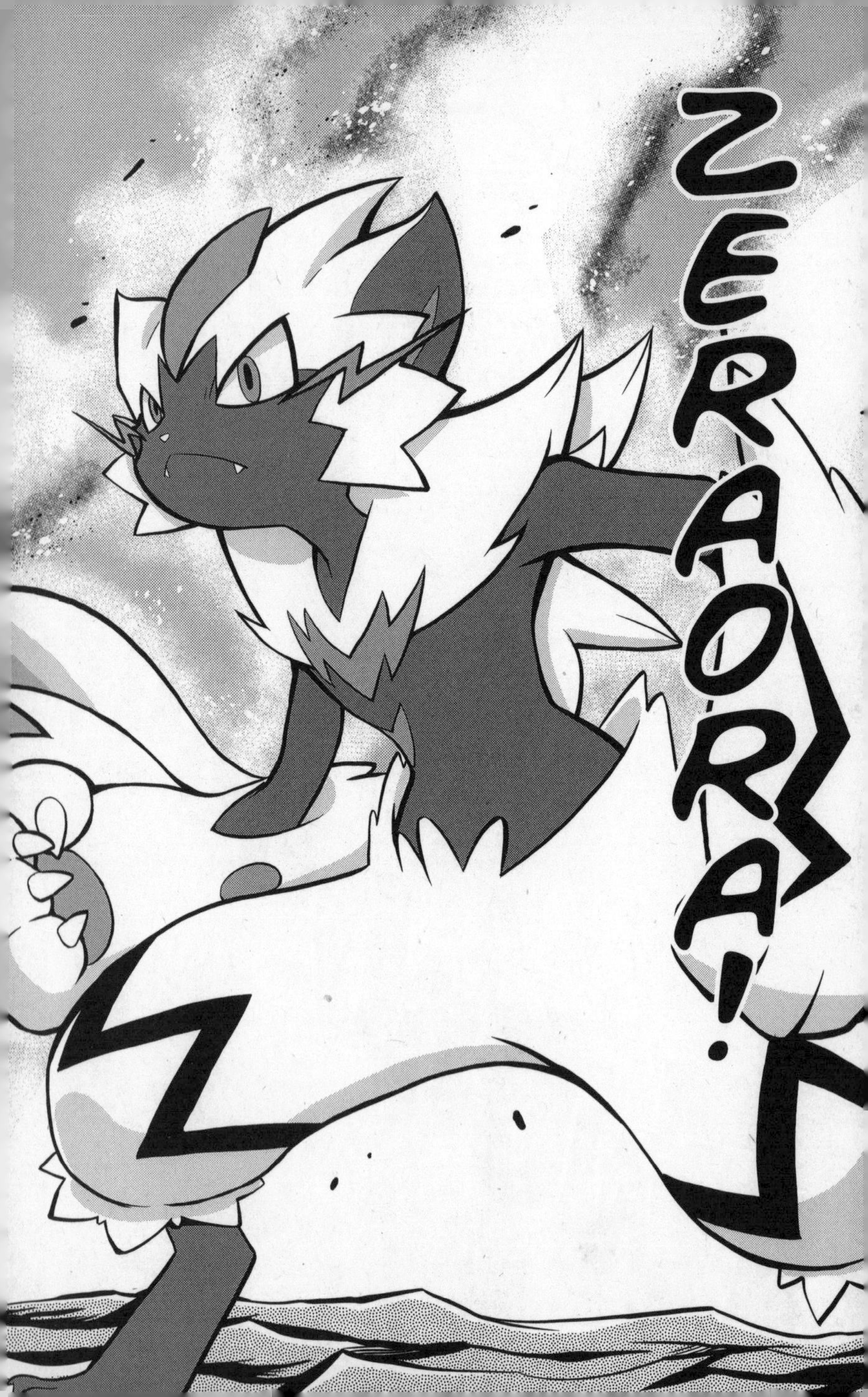
ZERAORA!

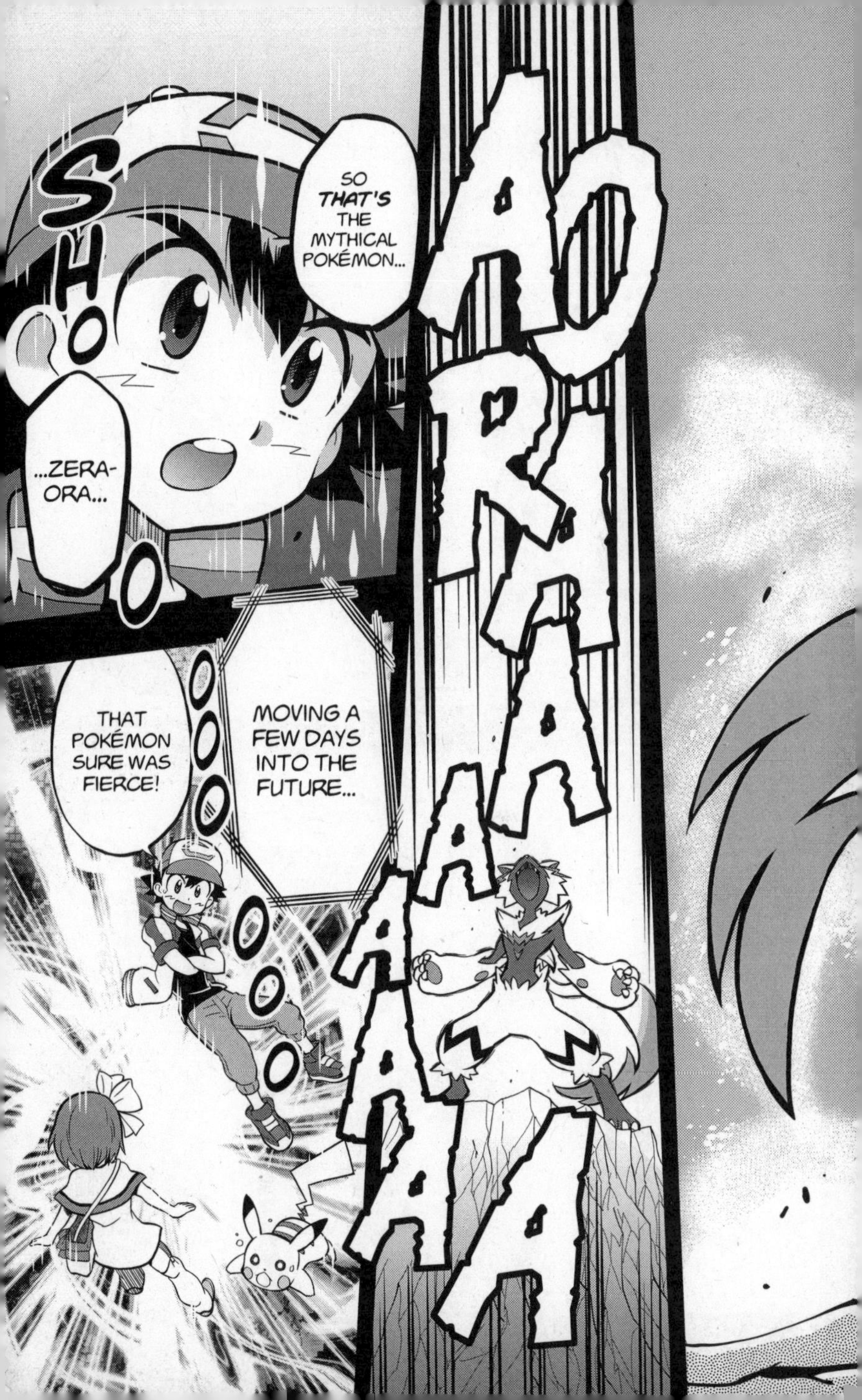
AORAAAAA
SHOO
SO THAT'S THE MYTHICAL POKÉMON...
...ZERA-ORA...
MOVING A FEW DAYS INTO THE FUTURE...
THAT POKÉMON SURE WAS FIERCE!

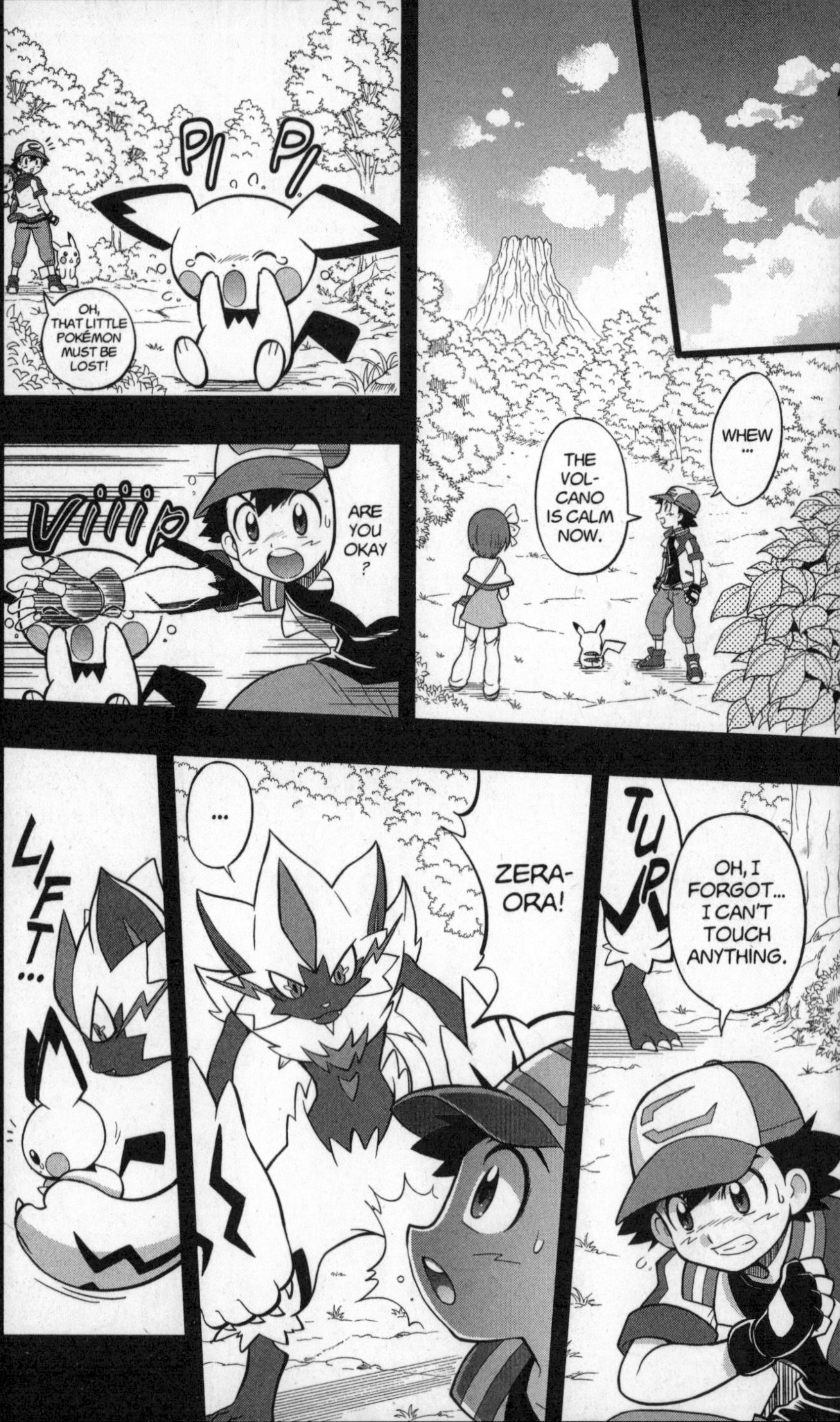
WHEW...
THE VOL-CANO IS CALM NOW.
PI PI
OH, THAT LITTLE POKÉMON MUST BE LOST!
ARE YOU OKAY?
VIIIP
TUP
OH, I FORGOT... I CAN'T TOUCH ANYTHING.
...
ZERA-ORA!
LIFT...

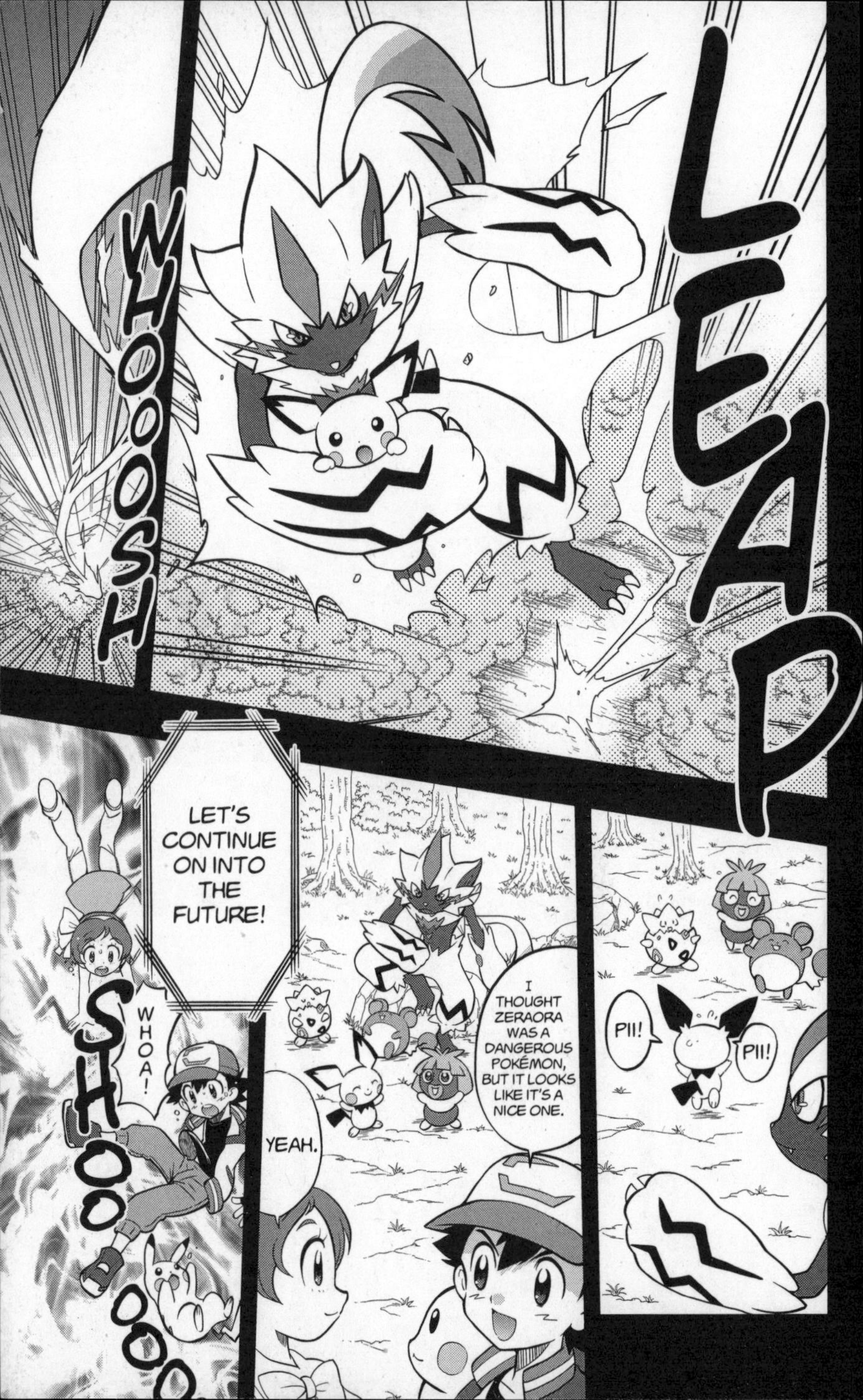
LEAP
WHOOSH
PII!
PII!
I THOUGHT ZERAORA WAS A DANGEROUS POKÉMON, BUT IT LOOKS LIKE IT'S A NICE ONE.
YEAH.
LET'S CONTINUE ON INTO THE FUTURE!
WHOA!
SHOOOOO

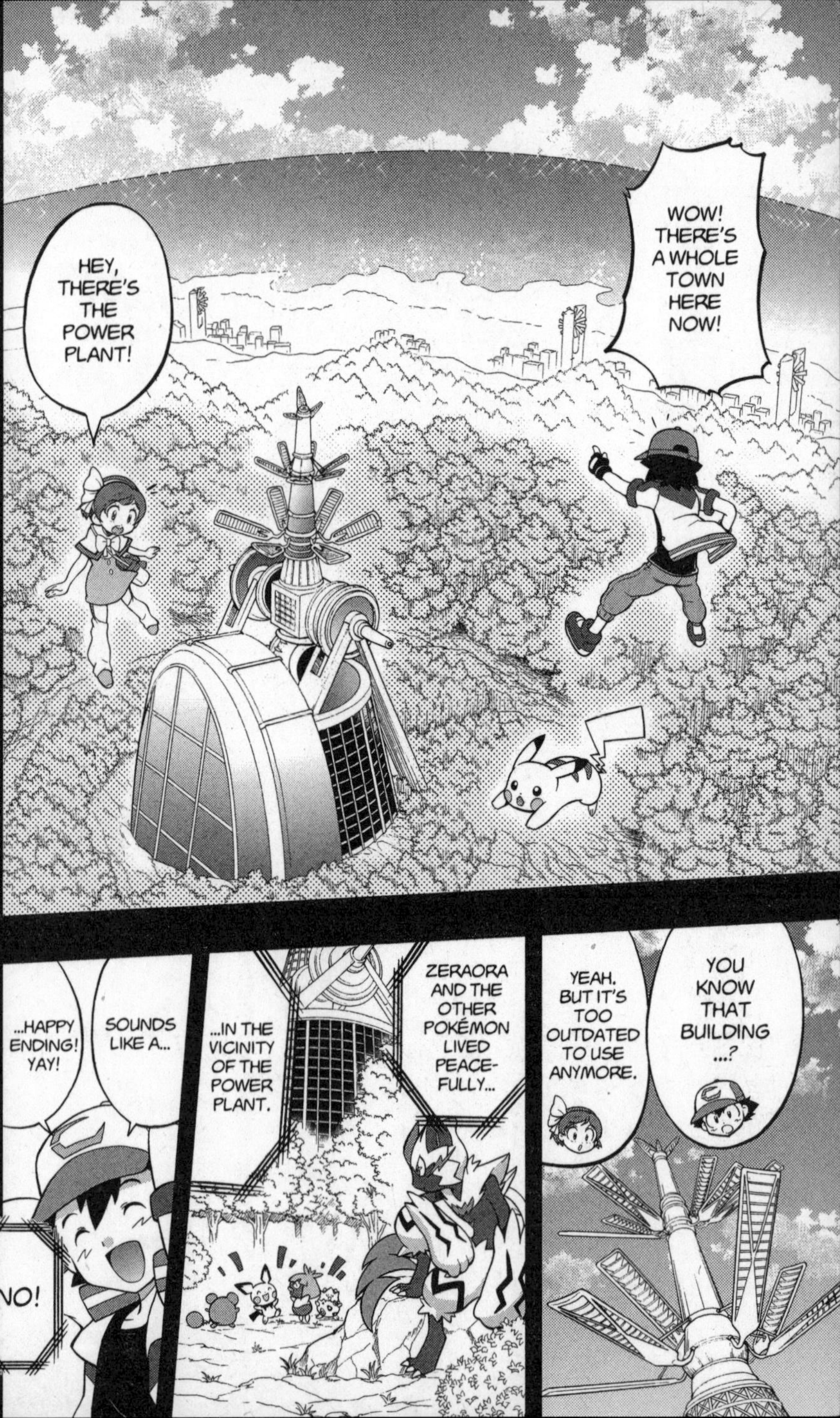
WOW! THERE'S A WHOLE TOWN HERE NOW!
HEY, THERE'S THE POWER PLANT!
YOU KNOW THAT BUILDING ...?
YEAH. BUT IT'S TOO OUTDATED TO USE ANYMORE.
ZERAORA AND THE OTHER POKÉMON LIVED PEACE-FULLY...
...IN THE VICINITY OF THE POWER PLANT.
SOUNDS LIKE A...
...HAPPY ENDING! YAY!
NO!

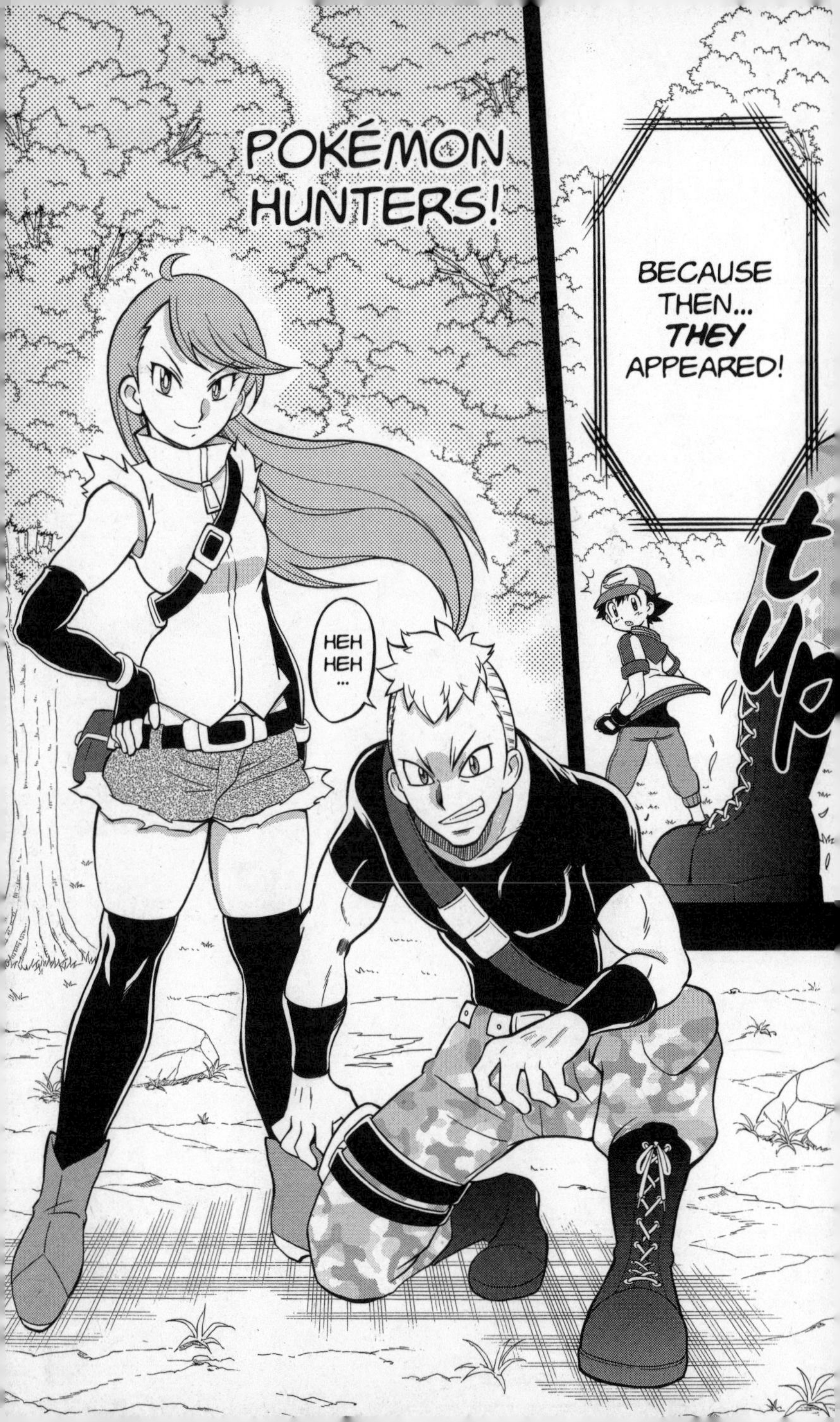
BECAUSE THEN... THEY APPEARED!
tup
POKÉMON HUNTERS!
HEH HEH ...

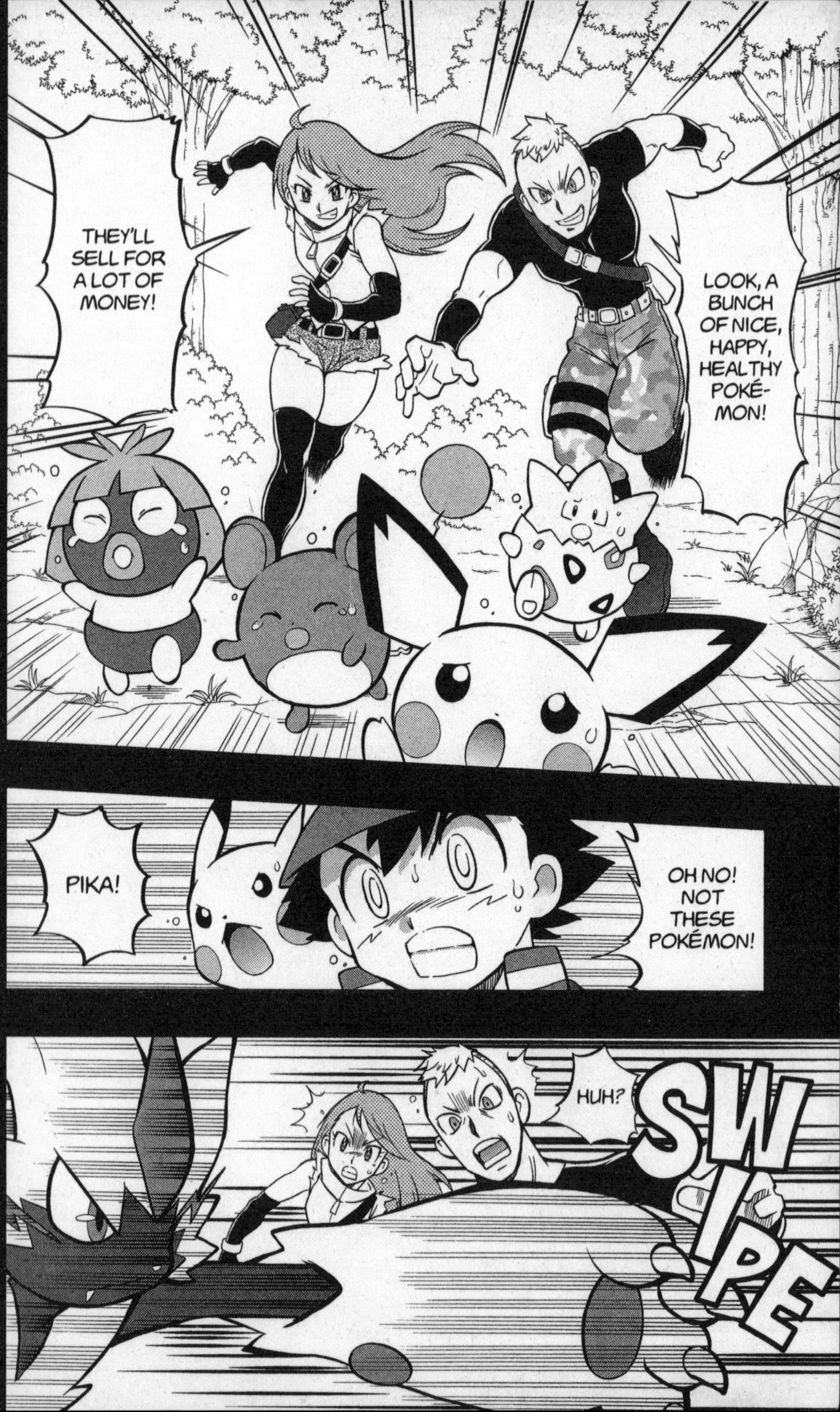
LOOK, A BUNCH OF NICE, HAPPY, HEALTHY POKÉ-MON!
THEY'LL SELL FOR A LOT OF MONEY!
OH NO! NOT THESE POKÉMON!
PIKA!
SWIPE
HUH?

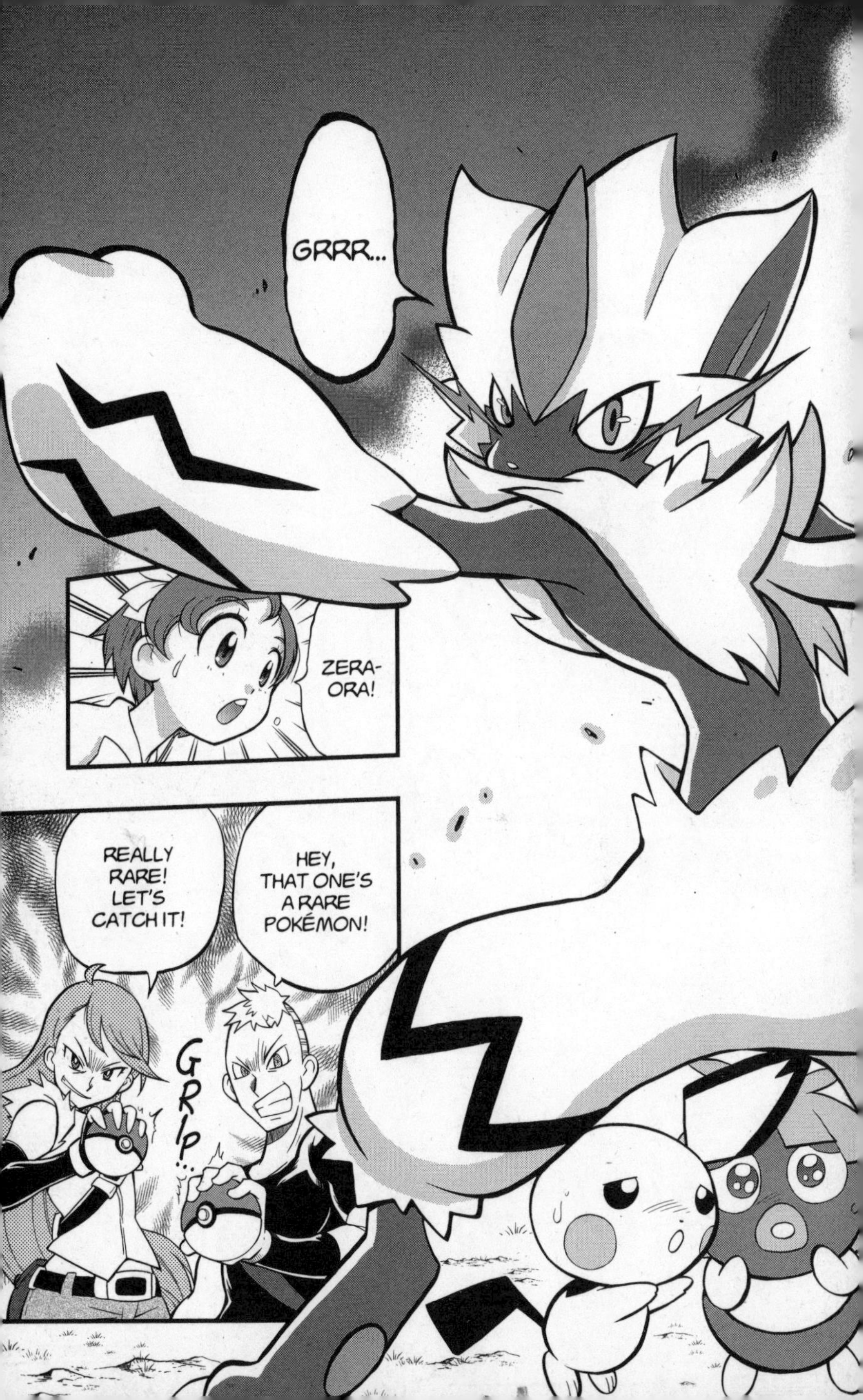
GRRR...
ZERA-ORA!
HEY, THAT ONE'S A RARE POKÉMON!
REALLY RARE! LET'S CATCH IT!
GRIP...

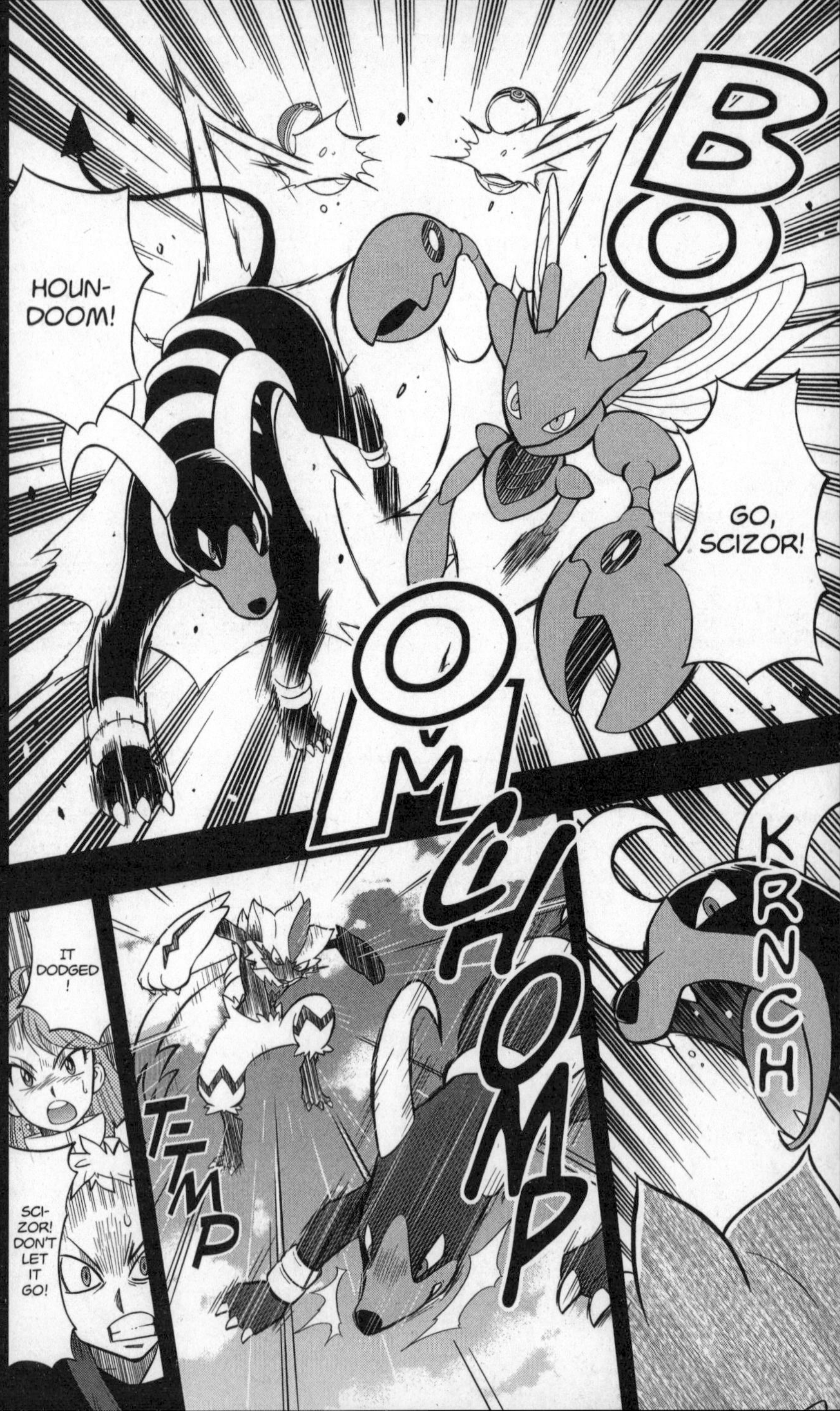
BOOM
GO, SCIZOR!
HOUN-DOOM!
KRNCH
CHOMP
T-TMP
IT DODGED!
SCI-ZOR! DON'T LET IT GO!

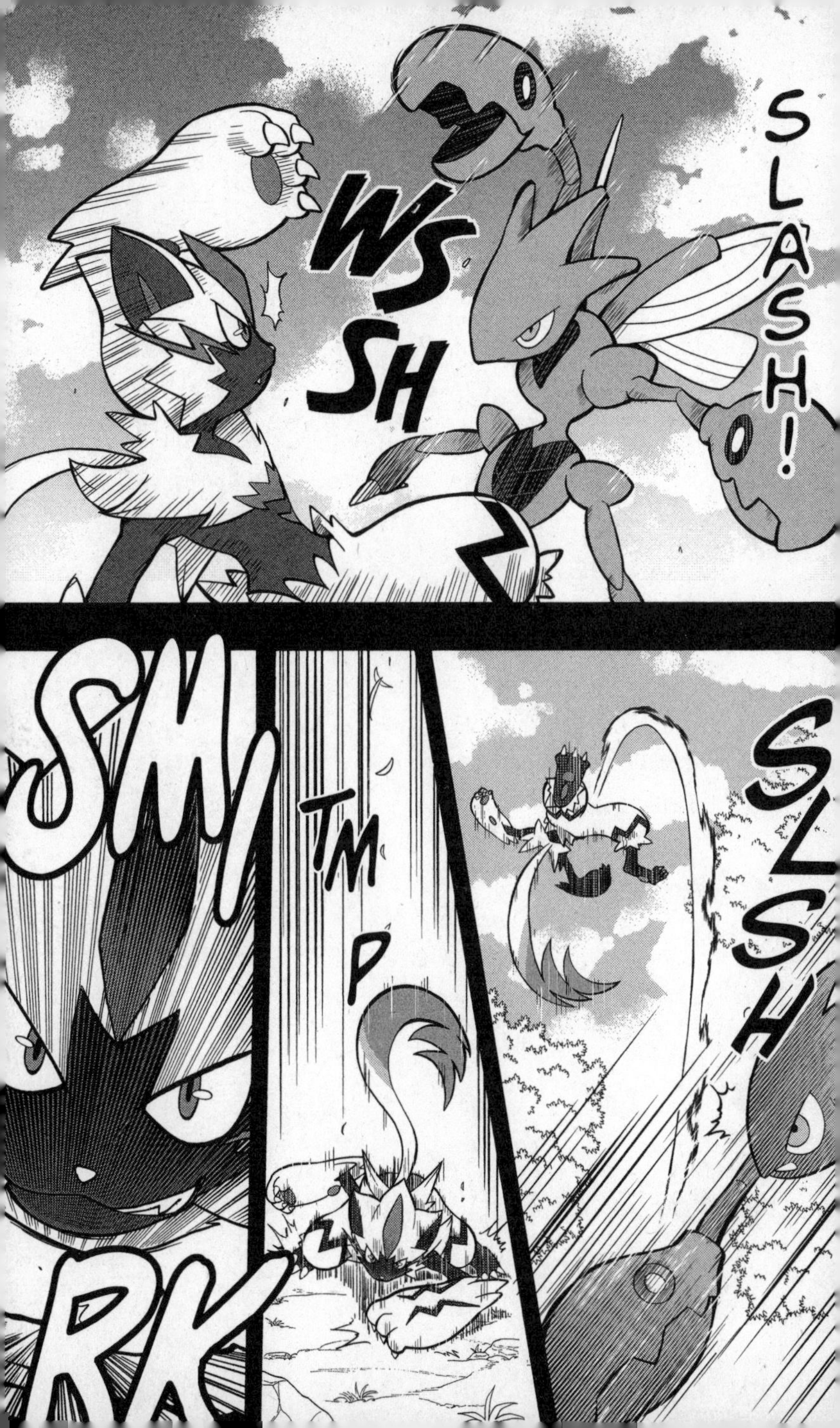
SLASH!
WSSH
SLSH
TMP
SHRK

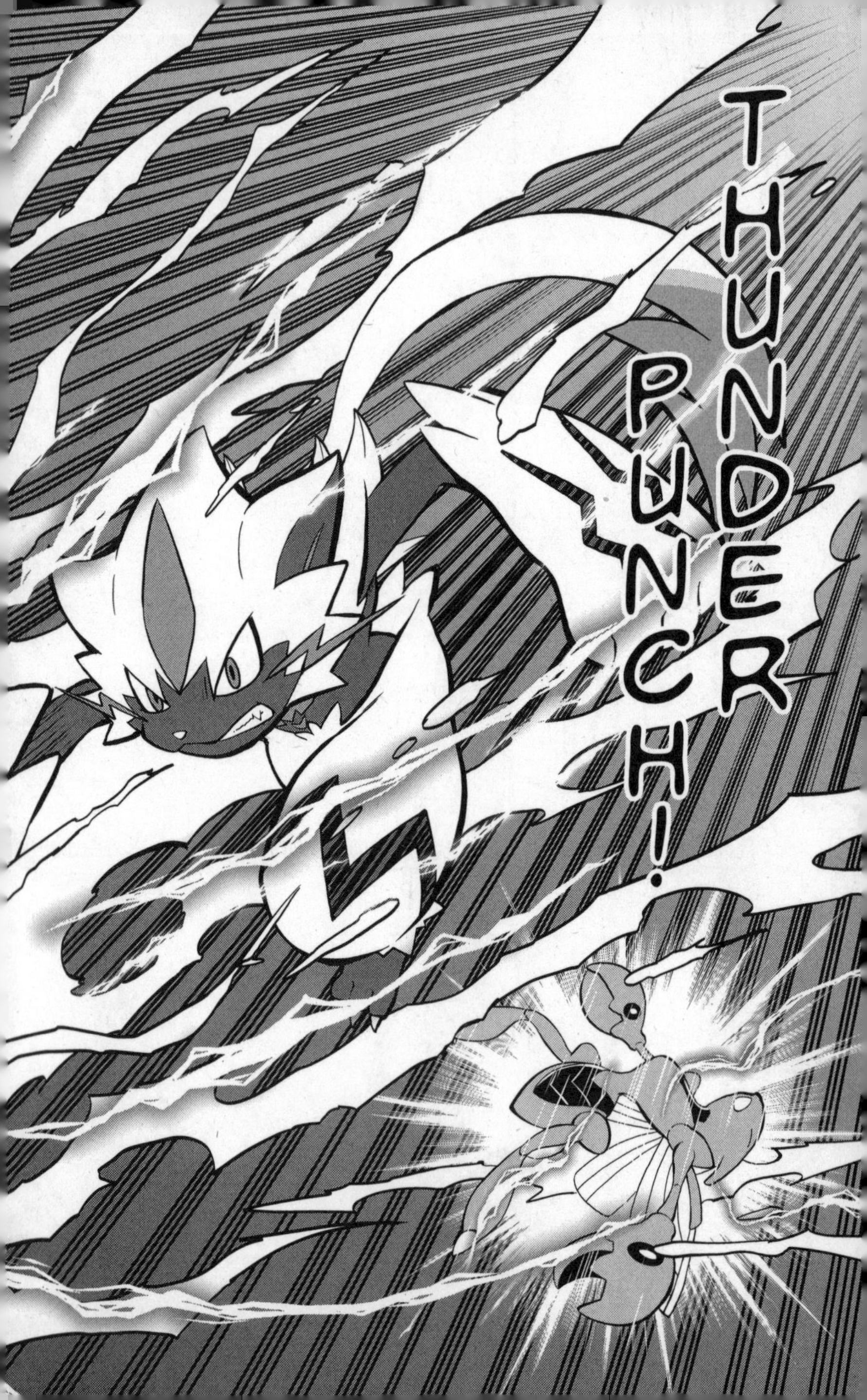
THUNDER PUNCH!

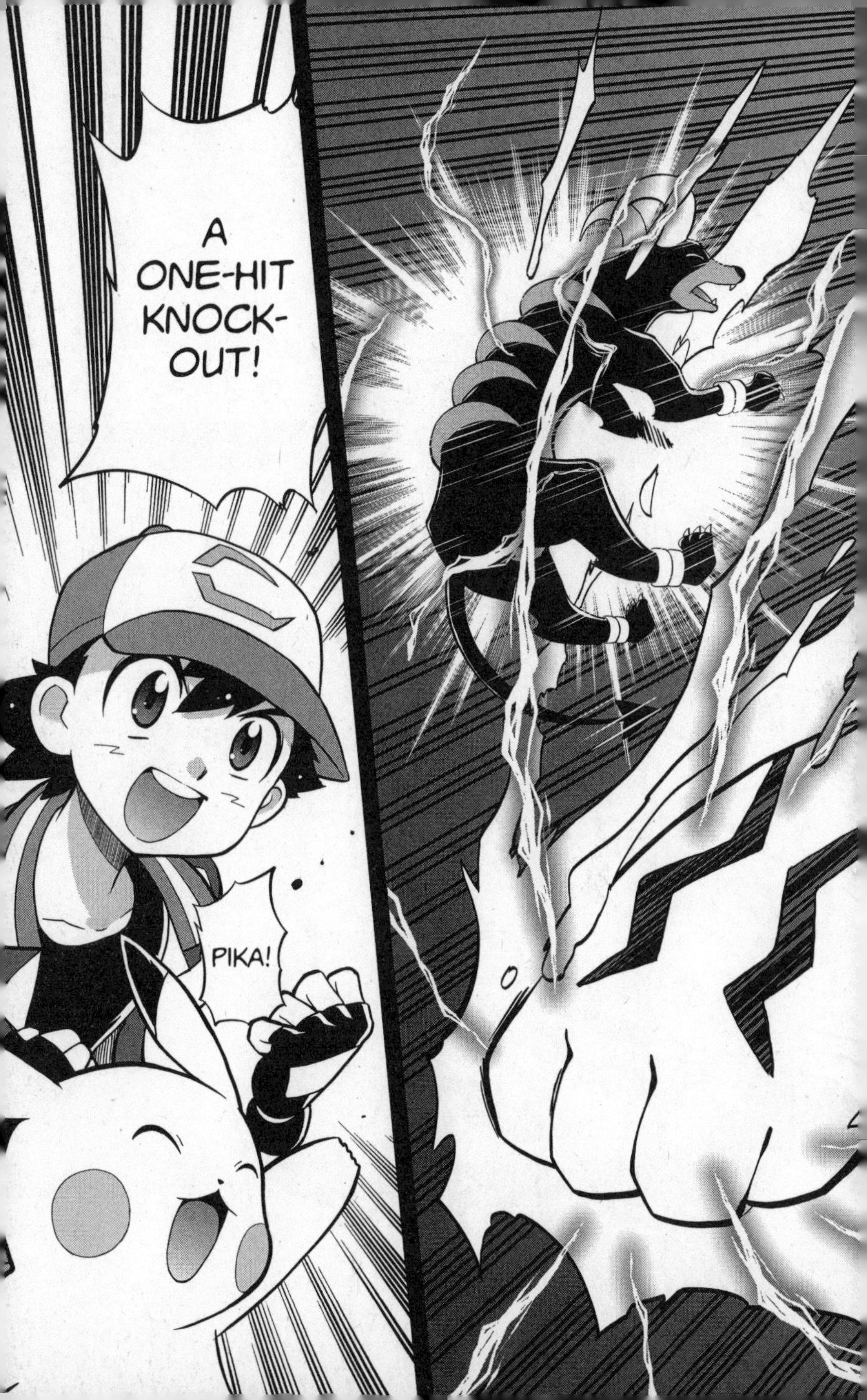
A ONE-HIT KNOCK-OUT!
PIKA!

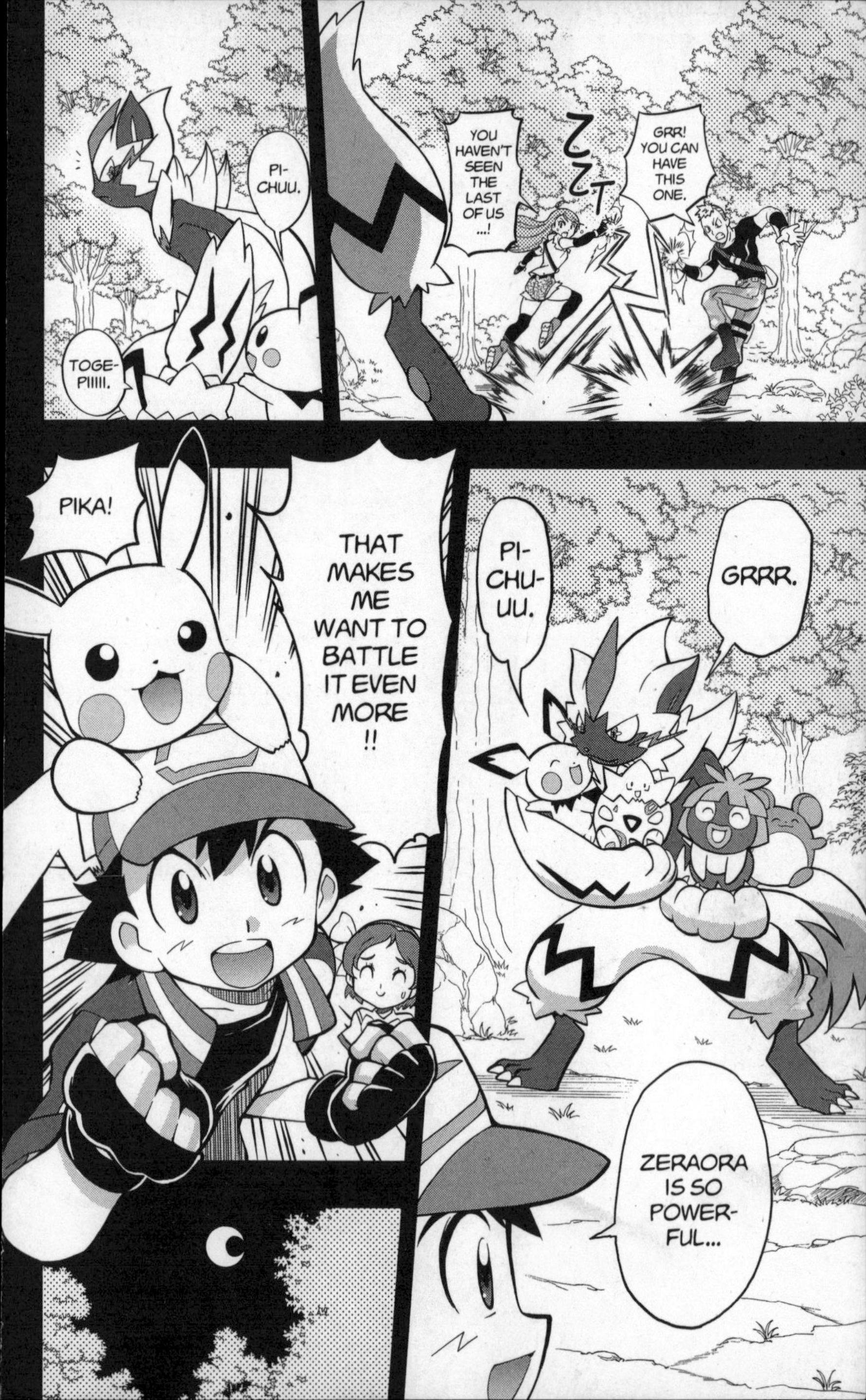
GRR! YOU CAN HAVE THIS ONE.
ZZT
YOU HAVEN'T SEEN THE LAST OF US ...!
PI-CHUU.
TOGE-PIIIII.
GRRR.
PI-CHU-UU.
ZERAORA IS SO POWERFUL...
THAT MAKES ME WANT TO BATTLE IT EVEN MORE!!
PIKA!

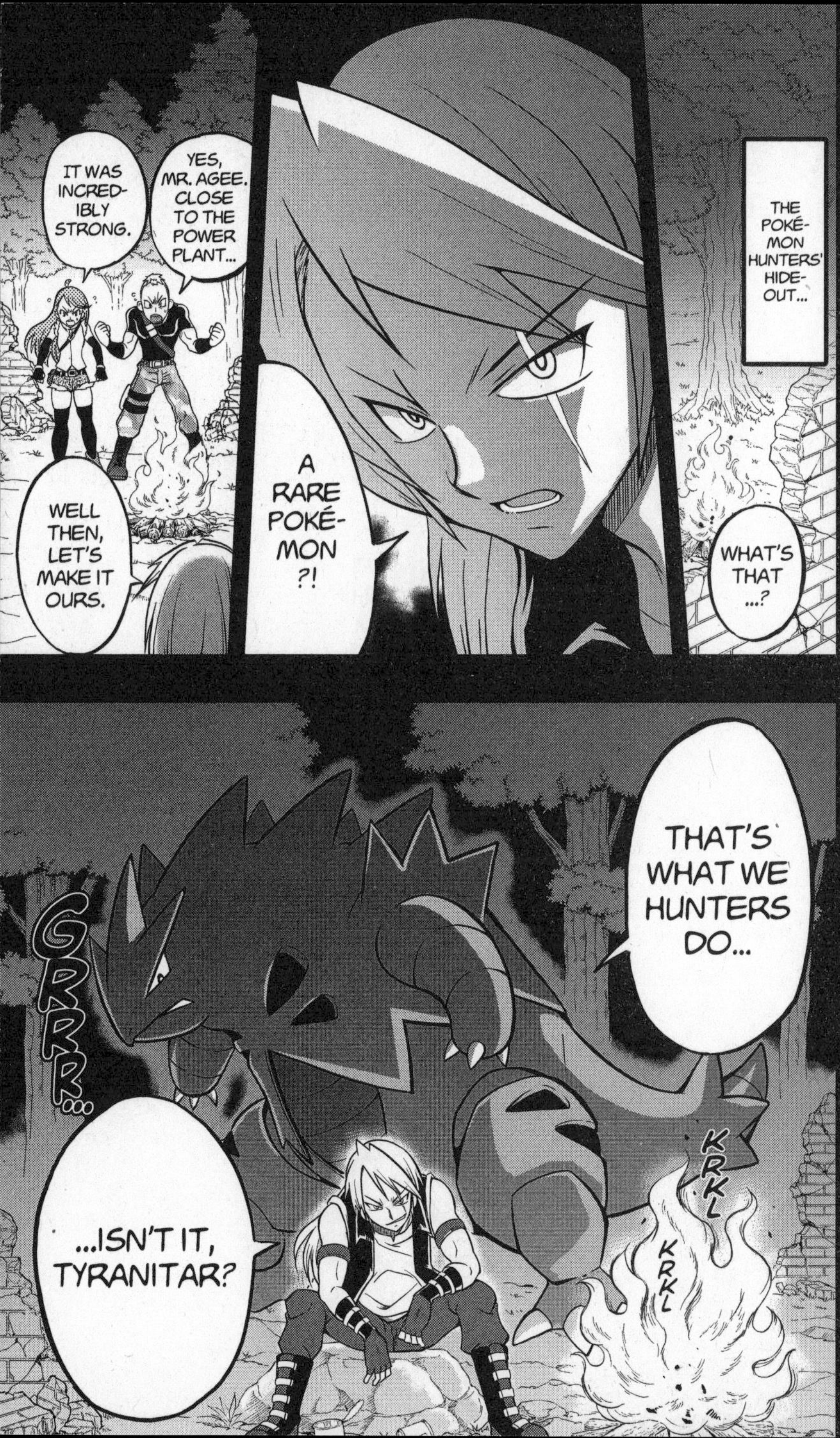
THE POKÉ-MON HUNTERS' HIDE-OUT...
WHAT'S THAT ...?
A RARE POKÉ-MON ?!
YES, MR. AGEE. CLOSE TO THE POWER PLANT...
IT WAS INCRED-IBLY STRONG.
WELL THEN, LET'S MAKE IT OURS.
THAT'S WHAT WE HUNTERS DO...
GRRR...
KRKL
KRKL
...ISN'T IT, TYRANITAR?

Chapter 2
Norbert's Courage

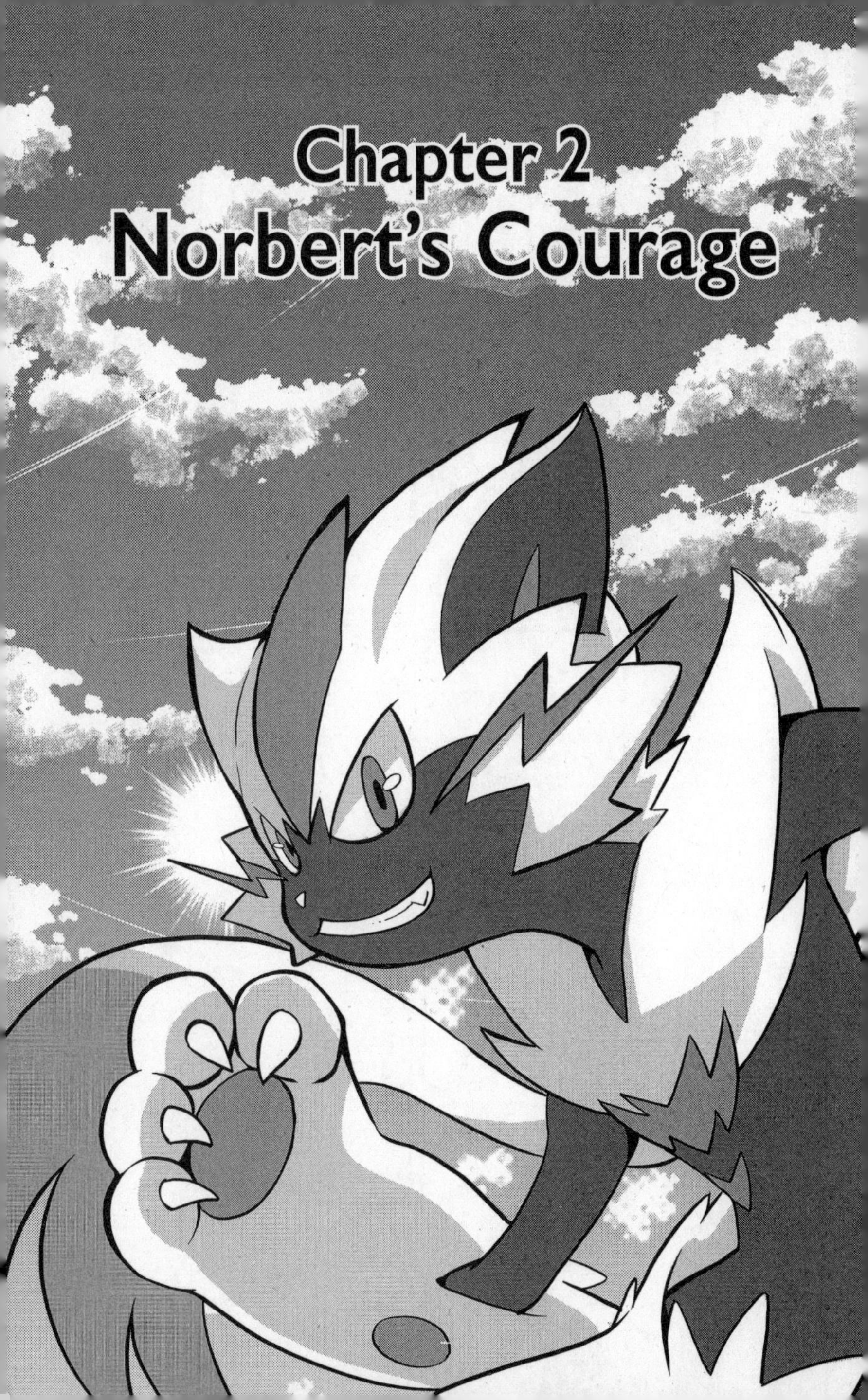

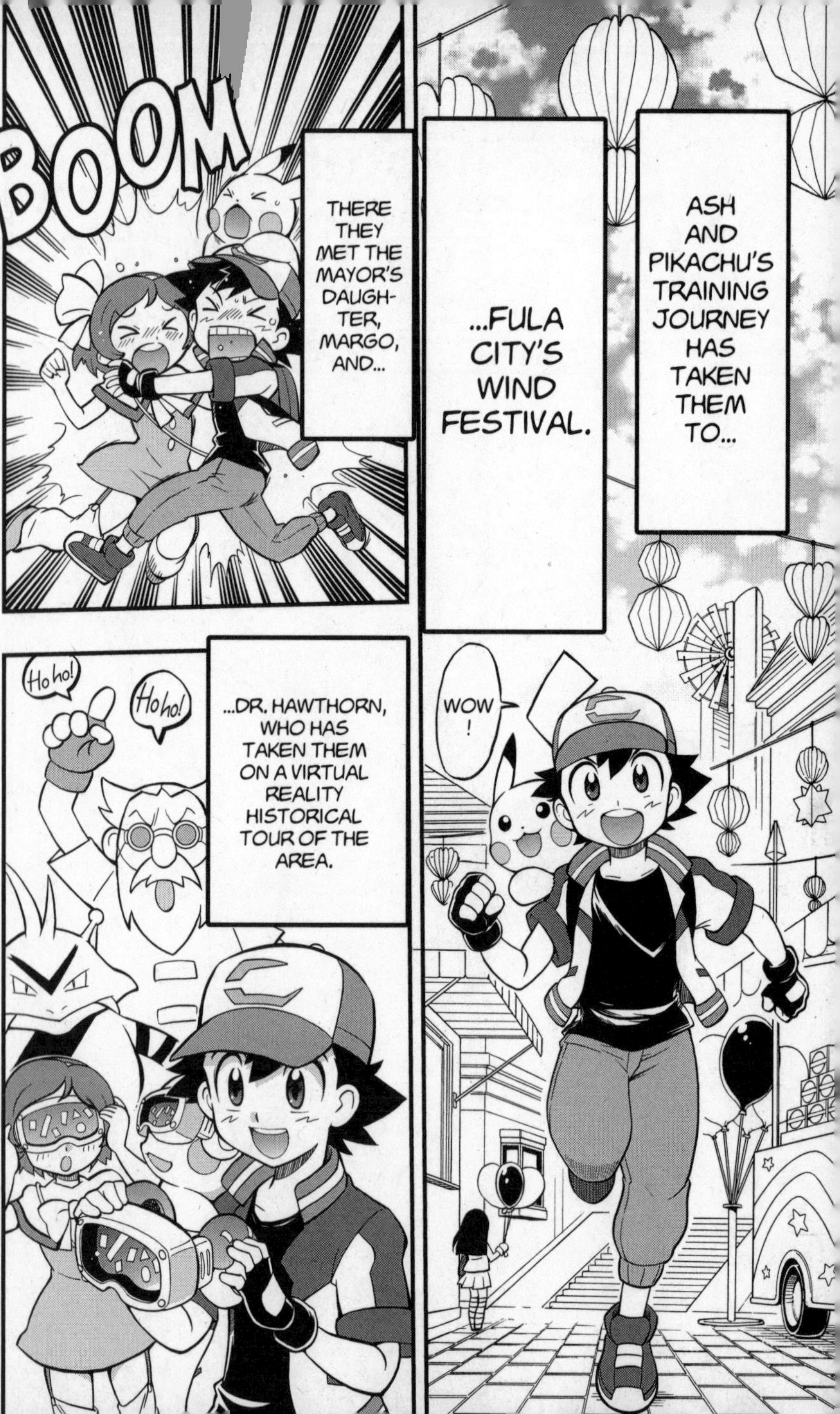
ASH AND PIKACHU'S TRAINING JOURNEY HAS TAKEN THEM TO...
...FULA CITY'S WIND FESTIVAL.
WOW!
THERE THEY MET THE MAYOR'S DAUGHTER, MARGO, AND...
BOOM
...DR. HAWTHORN, WHO HAS TAKEN THEM ON A VIRTUAL REALITY HISTORICAL TOUR OF THE AREA.
Ho ho!
Ho ho!

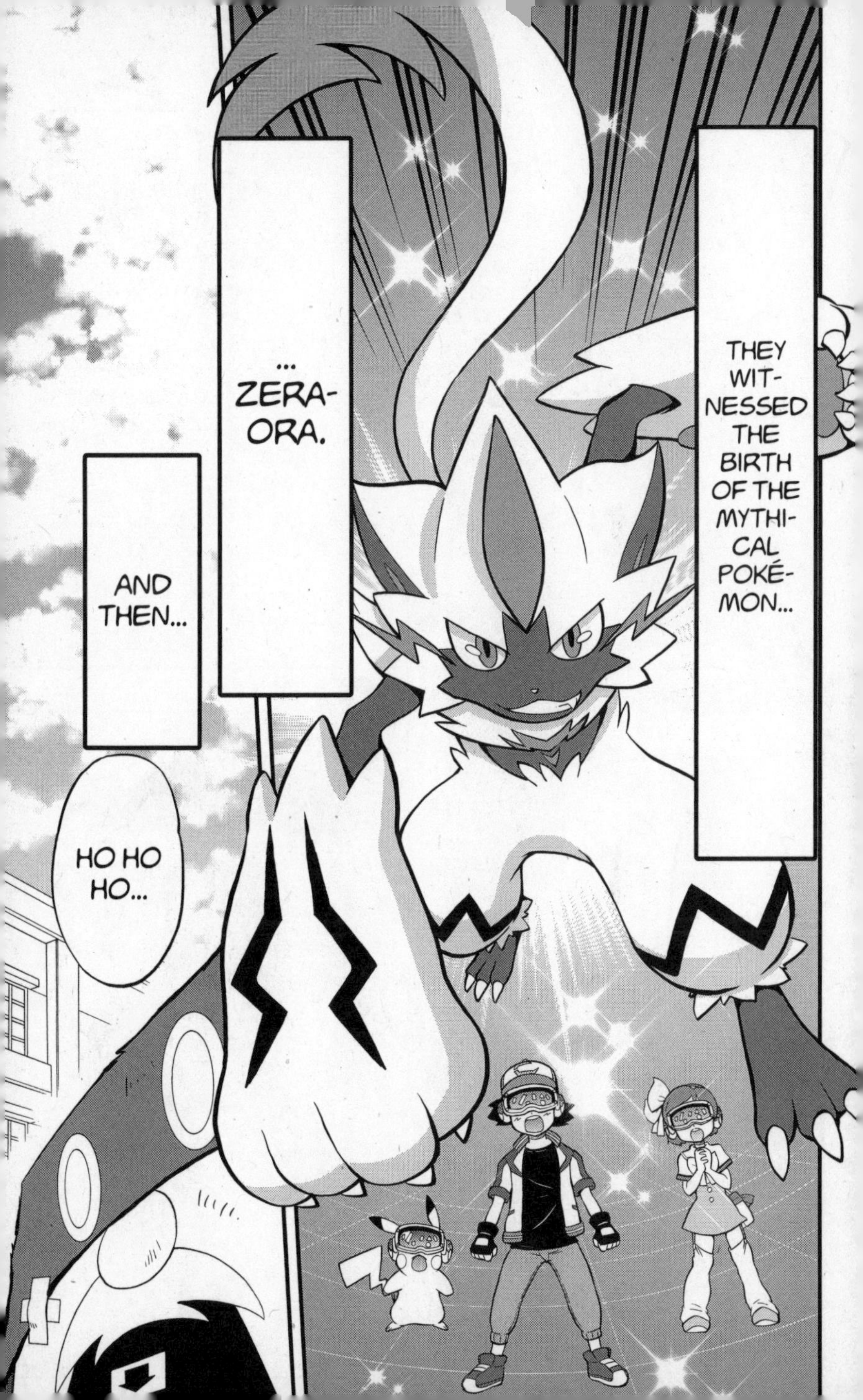
THEY WIT-NESSED THE BIRTH OF THE MYTHI-CAL POKÉ-MON...
... ZERA-ORA.
AND THEN...
HO HO HO...

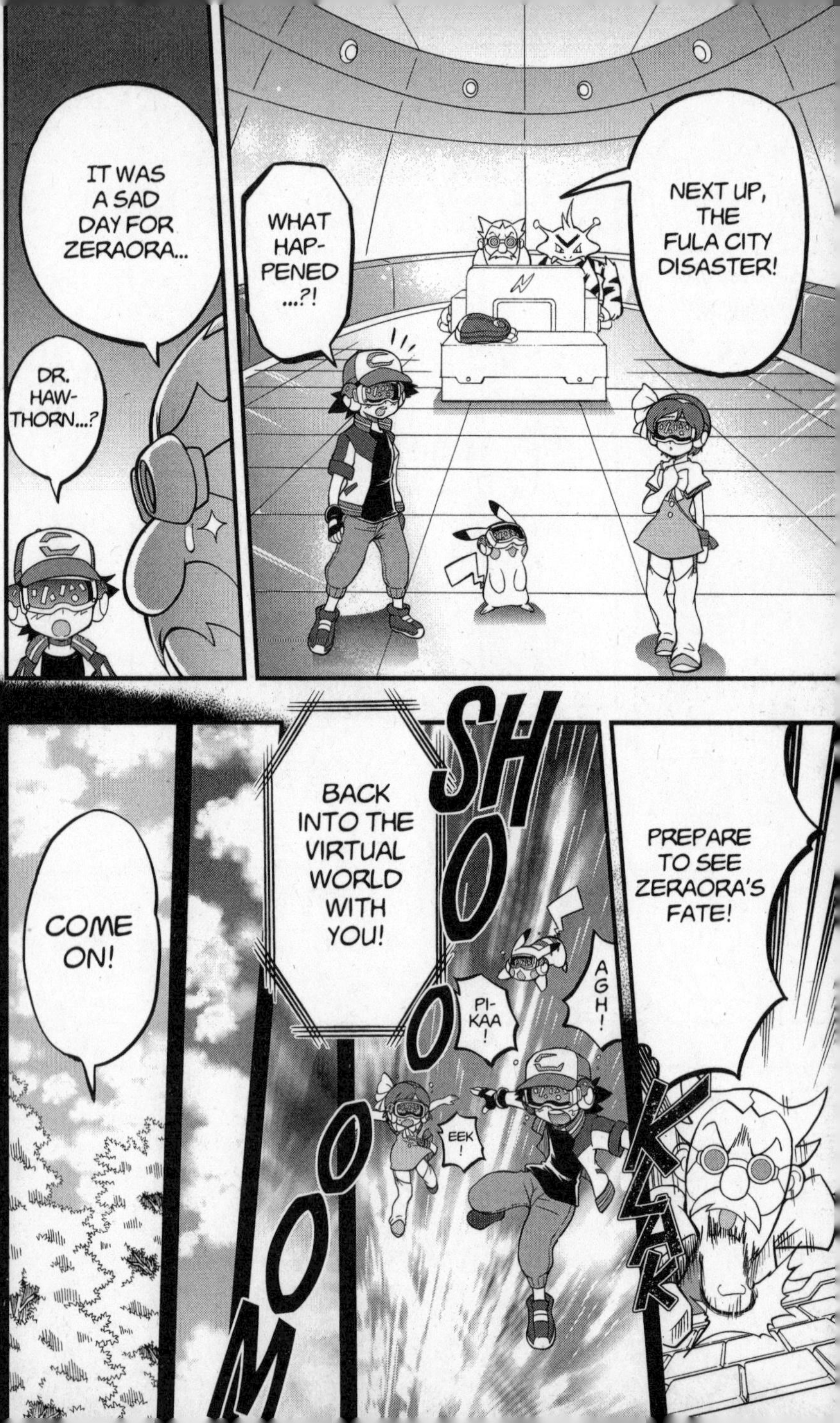
NEXT UP, THE FULA CITY DISASTER!
WHAT HAP-PENED ...?!
IT WAS A SAD DAY FOR ZERAORA...
DR. HAW-THORN...?
PREPARE TO SEE ZERAORA'S FATE!
KLAK
BACK INTO THE VIRTUAL WORLD WITH YOU!
SHOOOOOOOM
AGH!
PI-KAA!
EEK!
COME ON!

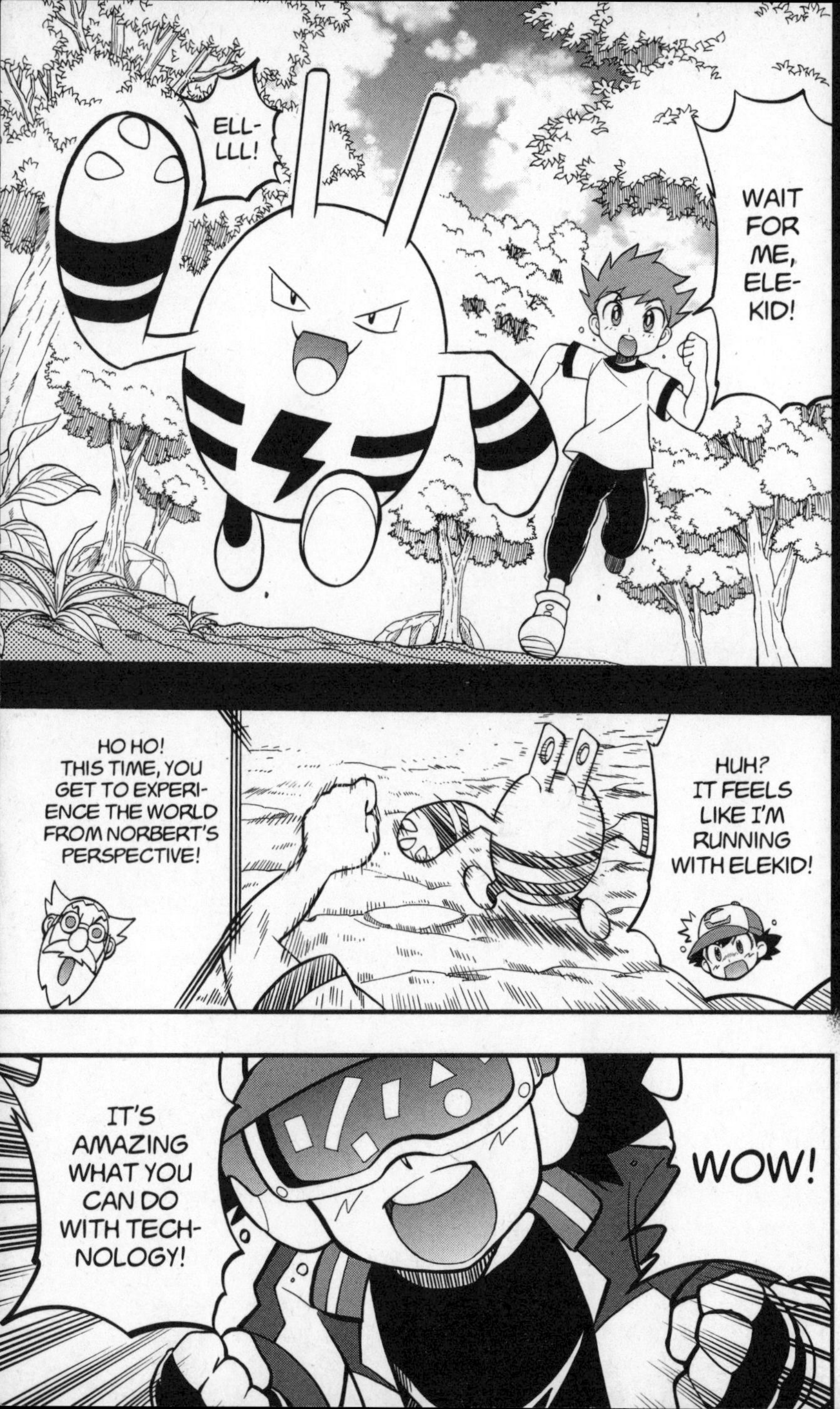
WAIT FOR ME, ELE-KID!
ELL-LLL!
HUH? IT FEELS LIKE I'M RUNNING WITH ELEKID!
HO HO! THIS TIME, YOU GET TO EXPERI-ENCE THE WORLD FROM NORBERT'S PERSPECTIVE!
WOW!
IT'S AMAZING WHAT YOU CAN DO WITH TECH-NOLOGY!

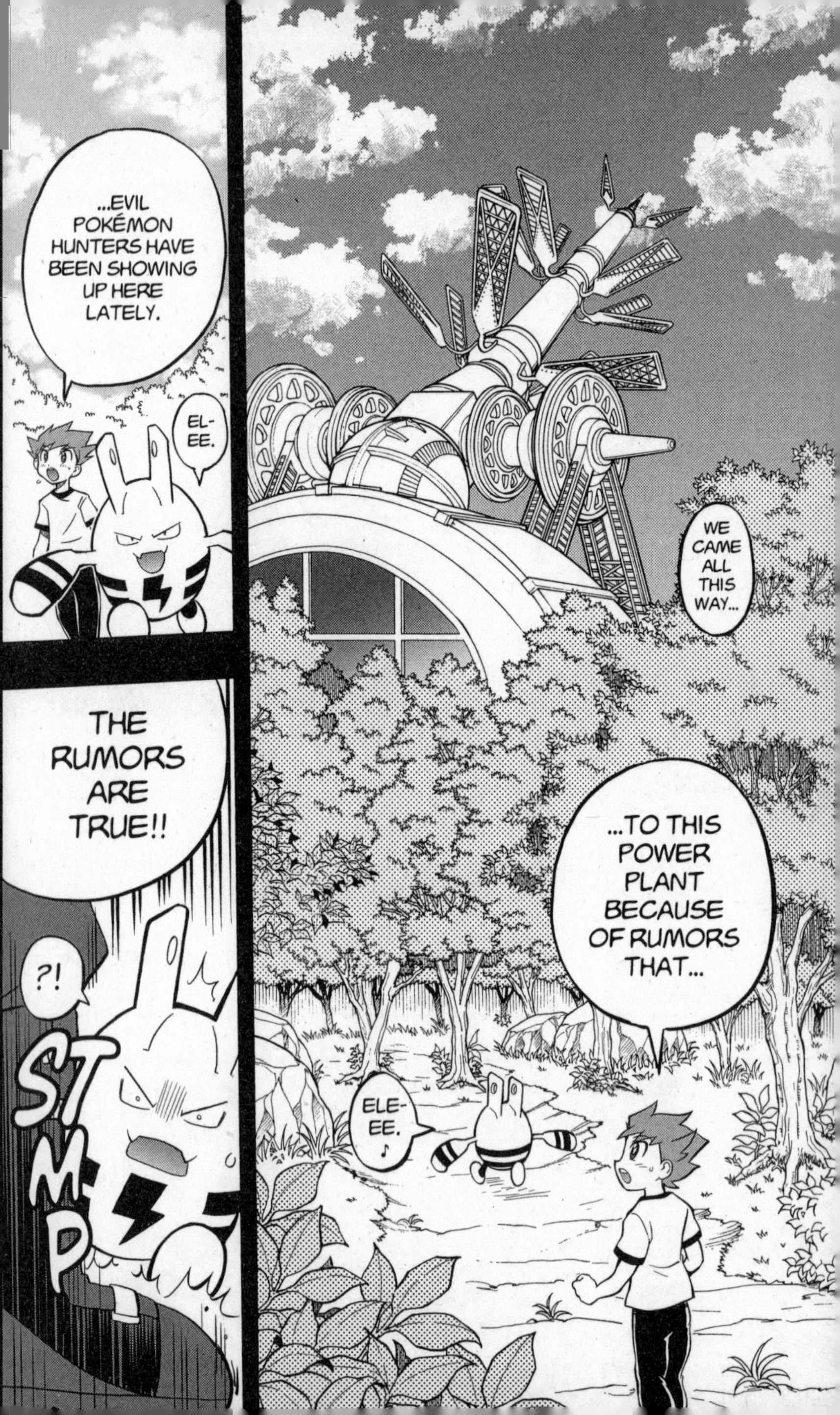
WE CAME ALL THIS WAY...
...TO THIS POWER PLANT BECAUSE OF RUMORS THAT...
ELE-EE. ♪
...EVIL POKÉMON HUNTERS HAVE BEEN SHOWING UP HERE LATELY.
EL-EE.
THE RUMORS ARE TRUE!!
?!
STMP

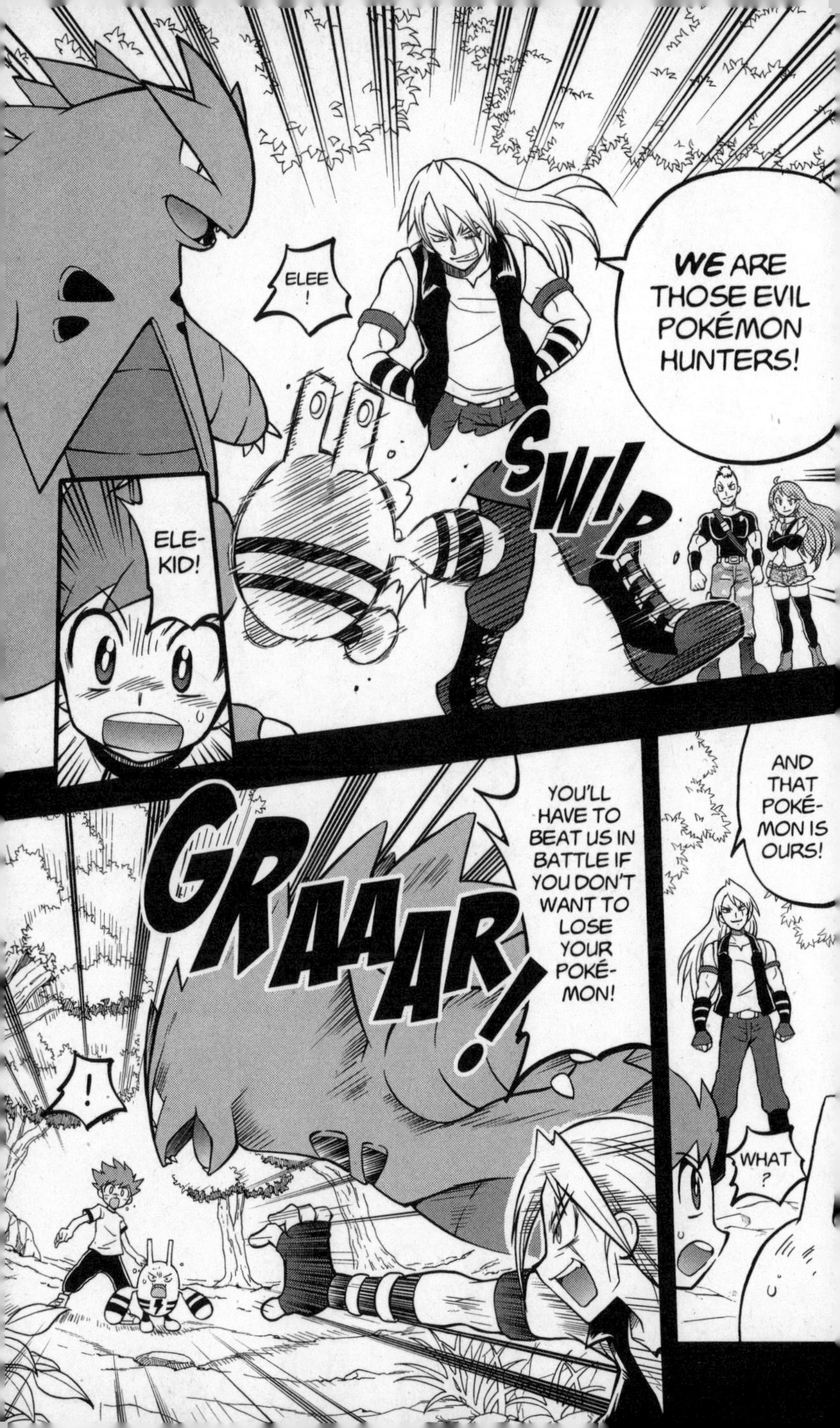
WE ARE THOSE EVIL POKÉMON HUNTERS!
ELEE!
SWIP
ELE-KID!
AND THAT POKÉMON IS OURS!
WHAT?
YOU'LL HAVE TO BEAT US IN BATTLE IF YOU DON'T WANT TO LOSE YOUR POKÉMON!
GRAAAR!
!

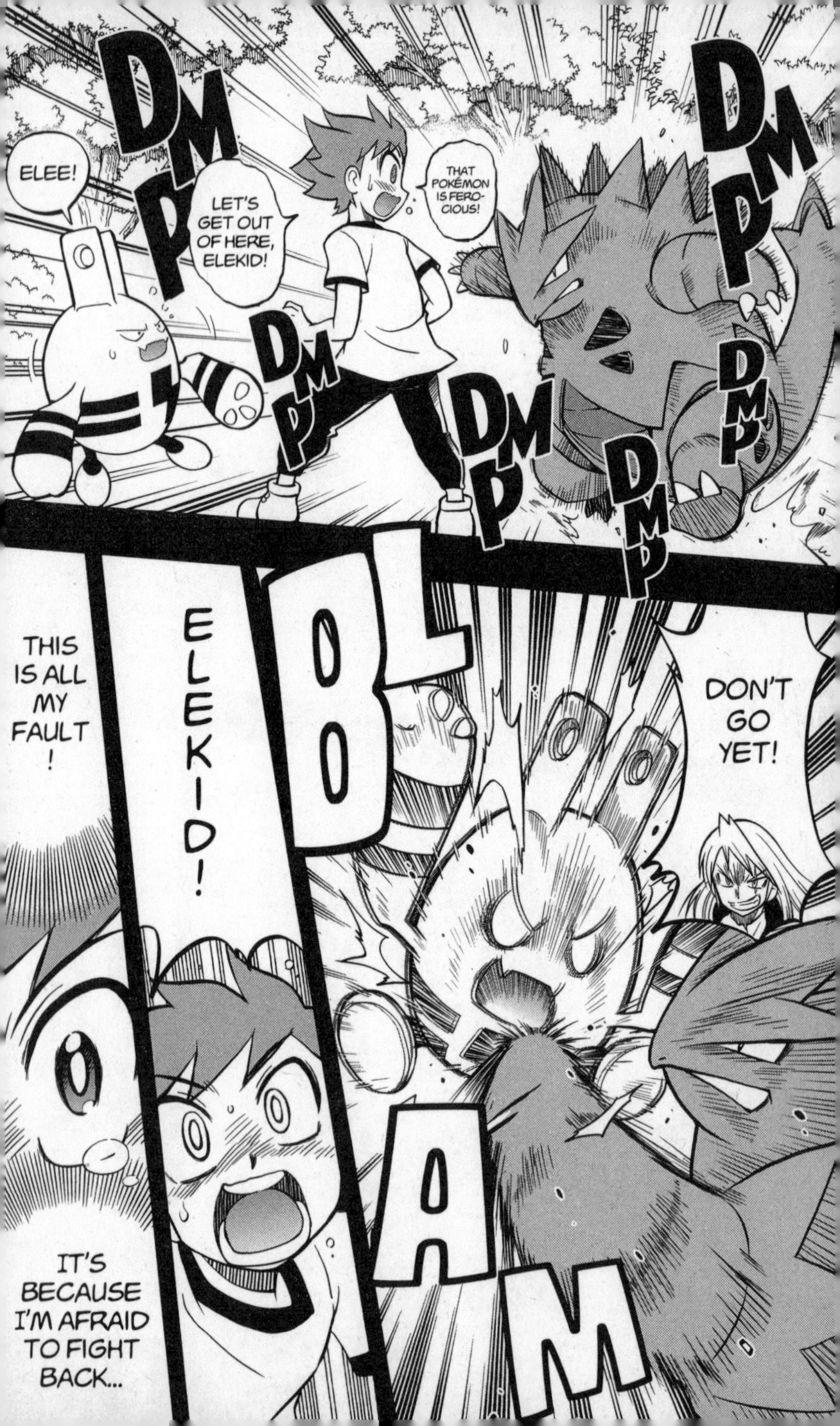
DMP
THAT POKÉMON IS FEROCIOUS!
LET'S GET OUT OF HERE, ELEKID!
DMP
ELEE!
DMP
DMP
DMP
DMP
DMP
DON'T GO YET!
BLOOAM
ELEKID!
THIS IS ALL MY FAULT!
IT'S BECAUSE I'M AFRAID TO FIGHT BACK...

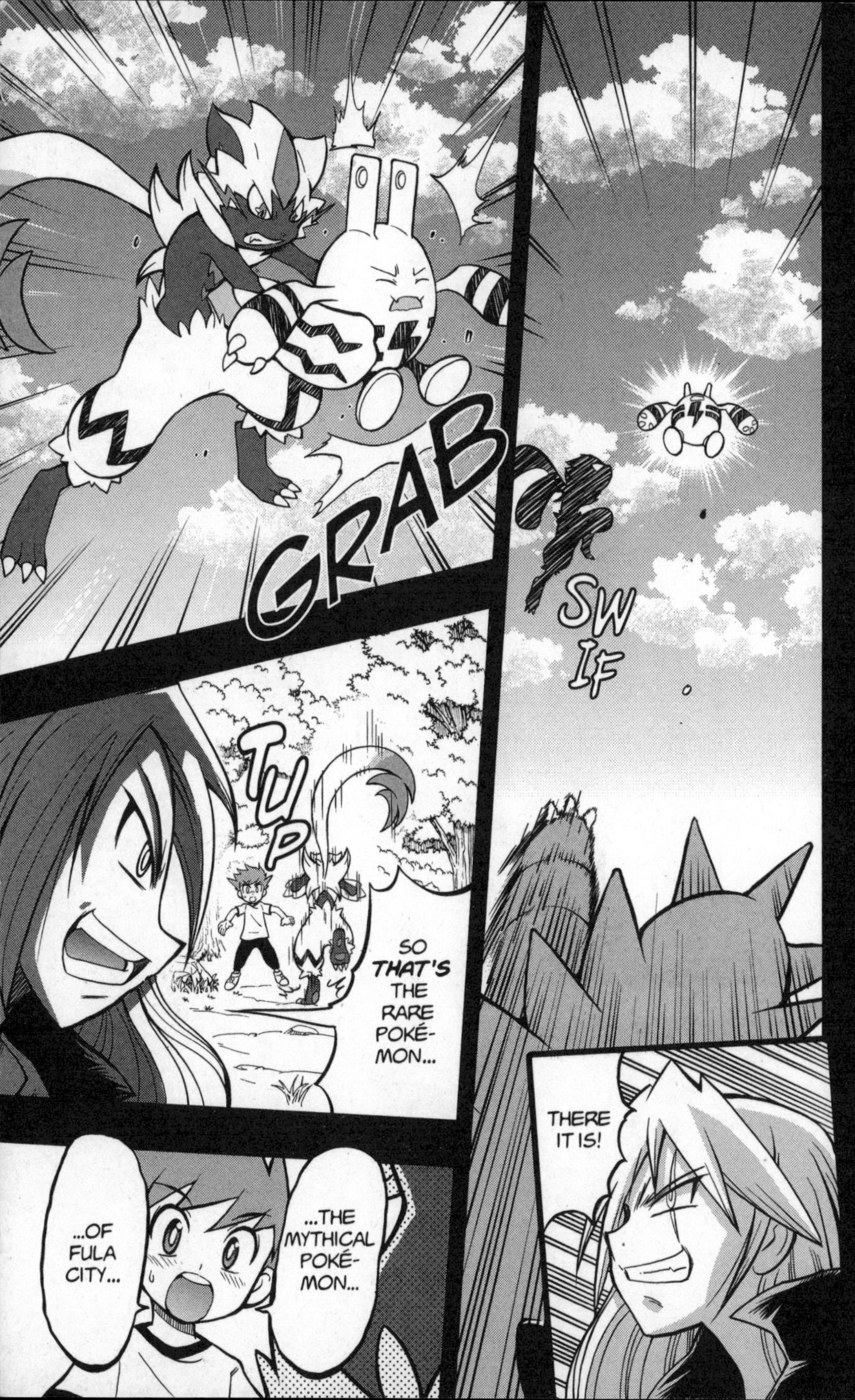
SWIF
GRAB
TUP
SO THAT'S THE RARE POKÉ-MON...
THERE IT IS!
...THE MYTHICAL POKÉ-MON...
...OF FULA CITY...

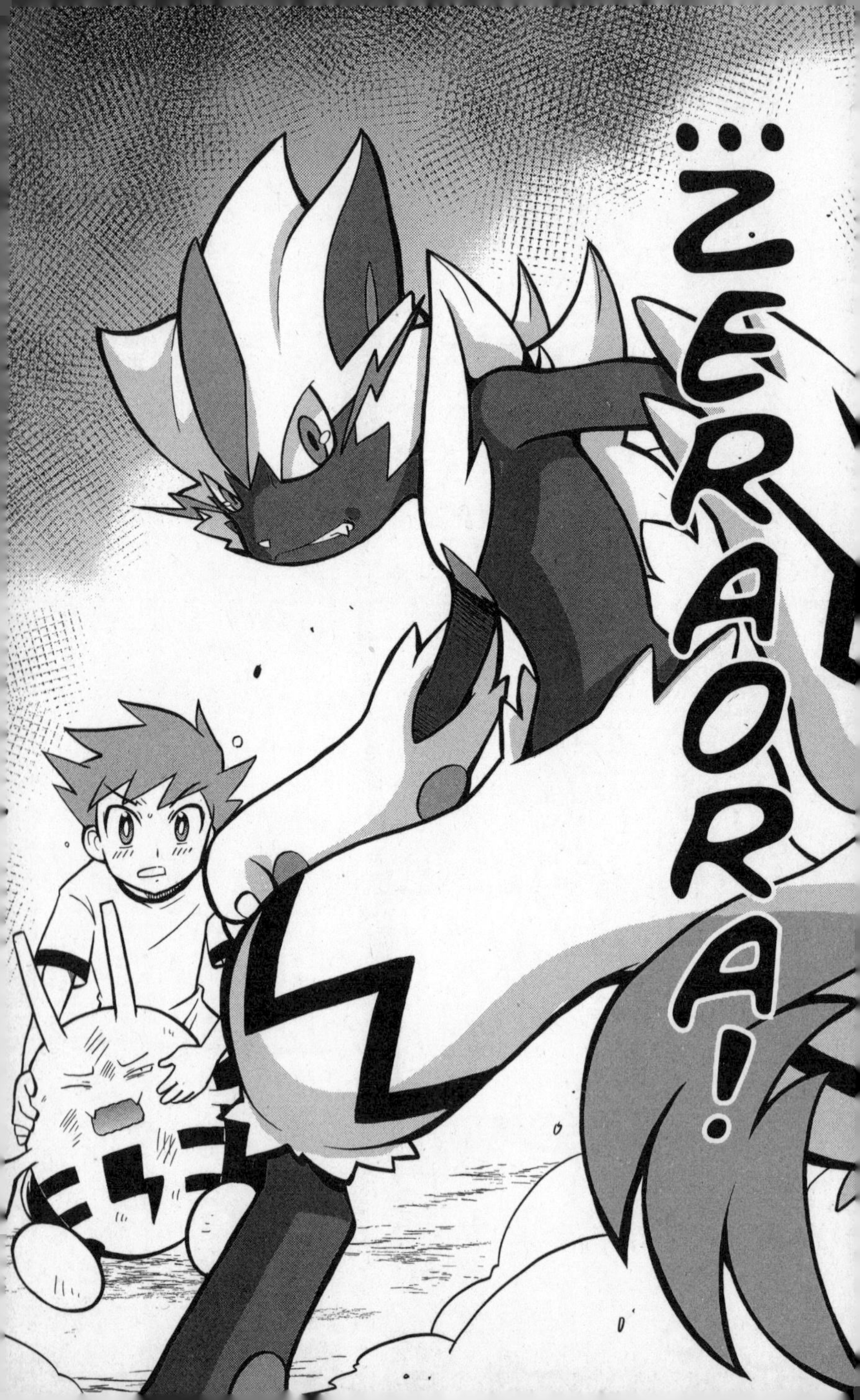
ZERAORA!

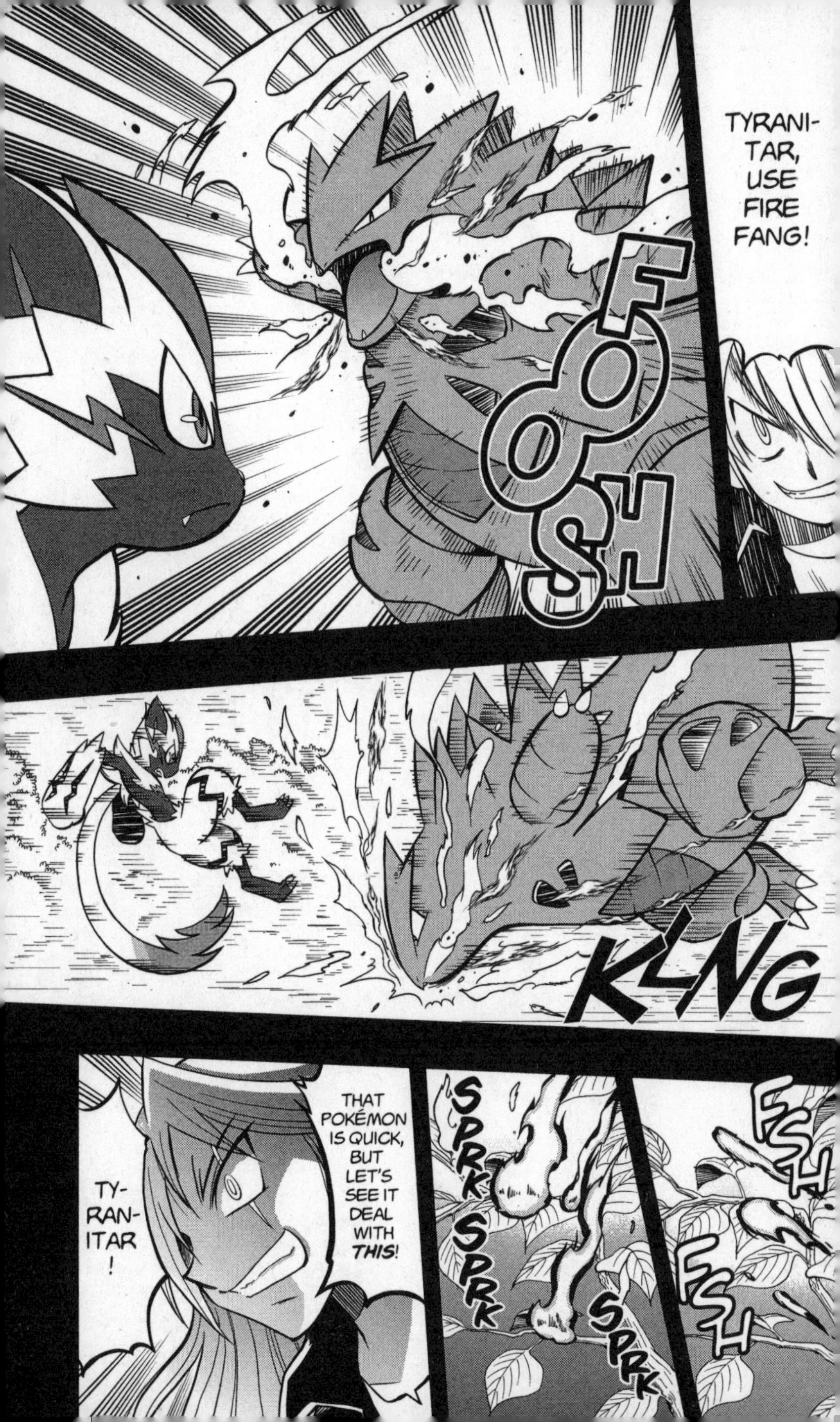
TYRANITAR, USE FIRE FANG!
FOOSH
KLNG
THAT POKÉMON IS QUICK, BUT LET'S SEE IT DEAL WITH *THIS*!
TY-RAN-ITAR!
SPRK SPRK SPRK SPRK
FSH FSH

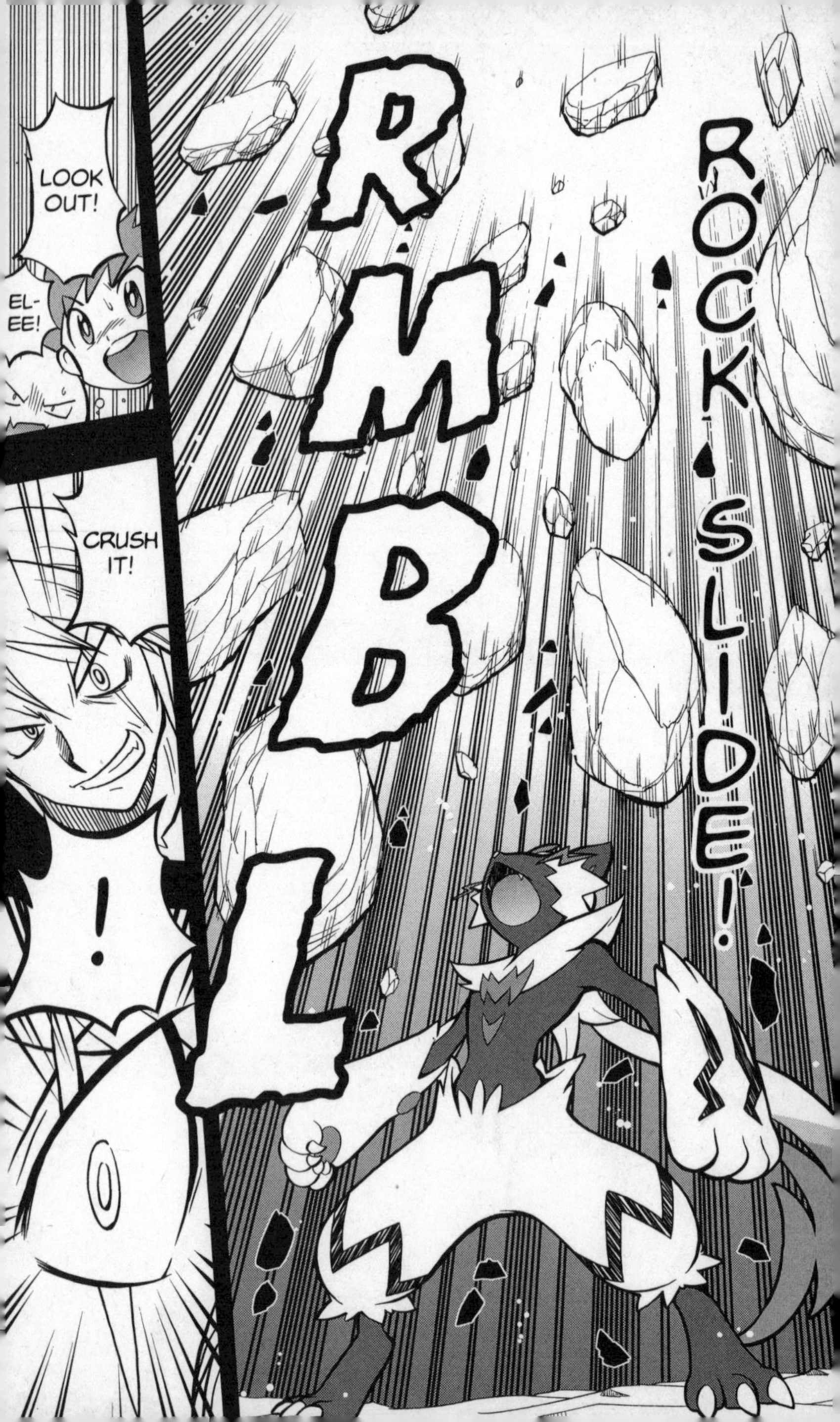
ROCK SLIDE!
RMBL
LOOK OUT!
EL-EE!
CRUSH IT!
!

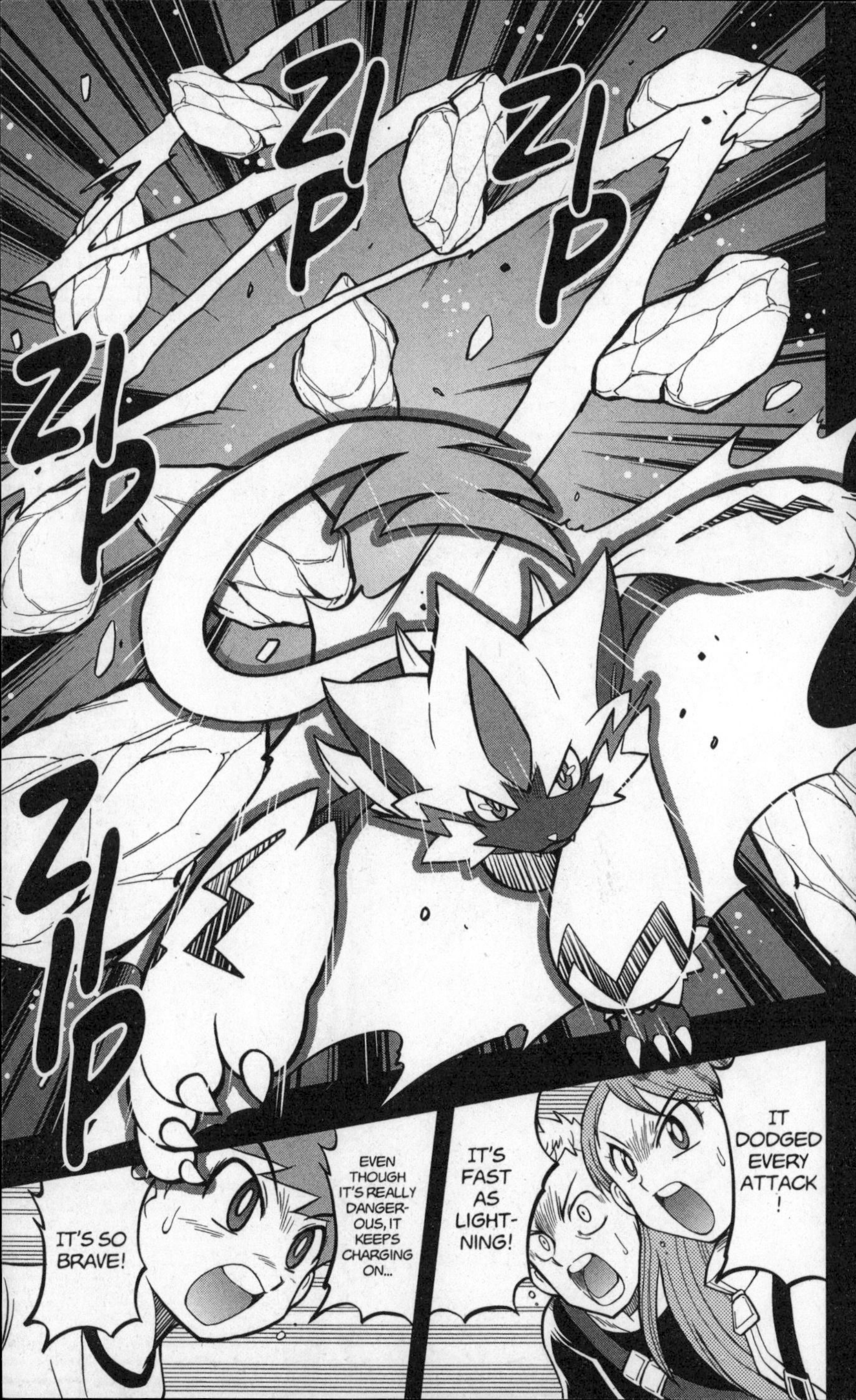
ZIP
ZIP
ZIP
ZIIP
IT DODGED EVERY ATTACK!
IT'S FAST AS LIGHTNING!
EVEN THOUGH IT'S REALLY DANGEROUS, IT KEEPS CHARGING ON...
IT'S SO BRAVE!

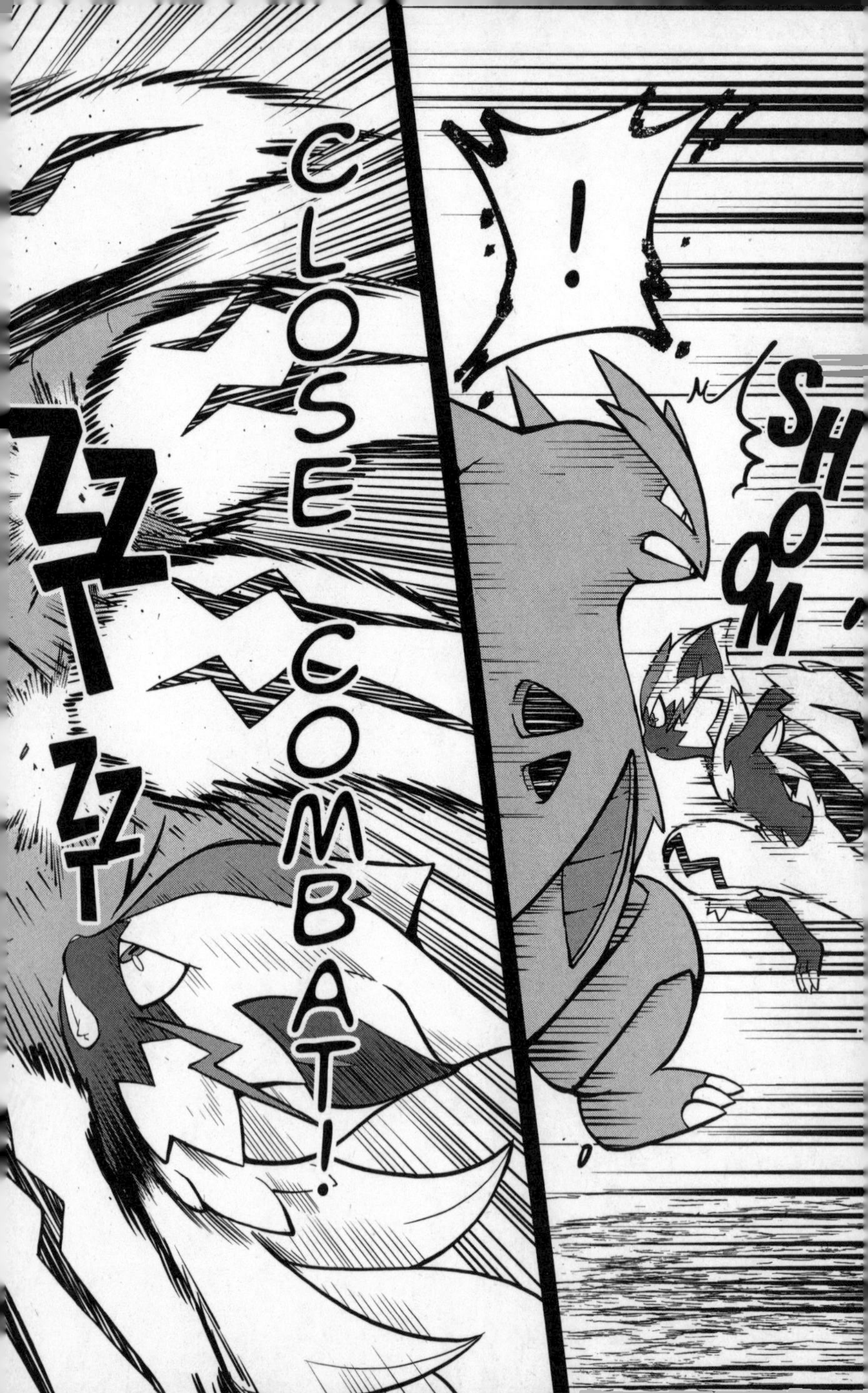
!
SHOOM
CLOSE COMBAT!
ZZT
ZZT

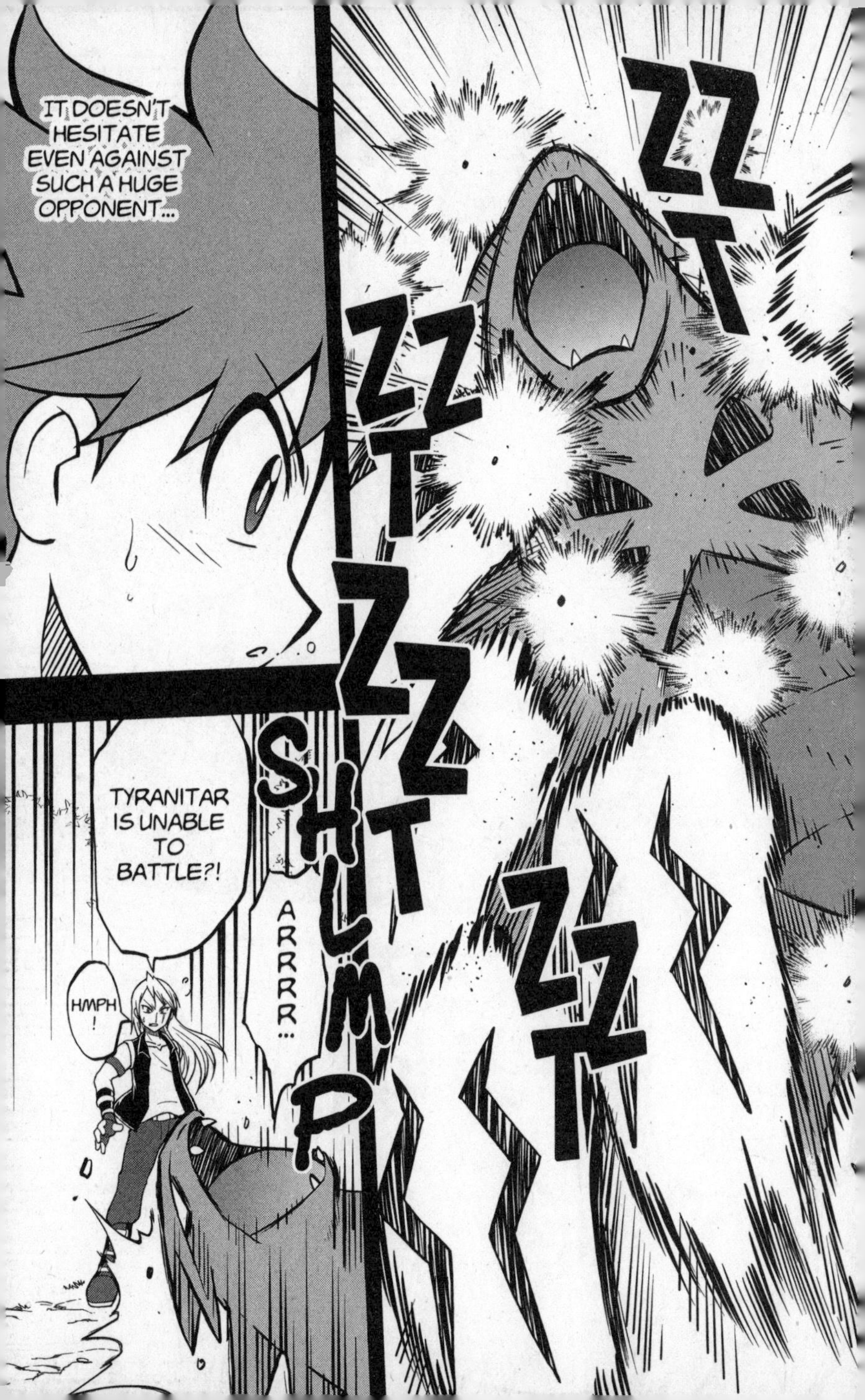

ZZT
ZZT
ZZT
ZZT
IT DOESN'T HESITATE EVEN AGAINST SUCH A HUGE OPPONENT...
SHLUMP
ARRRR...
TYRANITAR IS UNABLE TO BATTLE?!
HMPH!

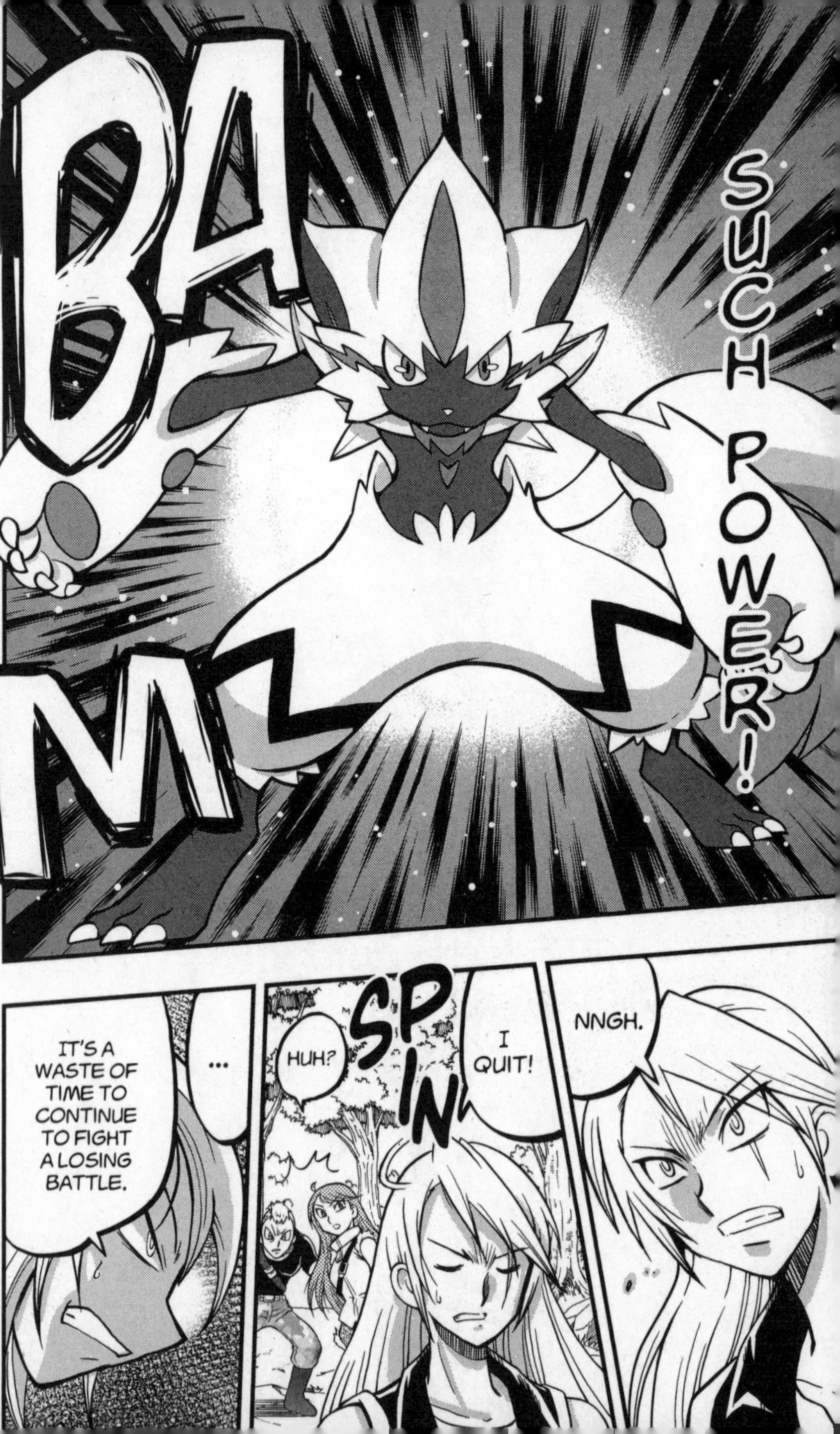
SUCH POWER!
BAM
NNGH.
I QUIT!
SPIN
HUH?
...
IT'S A WASTE OF TIME TO CONTINUE TO FIGHT A LOSING BATTLE.

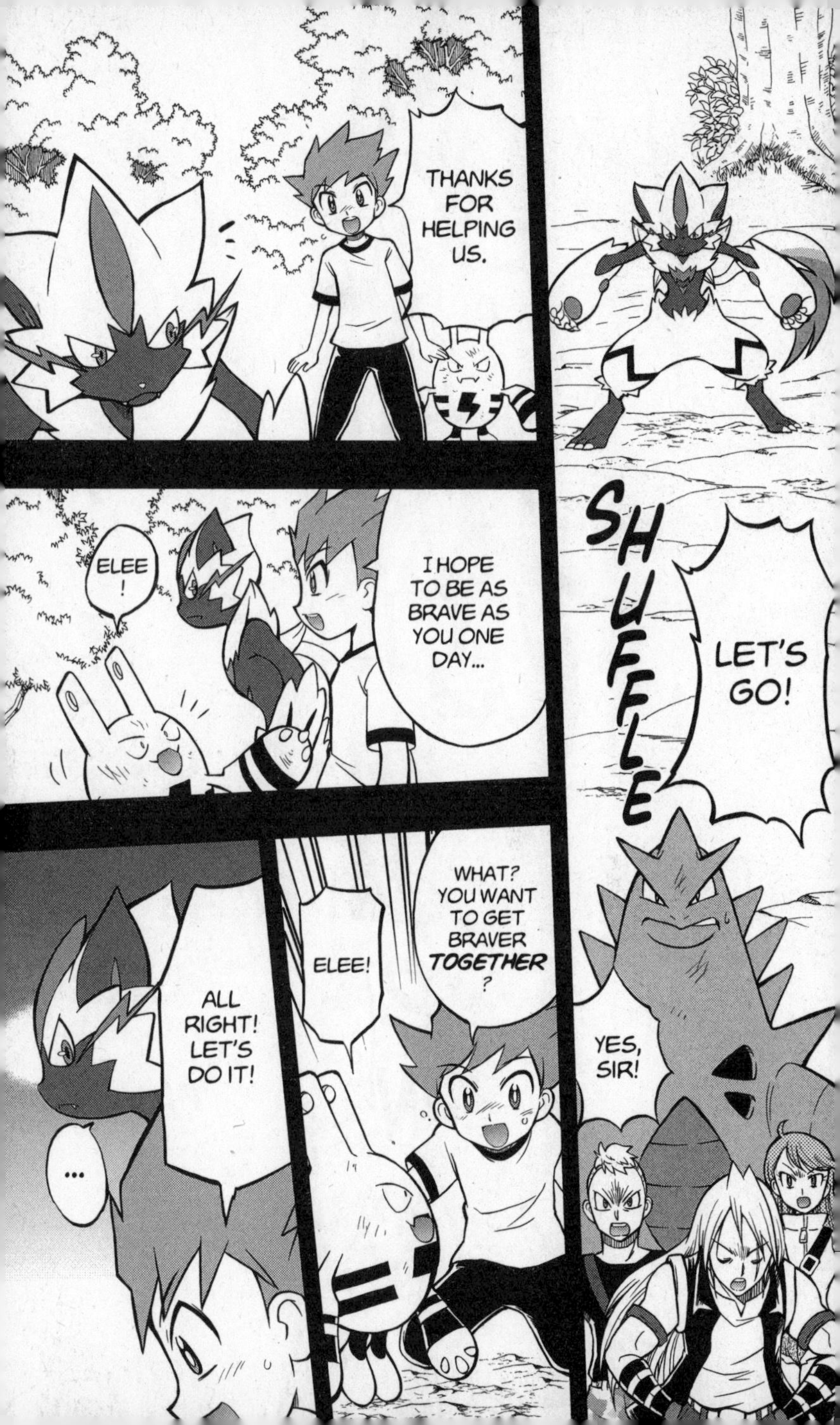
LET'S GO!
SHUFFLE
YES, SIR!
THANKS FOR HELPING US.
I HOPE TO BE AS BRAVE AS YOU ONE DAY...
ELEE !
WHAT? YOU WANT TO GET BRAVER ***TOGETHER*** ?
ELEE!
ALL RIGHT! LET'S DO IT!
...

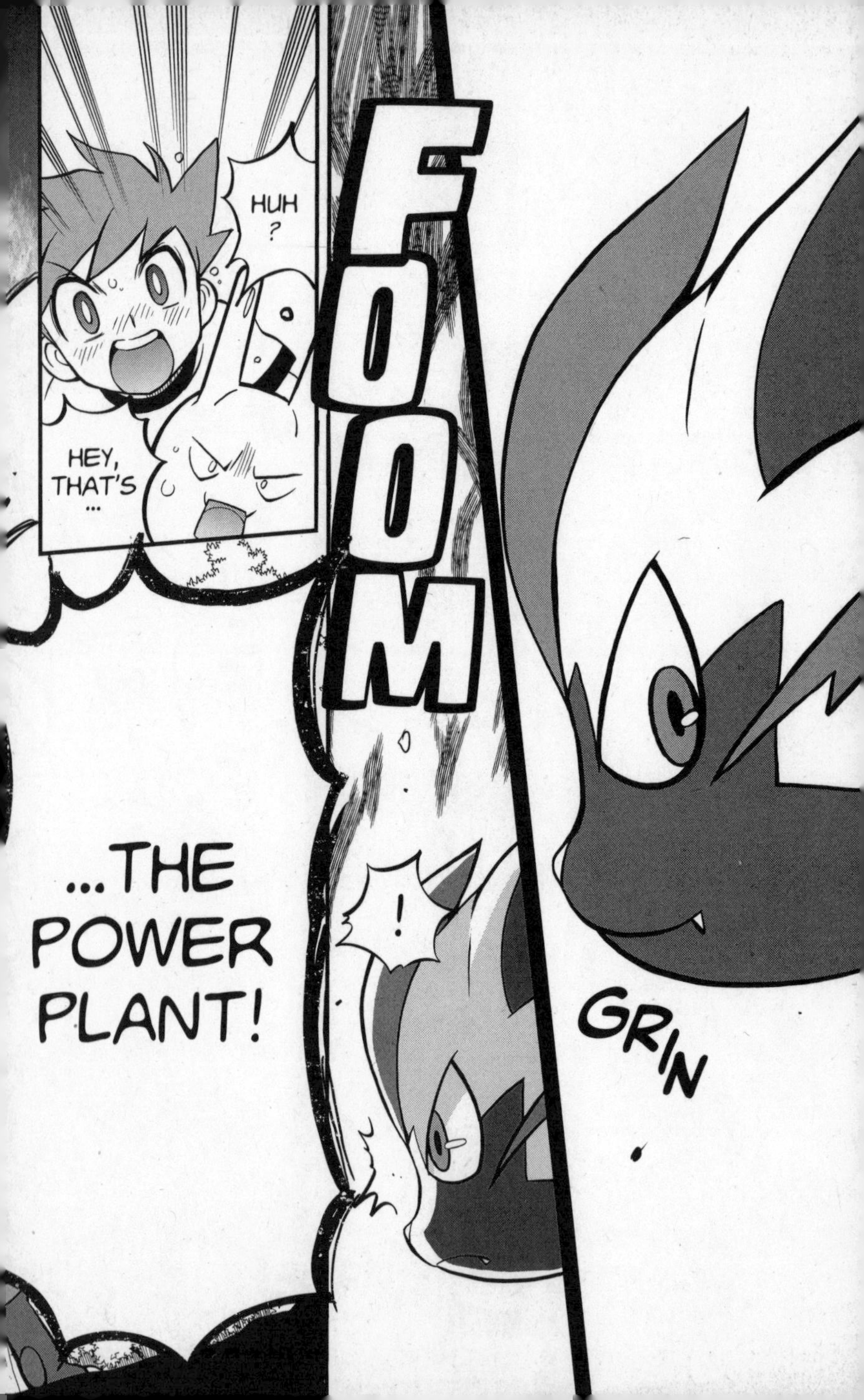
FOOM
!
GRIN
HUH?
HEY, THAT'S ...
...THE POWER PLANT!

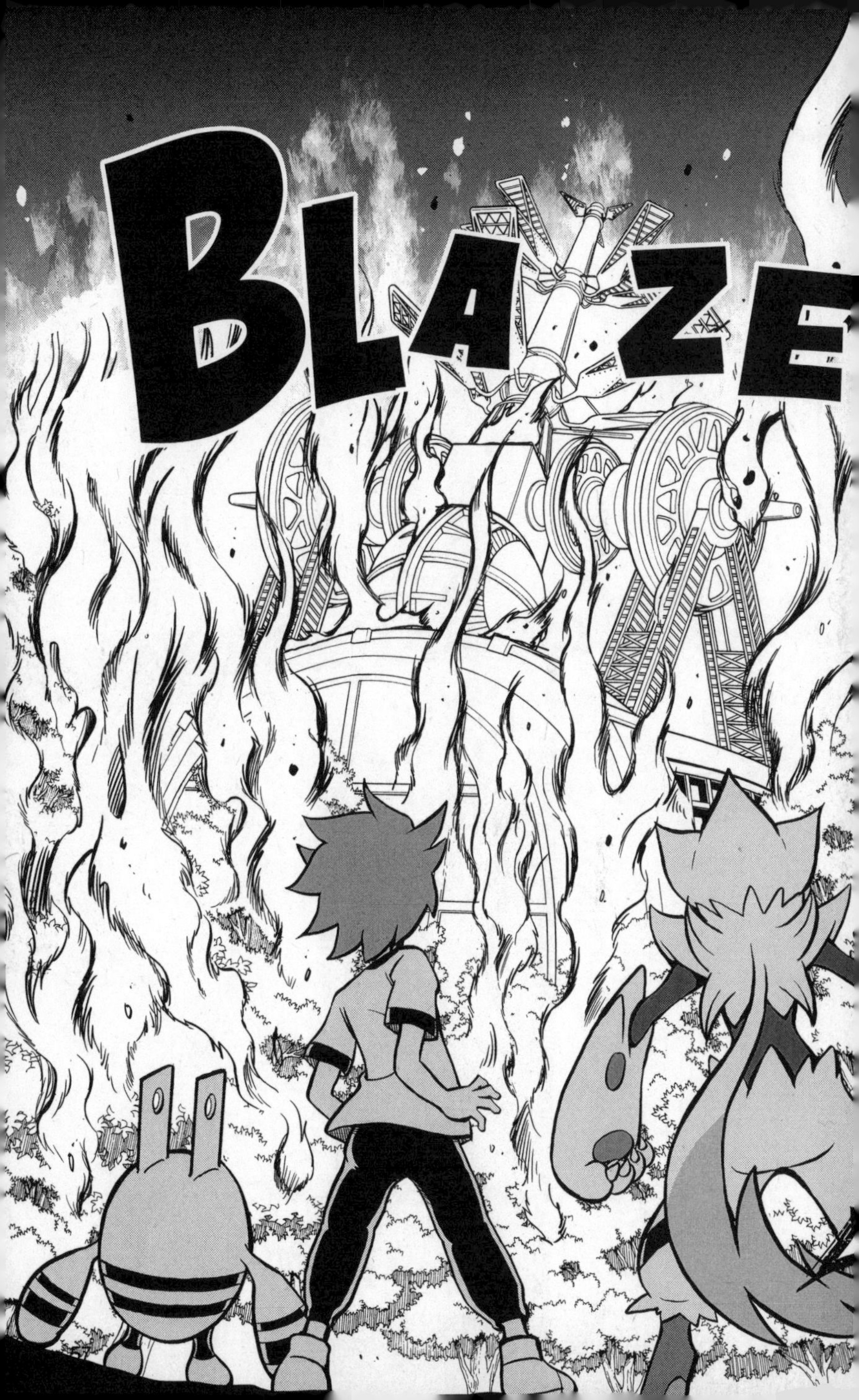
BLAZE

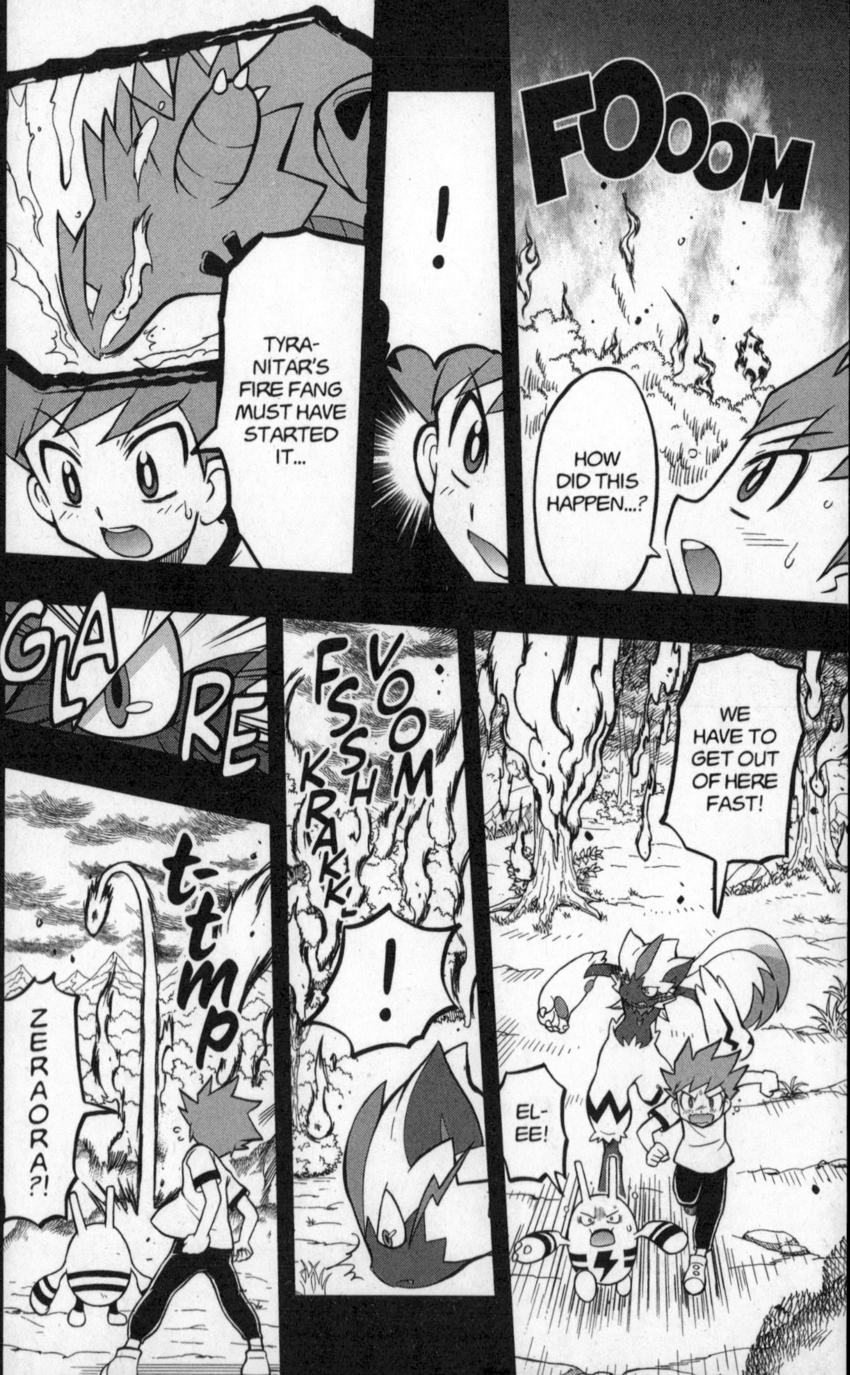
FOOOM
HOW DID THIS HAPPEN...?
!
TYRA-NITAR'S FIRE FANG MUST HAVE STARTED IT...
WE HAVE TO GET OUT OF HERE FAST!
EL-EE!
VOOOM
FSSSHH
KRAKKK
!
GLARE
t-ttmp
ZERAORA?!

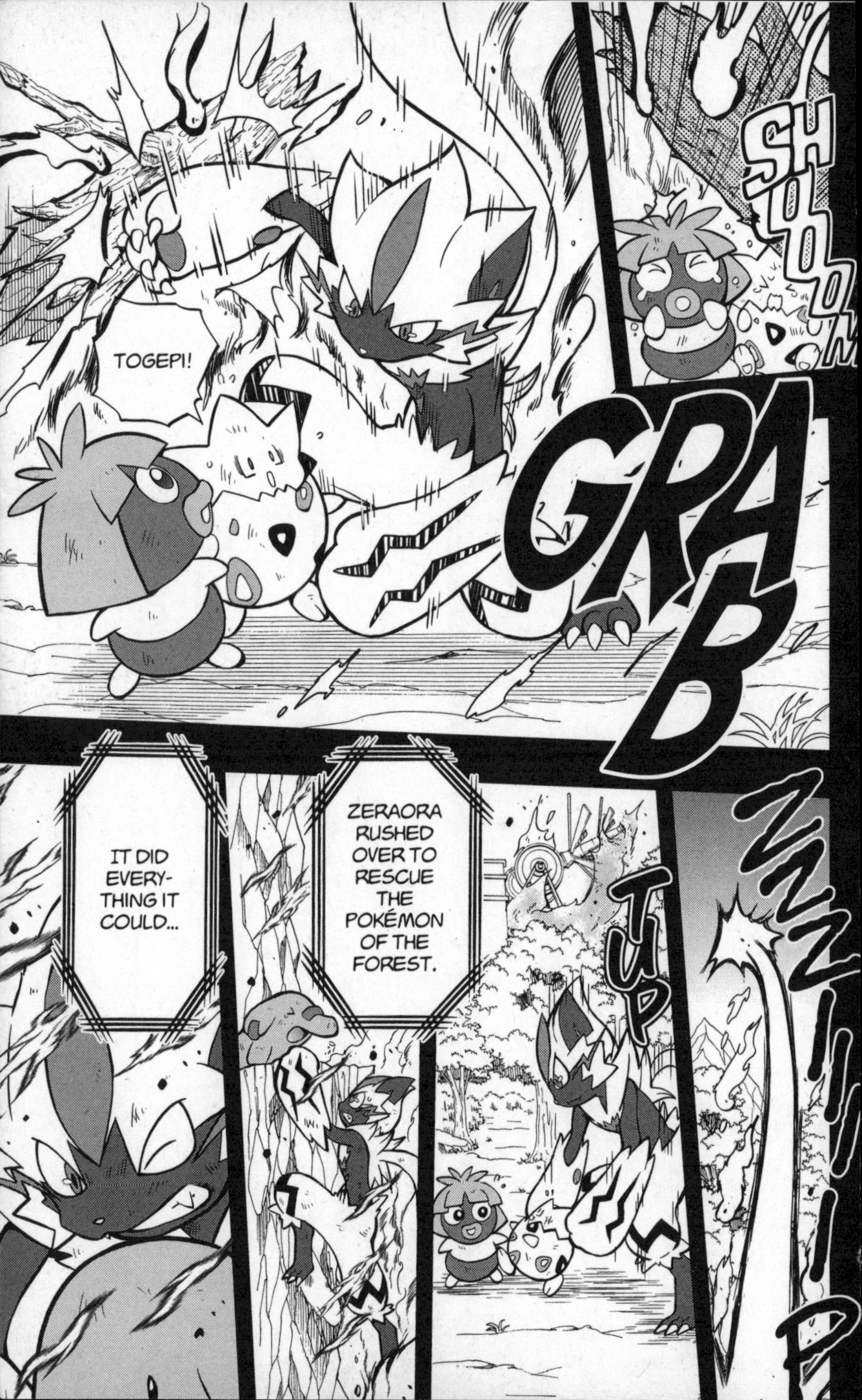
SHOOOM
TOGEPI!
GRAB
ZWIIIIP
TUP
ZERAORA RUSHED OVER TO RESCUE THE POKÉMON OF THE FOREST.
IT DID EVERY-THING IT COULD...

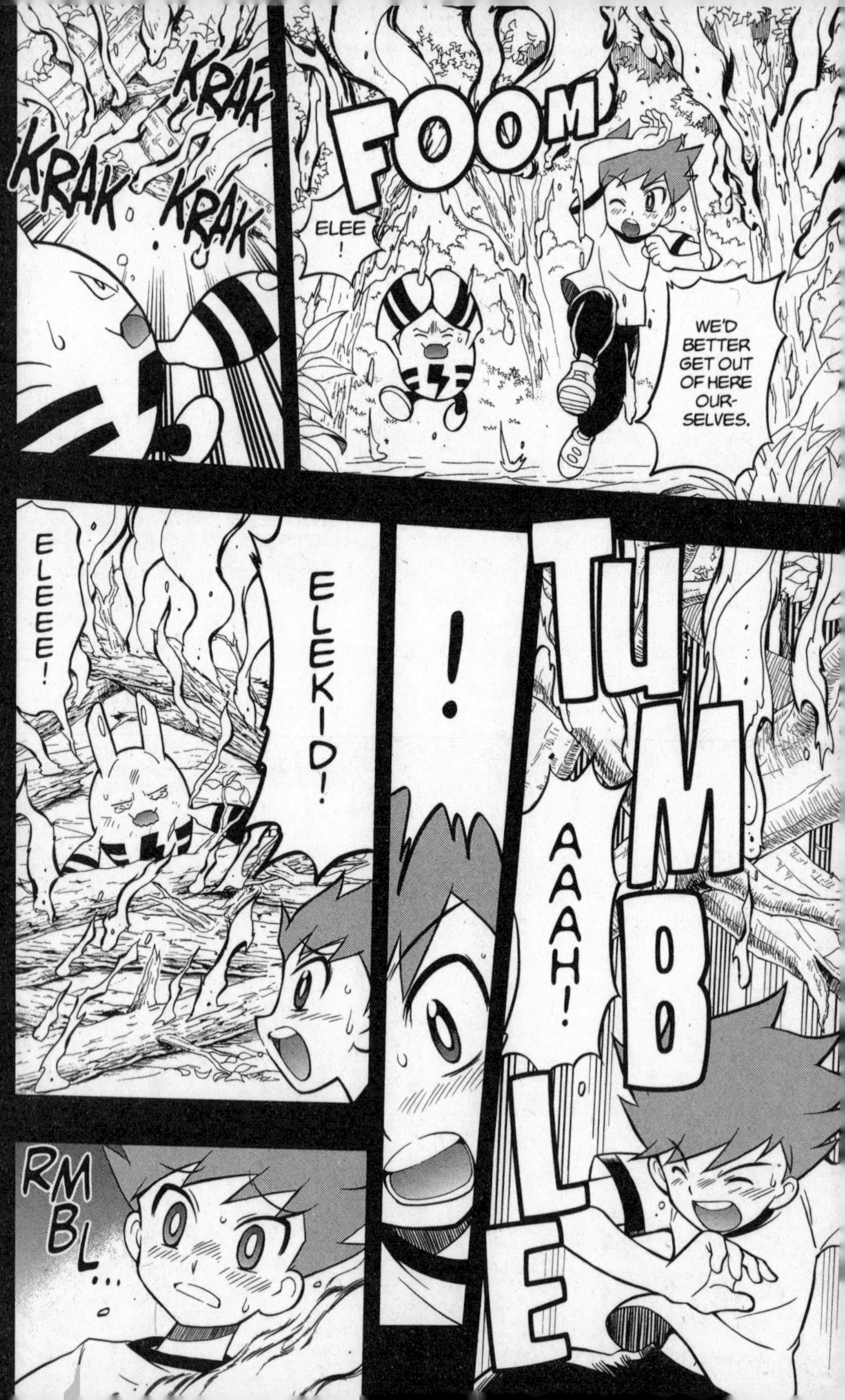
FOOM
ELEE!
WE'D BETTER GET OUT OF HERE OURSELVES.
KRAK
KRAK
KRAK
KRAK
TUMBLE
AAAH!
!
ELEKID!
ELEEE!
RMBL...

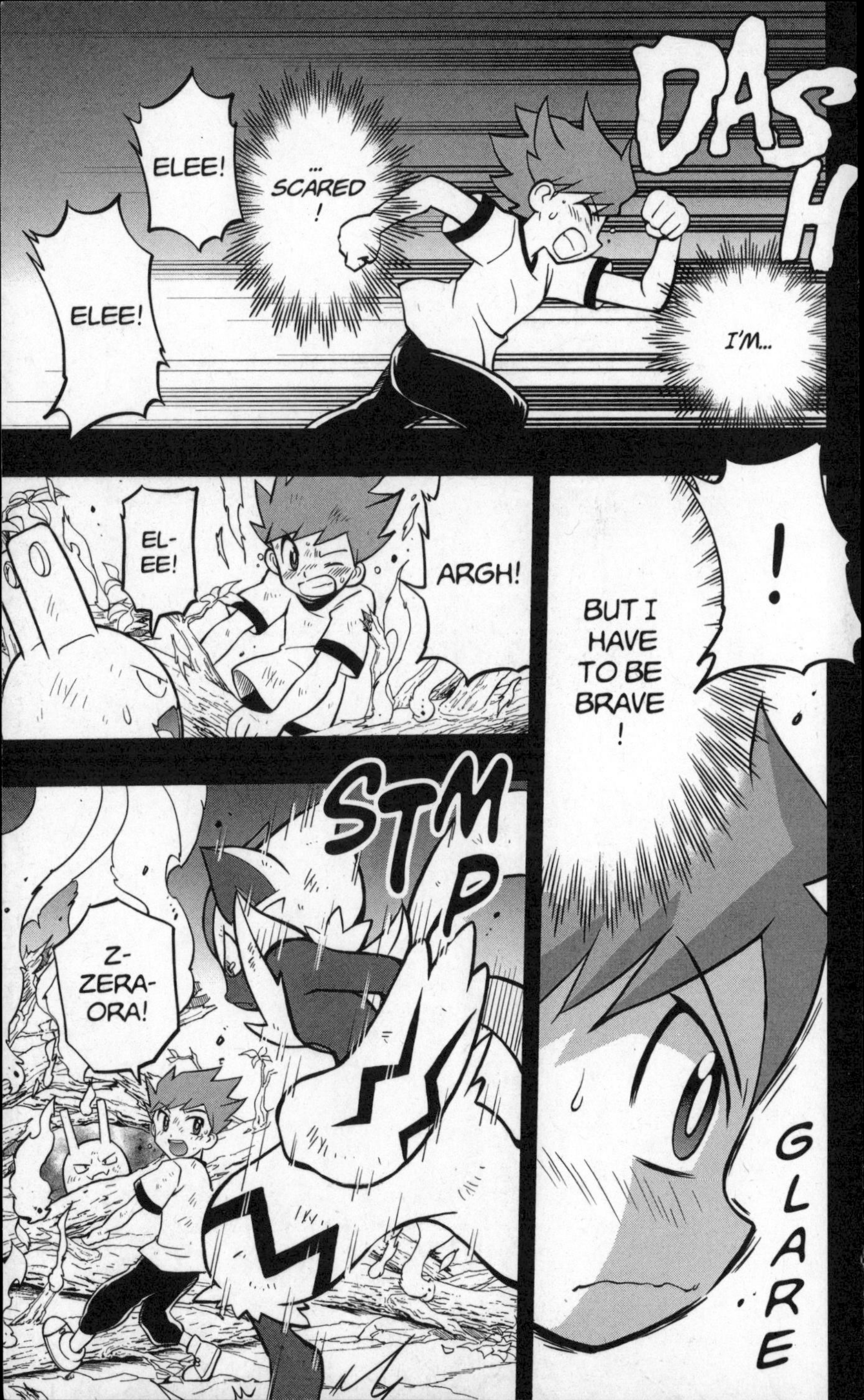
DASH
I'M...
... SCARED!
ELEE!
ELEE!
!
BUT I HAVE TO BE BRAVE!
GLARE
ARGH!
EL-EE!
STMP
Z-ZERA-ORA!

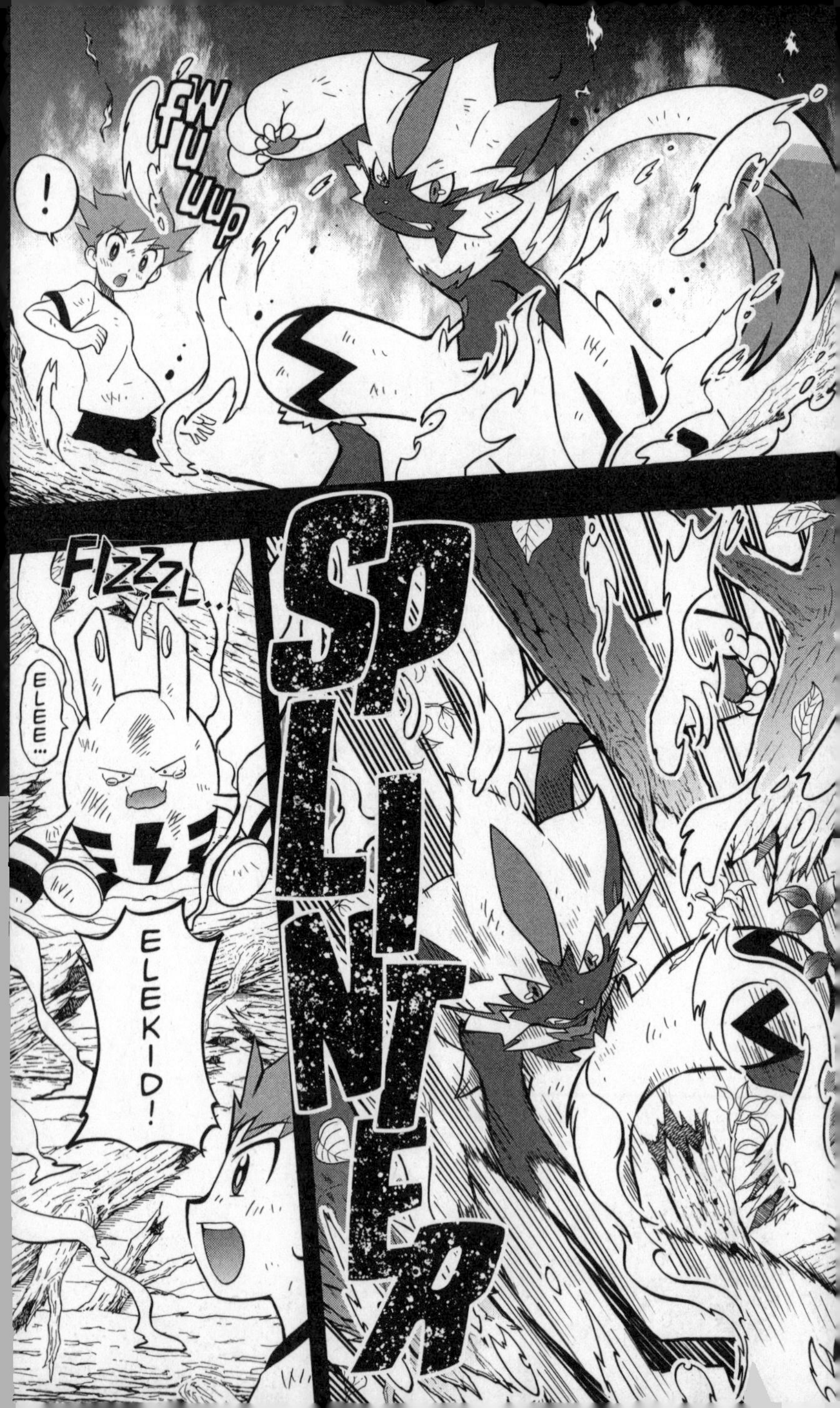

FWUUUP
!
SPLINTER
FIZZZL...
ELEEE...
ELEKID!

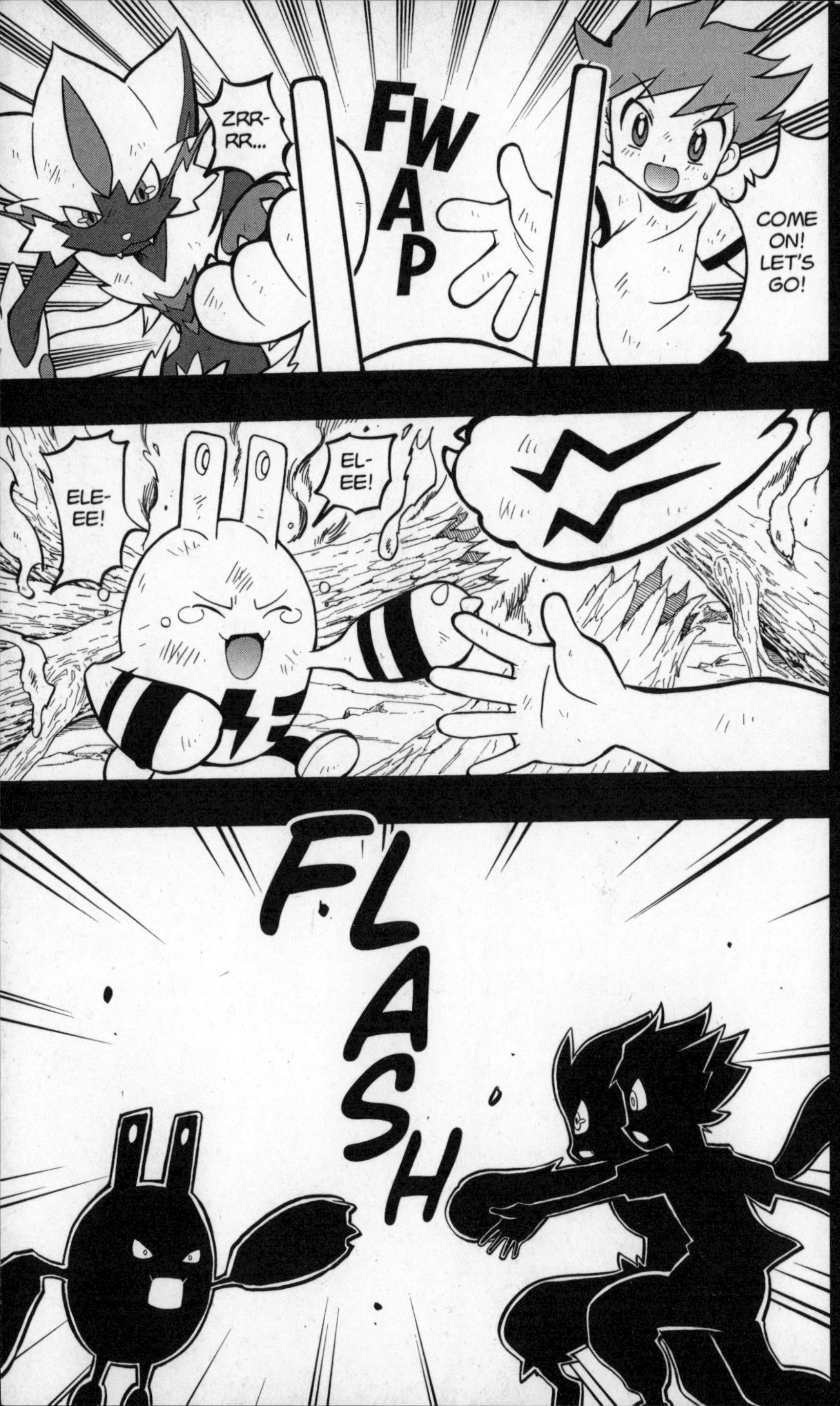
COME ON! LET'S GO!
FWAP
ZRR-RR...
EL-EE!
ELE-EE!
FLASH

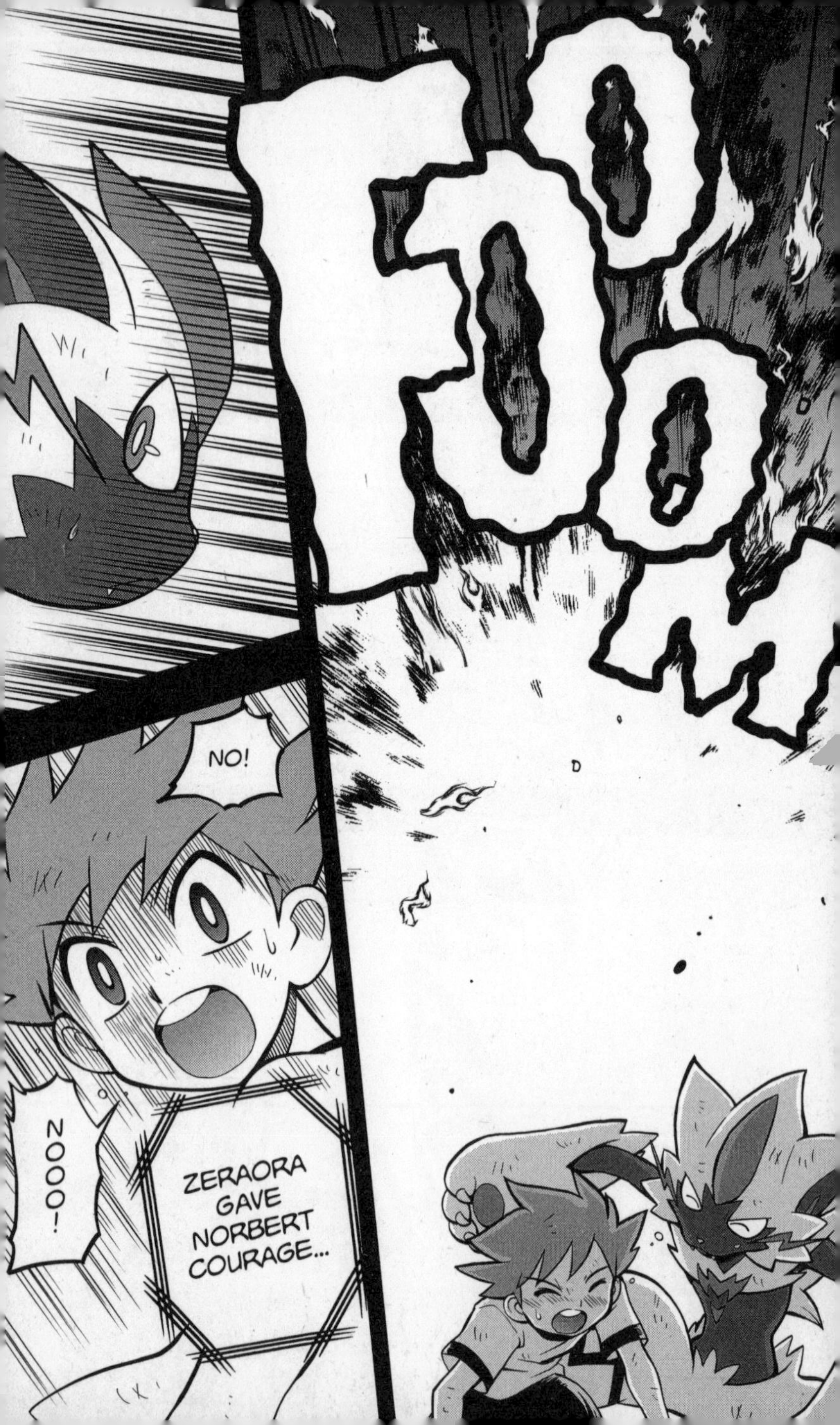
FOOM
NO!
NOOOO!
ZERAORA GAVE NORBERT COURAGE...

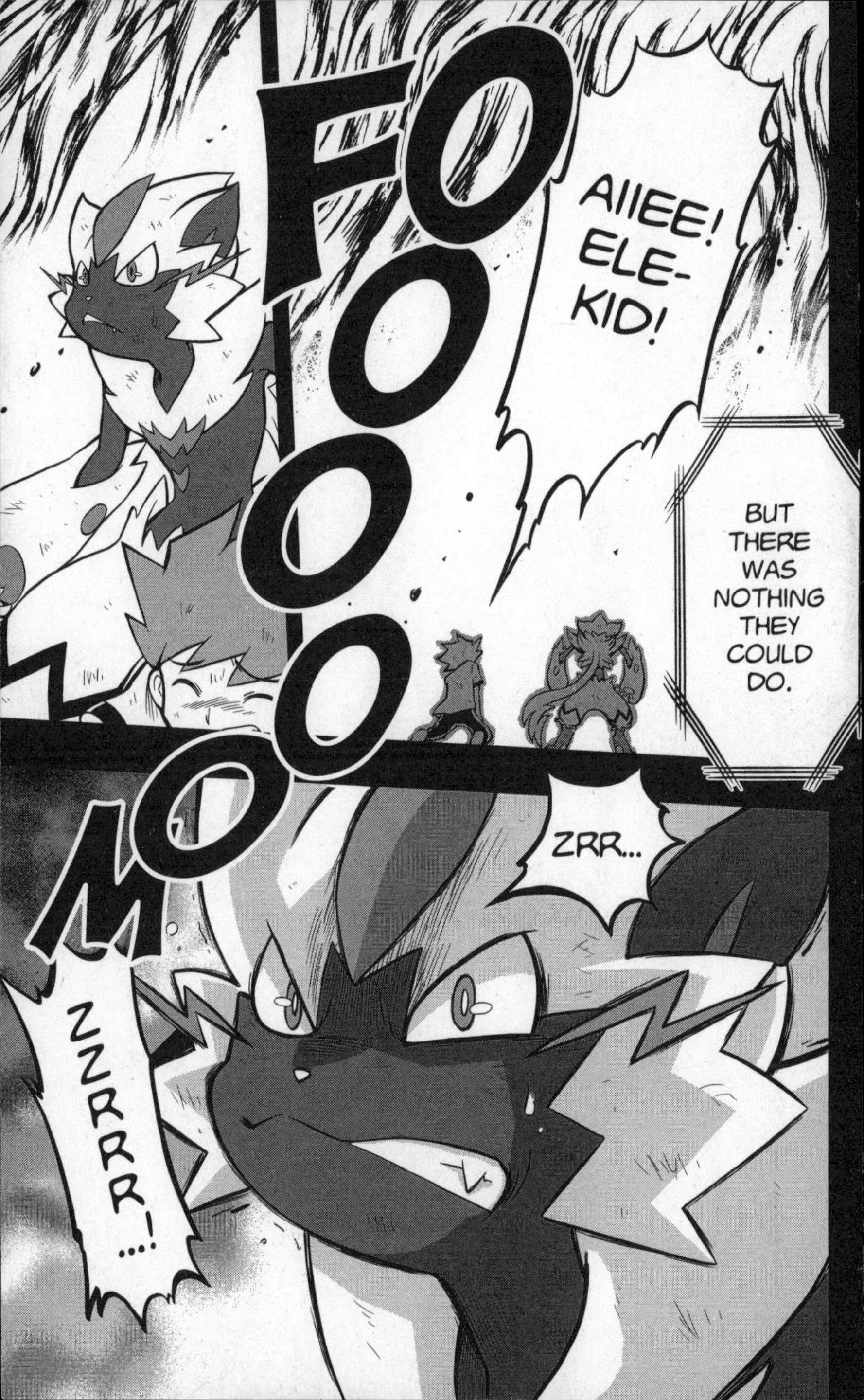
AIIEE! ELE-KID!
FOOOOOOM
BUT THERE WAS NOTHING THEY COULD DO.
ZRR...
ZZRRR...!

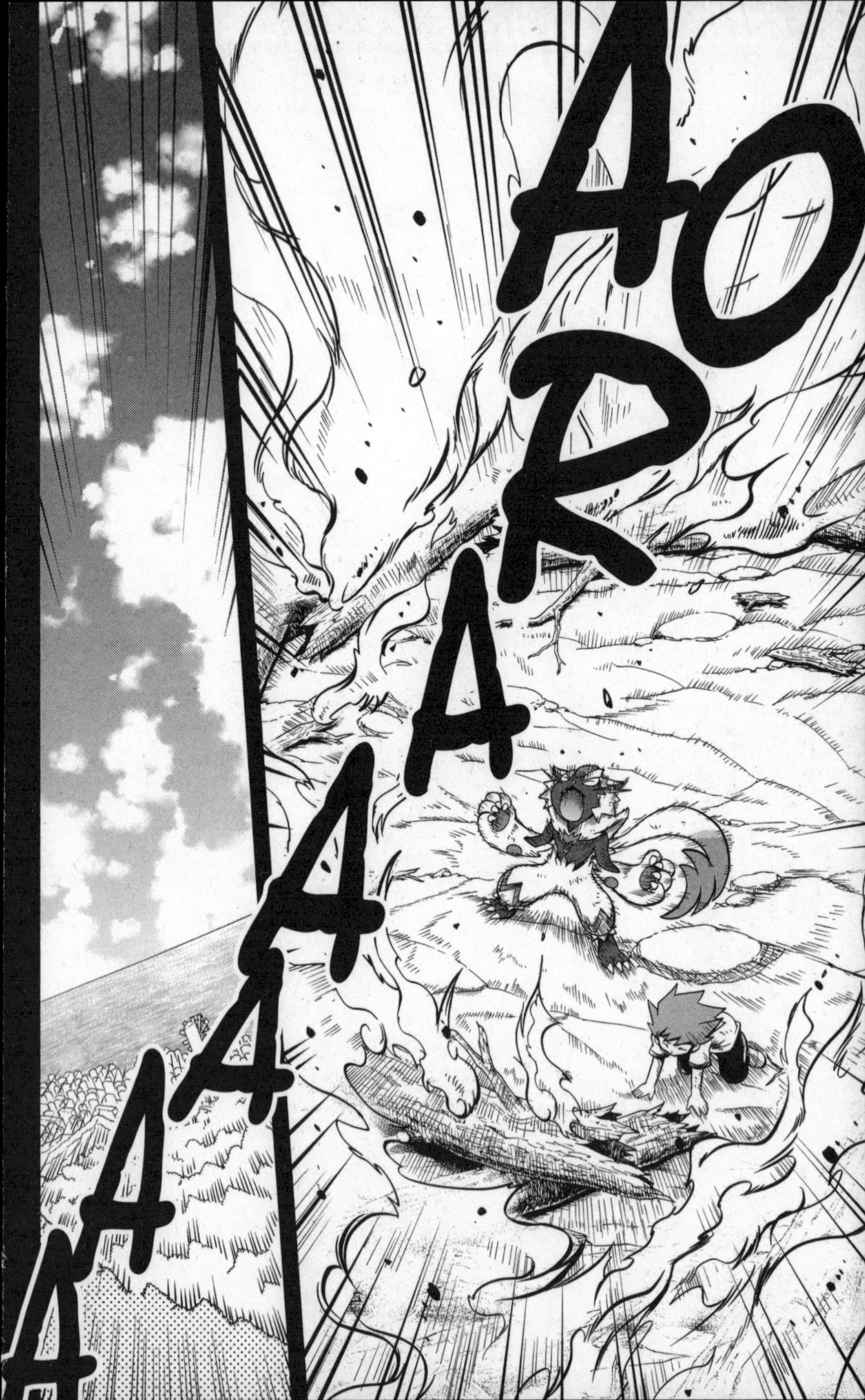
AOORAAAAAA

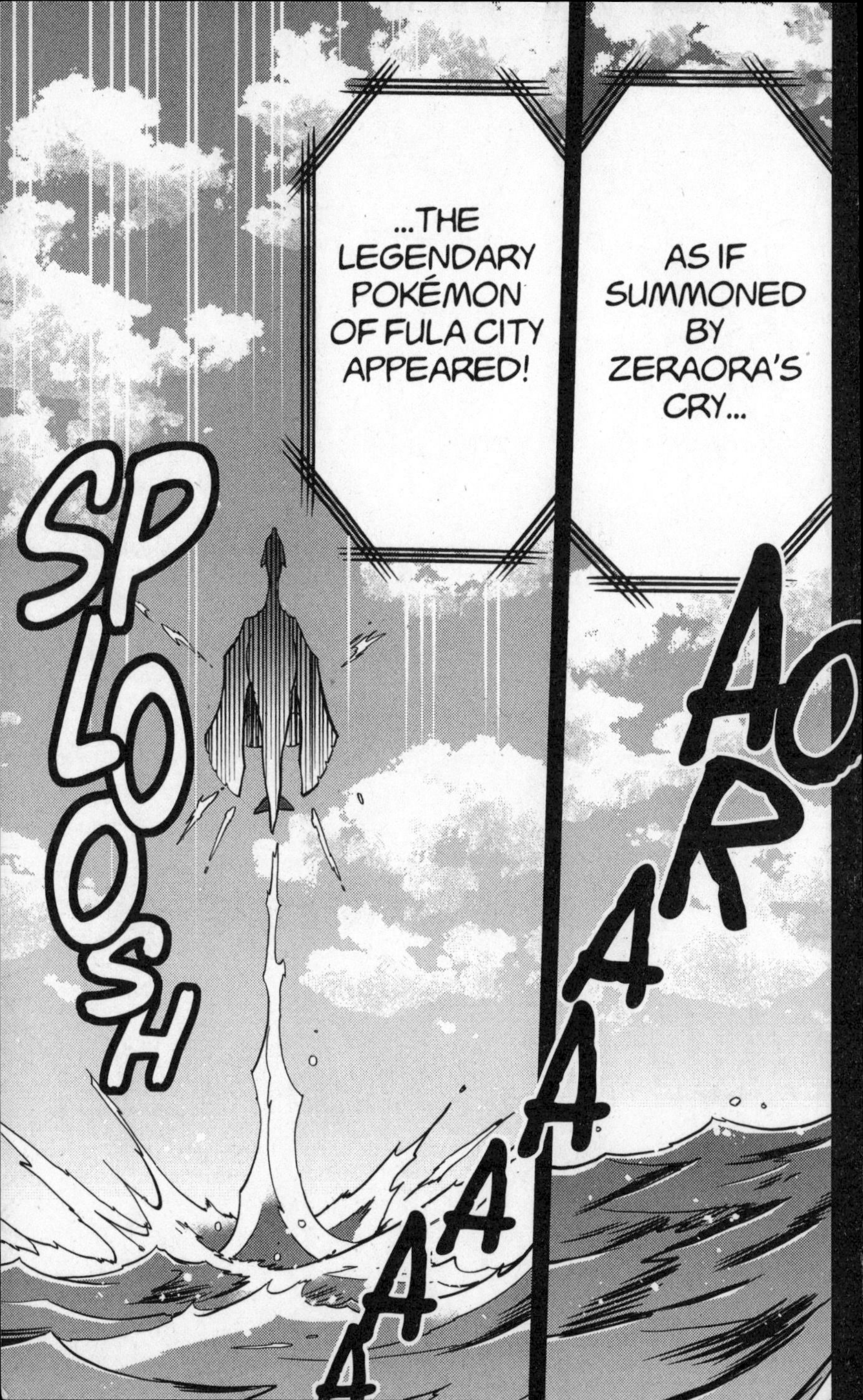
AS IF SUMMONED BY ZERAORA'S CRY...
...THE LEGENDARY POKÉMON OF FULA CITY APPEARED!
SPLOOSH

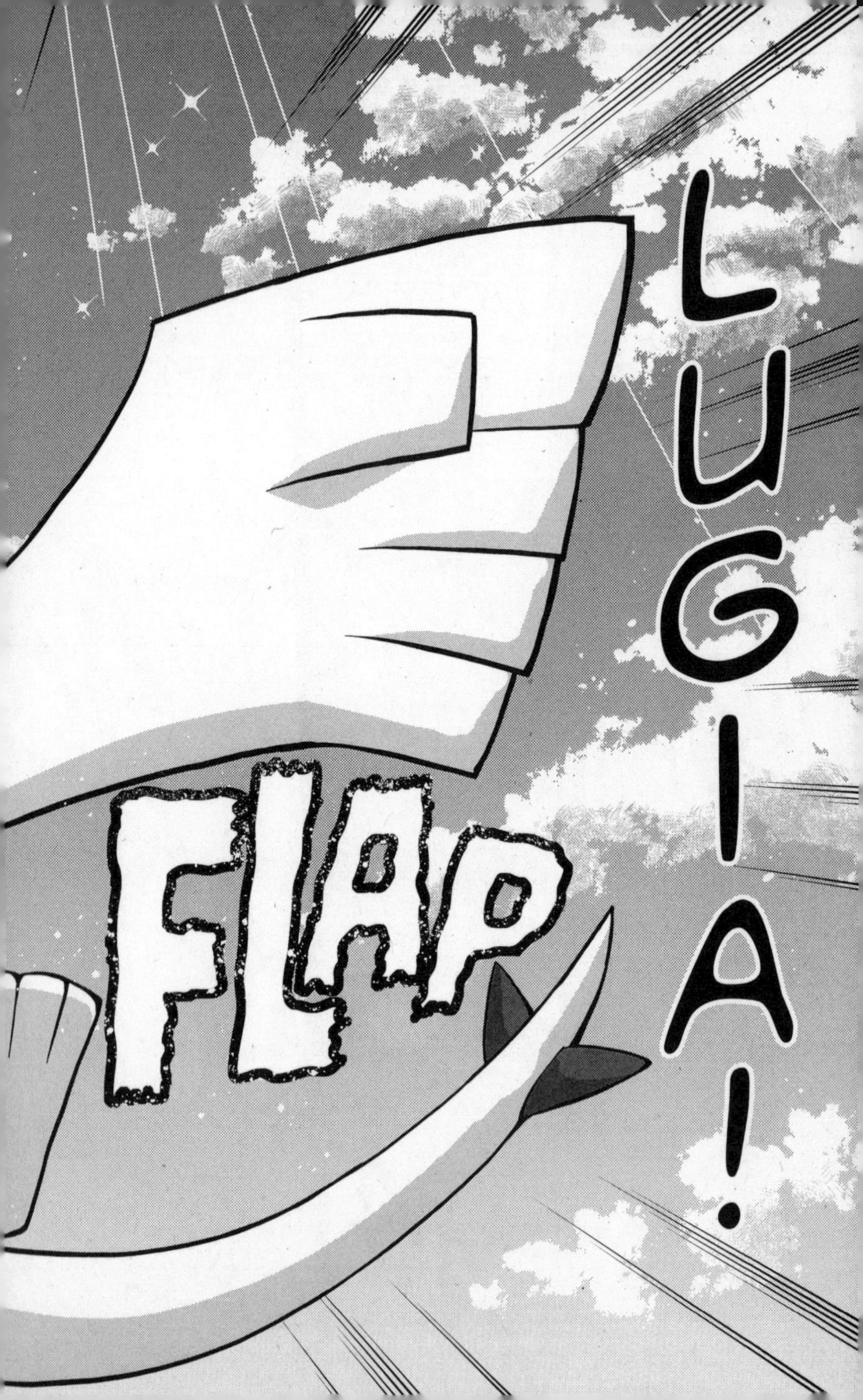
LUGIA!
FLAP

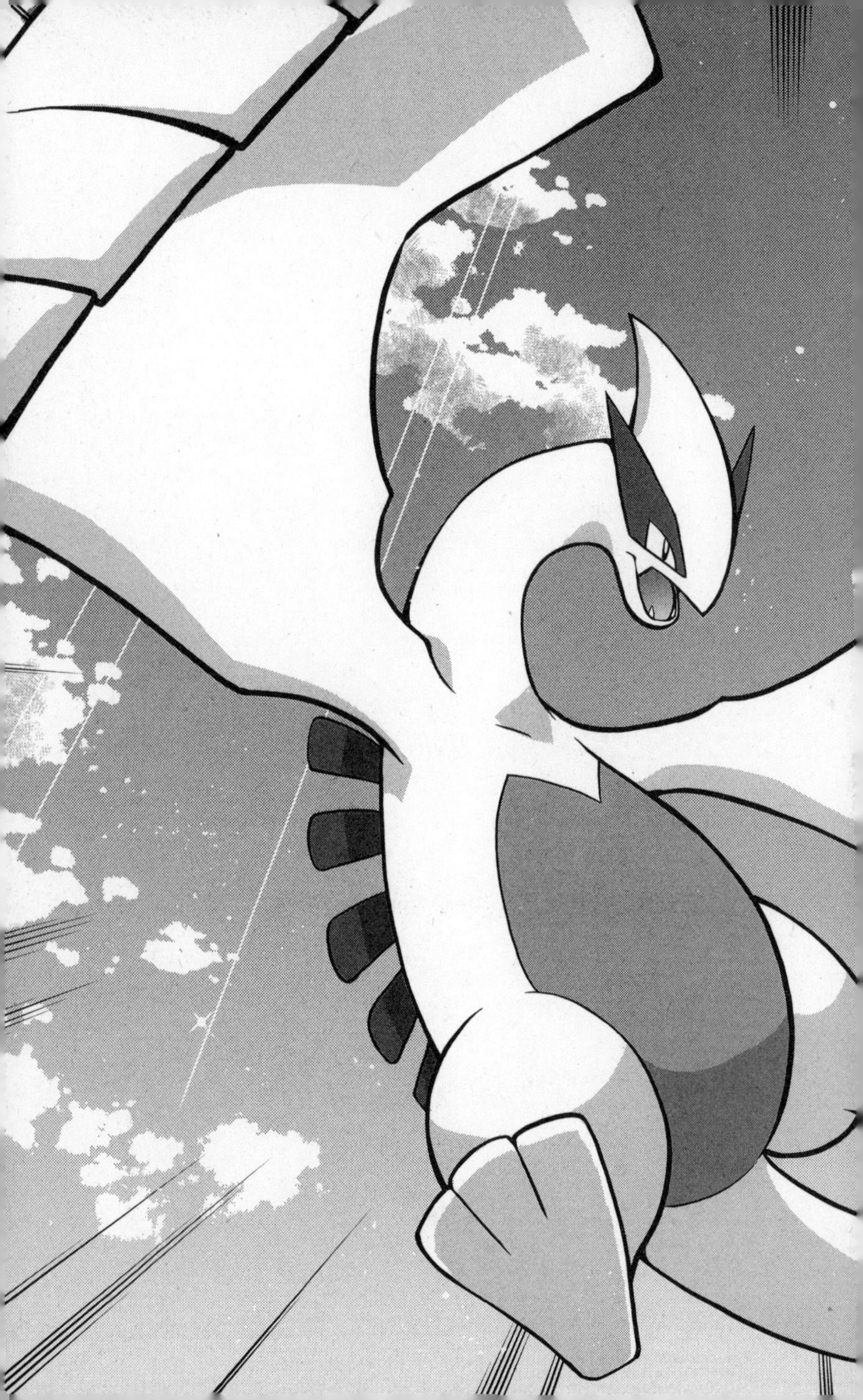

Chapter 3
Zeraora vs. Lugia

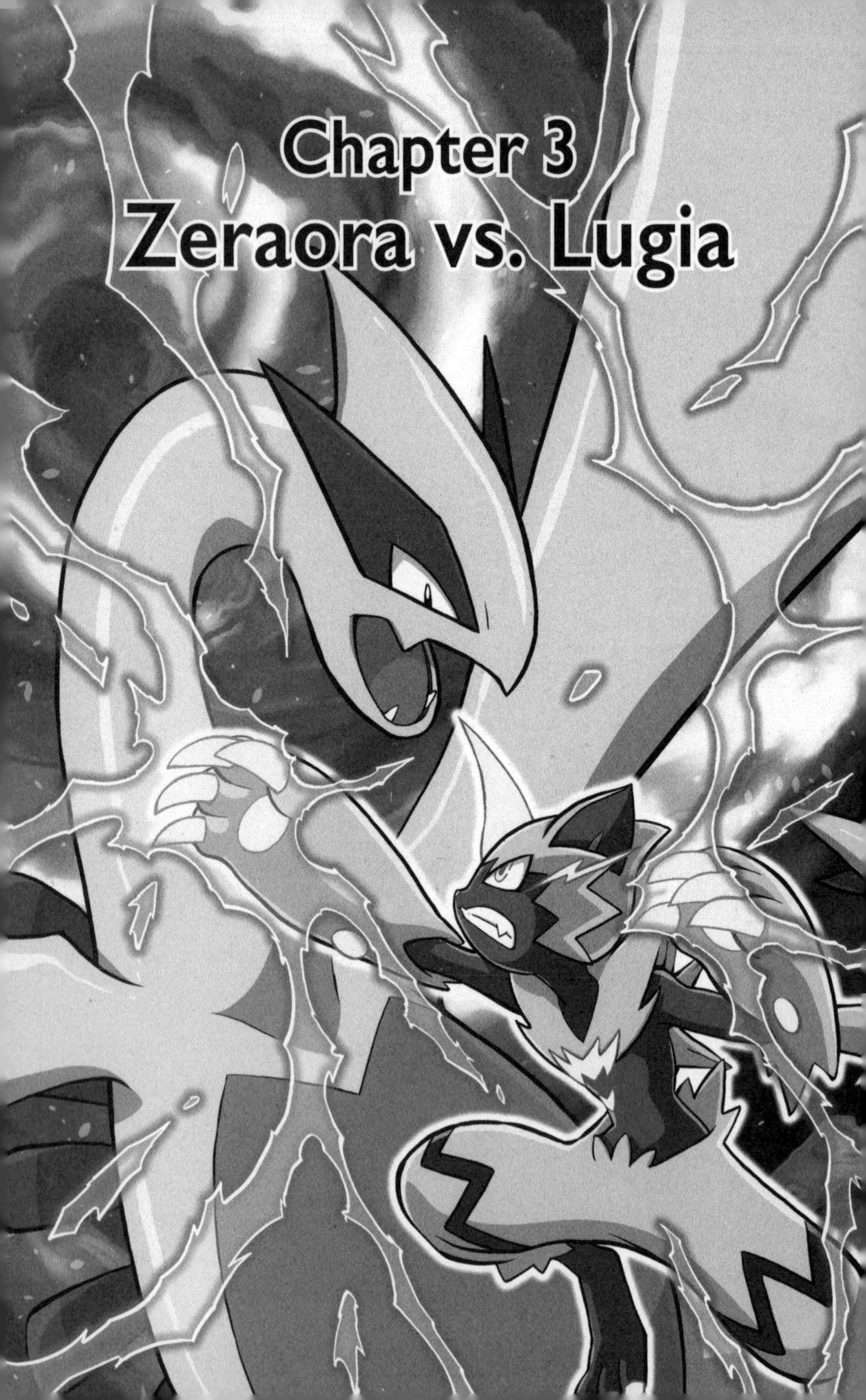

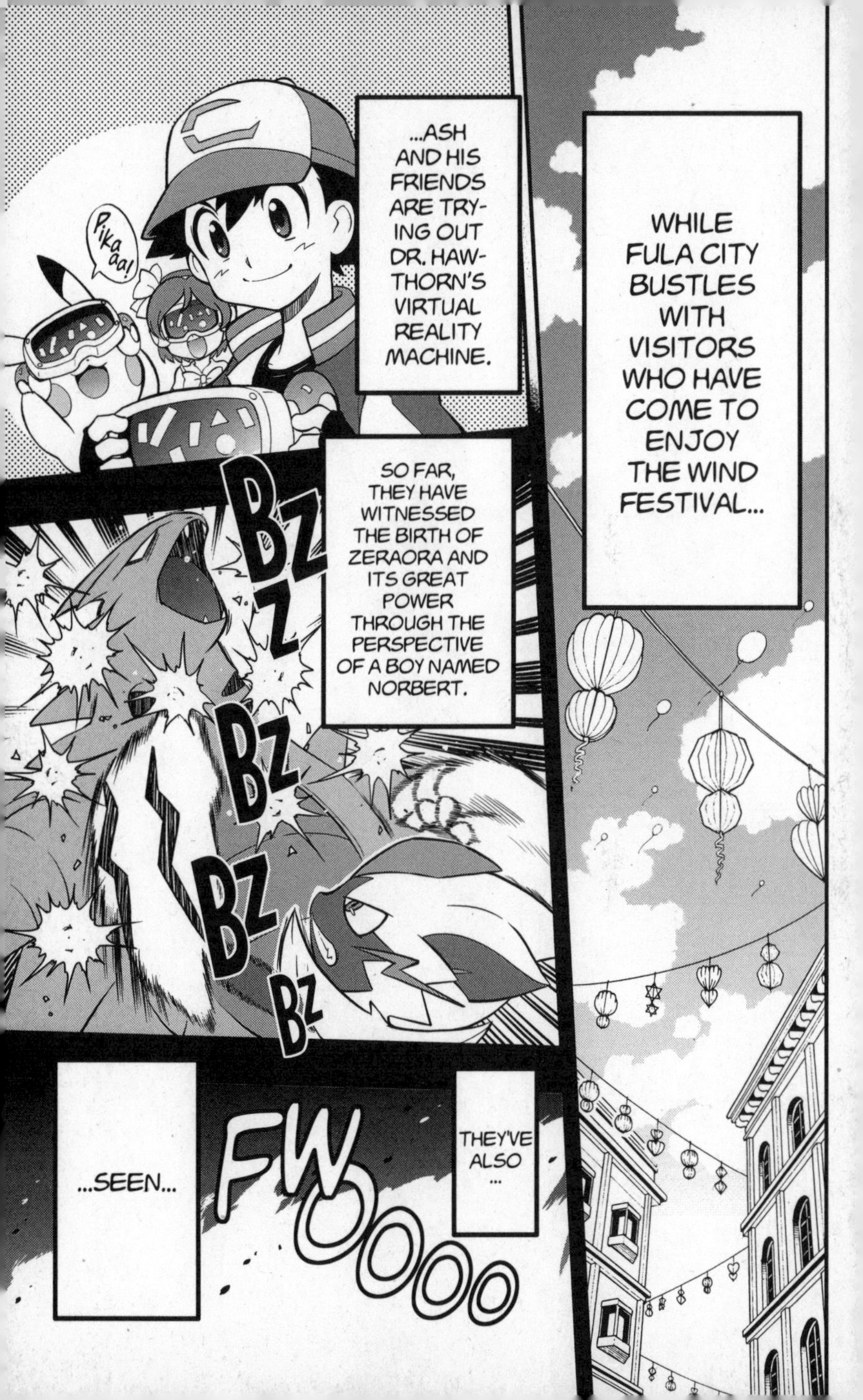
WHILE FULA CITY BUSTLES WITH VISITORS WHO HAVE COME TO ENJOY THE WIND FESTIVAL...
...ASH AND HIS FRIENDS ARE TRYING OUT DR. HAWTHORN'S VIRTUAL REALITY MACHINE.
Pikaaa!
SO FAR, THEY HAVE WITNESSED THE BIRTH OF ZERAORA AND ITS GREAT POWER THROUGH THE PERSPECTIVE OF A BOY NAMED NORBERT.
BZZ
BZ
BZ
BZ
THEY'VE ALSO ...
FWOOOOO
...SEEN...

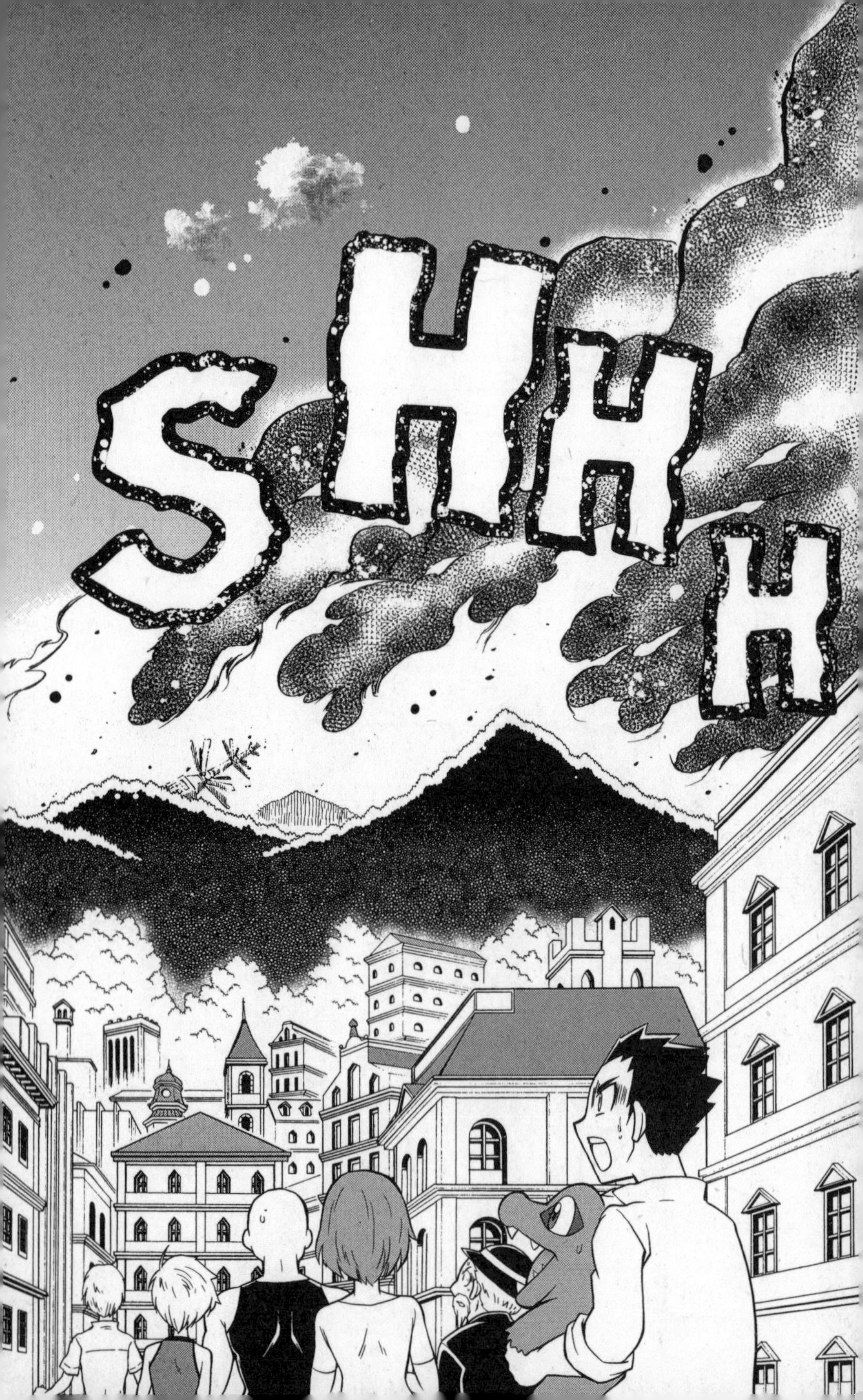
SHHHH

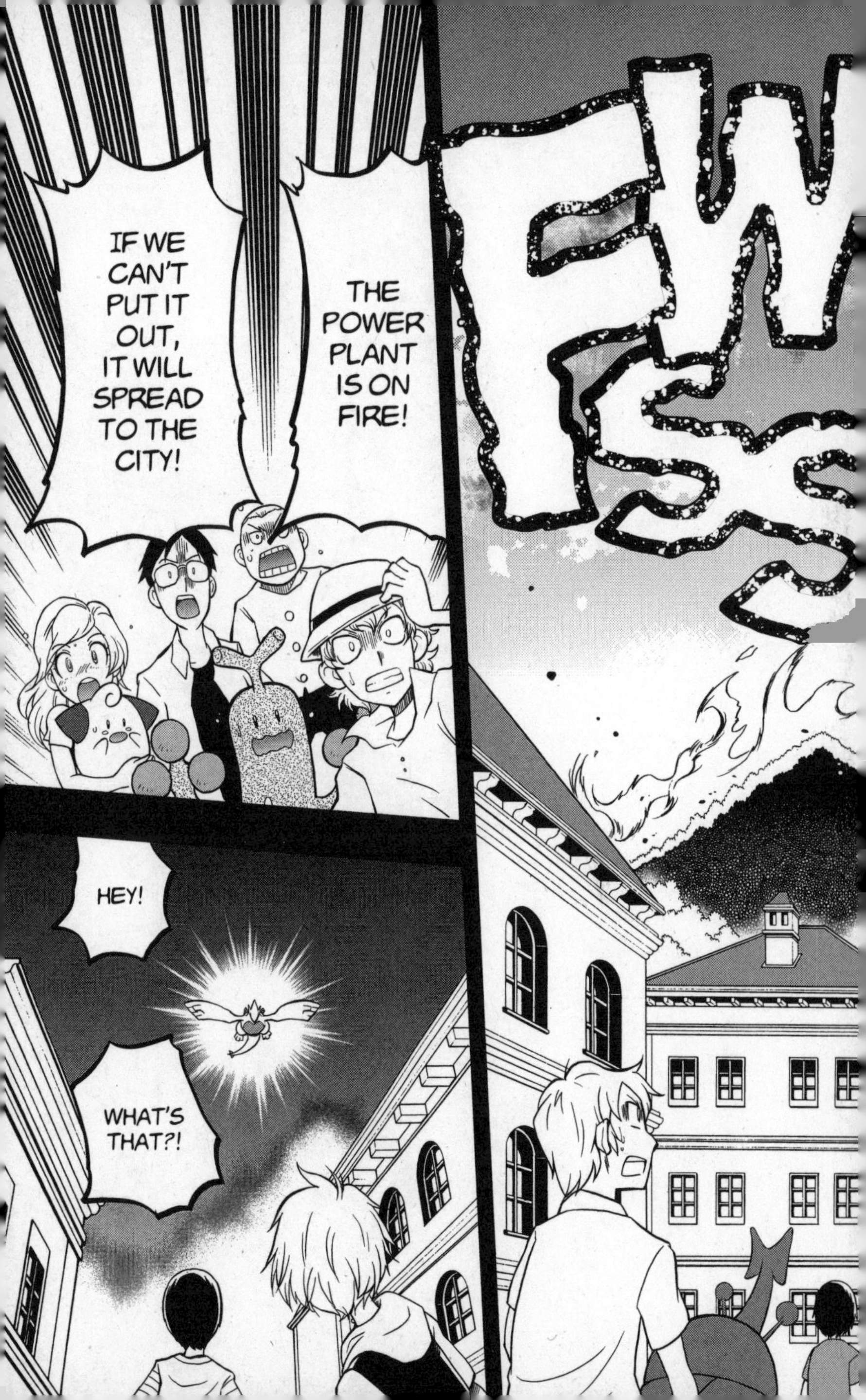
THE POWER PLANT IS ON FIRE!
IF WE CAN'T PUT IT OUT, IT WILL SPREAD TO THE CITY!
HEY!
WHAT'S THAT?!

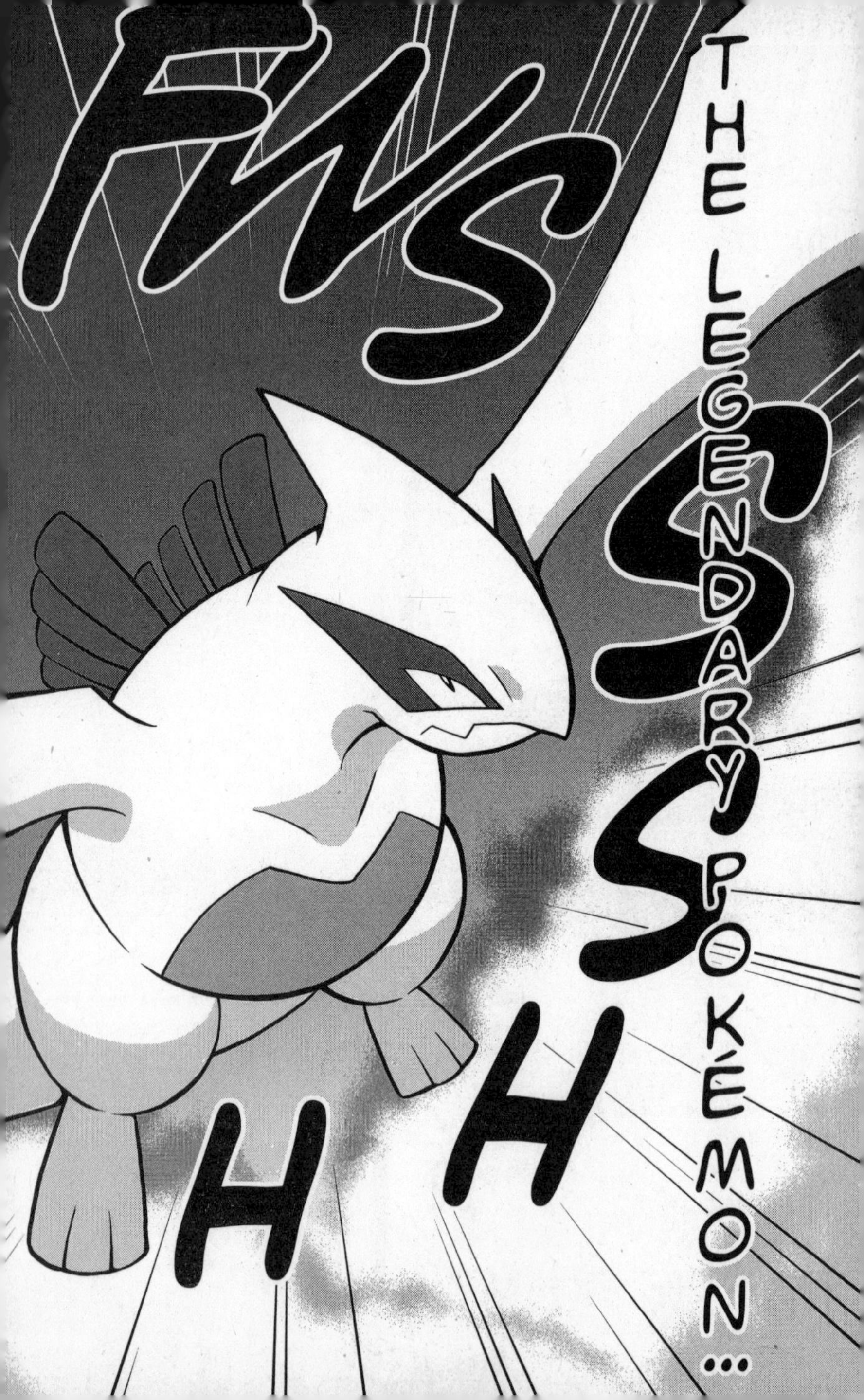
THE LEGENDARY POKÉMON...
FWSSSHH

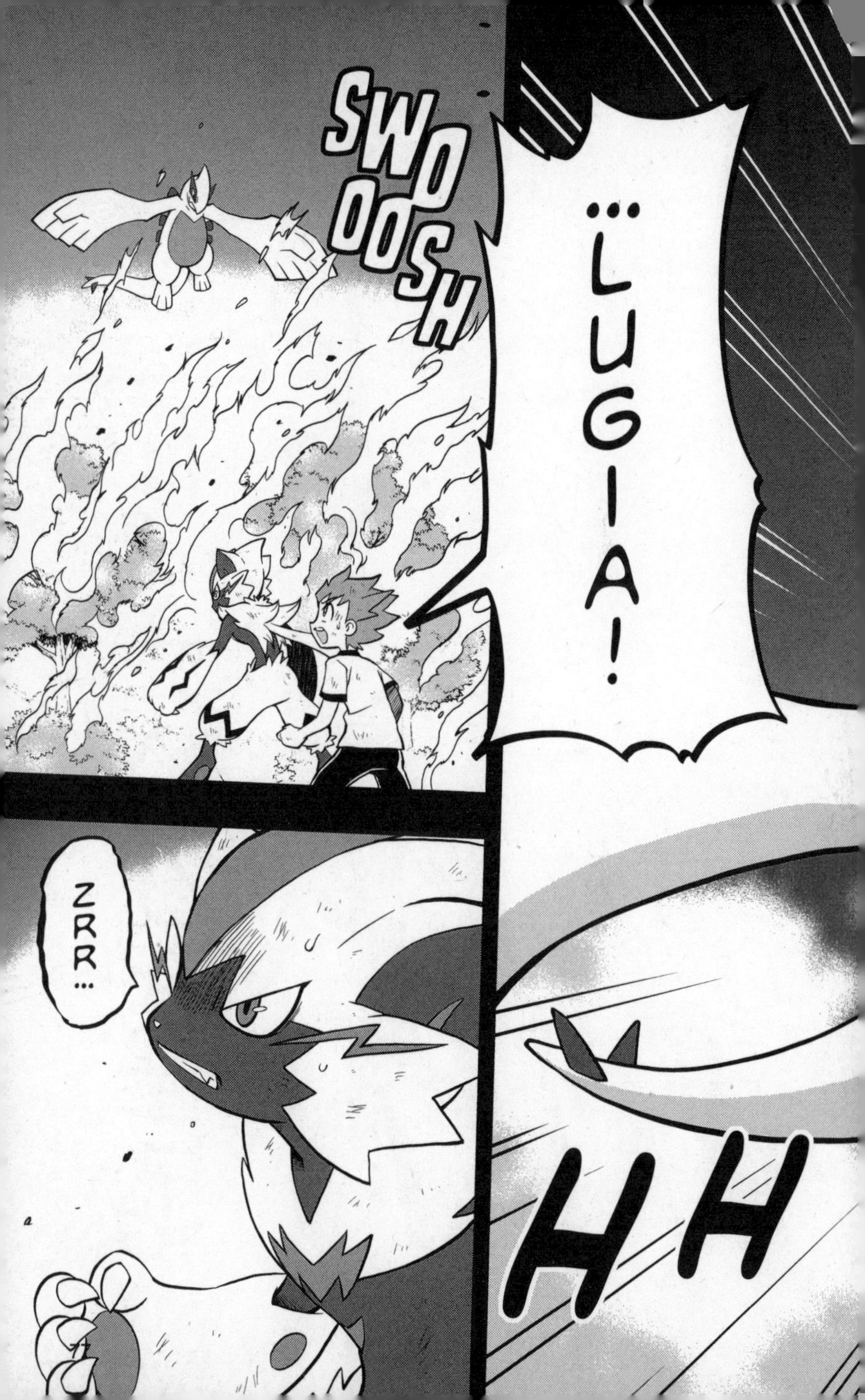

...LUGIA!
HH
SWOOOSH
ZRR...

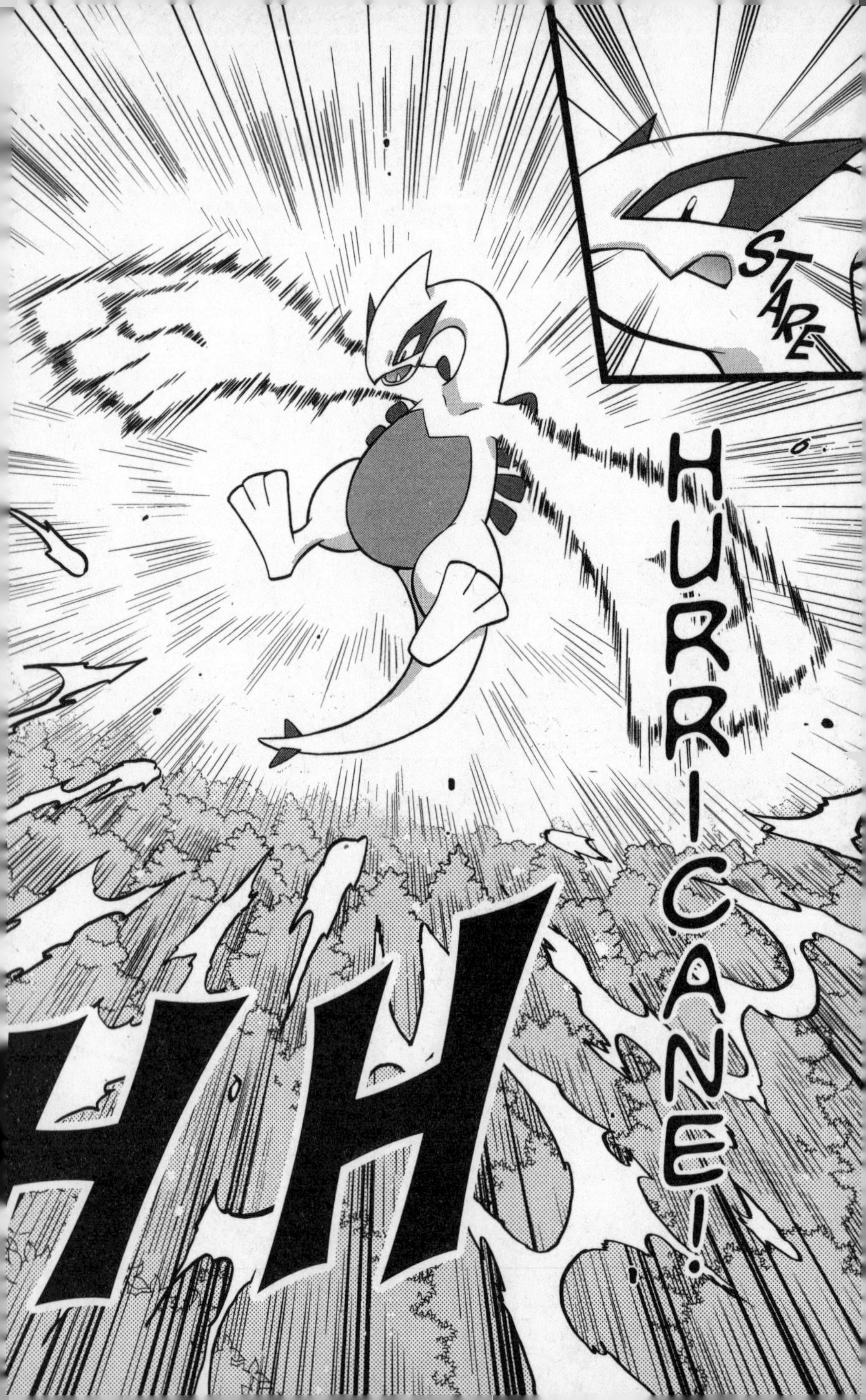
STARE
HURRICANE!

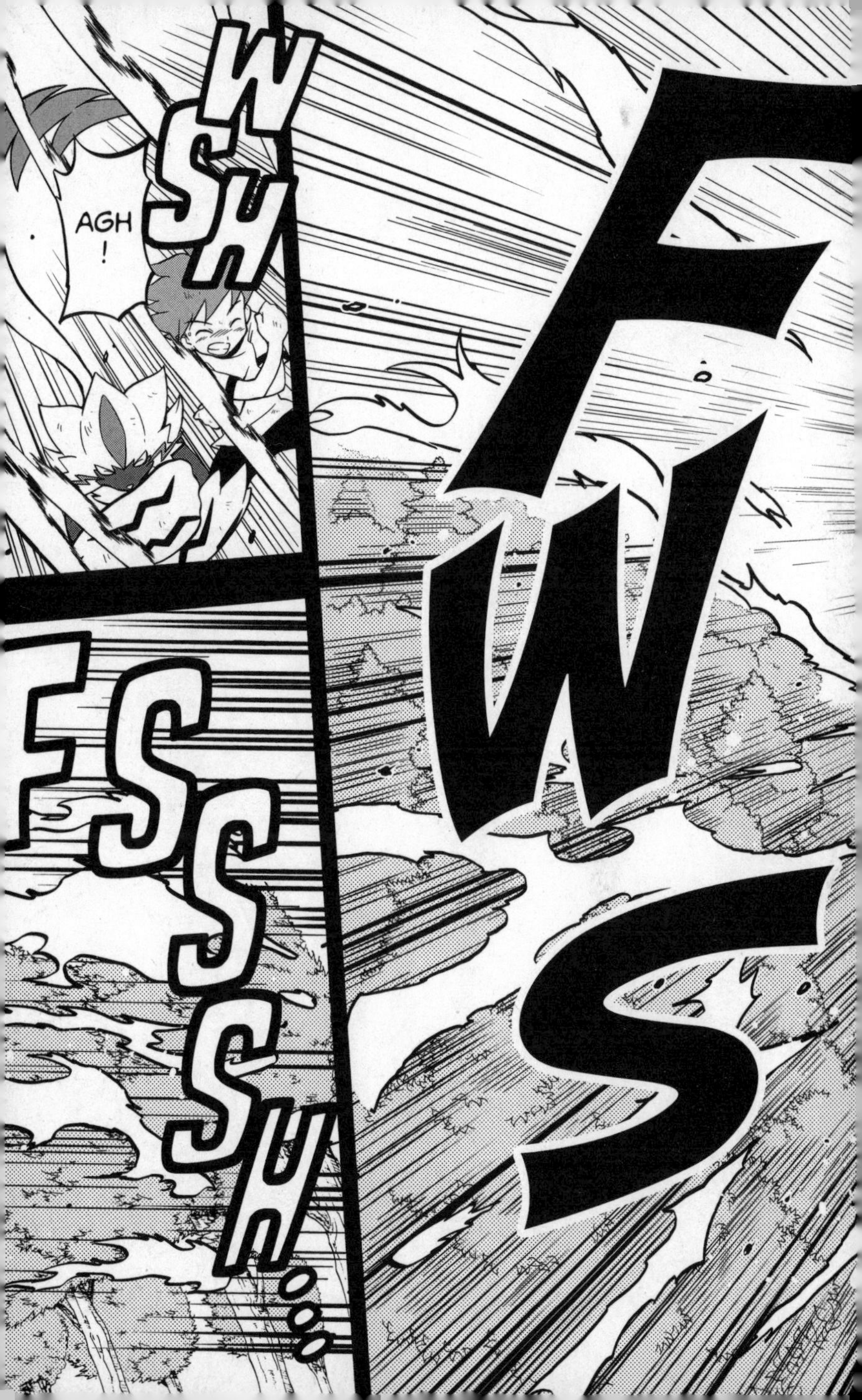
FWS
WSH
AGH!
FSSSH...

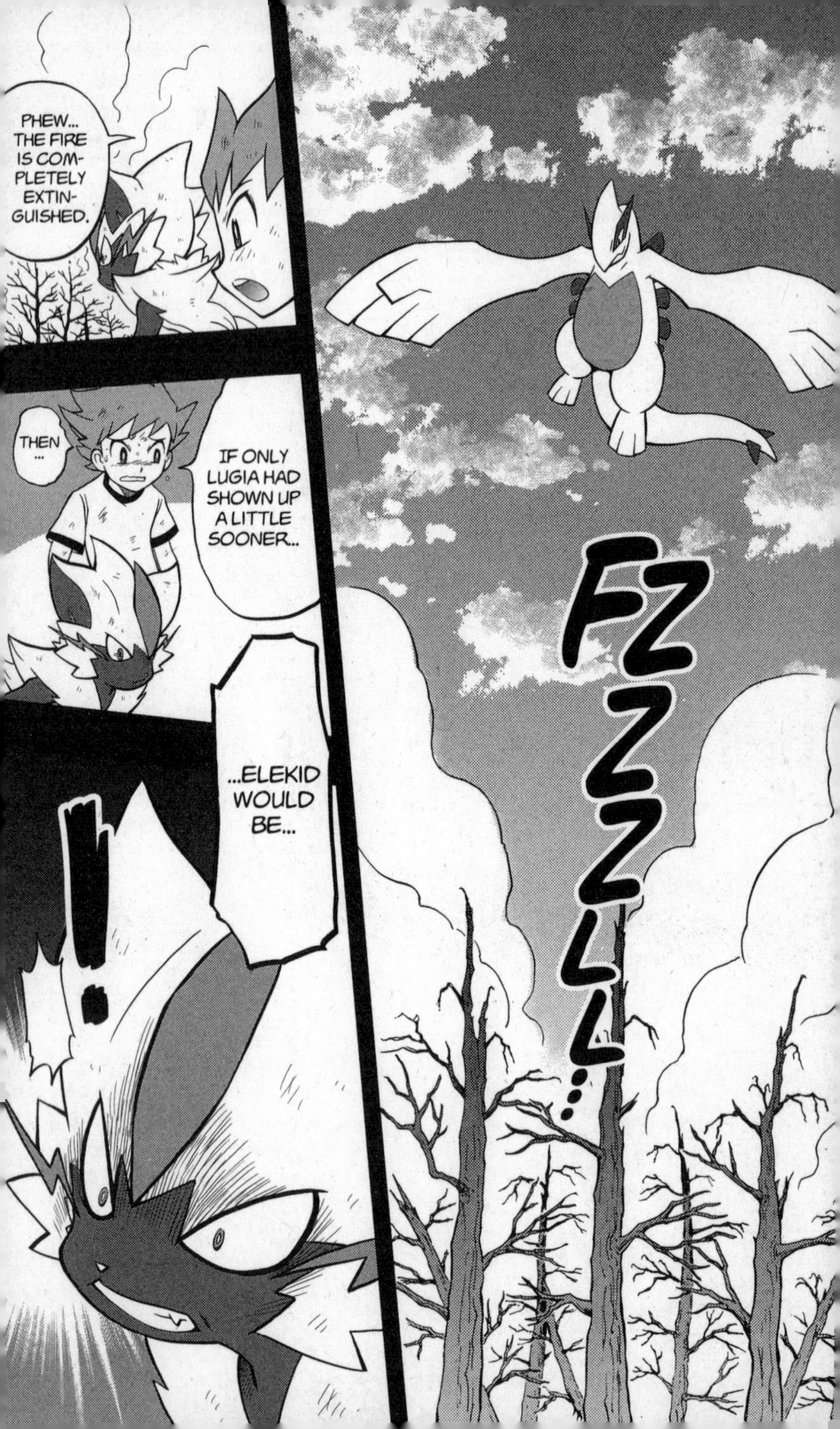
FZZZLLL...
PHEW... THE FIRE IS COMPLETELY EXTINGUISHED.
IF ONLY LUGIA HAD SHOWN UP A LITTLE SOONER...
THEN ...
...ELEKID WOULD BE...
!!

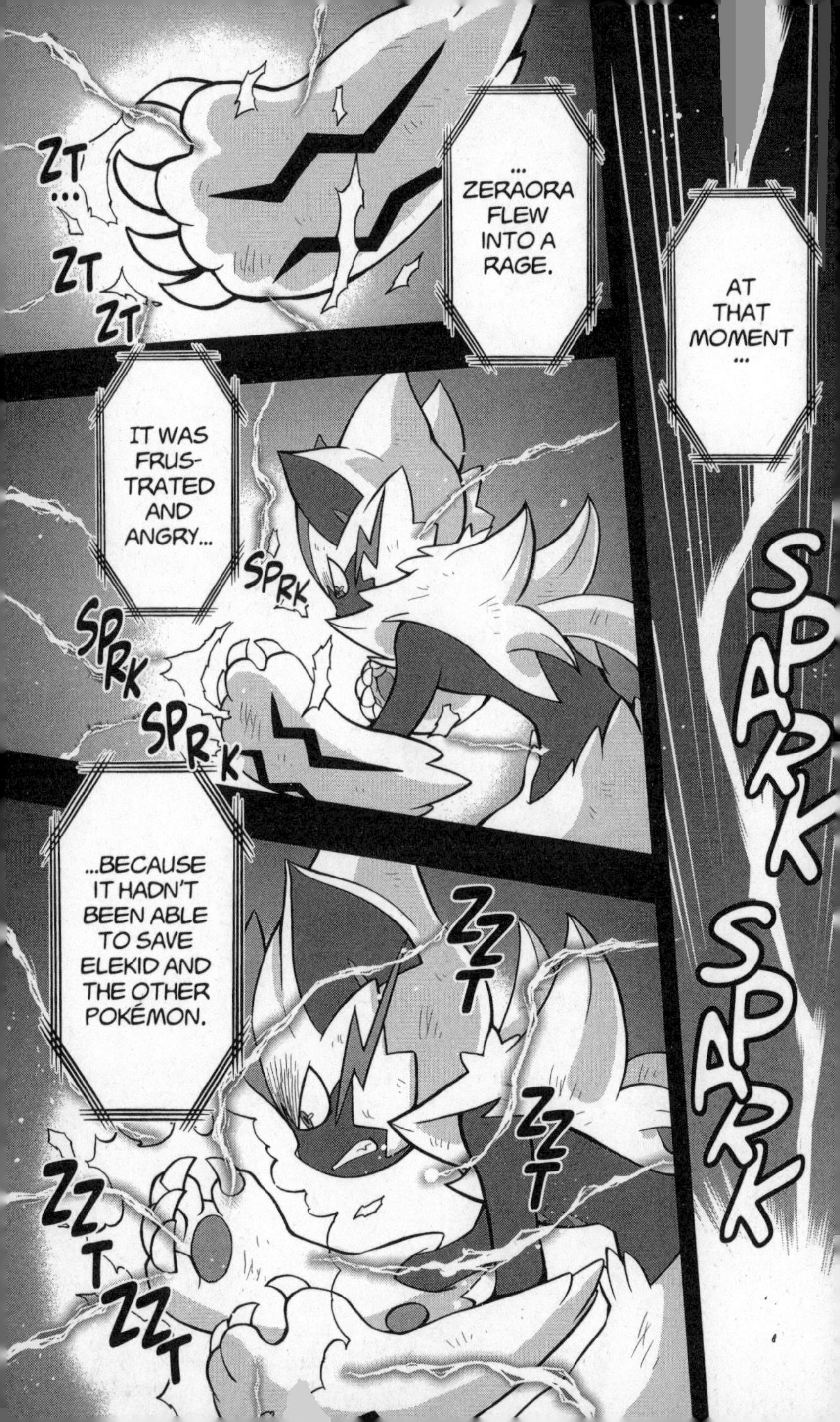
AT THAT MOMENT...
SPARK
SPARK
...ZERAORA FLEW INTO A RAGE.
ZT... ZT
ZT
IT WAS FRUS-TRATED AND ANGRY...
SPRK
SPRK
SPRK
...BECAUSE IT HADN'T BEEN ABLE TO SAVE ELEKID AND THE OTHER POKÉMON.
ZZT
ZZT
ZZT
ZZT

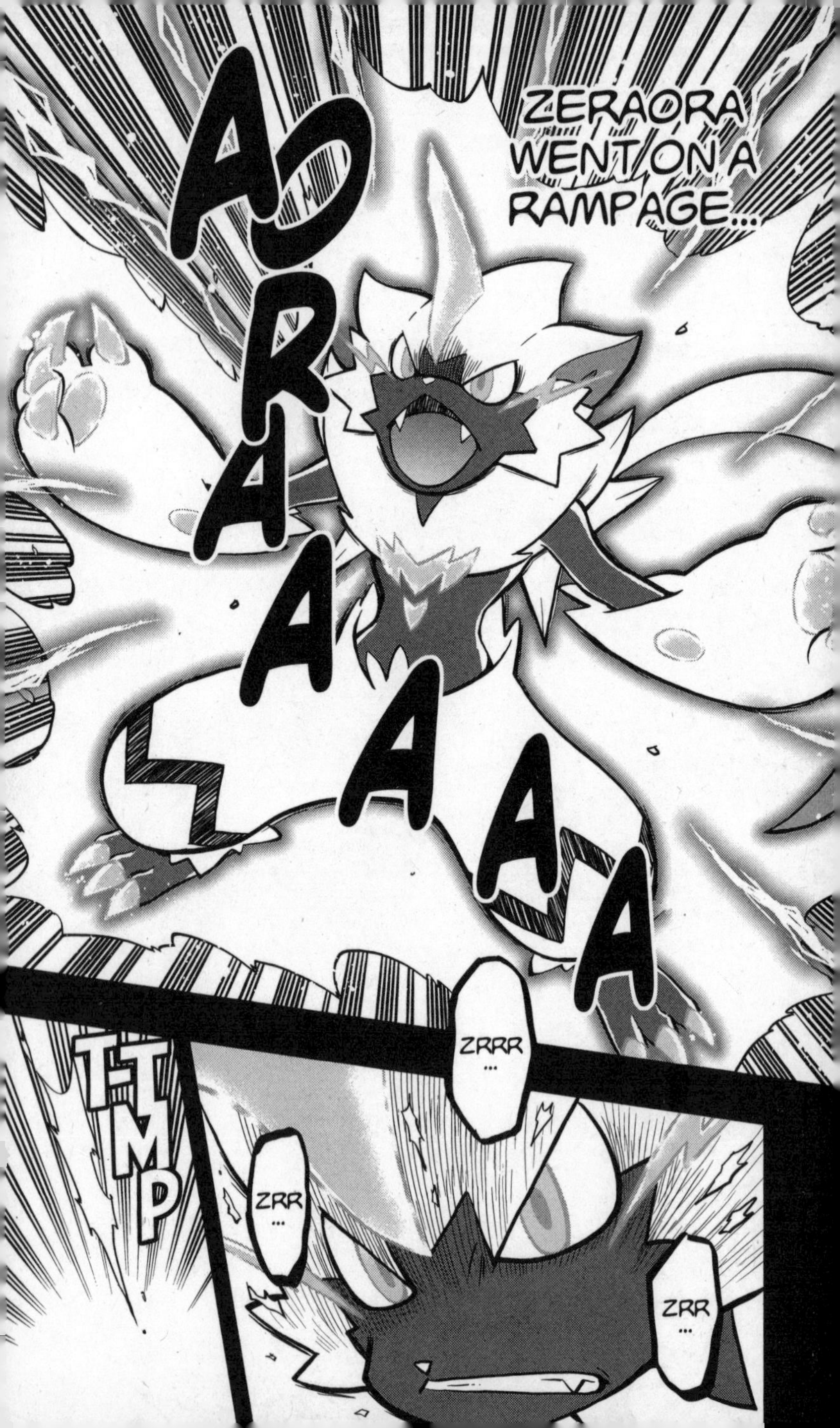
ZERAORA WENT ON A RAMPAGE...
AGRAAAAA
ZRRR ...
T-T-TMP
ZRR ...
ZRR ...

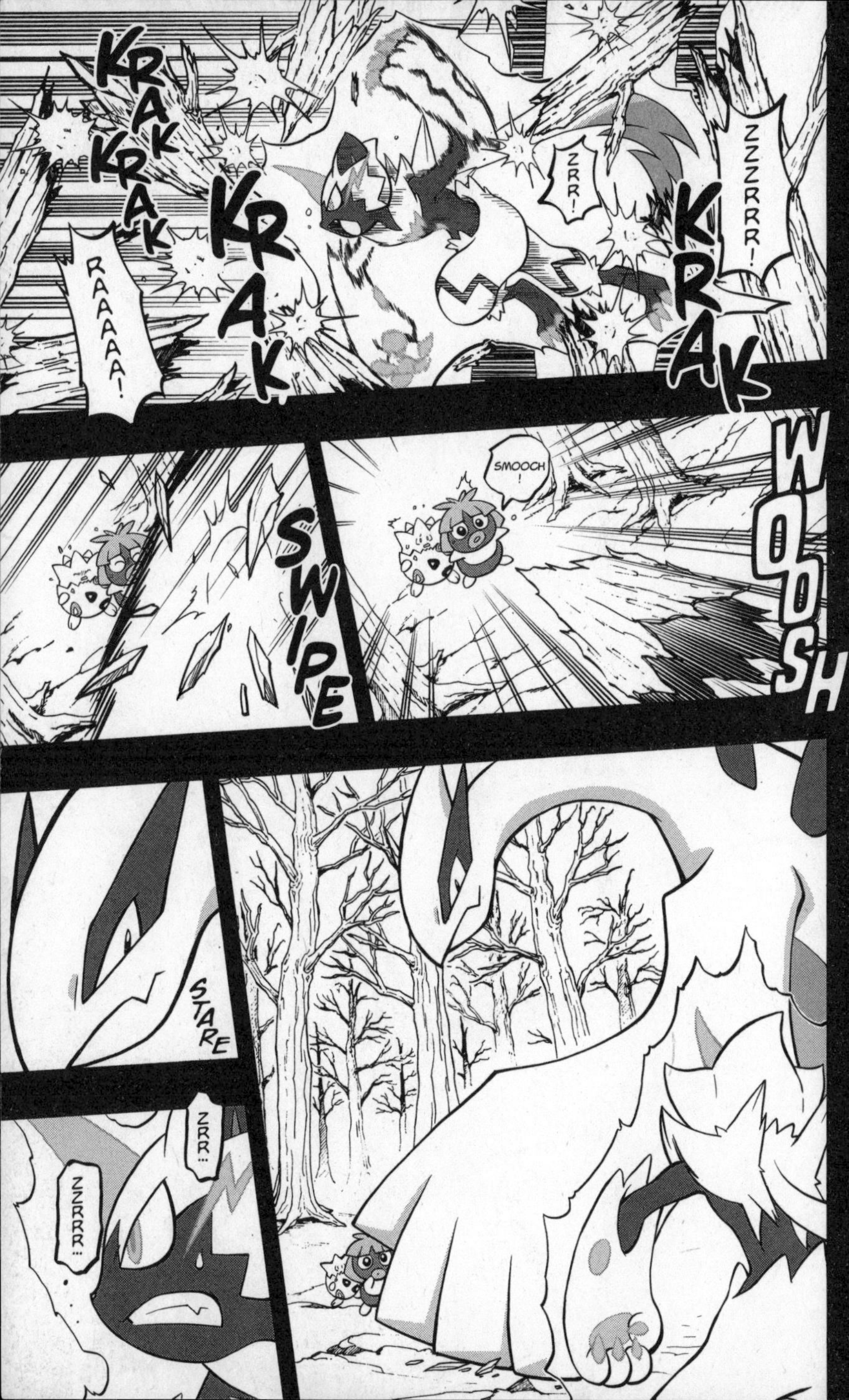
ZZZRRR!
KRAK
ZRR!
KRAK
KRAK KRAK KRAK
RAAAAAA!
WOOSH
SMOOCH!
SWIPE
STARE
ZRR...
ZZRRR...

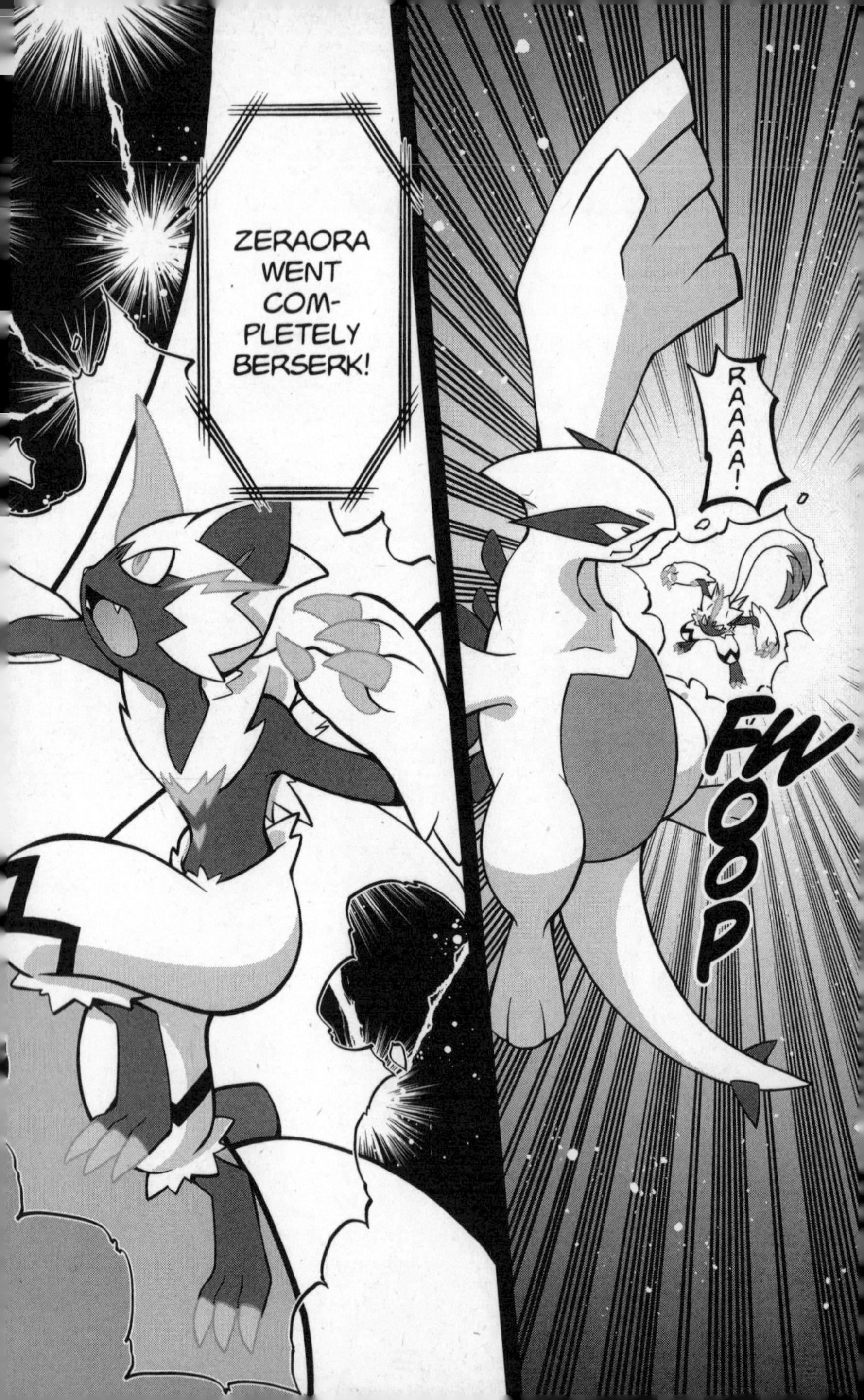
RAAAAA!
FWOOP
ZERAORA WENT COM-PLETELY BERSERK!

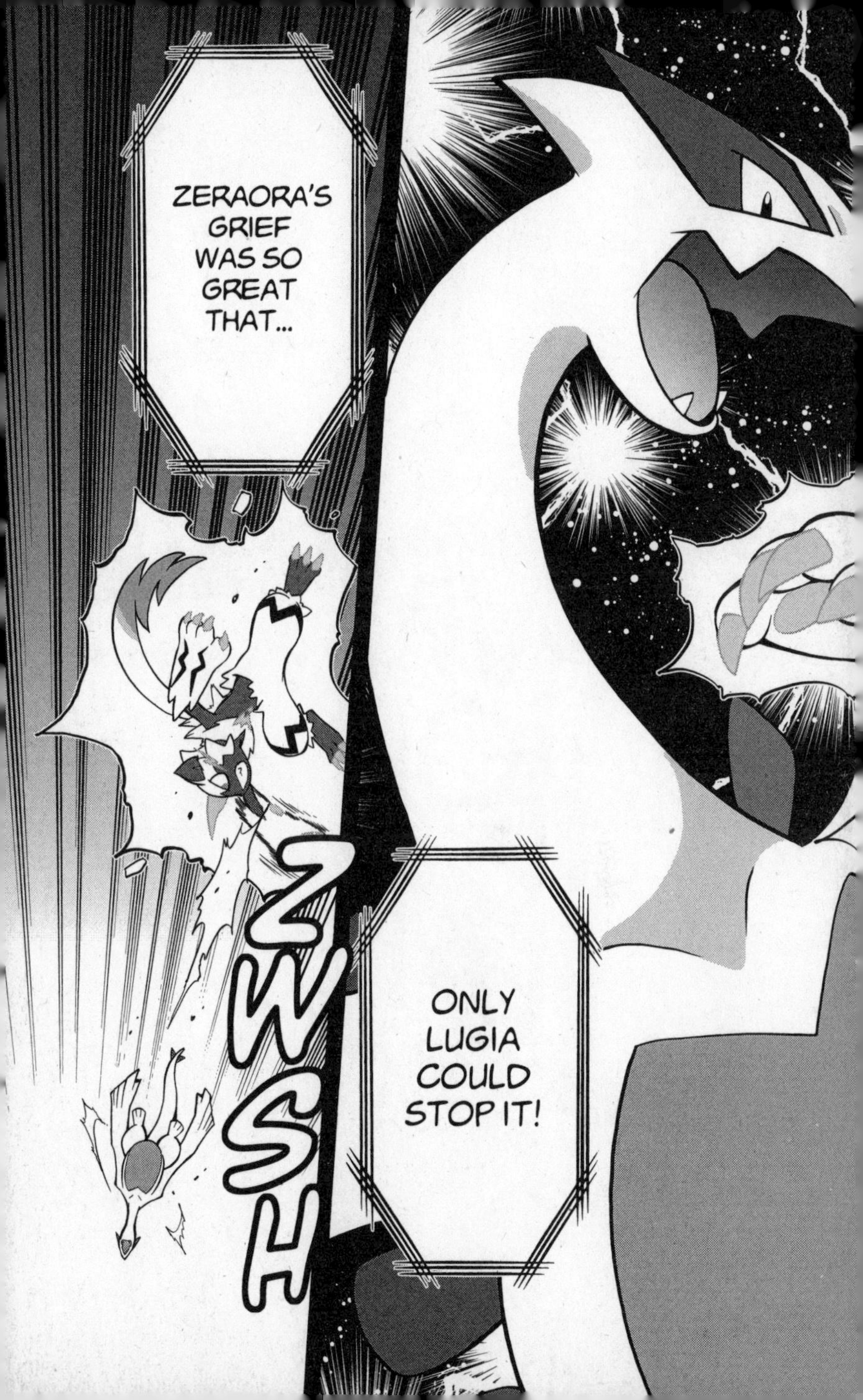
ZERAORA'S GRIEF WAS SO GREAT THAT...
ZWSH
ONLY LUGIA COULD STOP IT!

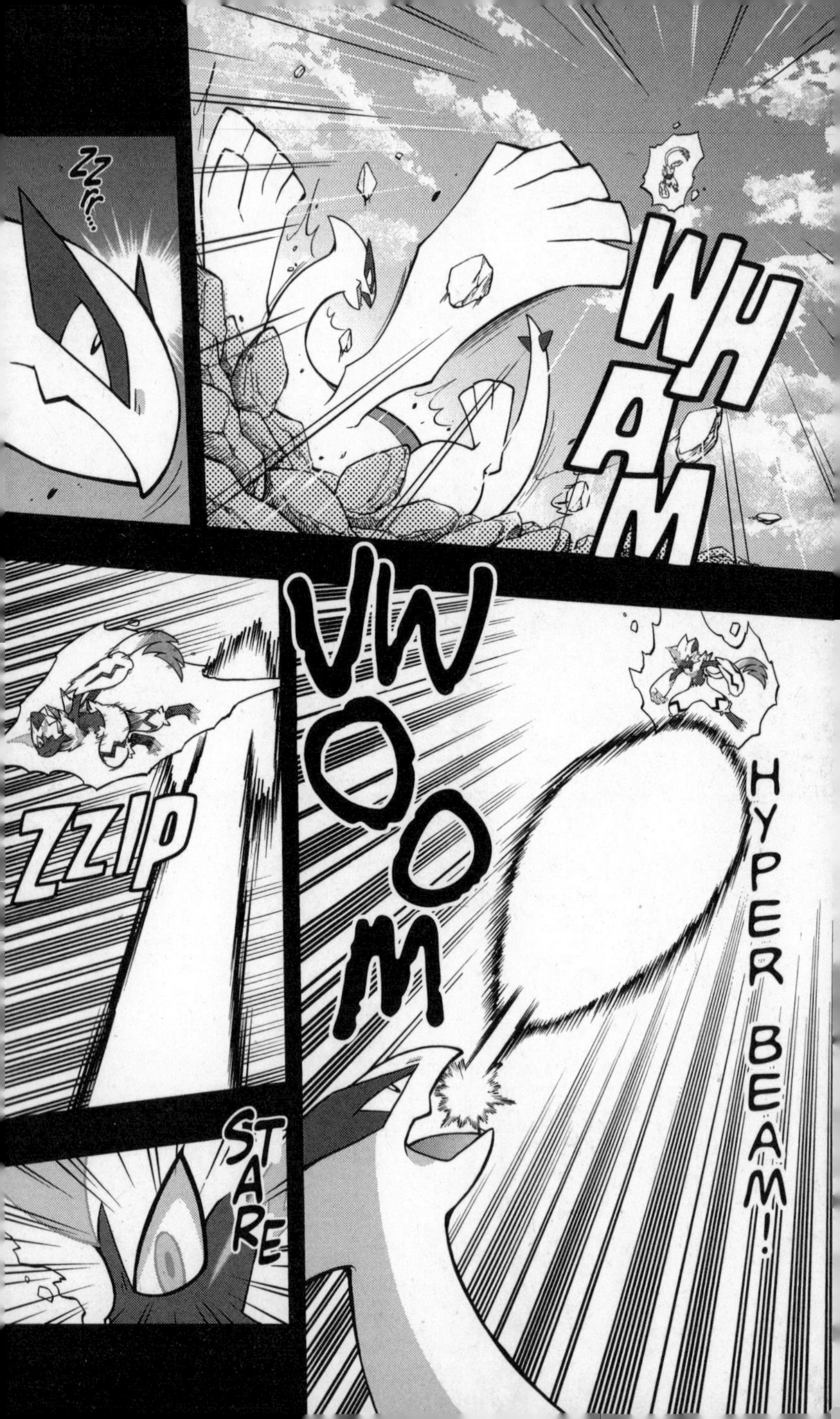
WHAM
Zzrr...
HYPER BEAM!
VWOOOM
ZZIP
STARE

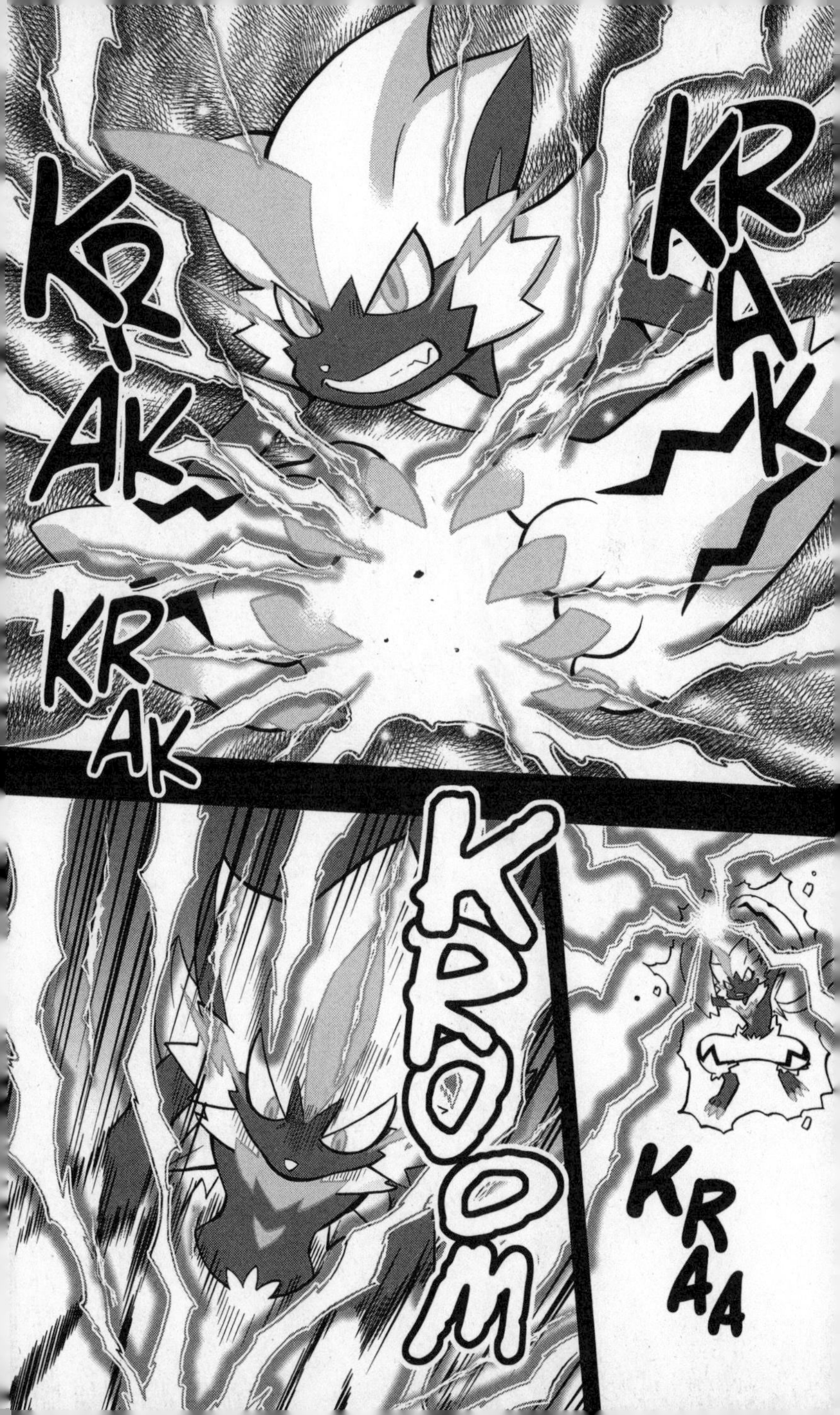
KRAK
KRAK
KRAK
KRAA
KROOM

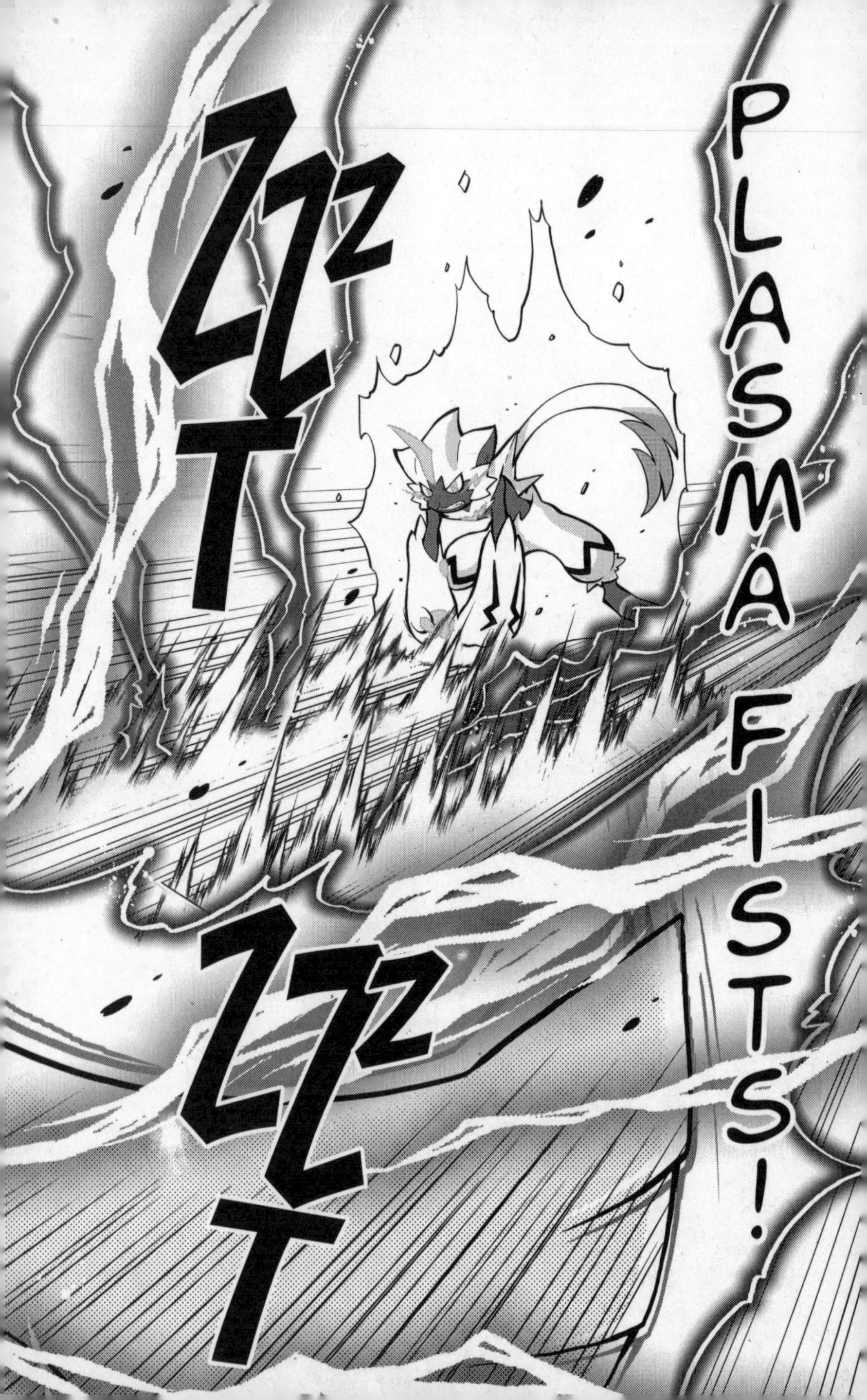
PLASMA FISTS!
ZZZT
ZZZT

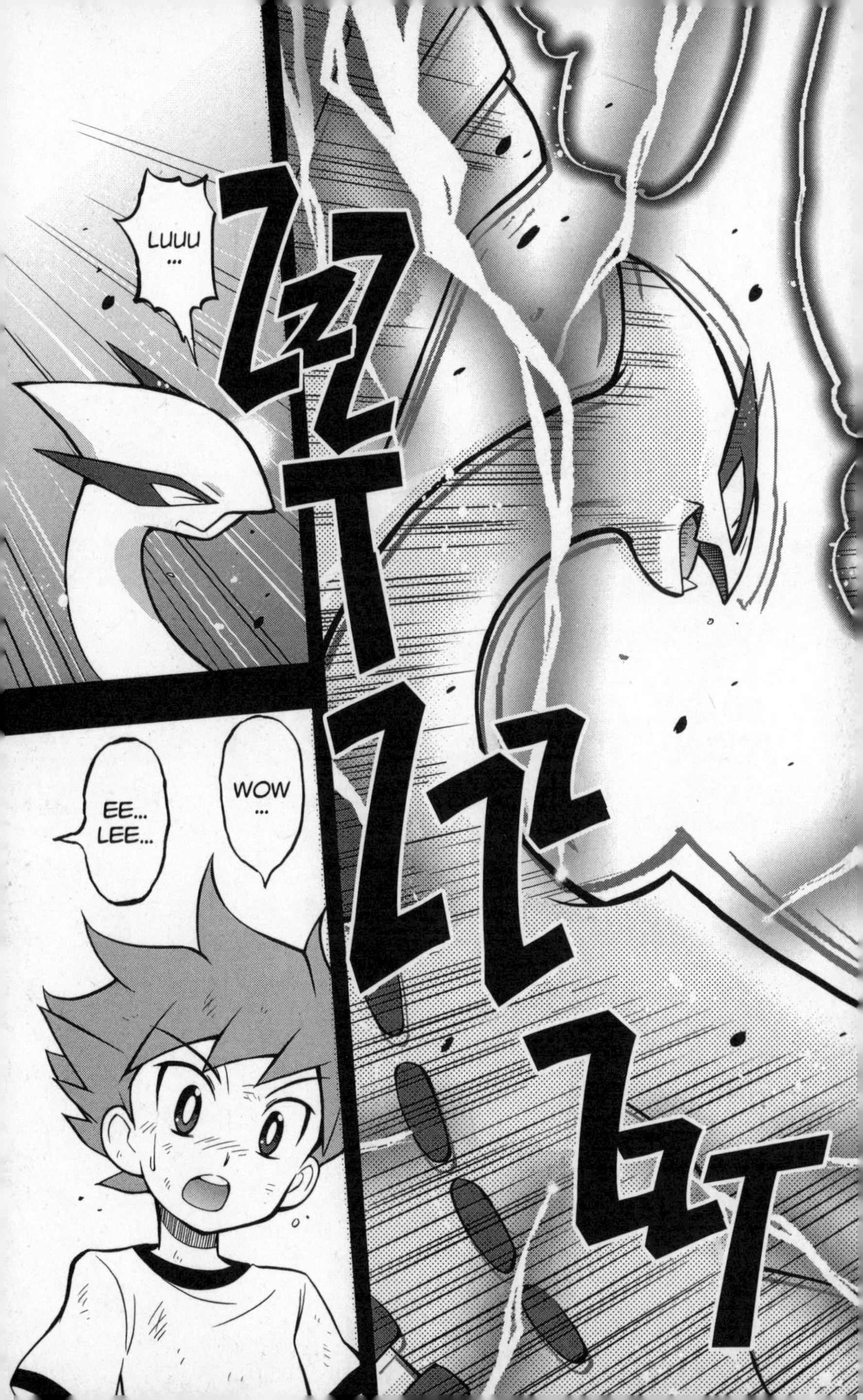
ZZZZT
ZZZZT
LUUU...
WOW...
EE... LEE...

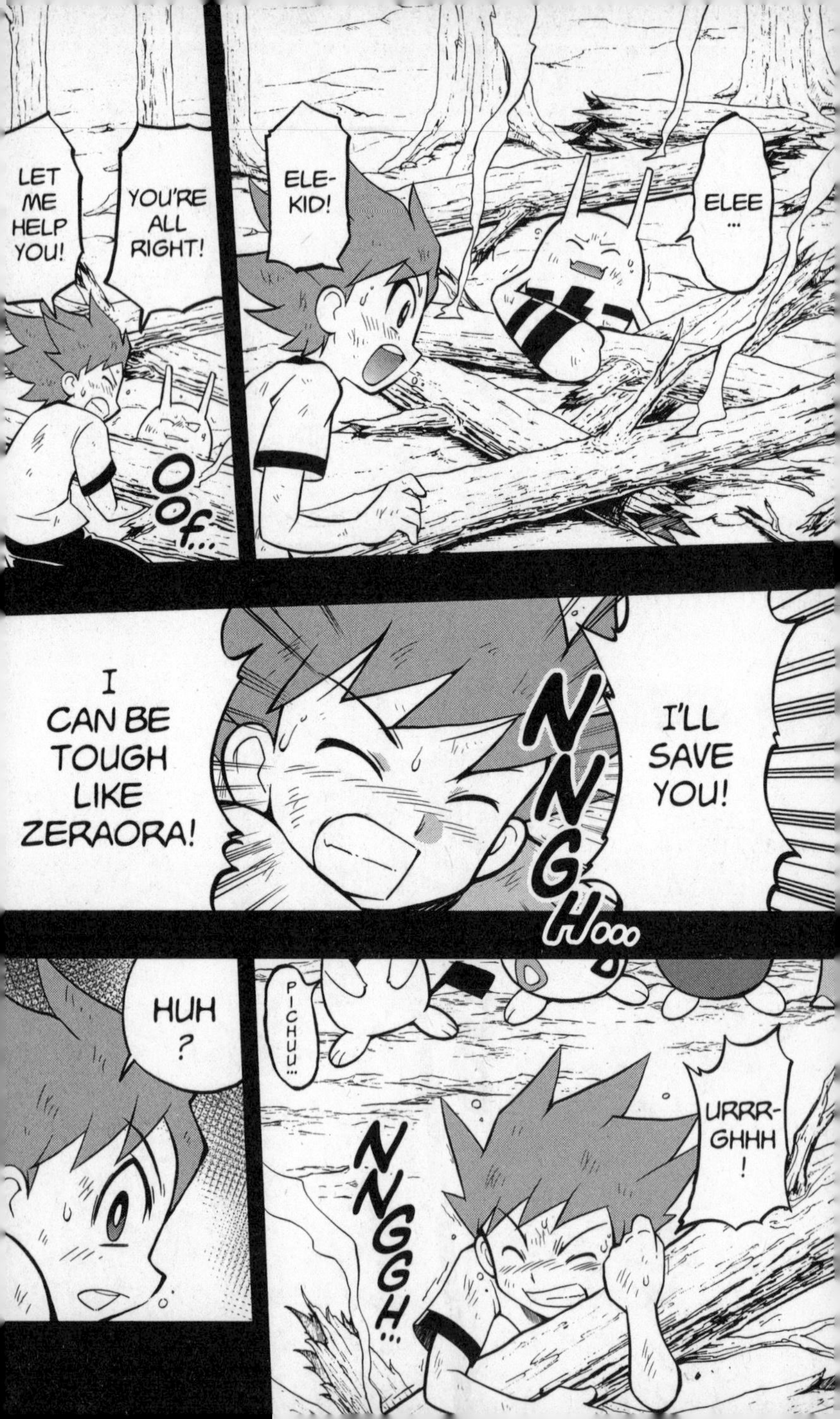
ELEE ...
ELE-KID!
YOU'RE ALL RIGHT!
LET ME HELP YOU!
OOF...
I'LL SAVE YOU!
NNGH...
I CAN BE TOUGH LIKE ZERAORA!
URRR-GHHH!
PICHUU...
NNGGH!!
HUH?

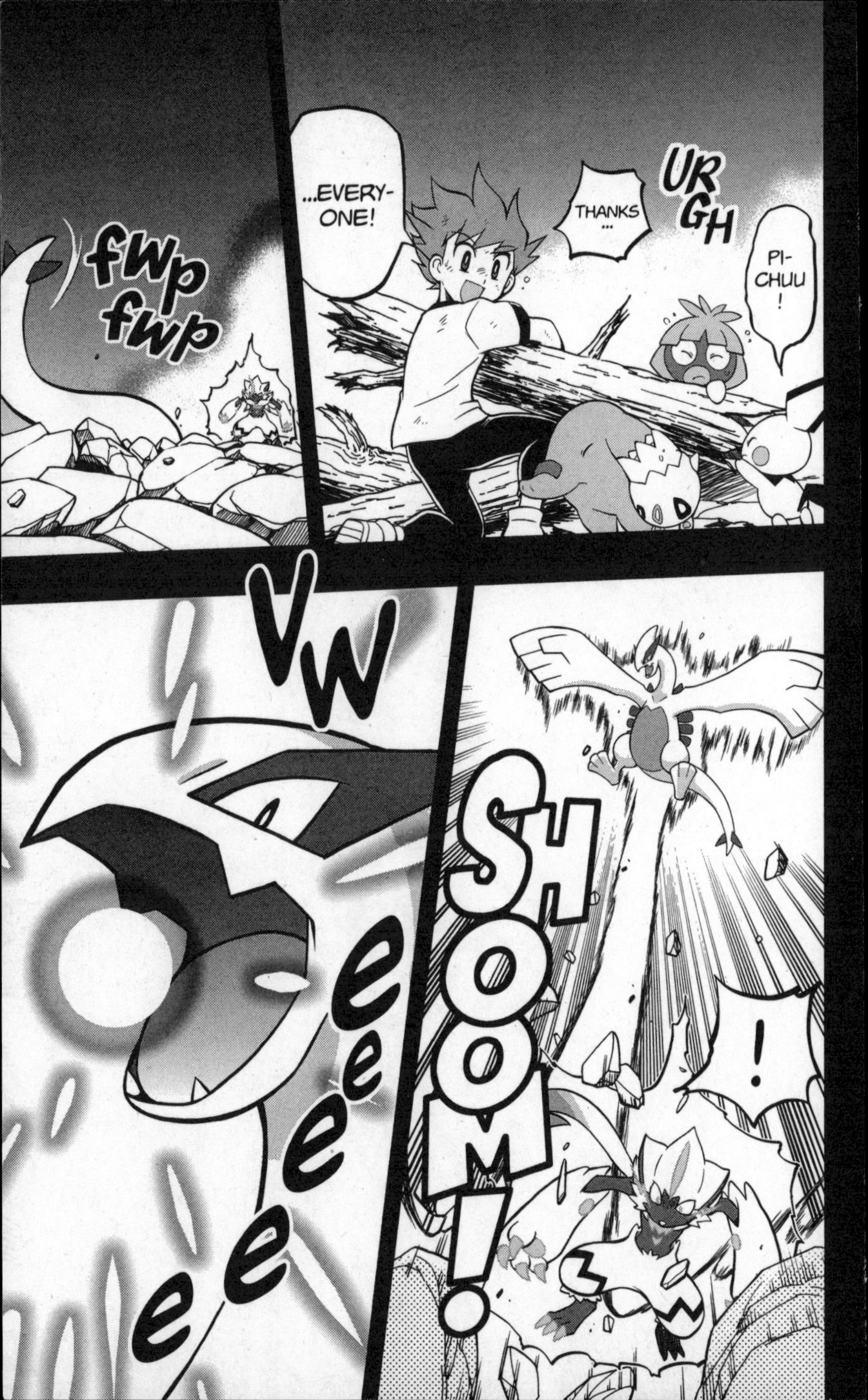
PI-CHUU!
URGH
THANKS...
...EVERY-ONE!
fwp fwp
SHOOOM!
!
VW
eeeeeee

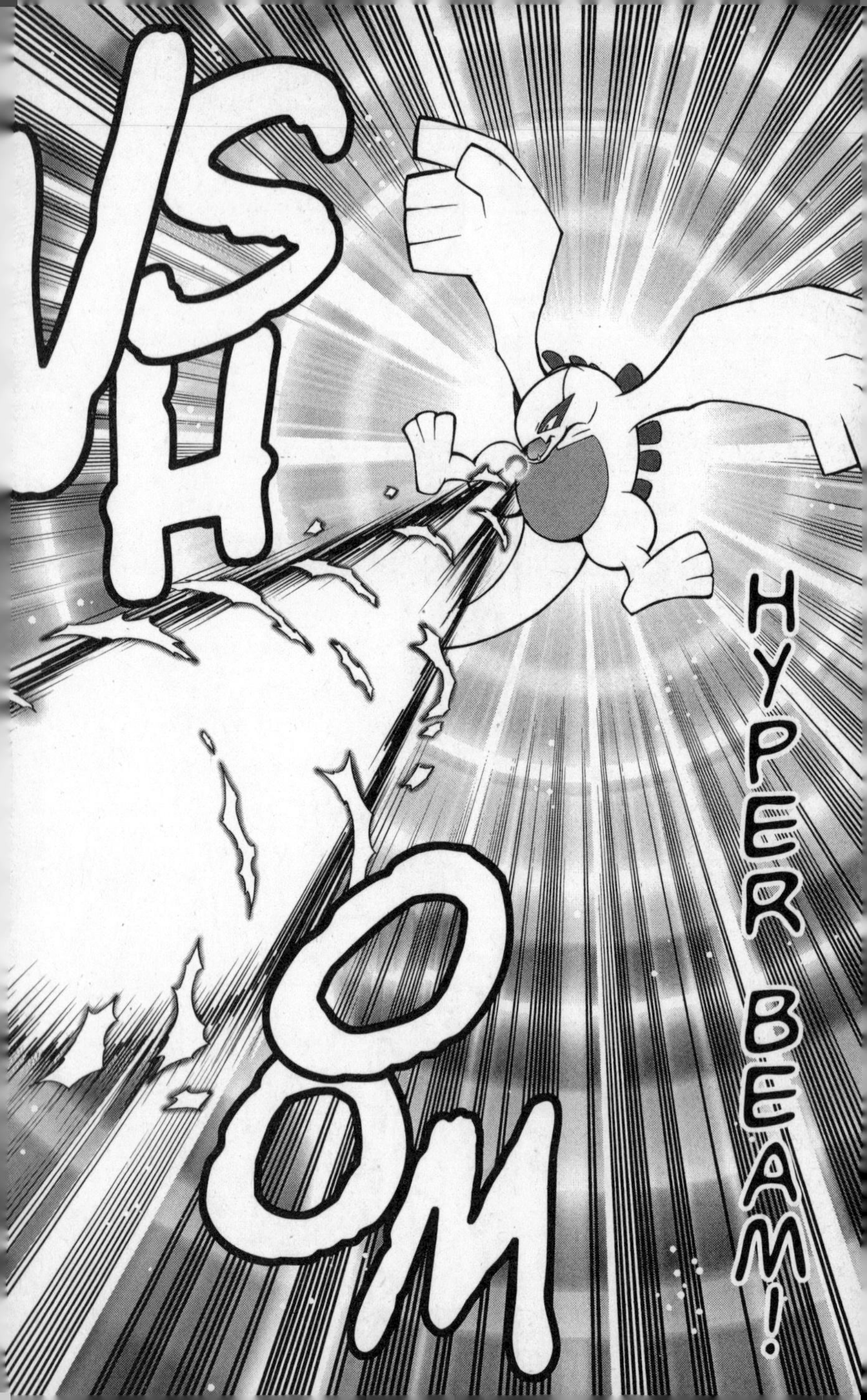
HYPER BEAM!
VSHOOM

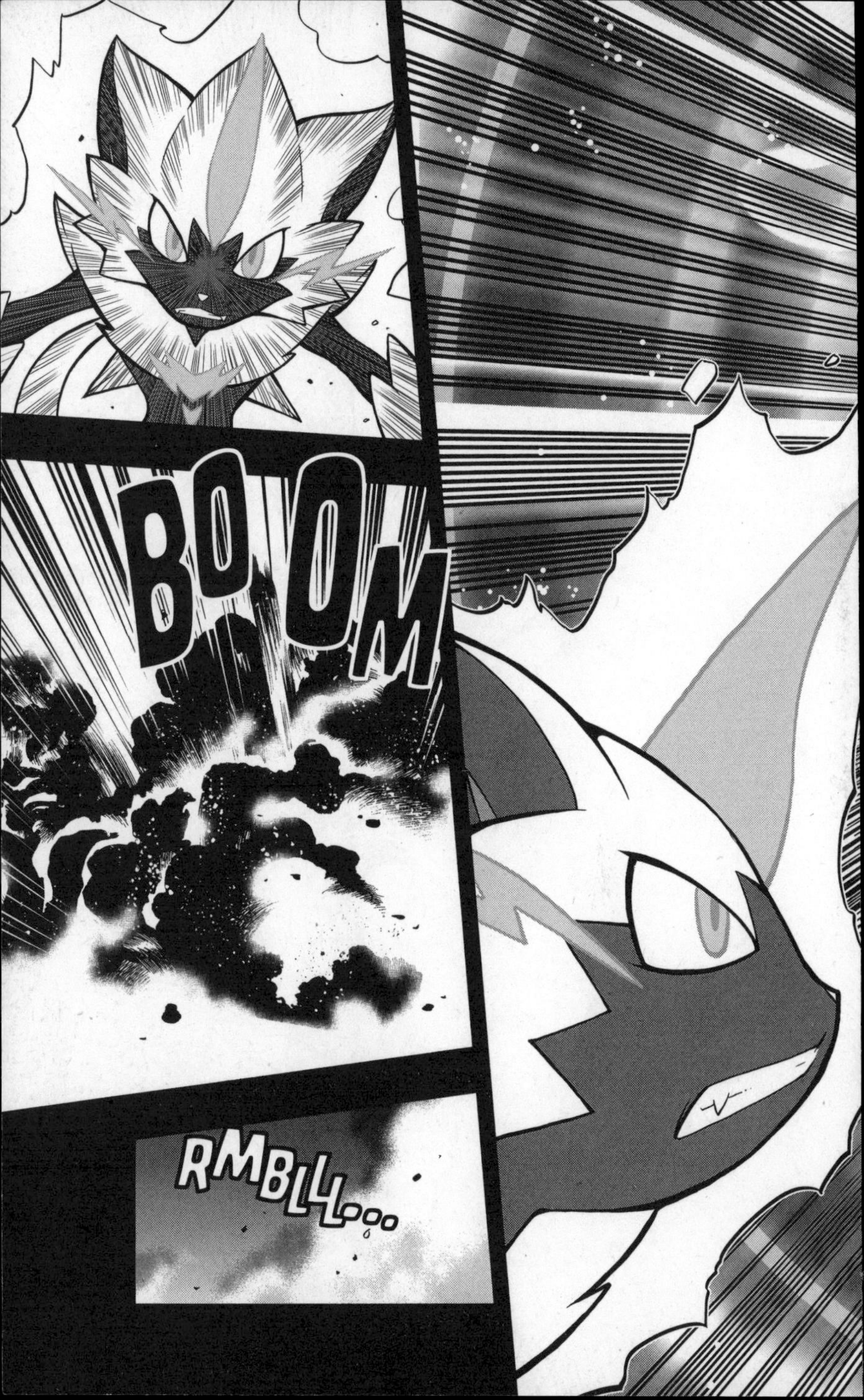
BOOOM
RMBLL...

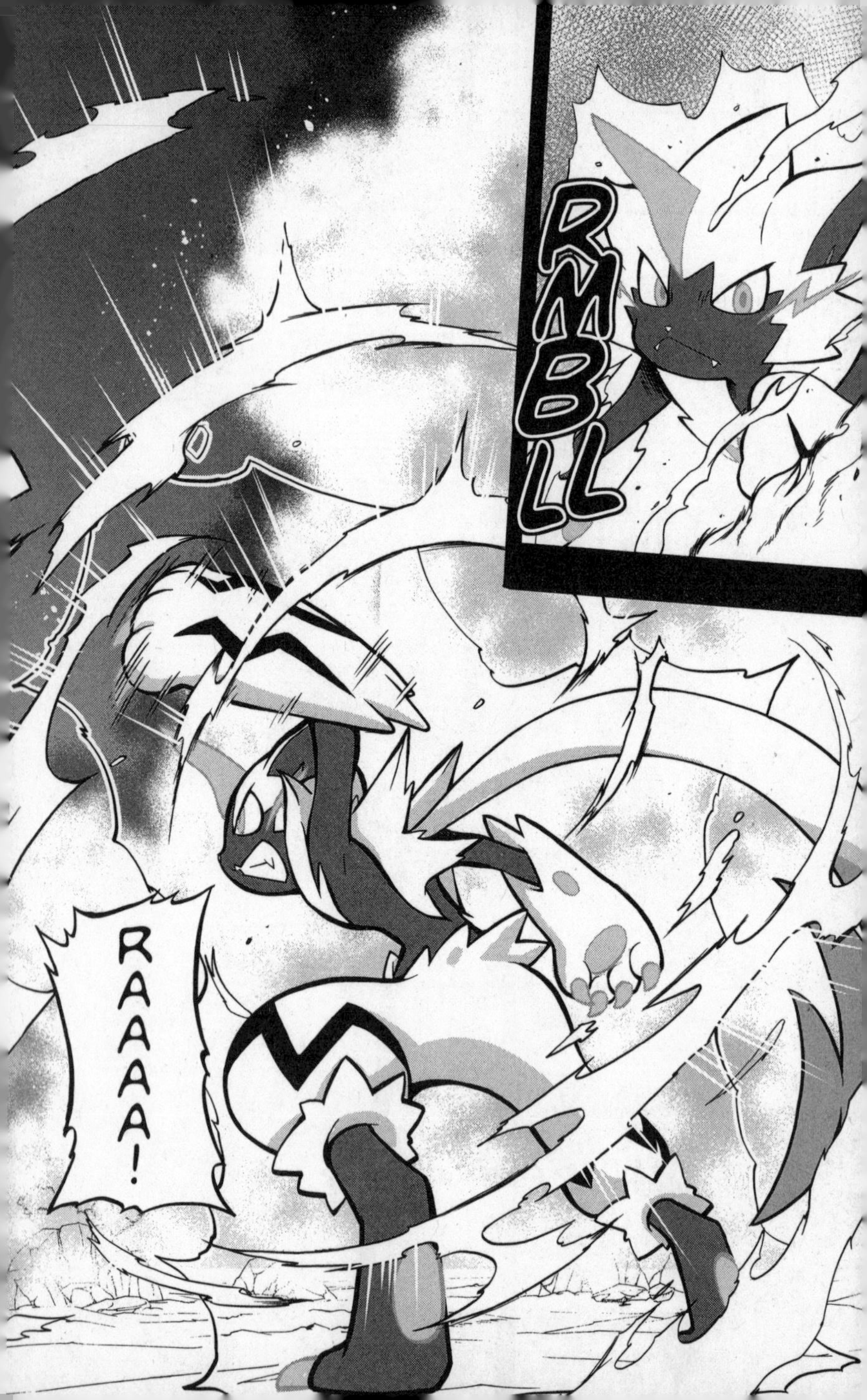
RMBLL
RAAAA!

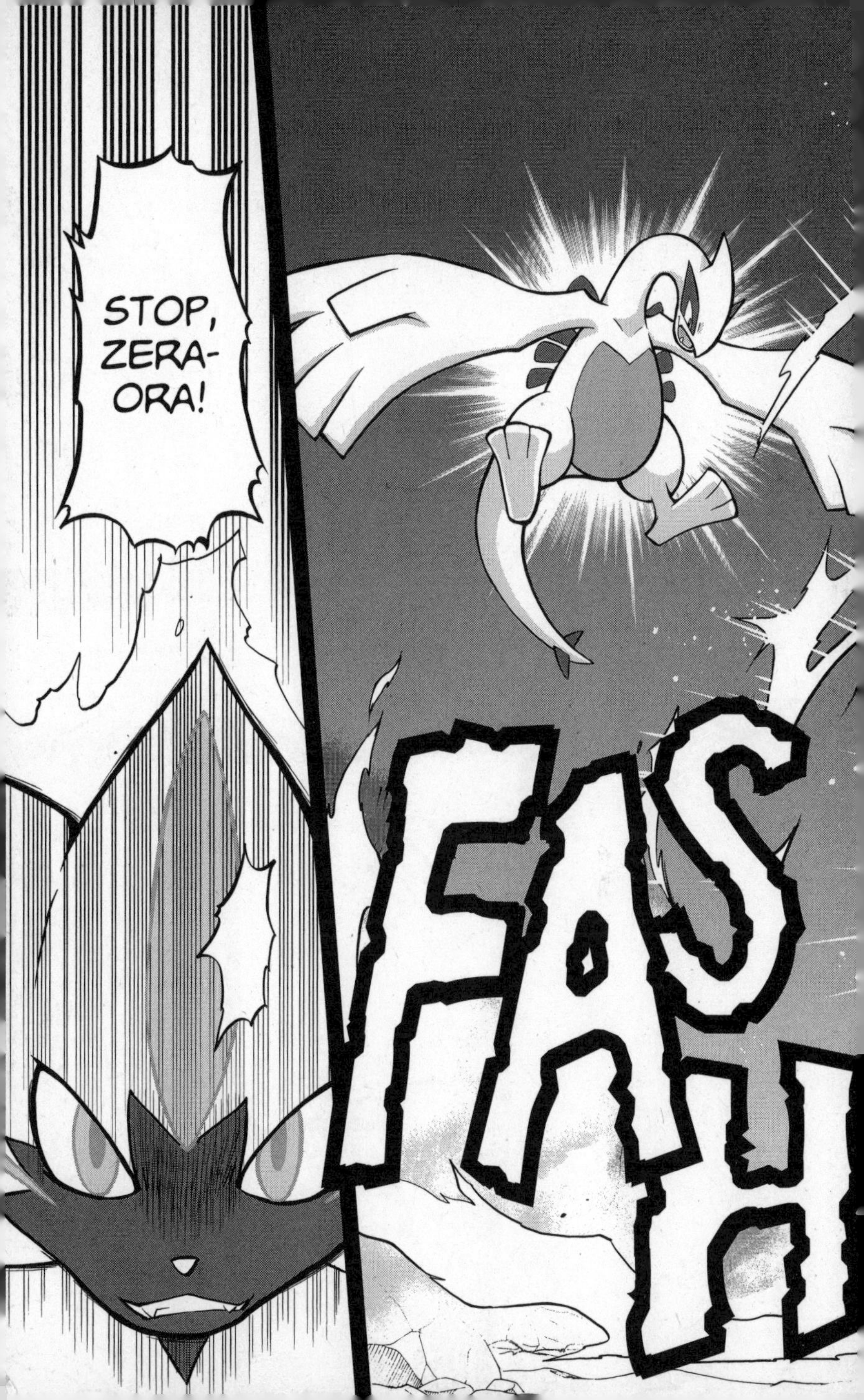
FLASH
STOP, ZERA-ORA!

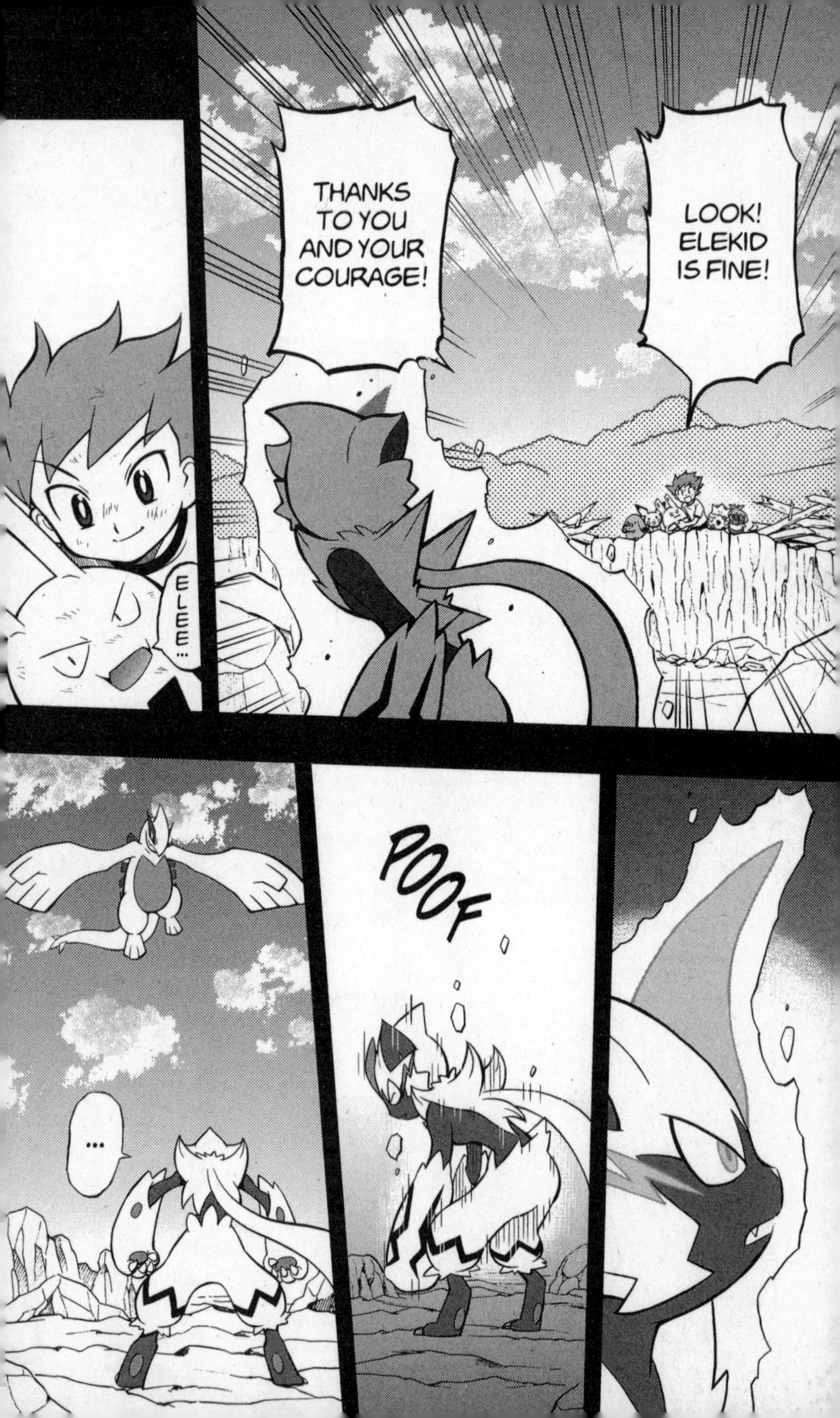
LOOK! ELEKID IS FINE!
THANKS TO YOU AND YOUR COURAGE!
ELEE...
POOF
...

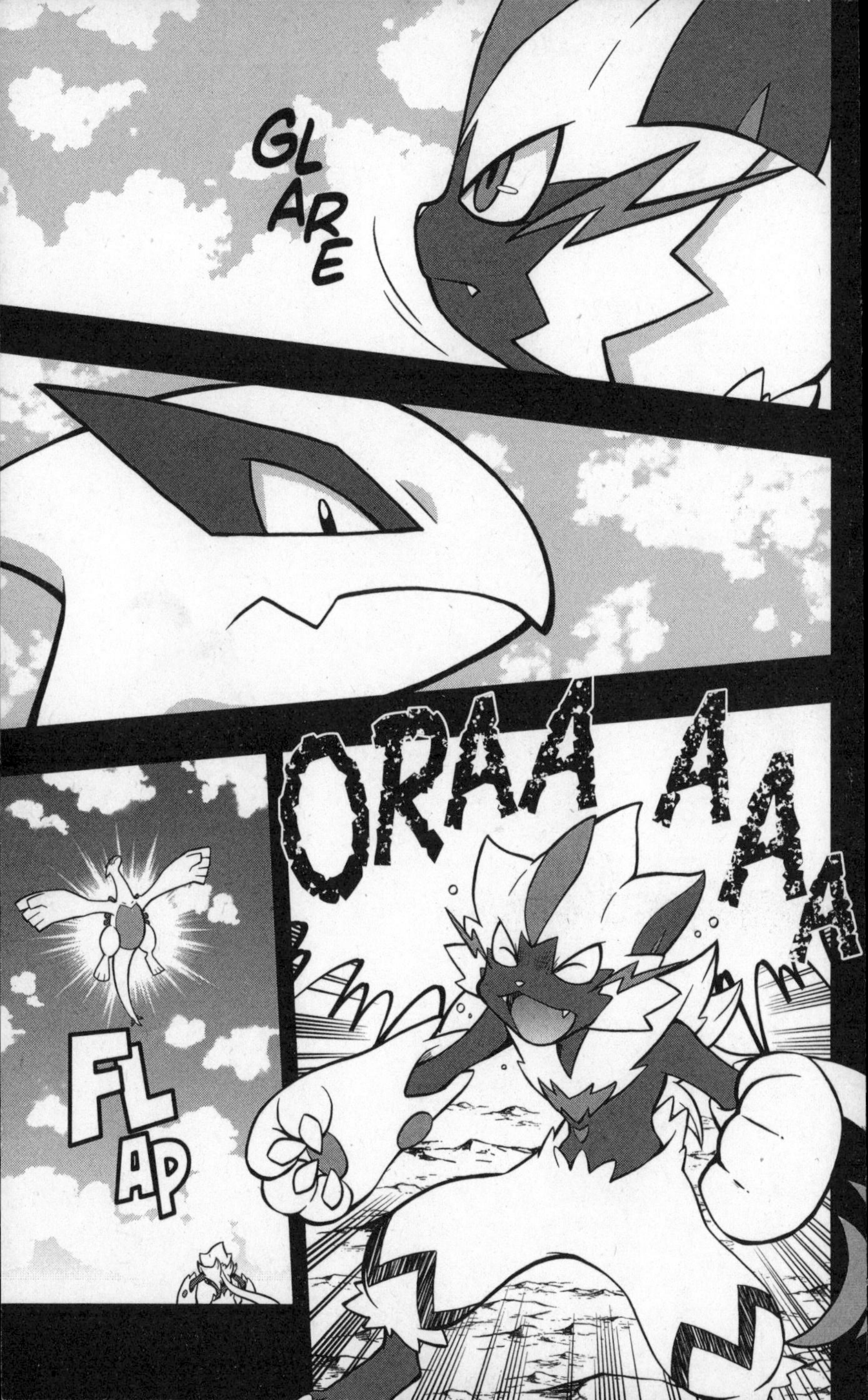
GLARE
ORAAAAA
FLAP

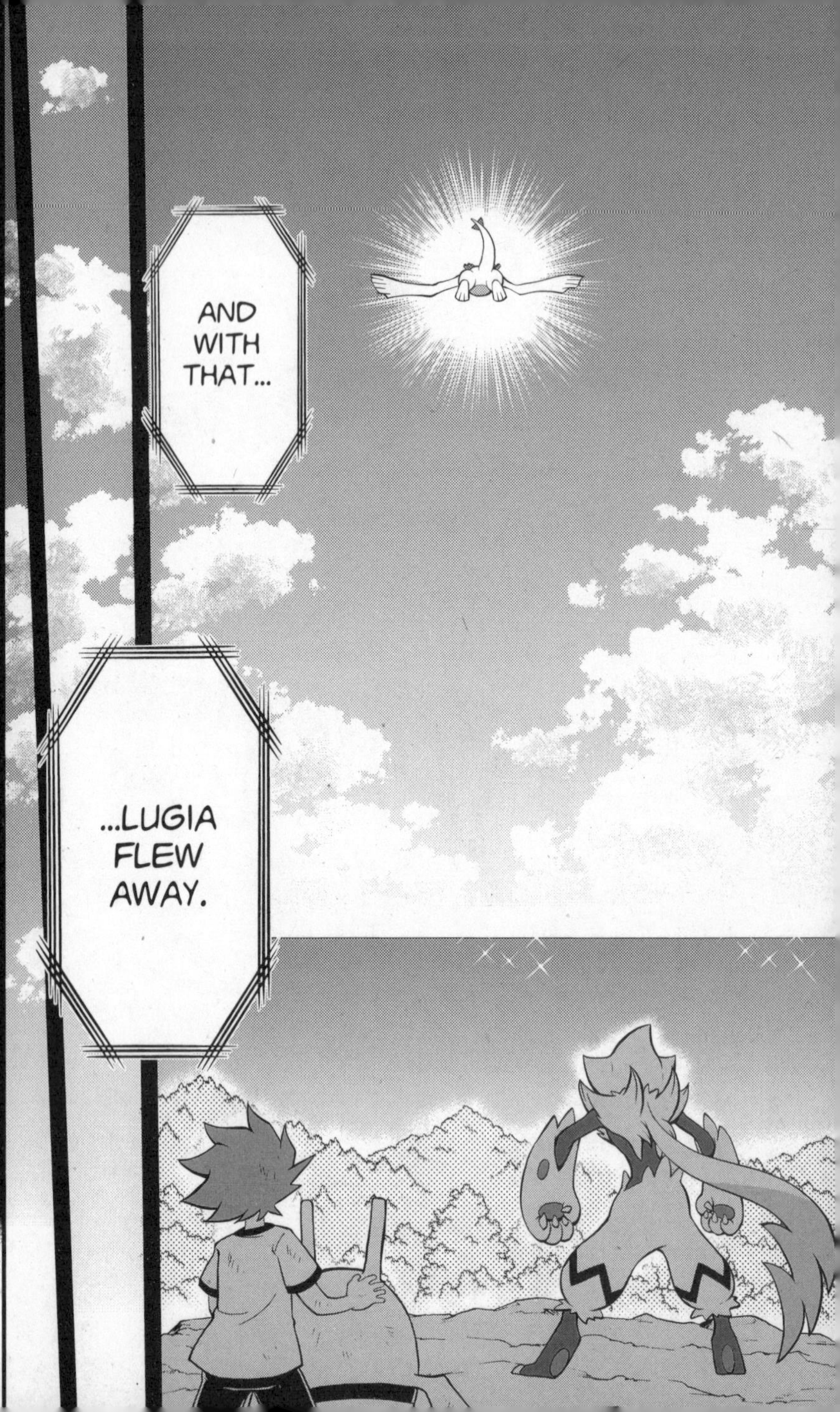
AND WITH THAT...
...LUGIA FLEW AWAY.

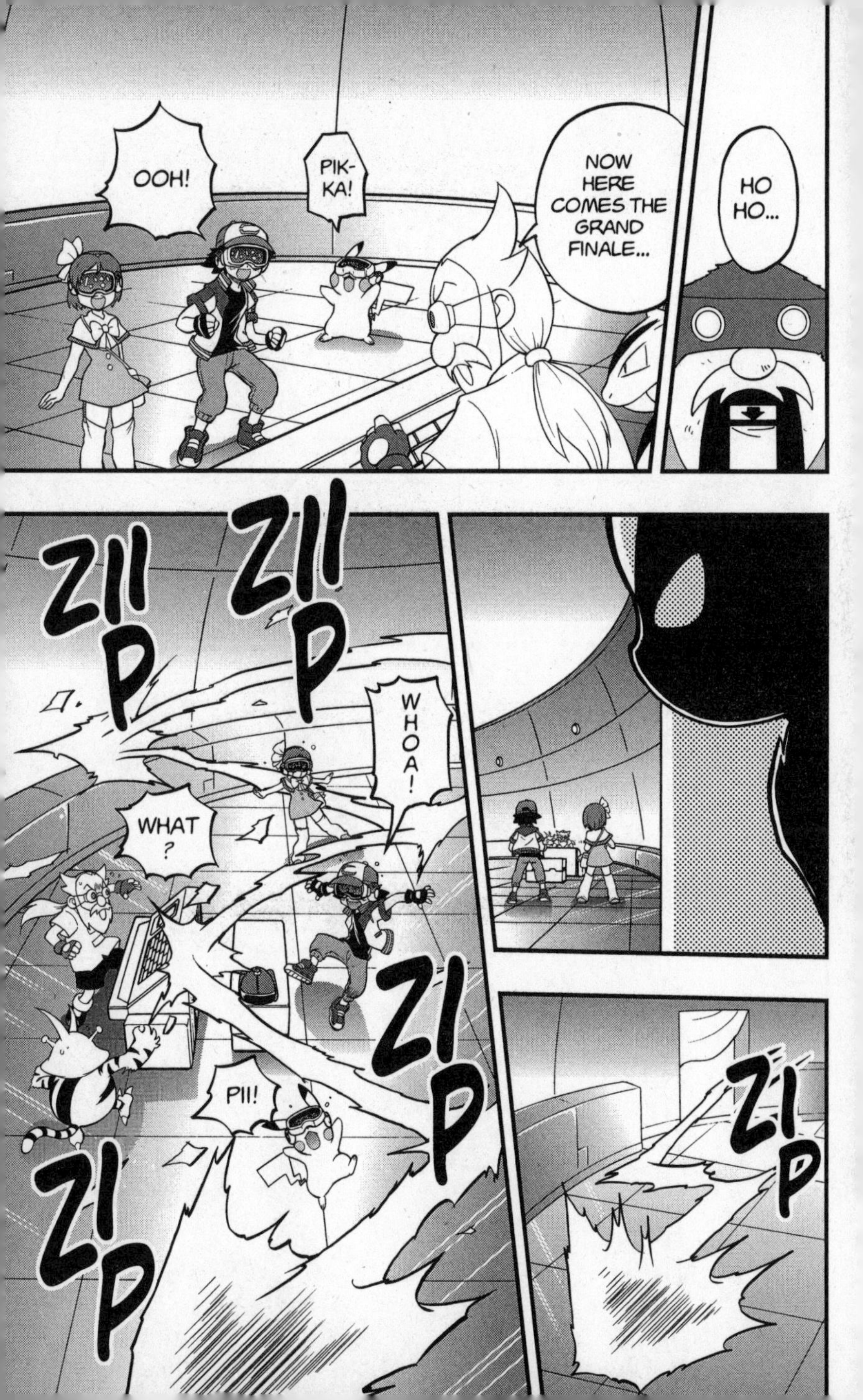
HO HO...
NOW HERE COMES THE GRAND FINALE...
PIK-KA!
OOH!
ZIP
ZIIP
ZIIP
WHOA!
WHAT?
ZIP
PII!
ZIP

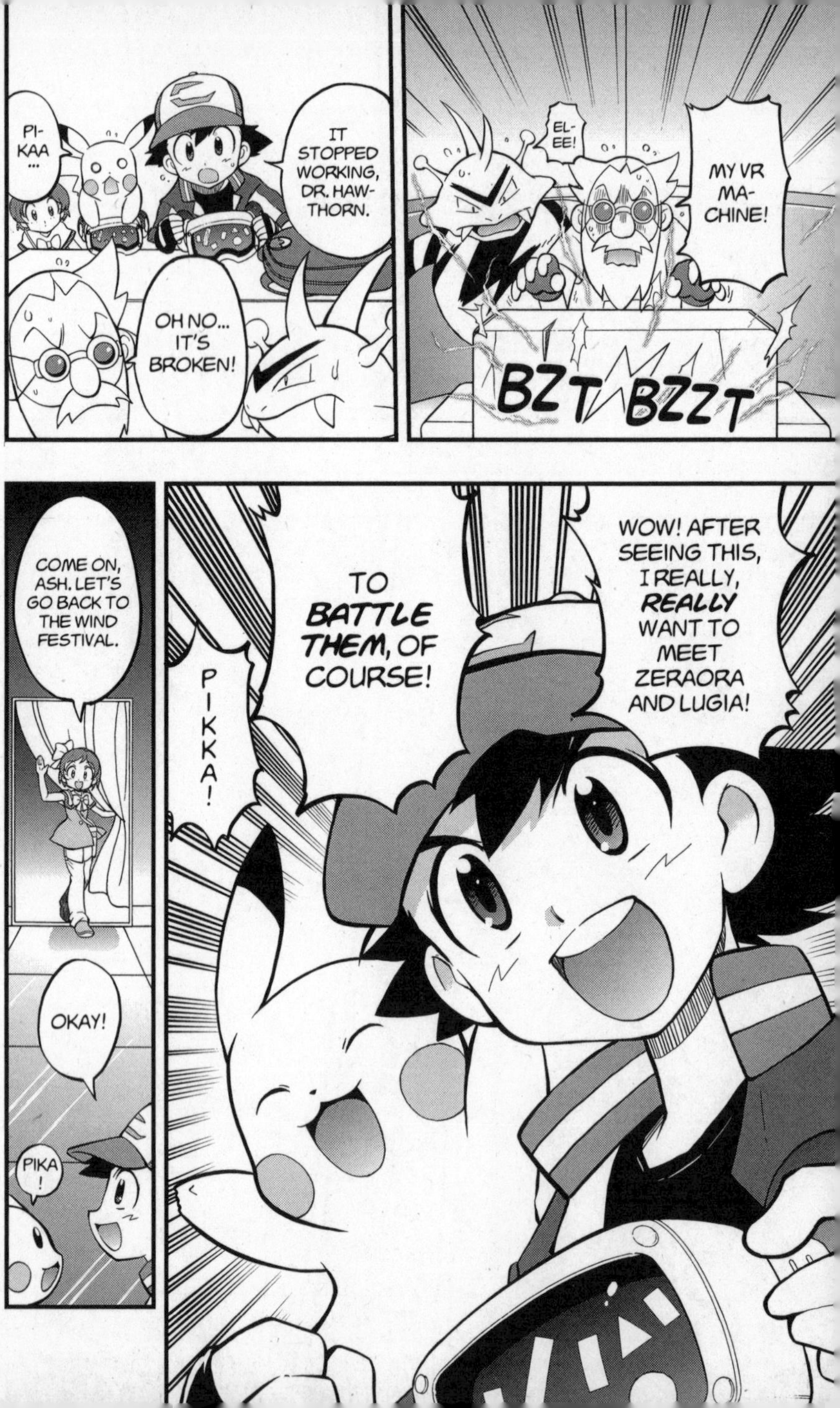
MY VR MA-CHINE!
EL-EE!
BZT BZZT
IT STOPPED WORKING, DR. HAW-THORN.
PI-KAA...
OH NO... IT'S BROKEN!
WOW! AFTER SEEING THIS, I REALLY, REALLY WANT TO MEET ZERAORA AND LUGIA!
TO BATTLE THEM, OF COURSE!
PIKKA!
COME ON, ASH. LET'S GO BACK TO THE WIND FESTIVAL.
OKAY!
PIKA!

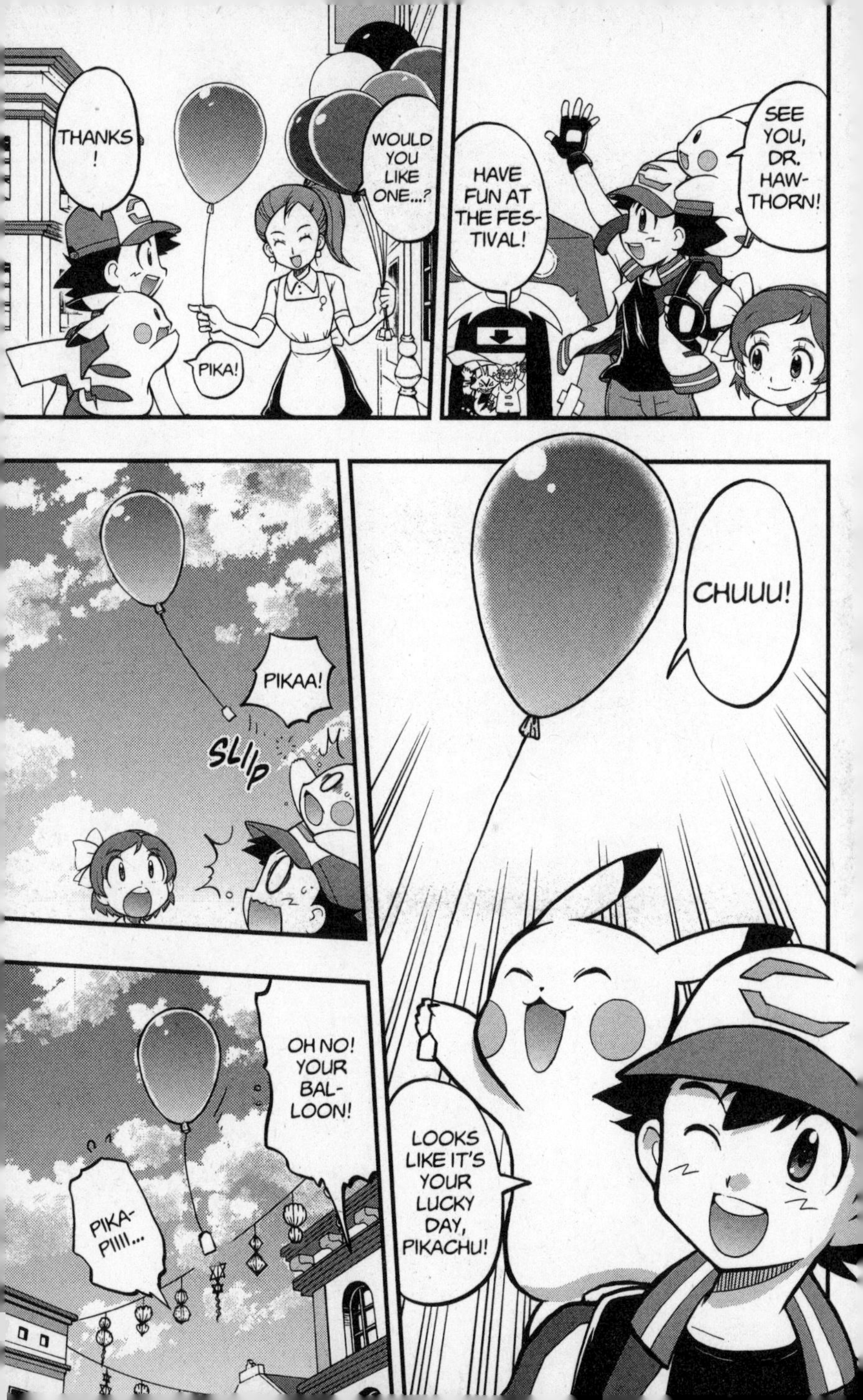

SEE YOU, DR. HAW-THORN!
HAVE FUN AT THE FES-TIVAL!
WOULD YOU LIKE ONE...?
THANKS!
PIKA!
CHUUU!
LOOKS LIKE IT'S YOUR LUCKY DAY, PIKACHU!
PIKAA!
SLIIP
OH NO! YOUR BAL-LOON!
PIKA-PIIII...

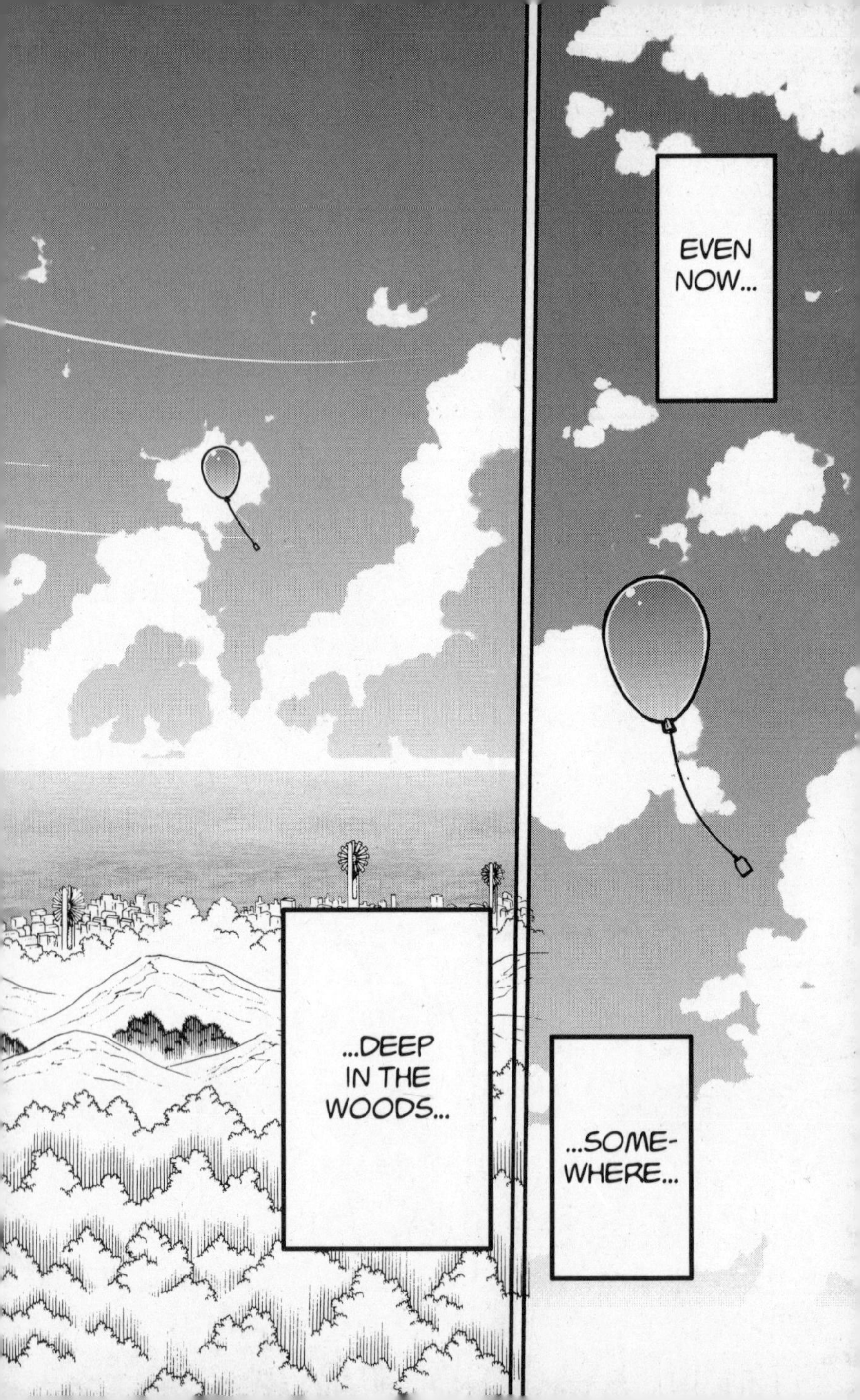
EVEN NOW...
...SOME-WHERE...
...DEEP IN THE WOODS...

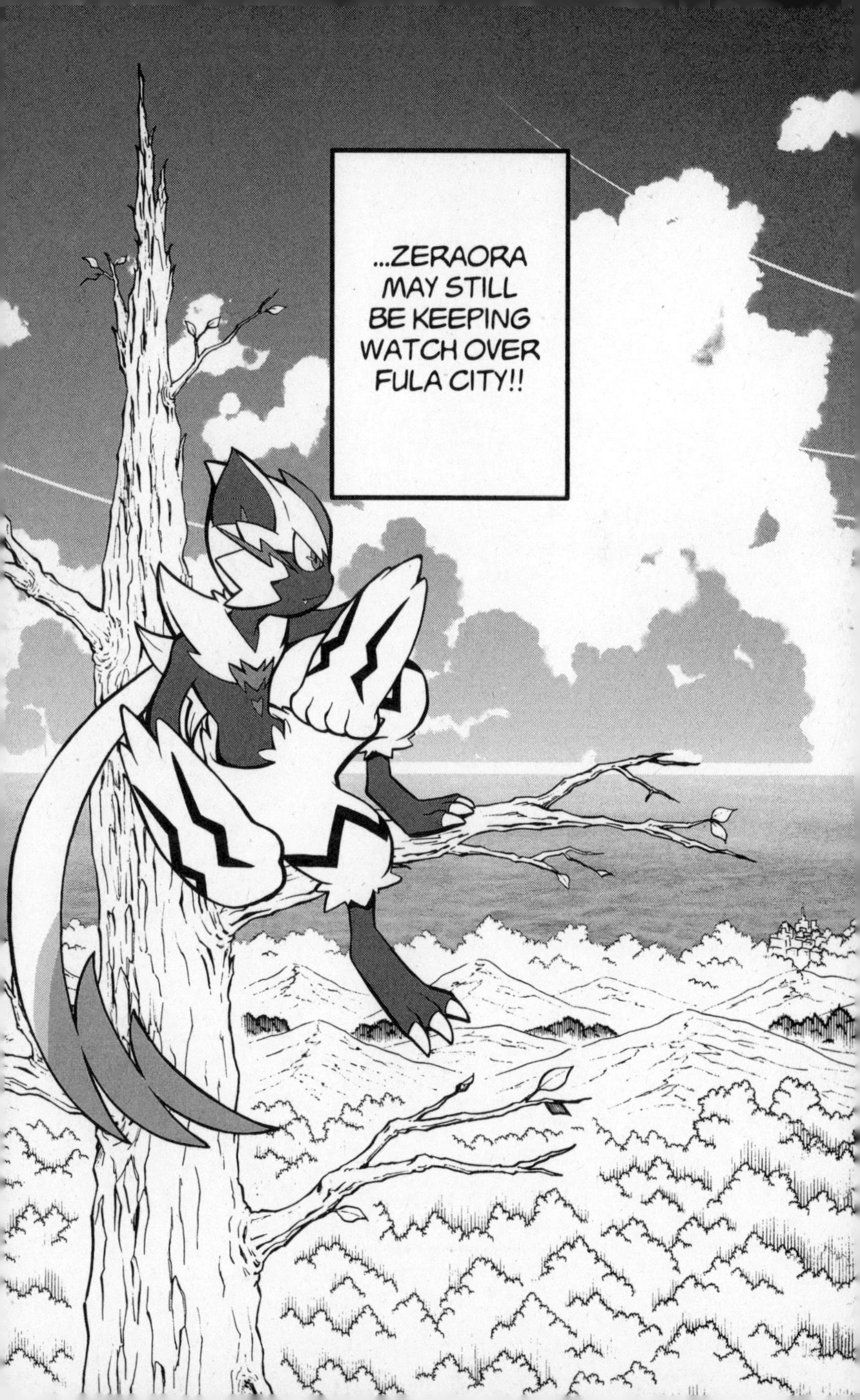
...ZERAORA MAY STILL BE KEEPING WATCH OVER FULA CITY!!

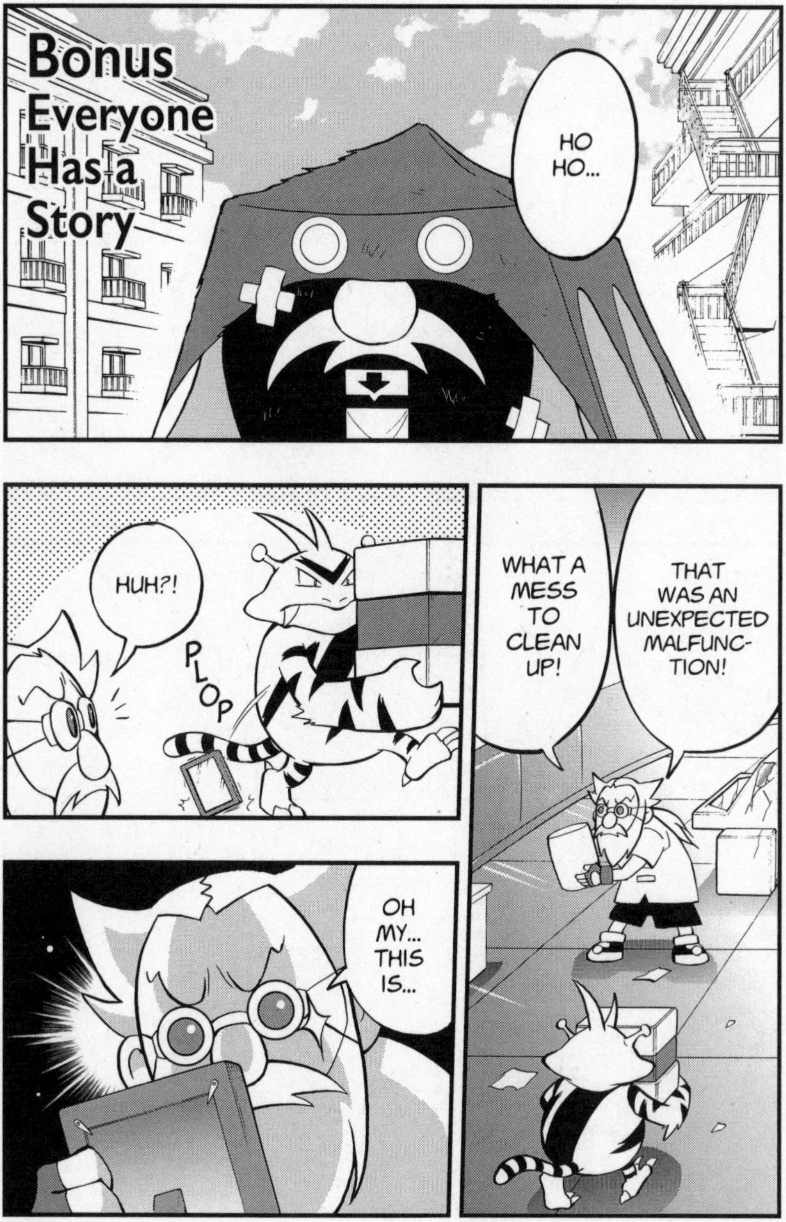
Bonus
Everyone Has a Story
HO HO...
THAT WAS AN UNEXPECTED MALFUNCTION!
WHAT A MESS TO CLEAN UP!
HUH?!
PLOP
OH MY... THIS IS...

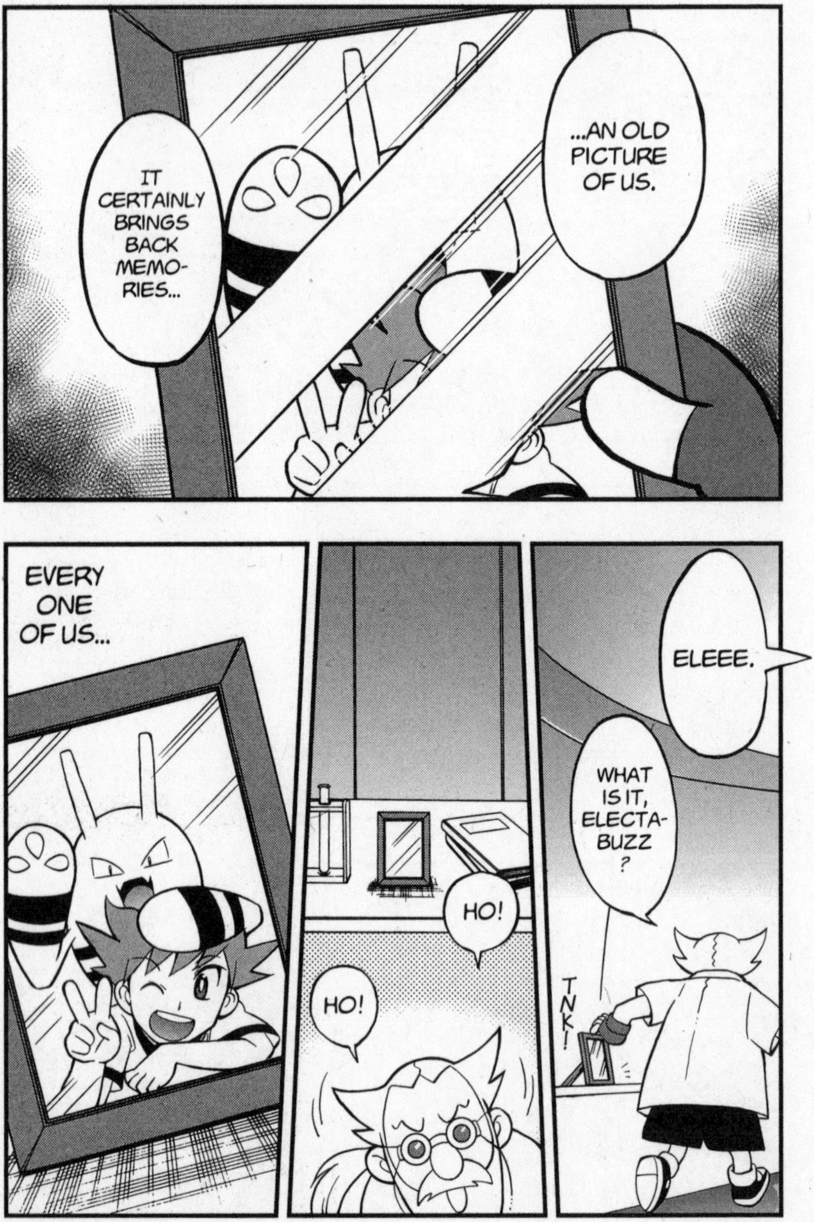
...AN OLD PICTURE OF US.
IT CERTAINLY BRINGS BACK MEMORIES...
ELEEE.
WHAT IS IT, ELECTABUZZ?
TNK!
HO!
HO!
EVERY ONE OF US...

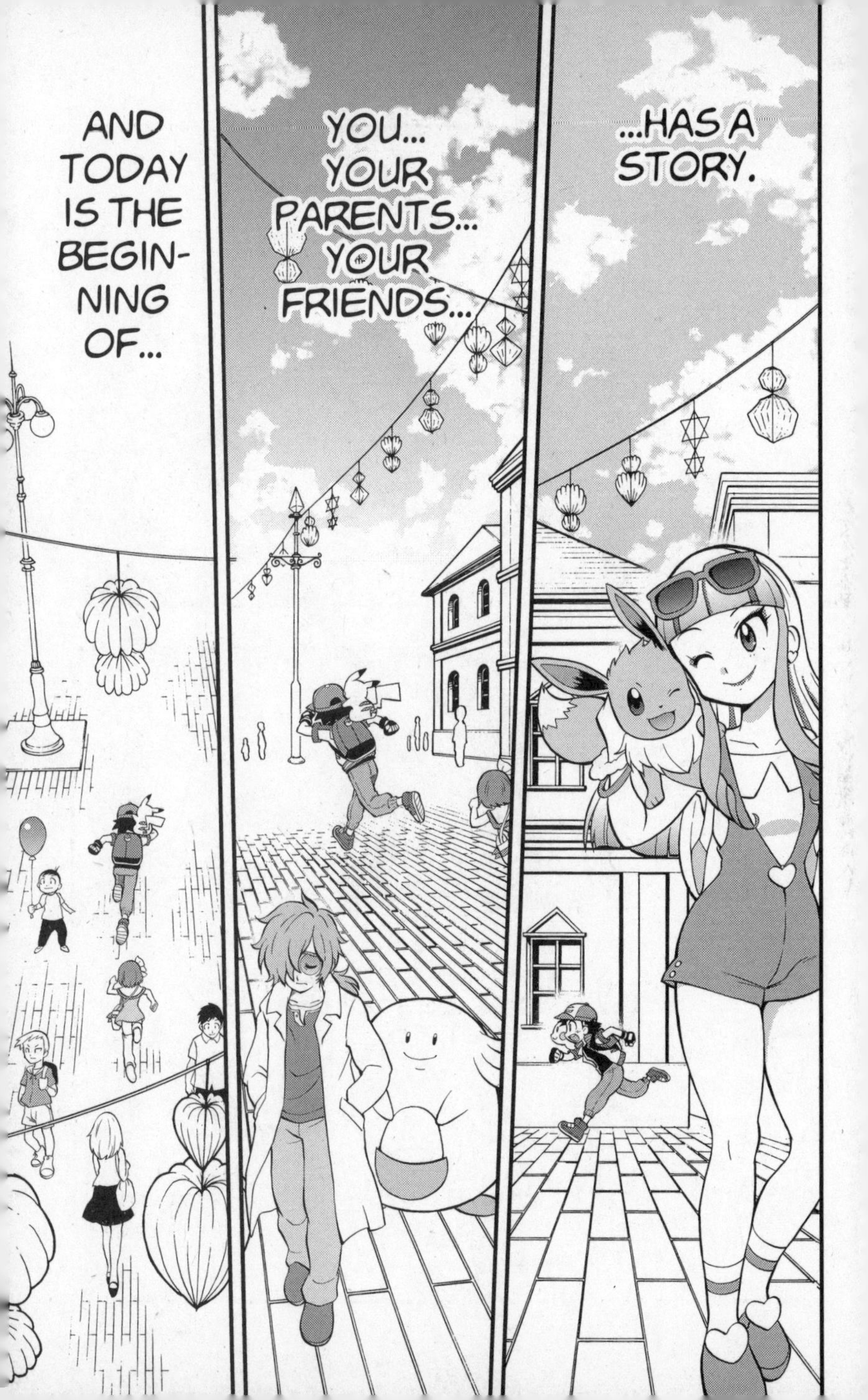
AND TODAY IS THE BEGIN-NING OF...
YOU... YOUR PARENTS... YOUR FRIENDS...
...HAS A STORY.

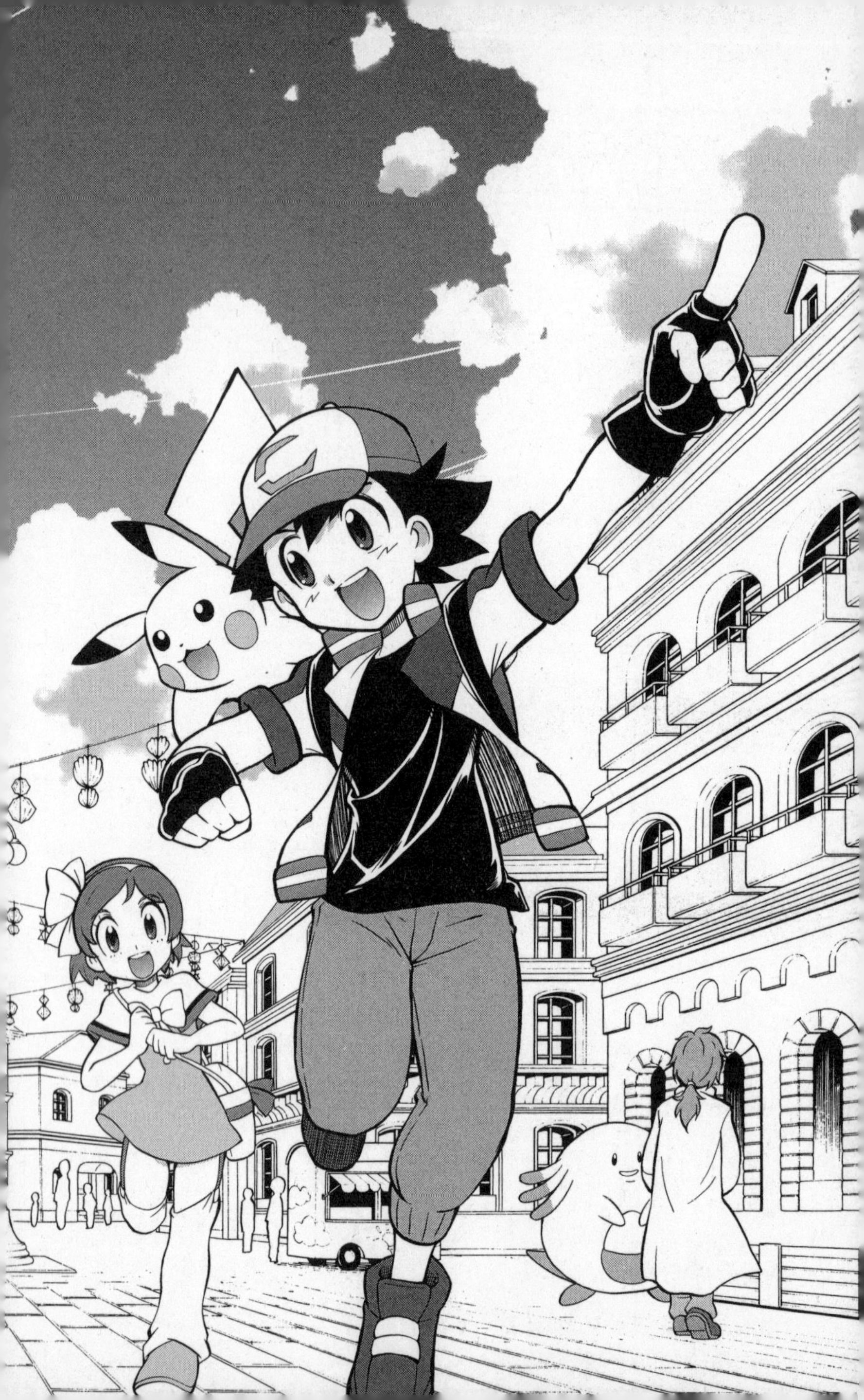

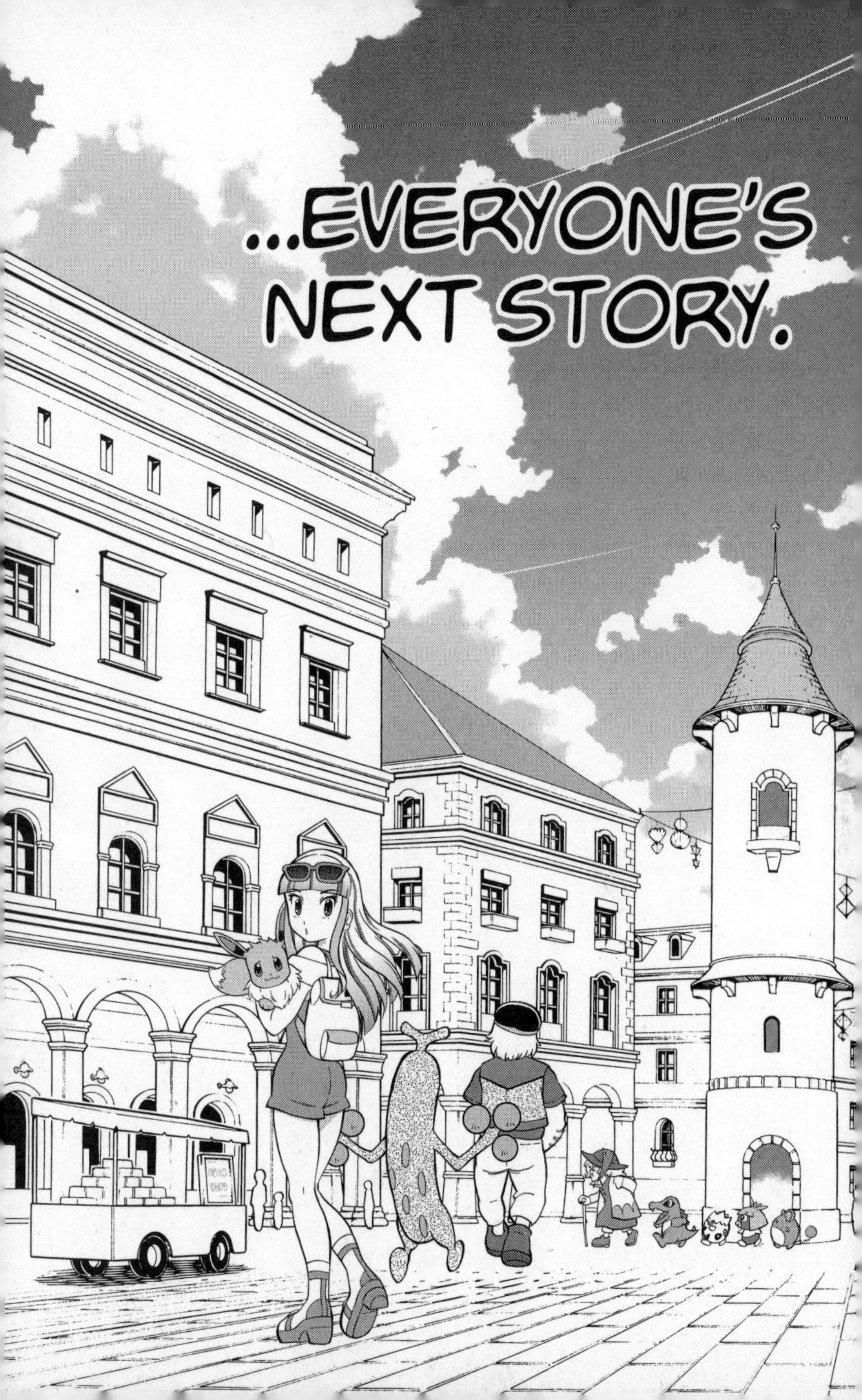
...EVERYONE'S NEXT STORY.

On the following pages, you can see the preview for the graphic novel you just read!

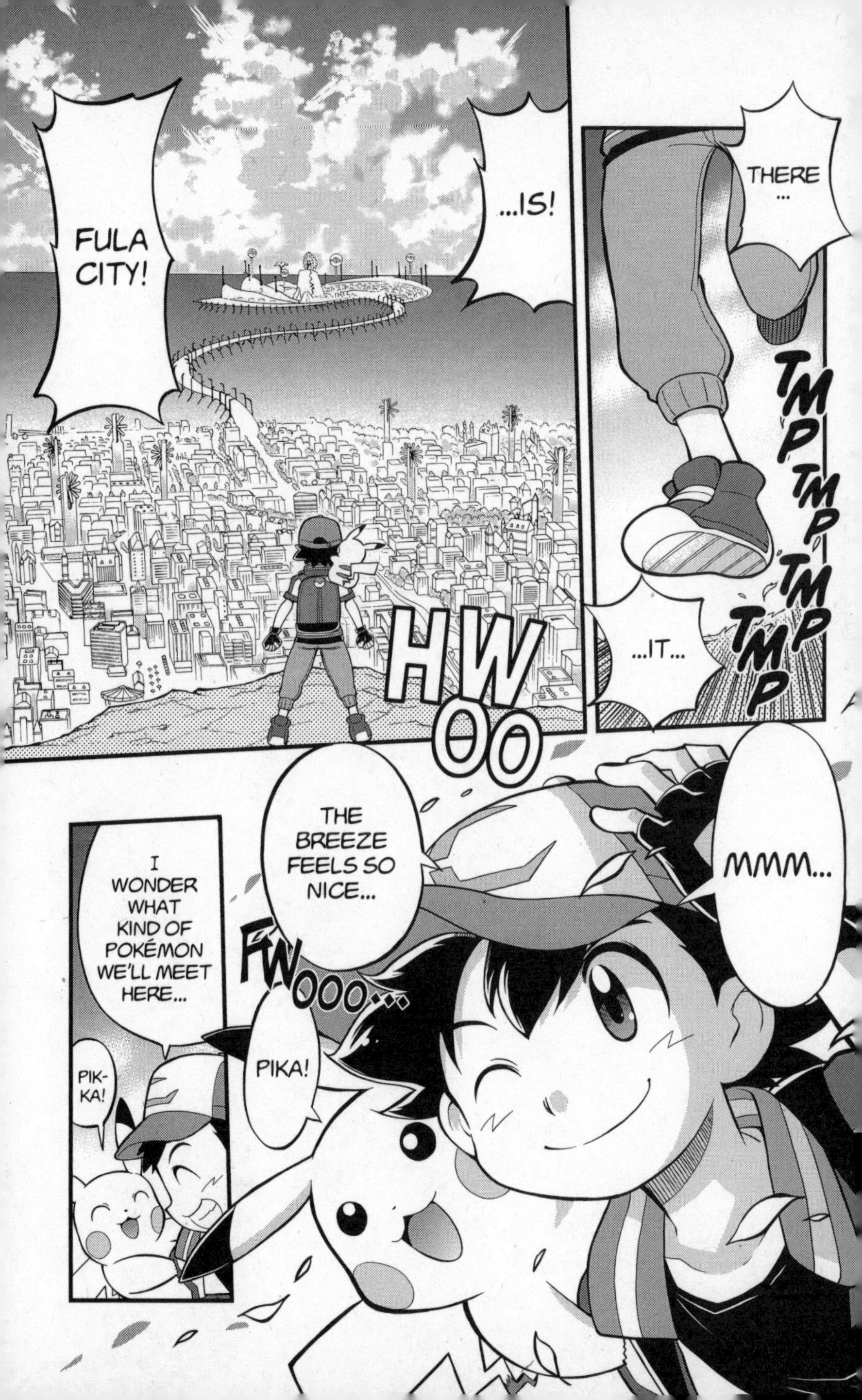
THERE ...
TMP TMP TMP TMP TMP
...IT...
...IS!
FULA CITY!
HWOO
MMM...
THE BREEZE FEELS SO NICE...
FWOOO...
PIKA!
I WONDER WHAT KIND OF POKÉMON WE'LL MEET HERE...
PIK-KA!

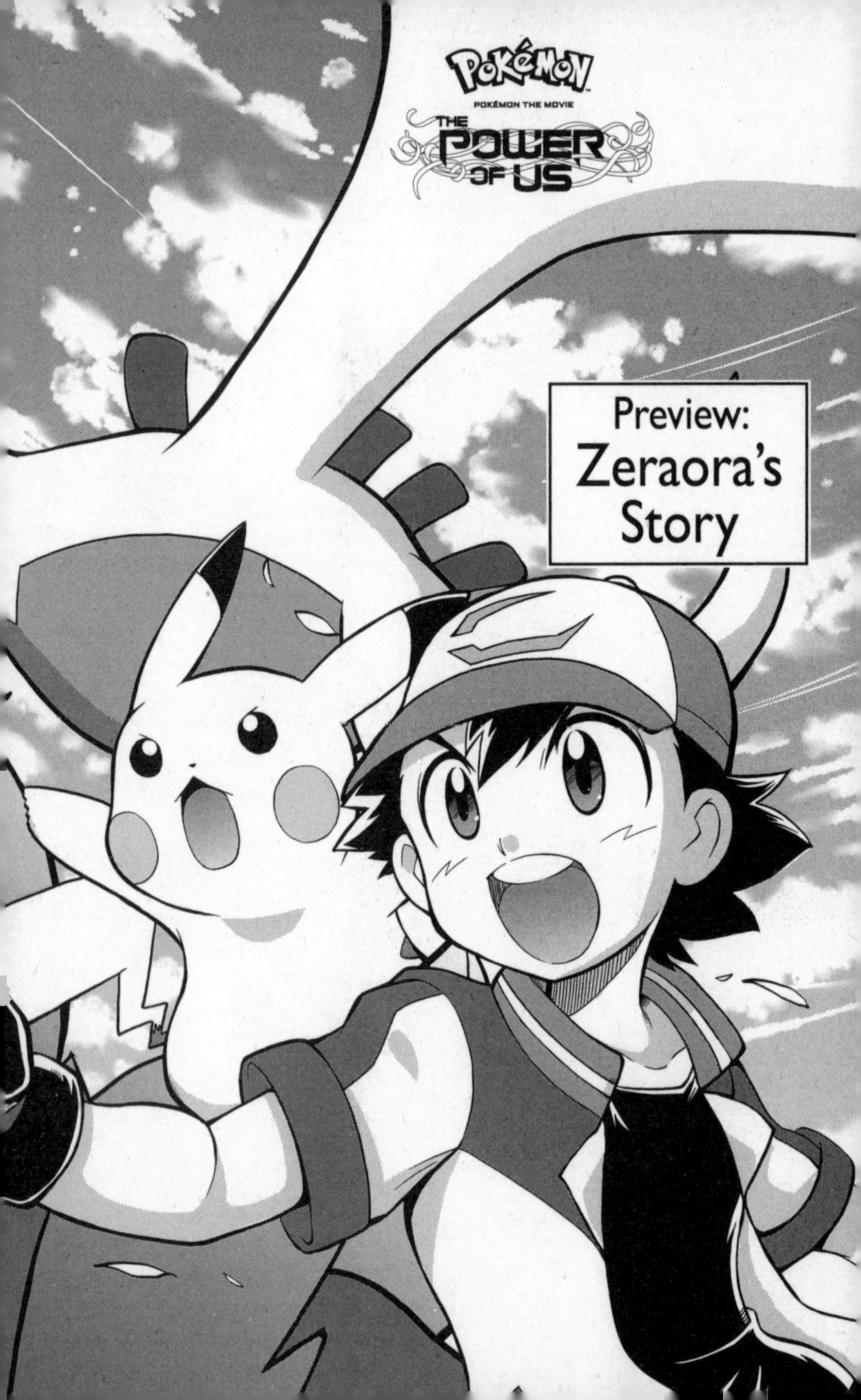
POKÉMON
POKÉMON THE MOVIE
THE POWER OF US
Preview: Zeraora's Story

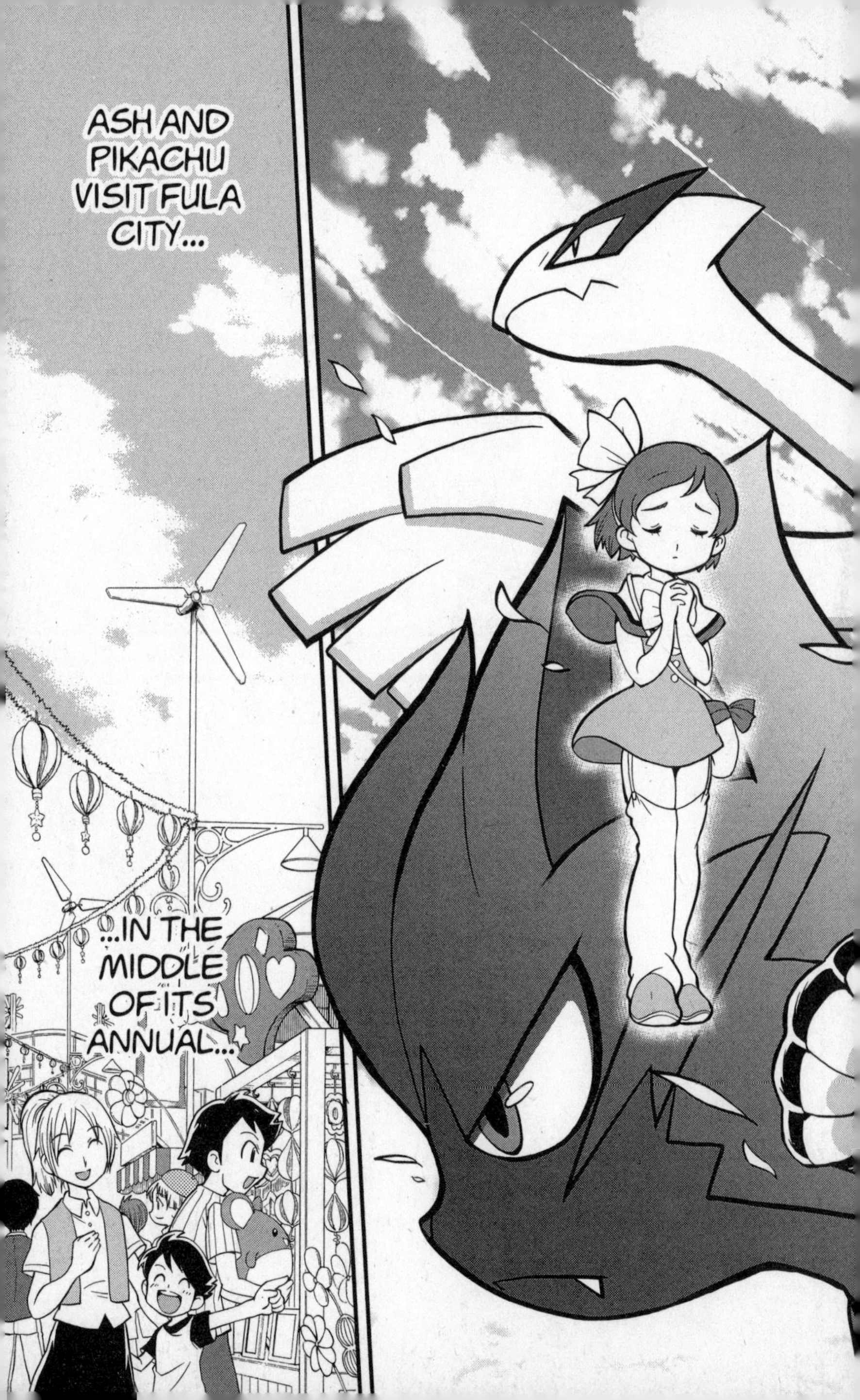
ASH AND PIKACHU VISIT FULA CITY...
...IN THE MIDDLE OF ITS ANNUAL...

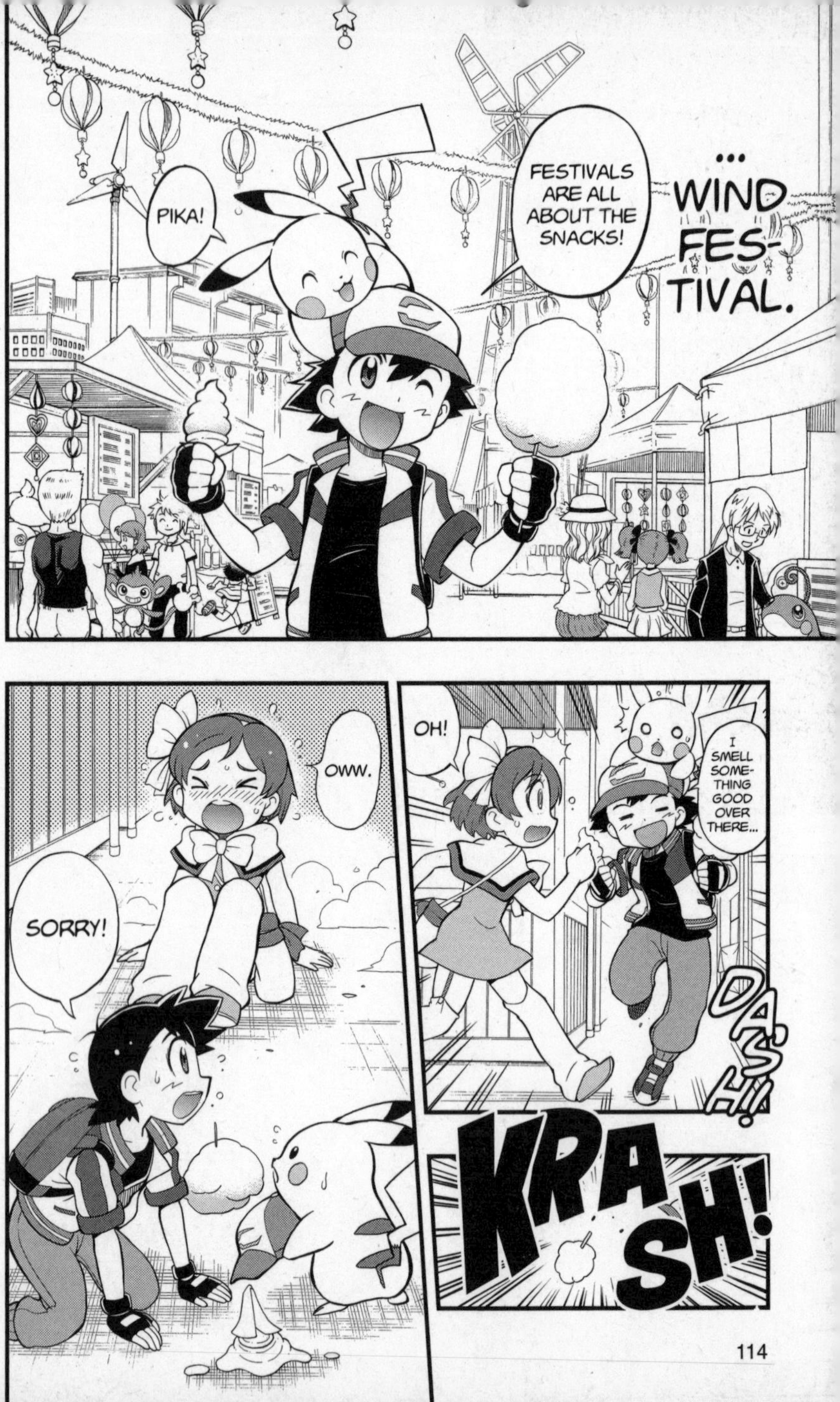
...WIND FESTIVAL.
FESTIVALS ARE ALL ABOUT THE SNACKS!
PIKA!
I SMELL SOMETHING GOOD OVER THERE...
OH!
DASH!
KRASH!
OWW.
SORRY!

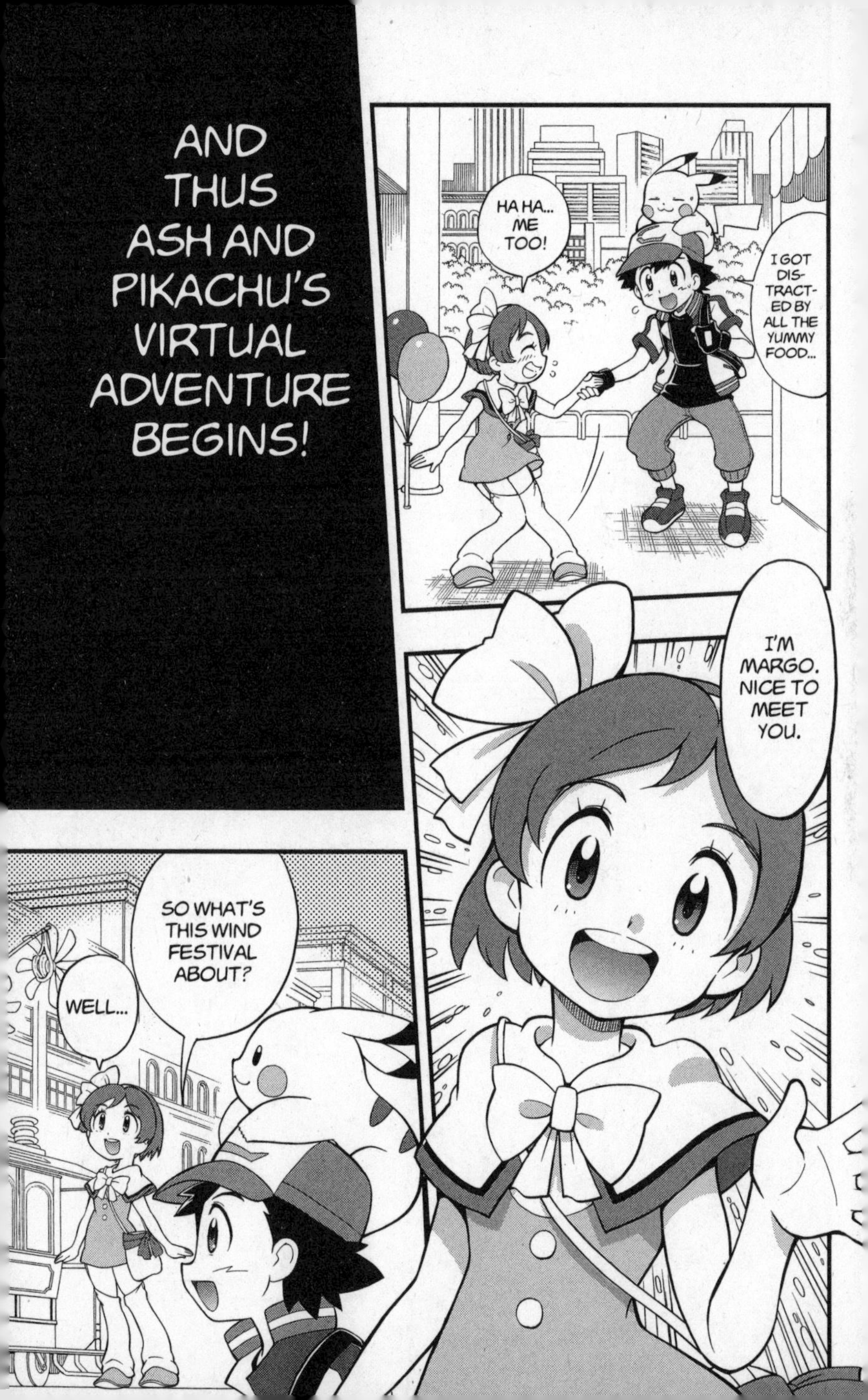
I GOT DIS-TRACT-ED BY ALL THE YUMMY FOOD...
HA HA... ME TOO!
I'M MARGO. NICE TO MEET YOU.
AND THUS ASH AND PIKACHU'S VIRTUAL ADVENTURE BEGINS!
SO WHAT'S THIS WIND FESTIVAL ABOUT?
WELL...

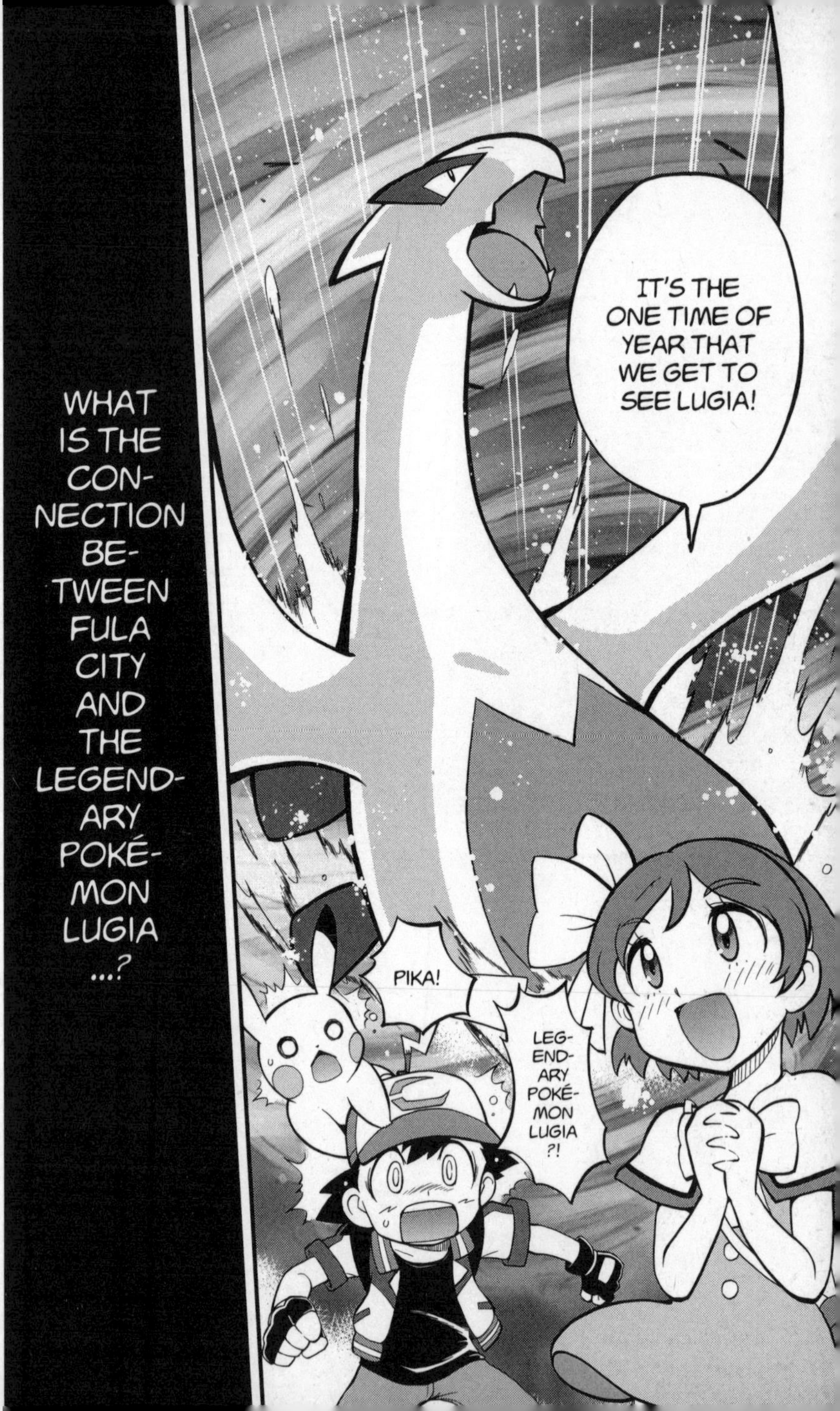
IT'S THE ONE TIME OF YEAR THAT WE GET TO SEE LUGIA!
LEG-END-ARY POKÉ-MON LUGIA ?!
PIKA!
WHAT IS THE CON-NECTION BE-TWEEN FULA CITY AND THE LEGEND-ARY POKÉ-MON LUGIA ...?

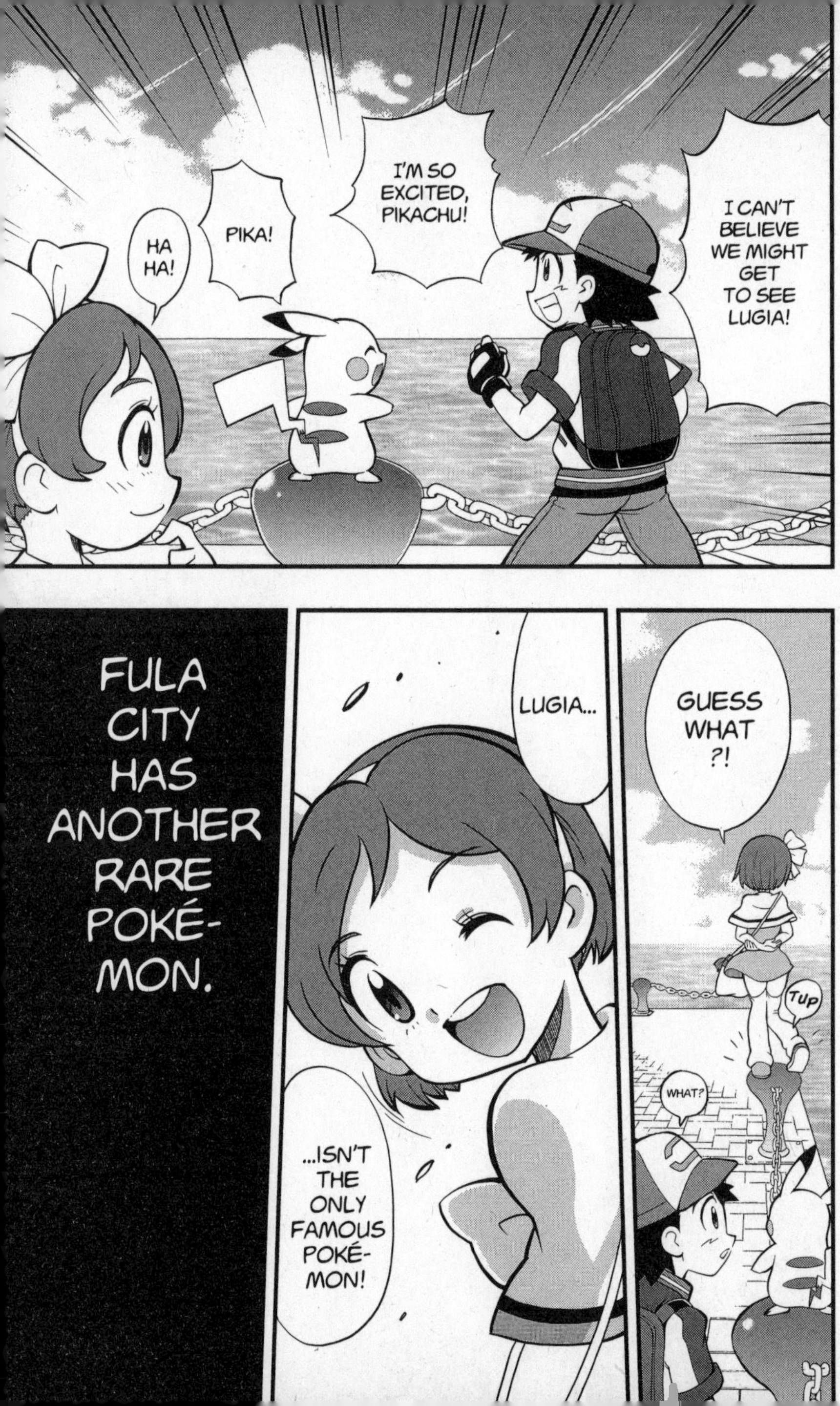
I CAN'T BELIEVE WE MIGHT GET TO SEE LUGIA!
I'M SO EXCITED, PIKACHU!
PIKA!
HA HA!
GUESS WHAT ?!
TUP
WHAT?
LUGIA...
...ISN'T THE ONLY FAMOUS POKÉMON!
FULA CITY HAS ANOTHER RARE POKÉMON.

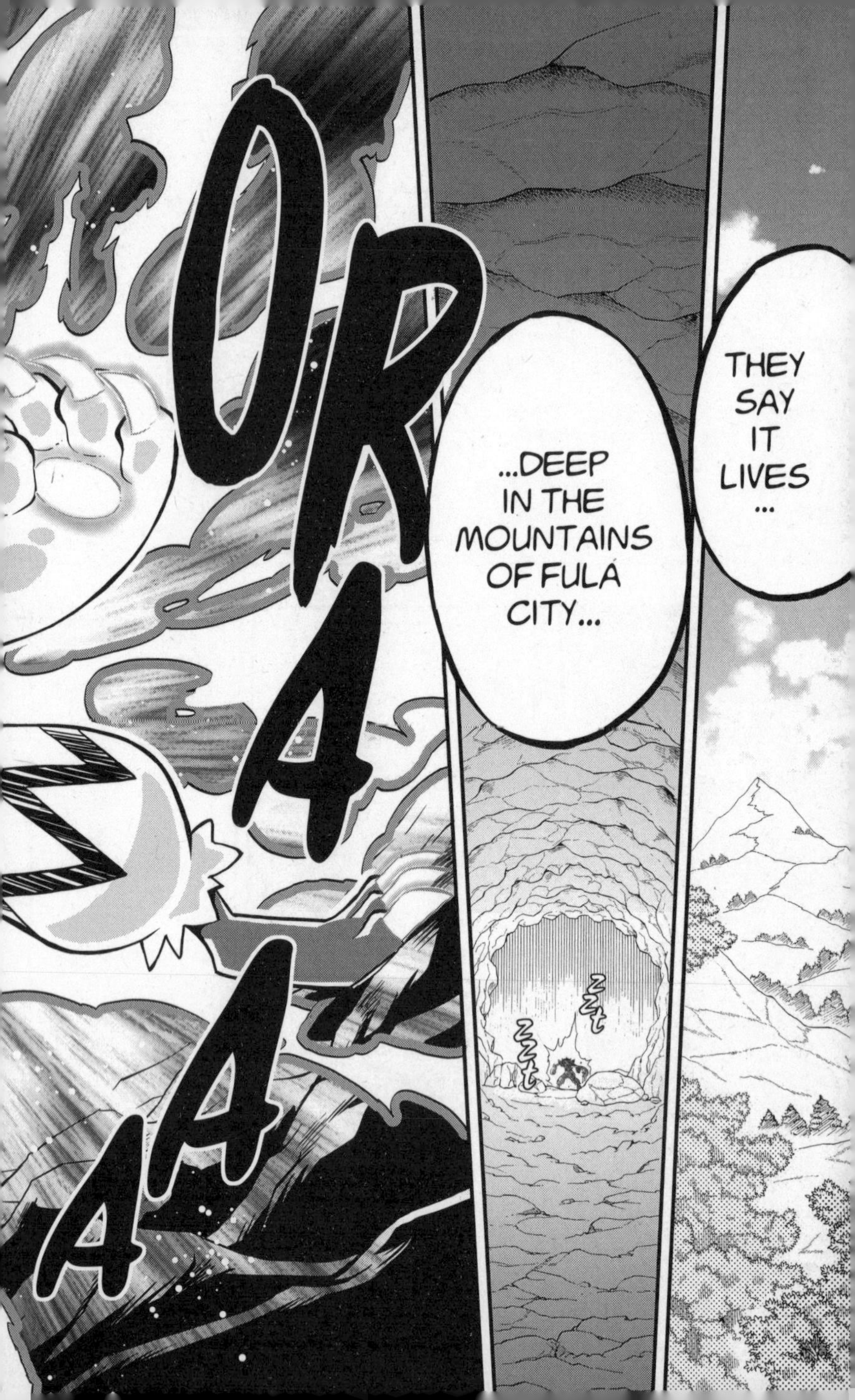
THEY SAY IT LIVES ...
...DEEP IN THE MOUNTAINS OF FULA CITY...
ZZt
ZZt
ORAAAAA

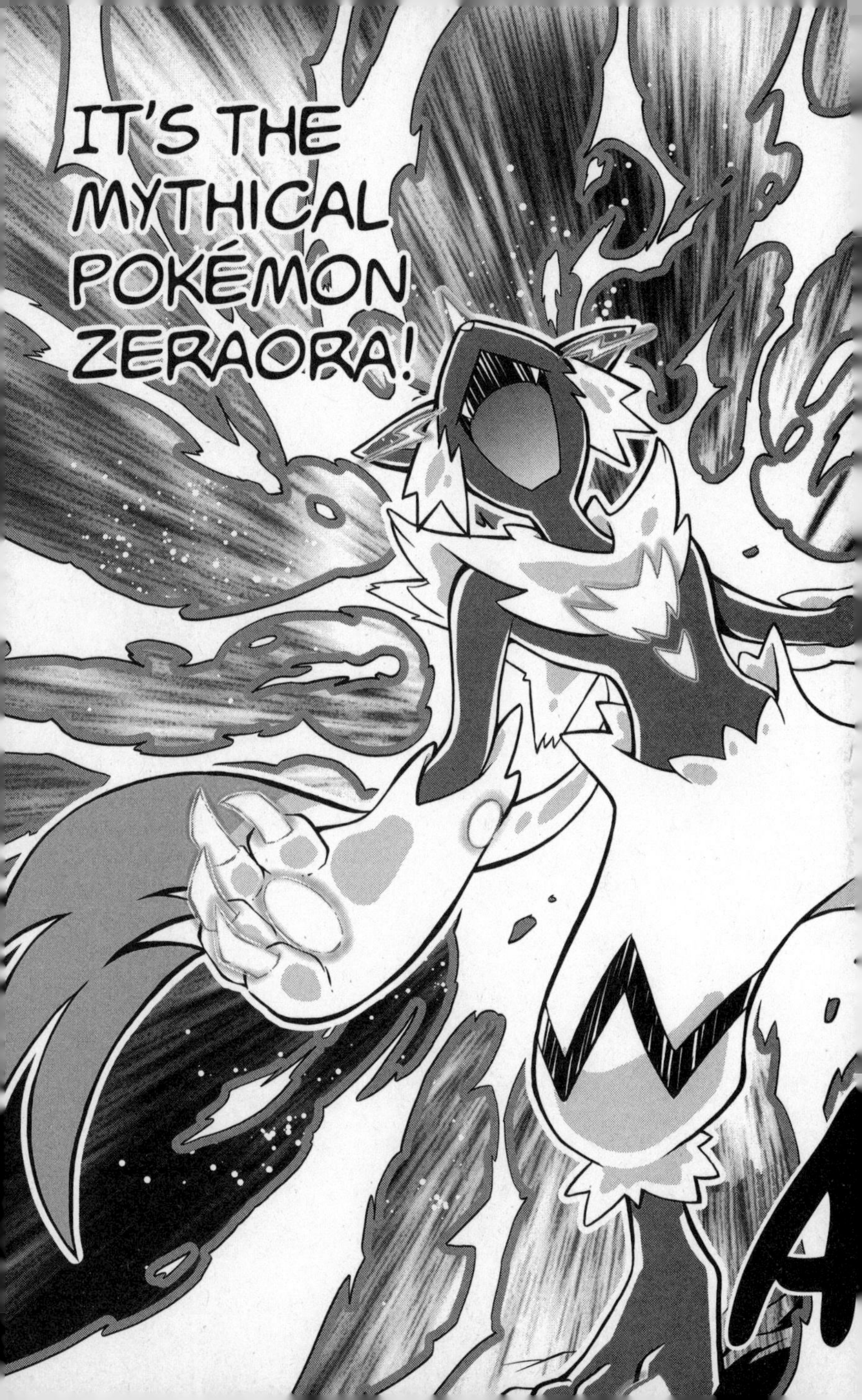
IT'S THE MYTHICAL POKÉMON ZERAORA!

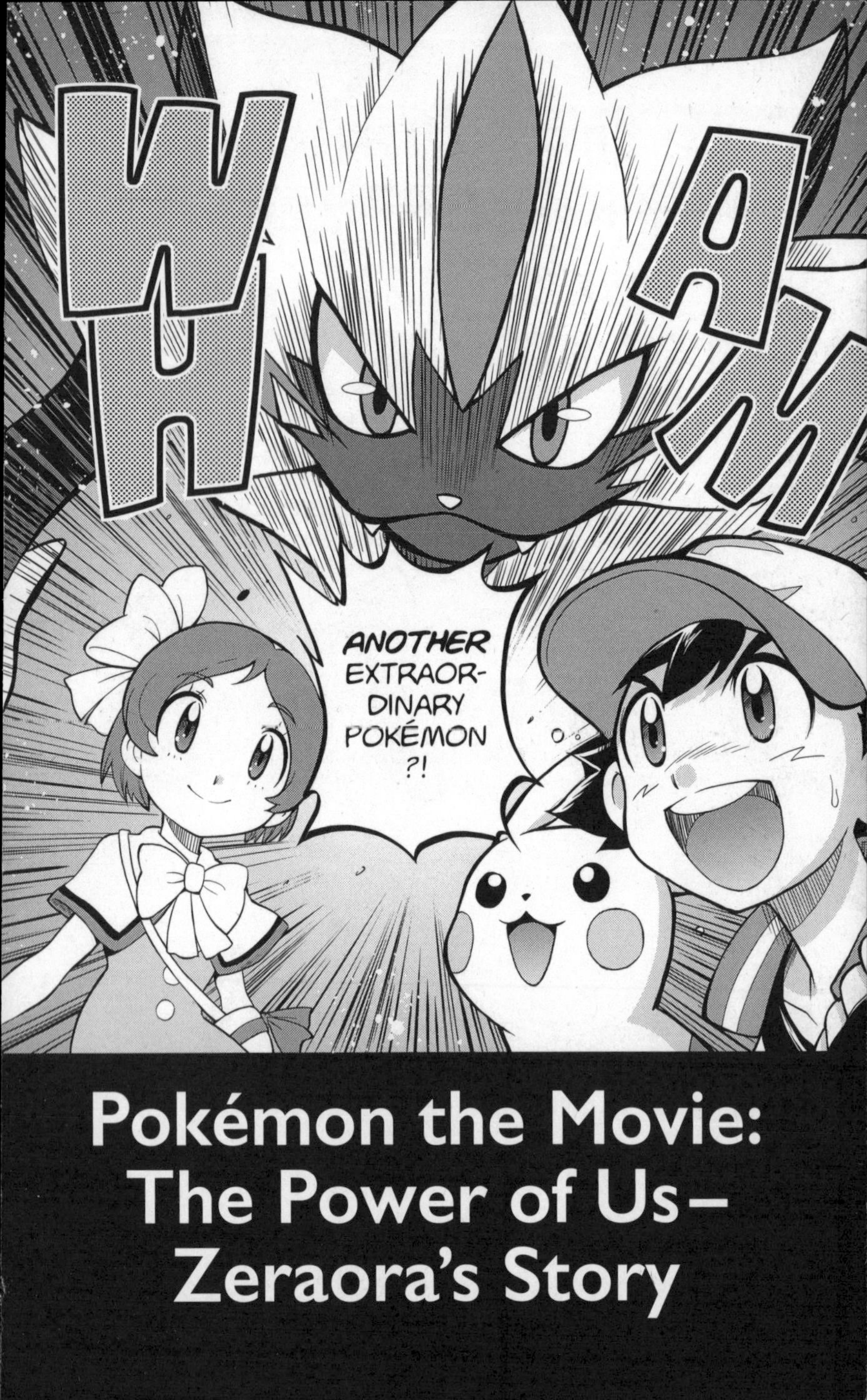
WHAM
ANOTHER EXTRAOR-DINARY POKÉMON?!

Pokémon the Movie: The Power of Us– Zeraora's Story

Special Thanks

Momoe Okabe
Yuki Fukahori
Kujira C.
Tetsuya Kawaishi

Yuta Imamura
(editor)

To everyone
who helped make
this manga…
Thank you
very much!

THE END

This story is all about Zeraora! You'll learn all of Zeraora's secrets! I hope you enjoy this graphic novel. On a side note, have you ever dreamed of squeezing Zeraora's paws...? I want to soooo much!

KEMON KAWAMOTO

POKÉMON THE MOVIE

THE

POWER

OF US

Zeraora's Story

VIZ MEDIA EDITION
STORY AND ART BY **Kemon Kawamoto**

©2019 Pokémon.
©1998–2018 PIKACHU PROJECT.
TM, ®, and character names are trademarks of Nintendo.
GEKIJOBAN POCKET MONSTERS MINNA NO MONOGATARI GAIDEN EPISODE ZERAORA
by Kemon KAWAMOTO
© 2018 Kemon KAWAMOTO
All rights reserved.
Original Japanese edition published by SHOGAKUKAN.
English translation rights in the United States of America,
Canada, the United Kingdom, Ireland, Australia
and New Zealand arranged with SHOGAKUKAN.

Original Cover Design/Plus One

Translation & Adaptation/Emi Louie-Nishikawa
Touch-up & Lettering/Susan Daigle-Leach
Design/Natalie Chen
Editor/Annette Roman

Printed in the U.S.A.

Published by VIZ Media, LLC
P.O. Box 77010
San Francisco, CA 94107

10 9 8 7 6 5 4 3 2 1
First printing, June 2019

viz.com

PARENTAL ADVISORY
POKÉMON THE MOVIE: THE POWER
OF US is rated A and is suitable for
readers of all ages.

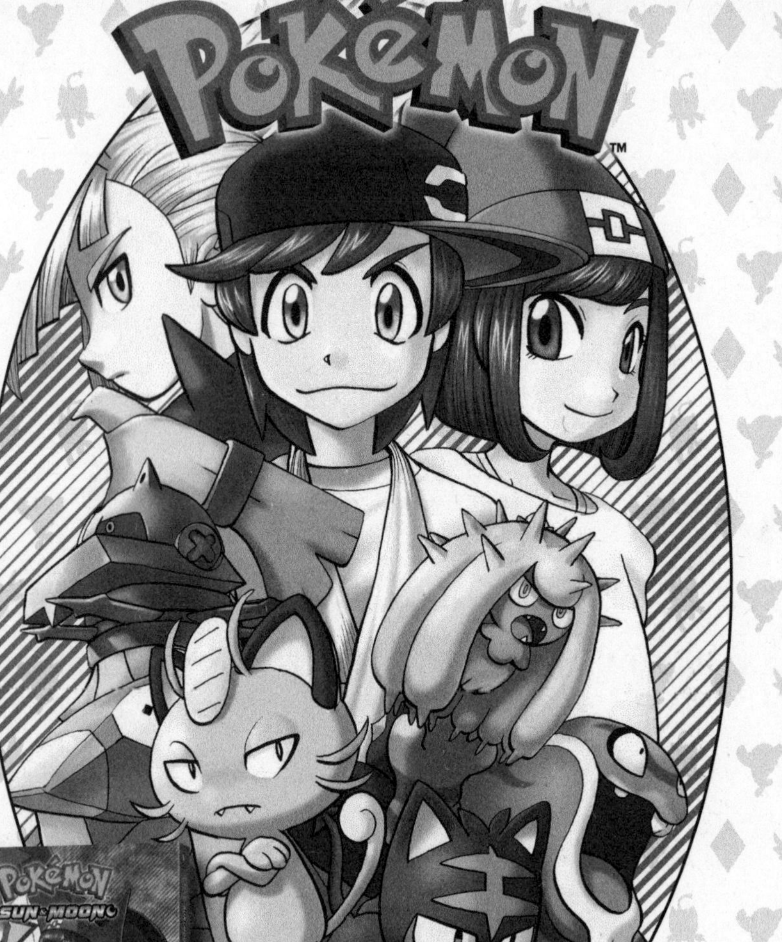
POKéMON™
SUN & MOON

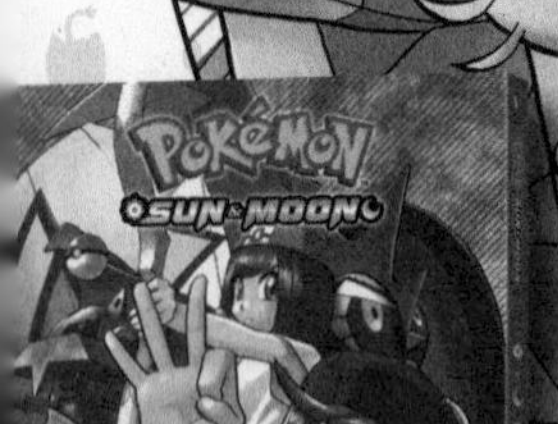
POKéMON
SUN & MOON
1
Hidenori Kusaka
Satoshi Yamamoto

Begin your Pokémon Adventure here in the Kanto region!

POKÉMON ADVENTURES

RED & BLUE BOX SET

Story by **HIDENORI KUSAKA**   Art by **MATO**

Includes
**POKÉMON
ADVENTURES**
Vols. 1-7
and a collectible
poster!

All your favorite Pokémon game characters jump out of the screen into the pages of this action-packed manga!

Red doesn't just want to train Pokémon, he wants to be their friend too. Bulbasaur and Poliwhirl seem game. But independent Pikachu won't be so easy to win over!

And watch out for Team Rocket, Red... They only want to be your enemy!

Start the adventure today!

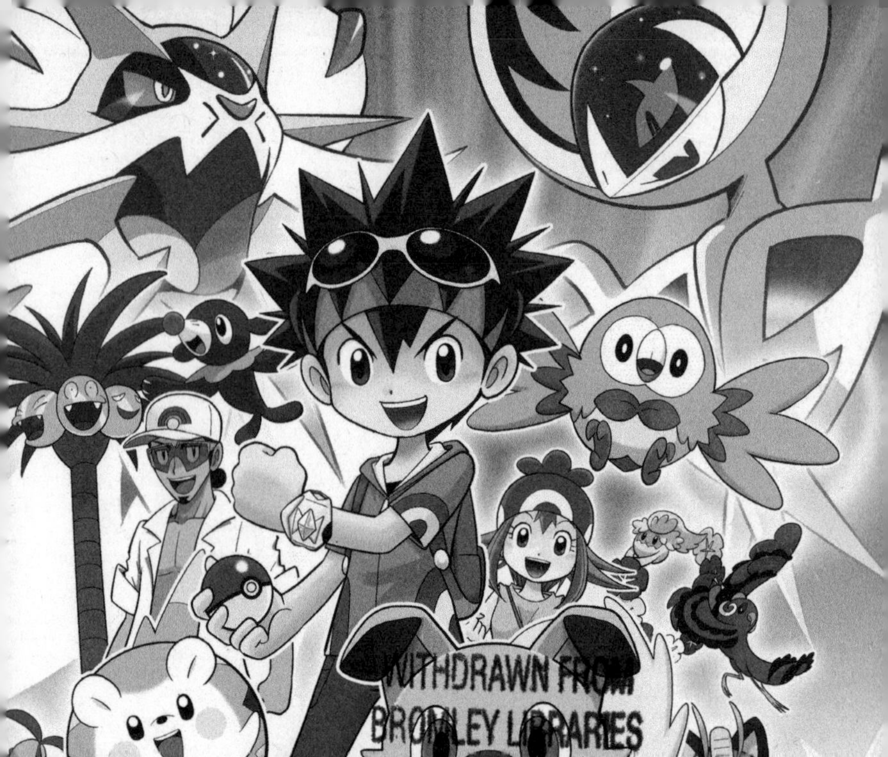

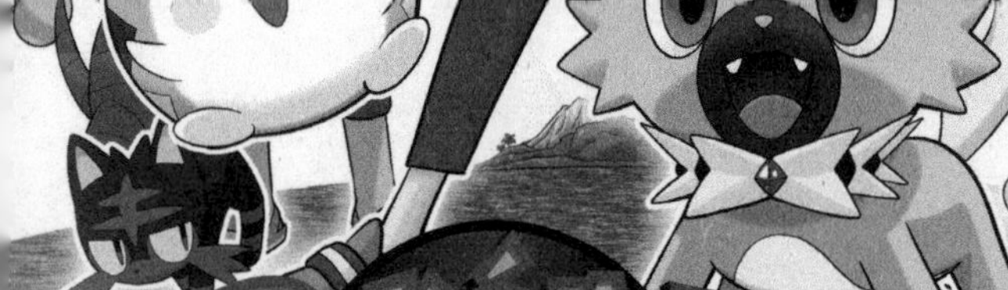
POKÉMON™
HORIZON
SUN & MOON

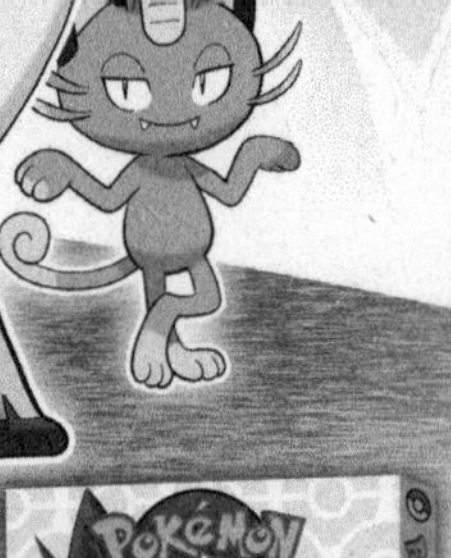
Pokémon
HORIZON
SUN & MOON
01
Story & Art
TENYA YABUNO

Akira's summer vacation in the Alola region heats up when he befriends a Rockruff with a mysterious gemstone. Together, Akira hopes they can achieve his newfound dream of becoming a Pokémon Trainer and master the amazing Z-Move. But first, Akira needs to pass a test to earn a Trainer Passport. This becomes more difficult when Rockruff gets kidnapped! And then Team Kings shows up with—you guessed it—evil plans for world domination!

Story & Art
TENYA YABUNO

VIZ

RATED A ALL AGES